CARRION

CARRION

Gary Haynes

WARNER BOOKS

To Karen, for Eleanor, and everything

A *Warner* Book

First published in Great Britain in 1994 by Warner Books

Copyright © Gary Haynes 1994

The moral right of the author has been asserted.

A CIP catalogue record for this book is available from the British Library.

ISBN 0 7515 0898 5

Typeset by Hewer Text Composition Services, Edinburgh
Printed in England by Clays Ltd, St Ives plc

Warner Books
A division of Little, Brown and Company (UK)
Brettenham House
Lancaster Place
London WC2E 7EN

Contents

Prologue

July 27, 1964.

Emma Trooper had sixty seconds to live.

She did not know it at the time, but she simply assumed that the axe turning the bedroom door into splinters would soon turn on her.

Wielding the axe was her mad husband, Ethan. Emma had no idea why he had gone berserk. She only knew that he was not after her, that his demented screams called out for their youngest son. 'You can run, Nathan!' he bellowed. 'You can try and run, but you can't hide, sonny, you just can't hide from me! You hear, boy?'

Emma closed her eyes to the madness. Ethan, she prayed, please don't. Fear constricted her throat; she could hardly breathe.

Her husband clearly had no such difficulties. 'Come on out, Nathan! Daddy's got you a *big* surprise!' He laughed, dragged the axe from the door, and swung it again. 'Can't hide, Nathan! Open the door for Daddy, kiddo, and get your big, *fat*, surprise!'

Emma tried to scream, but could not. Her throat felt as if it was lined with cement. She knew she should do something, *anything*, but was unable to move. Behind her, Nathan whimpered in the cupboard. She could not think of anywhere else to put him.

'Daddy wants to *come in*!' With that, the door exploded inwards. The man stood outlined in the doorway, grinning, his eyes mad and bloodshot. He was clean shaven, his hair freshly combed. Apart from the eyes (and the axe) he looked completely normal.

He paused to take a deep breath. 'Out of the way, Emma,' he ordered calmly. 'I need to see Nathan.'

Emma finally found her voice. Her vocal cords relaxed. She thought about the neighbours and the police, imagined the axe turned on her helpless son, and she screamed her heart out.

Unfortunately, she was too late. Her sixty seconds were up.

Her husband swung the axe with a negligent backstroke, turning the handle in mid-sweep so the gleaming blade would not make contact with his wife. He did not want to kill her, just shut her up.

The axe head struck with more force than the bone could bear. There was a hollow snap, and Emma's skull was crushed before she hit the wall. She left a dark trace of blood on the yellow wallpaper as she slid to the floor, eyes frozen open in surprise and death.

Her husband looked at his mistake without remorse. He was beyond feeling remorse now, had been since buying the axe that morning. He turned his attention to the room, eyebrows furrowed as he sought his prey. There was very little in the room: a bed, a wardrobe, a corpse. Very few places for the boy to hide.

Ethan bent and looked under the bed. There was nobody there.

'Nathan! Come to Daddy!'

Nathan had heard his mother scream, had heard the scream cut off at its peak, and he had heard the hollow impact as his mother had died. Nathan Trooper was not a stupid boy. He may have been paralysed with fear, but he was not stupid. He did not go to Daddy.

His father hefted the axe once more, took another deep breath, and advanced on the wardrobe. With one maniacal sweep of the axe he tore the door off its hinges. Nathan cowered in the corner, weeping dry tears of absolute terror and desolation.

'Daddy, please,' he begged. 'Please don't hurt me.'

His father raised the axe. 'This won't hurt, son,' he said gently, and almost sounded convincing. Then, as his mind plunged into the depths of insanity, he grinned again. 'Surprise!'

He lied. It did . . .

Ethan Trooper threw up six times. He wept and screamed and howled for mercy. He begged forgiveness for his sins, not just from God, but from his dead wife and son. When he heard the first siren he managed to pull himself together. He knew there would be questions he could not bear to answer. He discarded the bloody axe.

'May God have mercy upon my unworthy soul,' he said. Then he vaulted over the bannister at the top of the stairs, trailing rope like a falling anchor.

His feet reached the floor thirty minutes later when the police finally cut him down.

*

ID – the primitive animal instincts of the subconscious which are the basis for all psychic activity. Kept in check by the *ego* and the *super-ego*.

EGO – the conscious 'self'. Responsible for restraining the antisocial instincts of the *id*, and in turn tempered by the *super-ego*.

SUPER-EGO – part of the unconscious mind, a conscience for the *ego* and in turn the *id*.

Gary Haynes

Journal Entry, Ethan Trooper, January 15, 1962

'Removal of the restrictive super-ego, coupled with the closer linking of id to ego, will undoubtedly result in a greater mental capacity. However, with no conscience the animal instincts of the id will control the conscious mind. In a worst-case scenario, the individual will lose all restraint and be driven by pure primitive desires, without remorse or any sense of right or wrong, totally committed to the achievement of his ends – however perverse those ends may be. Since the id contains all that we know to be dark and hidden, the results of such a scenario would at best be unpredictable. At worst, they would be monstrous.

'In all honesty I cannot believe that this worst-case scenario will materialize in our experiment. As a result, I have decided to proceed with the research, despite Dr Franks' objections. However, in order to satisfy my colleague's concerns, I have agreed to maintain maximum security following the operations. We are both certain that in so doing, even the worst result can be rectified, and – if necessary – destroyed.'

BOOK ONE

TERROR FIRMA

CHAPTER ONE

William Wallis Makes a Call

Christmas Eve 1990, 11:25 p.m. London, England.

Ear-bursting volume, eye-splitting light shows, heaving bodies and a DJ on amphetamines. Schoolgirls dressed as twenty-five-year-olds, and who could tell the difference these days? Mini-skirts and skimpy tops and the occasional flash of forbidden flesh. The innocence of youth tarted up for the world to see.

And the world saw, stood to one side, propping up the bar. Single men bursting with ready cash, sexual tension, and a mind-boggling assortment of flavoured condoms. Married men with un-married lusts. A meat market under the guise of harmless fun.

In the midst of all this sat Bill Wallis – back straight, stomach sucked in, eyes wide and roving. Across his lips played a lascivious grin. His trousers bulged with desire.

As usual, with his wife away, Bill was out on the prowl.

Bill, thirty-six and a husband for six years, had a bad reputation: anything with two legs and a pulse was fair game. He had married his wife Anne for her money and her looks, and had spent all their time together cheating on her.

Bill thought people admired his errant ways. He thought he was God's gift to women. He thought a

3

large sphere of stellar matter radiated from his back passage. Bill thought his lovely wife was totally ignorant of all the affairs he'd had over the years, all the one-night stands, all the quiet visits to the clinics.

Only his last thought was correct.

His conversation openers were old and tired. His stomach bulged, and his hairline was rapidly receding. He smoked about thirty cigarettes a day and loved to eat pickled onions. Like most men, he did not even *think* about using mouthwash.

Bill was a boring, stupid, egotistical little man with nothing to offer the human race.

For the young girls in the bars, however, Bill Wallis had one redeeming feature – he was loaded. So if his stale personality failed to win the body of a nymphomaniac, then his full wallet usually did the trick. And even if all else failed, Bill never retreated alone. Because he had no qualms about paying for tail.

So, while his wife was visiting her wealthy and fortunately dying mother, Bill was touring the pubs and clubs around West London, trying to pick up a woman. The evening had been frustrating – the pubs were too quiet; the clubs were too noisy; and, to cap it all, he was too drunk.

He stood in a telephone box off Oxford Street, swaying merrily in the alcohol breeze, humming to himself. He was looking forward to a good screw, paid for with his wife's money. Sometimes Bill could not get over the irony of life.

Someone paced impatiently outside the cubicle, casting a shadow. Bill didn't care, they could wait. He fumbled the phone, the dialling tone droning hypnotically in his ears. Outside, the pacing footsteps faded and then disappeared. Bill looked over his shoulder at the street outside, saw nothing but dimly-lit pavement.

He dialled the number and, with the ringing tone in his ears, leaned back against the glass to relieve the strain on his unsteady knees. But the glass was freezing cold and it only made him shiver.

The ringing ended. He smiled in eager, drunken anticipation.

'Hello Bill.'

The smile froze on his face. 'Debbi?' he asked, surprised.

'No, Bill. Debbi isn't here.'

Bill struggled to free himself from the haze around his brain.

Hold on – why hadn't Debbi answered the phone? Debbi *always* answered the phone – it was her number, her flat, her occupation. And that wasn't Debbi's voice. In fact, that was nobody's voice. Nobody he knew, anyway. What was going on here?

'What's the matter, Bill? Cat got your tongue?'

Bill could hear his tired heart begin to race. Blood pounded in his ears and temples. He was suddenly, inexplicably, terrified. It was that voice – cold, dead, lacking inflection or emotion. He'd never heard a voice like it. But it conjured up images of death and graveyards at midnight in his whisky-logged mind.

Bill realized that the hairs on the back of his neck were standing on end. He sobered in an instant, driven to awareness by the rattlesnakes of fear which slithered in his stomach.

Why? he shrieked to himself. Why am I scared? What the hell is going on here? 'Who are you?' he managed to whisper.

Outside, the streetlight dimmed as a shadow passed in front of the door. Bill turned frantically, heart hammering painfully now, eyes bulging, palms sweating, bowels loosening.

'Don't piss yourself, buddy,' the phone taunted.

'Who are you?' he repeated, more loudly this time. 'Where's Debbi? How do you know my name?'

'Oh, I know many things, Bill. I know where you live. I know the names of all the women you've ever slept with. And there have been a lot of those, haven't there Bill? You've been a bad sinner. You're going to get what's coming to you, aren't you Bill?'

'What the hell is going on here?' he demanded. He had a chilling thought. 'Did Anne put you up to this?'

'Anne? No way, man.' The voice laughed, a sound from beyond the crypt. 'Feeling scared now, are you? Well, look behind you.'

Somebody outside, a shadow. Bill whirled, twisting his ankle. Unreasoning terror was rising in his stomach, throbbing in his skull. He knew he had to get out of there, and fast.

A shape, tall and blurred. A man. Thank Christ!

He dropped the receiver, no longer interested in listening to that tombstone voice, and pushed on the door.

It did not move.

He pushed again. Same result. Someone chuckled in his mind, a hollow, cadaverous laugh that filled his head with ice.

'Get a grip, Bill, you're losing it. Too much booze, too much lawless, sinning sex. Maybe it's time you paid the price.'

Shut up! Get out of my mind! The door is stiff, that's all. 'Well it was OK when you came in, Bill,' he whimpered to himself.

And then his bowels sank further as he saw liquid pouring in through the gap at the bottom of the glass panels. It was already settling in the concrete, collecting

6

in the corners, gushing over his shoes to pour out over the other side.

Someone pissing in my phone box! he thought with disgust.

He sniffed. His eyes widened. Adrenalin surged into his blood, shattering his drunkenness in a whirlwind of terror.

That isn't piss, he screamed silently. That's petrol!

'Hey! What the HELL!' He threw himself against the door, trying to manœuvre in the confined space. The door refused to budge. 'What the hell do you think you're doing?' he bellowed.

Jesus, he thought, one match in here and I'm history.

The petrol continued to pour in and fill the hollow in which he stood. Laughter echoed tinnily from the handset swinging on its yard of sprung steel. 'Time to pay the price, Billy-boy,' gloated the voice, but Bill could no longer tell whether it was coming from the telephone or directly inside his brain. Neither did he care – he just wanted to get out of the booth before it went up in smoke.

He smashed his shoulder into the glass door, bruising it, crying out in sudden pain. 'Let me out of here, damn you!'

Petrol fumes now assaulted his nostrils, bringing tears to his eyes. His struggles grew increasingly frantic. He hammered on the door, barged at it with his shoulder. Nothing worked. In sudden panic he kicked hard at the bottom pane of glass in the door, felt his big toe break and didn't care. The toughened glass shattered under the impact, sagging under its own weight as a web of cracks appeared. Bill kicked again, crying out at the pain in his foot, and glass flew all over the pavement. Cold air rushed in, buffeting the fumes. Blood poured down his left leg from a protruding shard of glass, but he didn't care. He just wanted OUT. Bending down, he used his elbow to make himself a hole big enough to crawl through.

And couldn't do it. He was too fat.

As suddenly as it had started, the flow of petrol stopped. Bill stared in disbelief at the puddle in which he crouched, aware that his arms, legs and backside were soaked with petrol. The cuts in his flesh were sheer agony, the petrol seeping into them sending spikes of torture along his nerves. He was moaning softly in fear and desperation, and as the silence grew outside he realized that all chances of escape were gone. His terror turned to despair. He gave up the fight, collapsed back in the puddle, one foot protruding through the hole he had managed to smash in the glass.

AND NOW I AM GOING TO DIE.

Surprisingly, the thought did not fill him with dread. His brain had gone numb. He was incapable of even pleading for mercy.

Outside, an unseen hand flicked the lid on a Zippo lighter, and with a harsh rasp the yellow flame burst into life. Bill was mesmerized by the glow as it danced in the darkness.

'No escape, Bill, whatever you do. You see, you can run, but you can't hide. You can never hide.'

Part of Bill's defeated mind tried to scream at him, tried to force him into one last ditch attempt at freedom. Run anyway! But he was deaf to the words – he simply sat there, watching the flame as it flickered in the hand of the man who was about to kill him.

The flame receded a few feet, then descended. 'Bye-bye Billy-boy,' came the voice from the telephone, as it swung lazily back and forth beside his face.

'Why?' Bill asked suddenly, more out of dazed curiosity than to delay the inevitable. 'Why me?'

Laughter sounded in his head. 'Why not, you dirty bastard? You deserve everything you get.' The laughter came again. 'Better get used to the flames, slimeball. You'll be burning in them for all eternity now I've consigned your soul to hell.'

There was a silent flare of blue flame. A streak of fire leapt six feet across the pavement and flew under the door into the phone booth. The petrol ignited with an ear-popping 'whoosh'. Bill's clothes caught fire, flames running up his trouser legs and jacket sleeves. His hair and eyebrows disappeared in a flash of burnt flesh, and as he opened his mouth to draw breath for a scream, blazing petrol fumes swarmed into his lungs. His skin started to melt, dripping from his fingers and face. An inhuman cry burst from his lips as his tongue turned to liquid fire in his mouth. His eyeballs exploded in the heat.

Within seconds the booth was consumed by flame. The plastic mouldings melted and ran onto the kicking husk on the concrete. Thirty seconds later all the remaining glass panels fractured in the blaze and blew out onto the tarmac. Sparks and burning tatters of cloth rose from the fire and landed in a nearby litter bin. Discarded garbage smouldered in the heat, then burst into flame as smoking globs of plastic spattered the street.

The shudders of the trapped man slowed and finally stopped. Flames licked at the concrete, consuming the remaining petrol and any combustible material in their reach. A bottle of petrol, dropped in the litter bin by the unseen killer, exploded. Shards of green plastic, some still boasting the slogan 'Keep Britain Tidy', burst from the casing around the bin and span off across the road.

At long last, blue lights flashed off walls and windows in the deserted street. The smell of melted plastic mingled with that of burnt flesh, a bitter aroma which clung to the clothes of the two policemen as they stood beside their car. The car radio crackled and hissed, the sound mixing with that of the dying fire.

Police Constable David Whitlock leaned forward to get a better look at the blaze. 'What the . . .?' The burning image cleared. He saw it for what it was, and vomited. Semi-digested hot dogs and Coke splashed the young constable's shoes. 'Oh shit,' he wheezed through bitter lips. His breakfast decided it was time to join his lunch on the pavement, curious to see what all the fuss was about.

His partner reached over to clap him on the back. 'Come on Dave,' he urged, 'bring it all up. No sense in doing half a job.'

Whitlock crouched in the gutter, hands on knees, nose full of vomit. The wind blew another whiff of burnt flesh into his face. 'Jesus Christ.' Retch. Gasp. Spit. 'Sonofabitch.'

Whitlock's partner reached into the car for the fire extinguisher. Standing back from the heat, the canister at arms' length, he turned the jet of CO_2 on the telephone box. Under the freezing onslaught of gas the plastic cracked, oozing down into a steaming pile which shrouded the burnt body within. Shattered glass littered the pavement. Smoke billowed up in stinking clouds, dissipating in the breeze.

The splash of headlight beams across the walls announced the arrival of another car. Doors slammed. Somebody coughed, hawked and spat into the gutter.

Chief Inspector John Daniels, dressed to the nines and unlucky enough to have been returning from a local concert, joined the gathering crowd around the destruction. 'Crazy season already, huh?' He sniffed, pulled a face. 'Right – better call this in.' He turned to the constable still crouched in the gutter. 'Pull yourself together man. Then get this area cordoned off.'

Dave Whitlock nodded. The queasiness in his stomach was bad, but nothing compared to the wrath of Inspector Daniels. He had a reputation for being a merciless, hard-nosed bastard, utterly contemptuous of human frailties. 'Right you are, sir.'

Passers-by started to crowd in against the three police-men, morbid fascination drawing them like moths around a flame. Daniels eyed them with disgust. Anything to break the boredom, he thought cynically, even some suicidal maniac with a petrol emotion. 'Constable!' he snapped. 'Get these bloody vultures out of here!'

'Yes sir.' The puke-stained policeman moved towards the crowd, calling out the usual platitudes like a farmer herding his sheep.

Daniels looked at his watch. It was half-past eleven, and the pubs were just turning out. 'What a way to end Christmas Eve,' he mumbled, then turned and walked back to his car. Something in his bowels told him it was going to be a long week.

CHAPTER TWO

Nathan Trooper Steals a Queen

Christmas Day 1990, 2:30 a.m. Cheshire, England.

As ever, England was in the grip of a wet Christmas. Perhaps the wettest place of all was Manchester in the dreary North-West, where moist Atlantic air ran inland to collide with the Pennine Hills and formed almost permanent rain-cloud. The townsfolk tended to be cheerfully, cynically, wet.

On the outskirts of town Nathan Trooper sat alone in his luxury two-bedroom flat. The starkness of the flat was testament to the man who lived there. There were no presents, no Christmas tree, no cards on the mahogany mantelpiece. Two thousand pounds' worth of hi-tech hi-fi stood idle. An expensive gas oven was all ready for the turkey and other delights Nathan would not be cooking, since they still sat on shelves in supermarkets Nathan never visited.

A casual observer would be stunned by the complete lack of seasonal cheer. They would probably deduce that Trooper was a miserable, self-centred bachelor. This was not quite the case. He just did not believe in Christmas. Nathan was an obsessively solitary man, painfully introverted, incapable of relating to others in any fashion considered normal.

Trooper was thirty-eight years old, single, childless,

parentless, friendless. That suited him fine. He could never understand why people insisted on surrounding themselves with other people. For him, company meant pain, headaches and nosebleeds; he simply could not cope with it. He lived in silence, apart from his music, and cherished darkness.

Everyone who met him – and few did, these days – left his presence with an overwhelming sense of *weirdness*. Nathan Trooper was strange. He recognised this fact, but preferred to think of himself as just different. It wasn't his fault. And he was quite happy if scornful strangers left him alone. That was, in fact, what he yearned for.

That evening, with gales lashing torrents of rain at his windows, surrounded by streets of sleeping children, Nathan sat alone. Cross-legged on the floor, just one small lamp casting subdued light in the room, he gazed at the chessboard in front of him on the low table. With a frown of concentration creasing his high forehead he reached out and took his opponent's queen. He allowed himself a slight smile. The game was going well.

A bottle of vodka stood on the table. Next to it was an array of chess pieces, no longer active in the game. The captured figurines, intricately carved out of hardwood, were predominantly black. That suited Nathan fine, since he was playing white.

The casual observer might think Nathan mad to compete against himself. But if the observer looked beyond his presumption, he might notice the strange expressions on Nathan's face, the erratic arm movements, the peculiar habit of laughing at nothing in particular. The observer would think Nathan was listening to someone, and would be disconcerted by this since he was absolutely alone in the house. The deduction, as usual, would be that Nathan Trooper was a strange man, perhaps even a little crazy.

brother had been dead for eight years.

CHAPTER THREE

Samuel Stevens Loses His Cool

Christmas Day, 1990, 5:00 p.m., Arizona, USA.

The United States: over 3000 miles coast to coast, a huge array of cultures and landscapes united under a single flag. From billionaire to beggar, skin-clad beach to snowy mountain top; icy, oily Alaskan waste to barren oily Texan wilderness. A land of extremes and extremists. To the west of centre, between the golden heartland of swaying corn and the Californian beaches of swaying flesh, lay Arizona: desert state, home of the Grand Canyon and countless species of rattlesnake. Spilling down from the high plateaux in the north-east, around the Canyon national park and away from the red fingers of rock exclaiming native America to the sky, Arizona dropped steadily south and west towards California and the West Coast Fever. Through the mountains and dusty plains ran 1000 miles of criss-crossed relentless highway, routes for the thirties' dustbowl migrants on their way to the dreams of the orange groves and away from the desolation of the mid-west. And those same dirty, dusty highways were home and inspiration for Patrolman Sam Stevens, veteran traffic cop.

Sam was thirty-six. He had lived and worked on those roads all his life. His father had owned a garage strategically placed in the middle of the desert. So strategically placed, in fact, that he now owned the garage, a diner, a motel and a burger bar. Plus enough people to work them for him so he could retire in style.

Sam had not inherited his father's flair for business, nor his devotion to money; he lacked the vision to exploit an opportunity. His father, after spending twenty years trying to mould his son into a worthy heir, had admitted defeat and let Sam go his own way. His final words on the matter had been, 'If my loins couldn't provide me with a successor, then I'm damned sure my capital will.'

Sam may have had the talents buried deep within him, but he was just not interested. His love was motorcycles, not money. His drug was speed on an open road, not the thrill of clinching a deal. If he had spent more time learning from his father instead of doing wheelies then things may have turned out differently.

What Sam had inherited were his father's looks. He was a large man, standing six feet two in his skin, with broad shoulders and a muscular body. He had a permanent golden tan which was the envy of everyone he arrested. His eyes were the bluest blue, his hair was blond, cropped short, and his teeth were straight and white. He looked like an advert for the American dream.

The traffic police valued Sam's looks and dedication. Having suffered years of ridicule about his enthusiasm and honesty, he was now highly respected. Indeed, he was worshipped by the rookies.

And Sam, in his own modest way, was proud of his achievements. He was proud of the service he had provided his country. Although his father never said as much, he was proud of Sam too. Besides, having a hero for a son was good for business.

So now, sixteen years on, Sam was famous in his small part of Arizona. He had the lowest accident rates of any patrolman in the state. Drivers breaking the law in Sam's patch did not just slow down when he caught them, they stopped. And then they got out of the car and read themselves their rights. Nobody argued – Sam never took chances these days. Besides, he had such an honest reputation that people were more inclined to apologize than argue.

His bosses liked him, most of his collars ended up liking him, and his wife loved him. As did his three adorable kids, who thought he was Dirty Harry rolled in with Indiana Jones.

Sam Stevens was a happy man . . .

As the sun began to sink on the horizon Sam headed home at a steady fifty-five miles an hour. He was returning from his father's house and the traditional Christmas visit, and was looking forward to some time with his kids. The coarse desert scrub passed him leisurely by on both sides, stretching far to both horizons and the distant hills, broken occasionally by the brave silhouette of a Joshua tree. The road ran forever before and behind him, hedged by the scrub and an occasional drooping wire fence way back from the tarmac. That road, more than the state, was his home.

It was warm, the wind was in his hair, and he had his favourite Iron Horse to carry him home. Sam was happy.

About ten miles from the small cluster of houses which formed his community, Sam noticed a car pulled over on the hard shoulder. It was on the westbound lane, parked neatly facing him as he headed east, apparently undamaged. It appeared to be deserted.

Sam was not a superstitious man. But when he saw that car the blood froze in his veins and his hair stood on end. His stomach churned and filled with fear. And his knuckles turned marble white as he gripped the handlebars. He did not know why; call it a premonition. But Sam knew he did not want to stop, that stopping would be a really bad idea. Sam had a bad feeling about the whole thing, and was having difficulty controlling his bladder.

I ain't gonna stop, he thought, I'm just gonna keep rolling 'til I get home, 'cos where I really wanna be right now is sitting with my babies, drinking ice-cold beer and thinking about anything *except* how bad this feels. I ain't gonna stop and say, 'Evening sir, having some trouble?' or any of *that* shit. This feels bad, and I don't want to end the day full of lead. Or worse.

The car was only a few hundred yards away now and Sam was disgusted to find the needle on his speedo pushing seventy.

Hey, calm down, man. Just 'cos you got the spooks that don't mean you can break the law. Take it easy.

He throttled back until his speed was within the law. He tried to feel better about this, but the spooks had not passed. In fact, it seemed the closer he got to the car the worse he felt. He was in a cold sweat now. Sitting there on his precious Harley in the middle of a deserted highway, Sam felt truly vulnerable for the first time in years. More so because he had no reason to feel like that – after all, it was only an empty car. Wasn't it?

And then, as he drew level with the vehicle and the chills and shakes reached breaking point, sixteen years of training fell back into place. *To Serve and Protect*, he reminded himself. It could be a woman with a baby, stranded out here in the middle of nowhere. Do your duty, Sam Stevens, or you may as well hand in your badge.

Another voice spoke up, one having trouble with its bowels.

But it's my day off and *I DON'T WANT TO BE
HERE*. If it's a mother and her baby then why the
hell does it feel like that car's been dumped there by
the Four Horsemen of the Apocalypse? *Please*, Sammy,
get your arse back home where it belongs before you
have an accident with it and spoil your pants. OK?

He passed the car, its malevolence sneaking by on
his left.

Sam's inner voices wrestled to gain control of his body.
Meanwhile, his automatic pilot cut in. Before he even
realized it, Sam had pulled over, dismounted and jacked
up the bike on its stand. Then he stood there for some
time, hands on hips, gazing back down the road into the
sunset, gripped by indecision and fear.

With one final, helpless sigh Sam surrendered and
strode off at a purposeful pace towards the abandoned
car. As his father used to say, 'When the time comes to
do something, do it. But do it right. Just remember, boy
– shit, or move on.'

'I'm doing it, Pa,' Sam mumbled to himself. 'And I'm
gonna do it right.' His right hand slipped inside his leather
jacket and closed around the comforting warmth of his
non-standard non-police issue .45 calibre Magnum. He
drew the weapon, his legs still pumping the tarmac away
behind him, and checked the load. Then, against his
better judgement but totally in tune with his instinct,
he slipped off the safety catch. He let the gun fall back
to his side as he walked, and the weight of it was pure
reassurance.

Two hundred yards. Halfway there.

He strode down the centre of the road, along the
white line, heading west. The road was deserted. The car
exhaust stared at him sullenly. His heart rate increased
to 120. His eyes scanned the horizon, constantly moving
behind his mirrored shades. He knew the sunglasses

would impair his vision, but since he was walking into the setting sun he needed all the glare protection he could get.

Then he noticed the noise.

Or rather, did not notice the noise. Eerie silence screamed at him, tense and expectant. Sam had lived in the desert for thirty-six years and had never once heard it fall totally silent. It sounded as if the abandonment of the car had triggered the death of every living creature in the area.

Except himself. For the only sounds he could hear were the thud of his boots on the road, the whistle of air in his lungs, and the pounding of his heart in his chest.

One hundred yards to go. Heart rate: 135.

Sam felt stranded in one of those hideous nightmares – where escape is only possible by fleeing down a corridor that gets longer as you rush along it, and where your feet are stuck in maple syrup.

Except, he reminded himself, I'm not exactly escaping. If my senses are correct then I'm running into, not away from, the danger.

Sam attempted a cheerful grin, failed miserably.

And then, just like the dreams, he was suddenly there. One moment he had a mile to go, the next he was right on top of the car and it was TIME (please God let me live through this).

Sam stopped his prayers, raised his pistol and went into action. Heart rate: 140.

The vehicle was now only ten yards away. The low sun dappled the windows with hateful reflections and filled the interior with shadows. Sam's sixth sense was working overtime, feeding him with primitive images. The ancestor within him would have fled from those dark shadows, but a million years of evolution had dulled that receptiveness – Sam had become the hunted, not the hunter. Part of him realized this, even when swamped by his twentieth-century mind. And Sam Stevens, traffic cop hero, paid attention to his instincts.

So Sam turned his fear into anger. And resolved to kick arse.

The car was of foreign manufacture, a Volkswagen. It had Pennsylvanian licence plates.

Long way from home, Sam noted.

It appeared undamaged, but Sam kept his mind open. No tyre marks on the road. Therefore no sudden skid. The two tyres he could see were unmarked, and the car was level on its wheels. Therefore no flat. The bonnet was down. All the doors were shut. Sam would have laid ten dollars to a dime that the gas tank wasn't empty, either. The engine was silent. No tell-tale cooling sounds.

Been here a while then, he concluded.

He walked carefully towards the rear of the car, veering right away from the road. He saw that there was a good two feet between the car and where the edge of the tarmac met the scrub. His gun was ready when he rounded the corner, in case someone was crouched in the blind spot, but there was nobody there.

Five yards. He stopped. Three sides clear. That only left the front. He crouched down on the balls of his feet, right hand free and ready with the gun, left hand supporting his weight. With a last look around – deserted, even the scrub to either side – he ducked his head and looked under the car.

The view was unobstructed. He could see all around the car at ground level, and all he saw was tarmac. So: abandoned.

But the frown had not lifted from his brow when he stood. He *knew* something was there, somewhere, waiting for him, listening for him. Even watching him, maybe. He scanned the scrub again, straining his eyes to catch a glimpse of movement, or reflected sunlight, or an imperfection in the flowing contours of the land.

Nothing.

If they're out there, he thought wryly, then they sure aren't keen to be seen. So they're either not out there, and I've been pissing myself for nothing, or they have good reason to be hiding.

Satisfied that nobody would leap from beside the vehicle to attack him, Sam withdrew a few yards and backed off. He knew he needed to see inside the car, but what he needed and what he wanted were two entirely different things. As it was, he couldn't see diddly-squat through the glass with the sun on it, so he would have to go around to the bonnet.

He sighed, wishing he could get a hold on his irrational fear, knowing he was no longer in control. His feet were heavy as he wandered around to the front of the car.

The view through the windscreen, looking east, revealed nothing. The road was deserted, the front seats were vacant, and the rear seat was empty except for an unoccupied baby chair.

Sam's frown deepened.

He backed away again, feeling decidedly edgy stood out there silhouetted against the skyline. His gaze flicked uncertainly between the car and the beckoning safety of his bike.

One abandoned foreign car. No crash. No accident. No driver. No passengers. No people. No gas?

Maybe he had been wrong. Maybe whoever it was had just run out of gas, decided to walk back to the garage ten miles away. That would at least explain why he had not seen them on his way home.

Maybe.

What it would NOT explain was why Sam just felt so *wrong* about the whole situation. It would NOT explain the unreasoned terror he sensed cackling at the edges of his sanity. Nor would it explain the utter certainty he had that he *was not alone* out here.

Sam forced himself to think.

OK. I've had a quick look. I can either have a *long* look, or I can high tail it the hell out of here. Maybe I'll drop in at the gas station on the way to check if anyone's stopped by. Or maybe I'll just lie on the road and cry myself awake, 'cos this really HAS to be a bad dream. I'll wake up soon, and Tracey will be beside me, and the kids will be all tucked up in bed. And maybe I'll just borrow one of her cigarettes, grab a beer and shoot some pool. Or put my gun to my head and blow my stupid brains out.

Anything but open one of them car doors.

He backed away a little further.

'Sammy, don't open those doors. I know you won't enjoy it.' Speaking aloud brought him back to himself slightly. 'What you don't touch can't hurt you, Sammy old boy.'

'You can bet your ass on that, mister.'

The voice came from out of the nothingness just behind Sam's left ear. He whirled, right hand rising to bring the .45 to bear, left hand outstretched to beat off any attack.

There was nobody there.

He span on the balls of his feet, doing a complete 360 degree turn. The road and scrub were deserted in all directions. Sam's heart was now hammering painfully in his chest. He felt on the verge of having a coronary. His palms were slick with sweat, and his light shirt was plastered to his wet skin. He stared at the world around him, wide-eyed and terrified.

JESUS! he screamed to himself. What the hell was THAT? He half expected to hear an answer to that question, a ghostly proof of his perceptions. But the eerie silence was his only reply.

Sam was at a total loss for the first time in his life. He had never felt so completely out of control.

'Jesus,' he repeated aloud. 'My nerves are shot to hell, and I'm squeezing this gun so hard I'll mould it a new grip.' He forced himself to relax. 'Just hearing things, I guess.'

Again, he cocked an ear at the empty air, almost hoping to catch a response. Go on, he thought, tell me I'm wrong.

Again, silence was his only answer.

He hawked up some phlegm and spat it onto the road. 'Sure is a lot of nothing around here,' he drawled. 'And what there's most nothing of is SENSE. I'm here in the middle of nowhere, there's all sorts of weird shit going on, I'm about to have a heart attack, and I need to change my pants.' He managed a sharp laugh. 'Nearly wet myself there. Getting a little trigger happy, too.'

He looked back at the car. It hadn't changed, hadn't moved. Hadn't sprouted legs and wings and taken to the sky. Which, he admitted, was something at least. Sam's thoughts came down from their adrenalin induced spiral and settled back into some form of normality. His heart slowed slightly – 130 – and he began to feel a little more in control.

'Right then Sam, let's sort this out.' He stepped back from the car a little further, as if putting distance between it and himself would actually reduce the fear in his mind.

Surprisingly, it did.

'Point one you're doing nobody no good out here. If someone tapped you on the shoulder asking for a light you'd like as not just blow his head clean off. And that's not just stupid, it's dangerous – a jumpy cop with a gun is as welcome as a flood in a tampon factory, and you know it. Point two – this is too weird for me. And I knew it would be weird as soon as I saw that damned car, right?

'Point three – there's nobody here.' Admitted. But what about all the ghosts and little monsters waiting just out of sight to pounce on me? 'Point Four—' He paused.

The silence was really getting to him now. It was just so unnatural, and it unsettled him more than the voice. He glanced at the horizon. The sun was sinking fast and it would soon be dark. 'Point 4,' he resumed, 'I don't want to be here when it gets dark. Somehow, don't ask me how, I just KNOW this is gonna get a whole lot worse in the dark.' And as far as I'm concerned it's bad enough already. 'So, wise guy, what do you suggest? Open those car doors or just leave while I'm still in one piece?' He smiled, which surprised him. 'I must admit, I'm rather keen to get moving. I think I've outstayed my welcome.'

That sentence was terminated by a sudden gust of wind. A single, lonely tumbleweed danced across the road, sounding like fingernails tapping on glass. The noise of the wind only deepened the silence around the car, which rocked gently on its suspension.

Sam felt the coldest chill of his life fill his bones. For a moment he was incapable of movement. His senses screamed death and he could swear he smelled decomposing flesh. His skin was an instant rash of goosebumps. His eyes iced over, his gaze fixed on the rear window of the car.

And for a moment, just for a moment, Sam thought he saw a face there. Or something.

But then it was gone.

The wind died as suddenly as it started. Sam felt some warmth return to his limbs, but he was shivering and his flesh was hard with the cold. The barrel of the .45 wavered. Sam still stared at the window, rooted to the spot with terror.

Please God let that have been a trick of the light. Please God let that car be empty. Please God let me out of this.

He tried to turn away but his petrified body would not respond to his brain. When at last he managed to turn his head, his eyes stayed locked in the same place, swivelling in their sockets.

SAMMY GET THE HELL OUT OF HERE! NOW SAMMY! GO!

His heart was hammering again. Fingers of ice were creeping over his shoulder-blades. A thousand evil eyes were regarding him from every shadow, waiting. Waiting for darkness to fall so they could rush at him, smother him, knock him down and tear him limb from limb, dance circles of demonic glee over his dismembered body in the moonlight, sink their fangs into his bloated heart and—

Dark shadows moved in the car. The Volkswagen shifted on its springs. A blood soaked hand appeared in the window.

Sam Stevens uttered a low moan of terror, turned, and fled.

Powerful legs pounded his feet on the tarmac, hurling his body away, back from the nightmare, down the road towards his Harley. Lungs sucked in huge volumes of air, feeding a thousand muscles with energy. Adrenalin surged into his bloodstream.

One hundred yards left, and the bike seemed a hundred miles away.

Sam put his head down and ran as if the Hordes of Hades were at his heels. An ankle turned painfully in a pothole, nearly spilling him, but he recovered and bounded on, ignoring the pain.

Somewhere in his mind something laughed.

'You can run. You can run. But you can't hide.'

Fifty yards and he was gasping for breath. The air wheezed from his overloaded lungs. He wanted to slow down.

Can't. Can't slow down. Got to run.

Five yards, and suddenly he was there, catching his skin on the exhaust pipe hard enough to tear his trouser leg and flesh. Blood welled from the cut. 'Bitch!' he wheezed. He realised with amazement that the exhaust was still hot. Sam kicked the bike off its stand, swung his leg over the seat and dropped onto the leather like a sack of bricks. The suspension protested slightly.

Down the road, four hundred yards away, stood the deserted car.

Sam fumbled for the kick start. His ankle was beginning to throb and he could feel the blood seeping down his shin.

Behind him a car door slammed.

He froze. Head down, one foot raised to kick down on the lever, other leg supporting the combined weight of him and the machine. Suspended in time, utterly motionless, a still photograph.

'Look around,' a voice called from a great distance, but Sam heard it clearly. The voice went well with the silence earlier: eerie, hollow, toneless and dead. 'Look around and face me, Sam.'

His head rose slowly, unwillingly. There was something hypnotic in the voice, something compelling and undeniable. A litany repeated in his mind: Don't look round, don't look round.

'You know it makes sense, Sam,' called the voice.

I know it doen't, Sam thought. Don't look. This isn't the movies, Sam. *Don't* look behind you.

Unbelievably he felt his head turning.

'Look around Sam. Come on, are you scared? A hero like you?'

Sam blinked. Yes, I'm scared. Scared of you. Whoever you are. *Whatever* you are.

He reached for his gun, realising it was no longer in his hand and that he could not remember holstering it. But the .45 sat snugly against his shoulder within its leather home, evidence of his reflexes and ingrained training: whenever possible, do *not* run with a loaded gun, or you'll probably blow your own foot off. But he was not running now. His fist closed around the butt of the pistol.

The voice laughed. It was the most hideous laugh Sam had ever heard. 'That won't do you any good, Sam.'

Stevens jerked back his head, surprised. What the hell . . .? His indignation rose like a mushroom cloud. He was beginning to realise he was not a participant in a fair game, and Sam *hated* cheats. Once again, this time at a critical moment, his fear turned to anger. Frozen muscles melted in the heat of his rage. The cloak of terror around his brain vaporized.

He grinned. 'If you can't beat 'em,' he said slowly, relaxing his leg on the kick start, 'fuck 'em.'

With a bellow of rebellion he rammed his foot down hard. The Harley roared into life. Sam did not turn round or look back. He did not even consider putting up a fight or stopping to see WHAT it was he was up against. He just kicked the bike into gear and let out the clutch. With a squeal of rubber the Harley slid out onto the road. There was a slight fishtail wobble on the rear end, the result of Sam's over eager clutch control, then he was racing up through the gears. The engine, still warm and eager, thundered beneath him, desperate to do his bidding and carry him home.

Thirty. Thirty-five. More throttle. Forty.

And then came the unmistakable sensation of warm breath on the back of his neck, a smell of foul, fetid lungs in his nostrils.

Sam screamed and lurched forward. The spasm of his muscles pulled the throttle towards him, and the motorcycle leapt madly under his backside. The clock span past sixty.

Something just by his left ear chuckled softly. Sam felt the exhalation on his skin, and once again the rank odour of decomposing lungs. Without even realising it, he wet himself.

A long claw tapped him gently on the cheek. Sam cringed away from it, yanking back further on the throttle. Even as he accelerated, however, Sam knew it would do no good. Because he was already doing seventy-five, and it was hovering right behind him as if he was still parked by the roadside.

Or rather, it was not hovering at all. He caught sight of the long shadow he cast in front of him, and there was no sign of the demon breathing down his neck.

The paradox caused Sam to scream again in fear. And the claw dug deep into his cheek and tore off a large flap of skin.

Sam nearly passed out, so great was the pain. Blood gushed from the wound, and the teeth on his left jaw began to ache as the wind whistled against the nerves. The piece of skin hung uselessly against his face, flapping painfully, dripping crimson rain. 'Oh shit,' he moaned through the blood, 'oh shit oh shit oh shit.'

In a last desperate attempt at escape he gave the bike everything it could take. If he was going to die, then he figured he may as well die doing 125 than wetting his pants on the hard shoulder. So despite the pain, despite the certainty that he would never see his family again or get home alive, Sam Stevens opened his mouth and laughed in the face of Death. This was his dream – the speed, the wind in his face, the fury of the road.

Sam laughed like he had never laughed before, so hard that he gasped for breath as the passage of air tore the wind from his lungs. Yet he had never felt so *alive*.

Imperceptibly at first, but then more rapidly, the breath on his neck cooled. Until all that remained was his laughter tumbling into the slipstream. For a while he could not believe it, simply sat there enjoying the respite while he waited for another attack. But then, through the adrenalin fizz in his blood, he sensed his fear slacken. The power of the beast dropped off miraculously as he pulled away, until at last he felt no more of its presence.

Then, and only then, did he allow himself to take a quick peek over his shoulder. The road was deserted, the car gone or dropped out of sight. Either way, he felt no more terror. He thought he might make it home after all. His smile widened, and he was so jubilant he no longer even felt any pain in his cheek.

Without warning the voice spoke again in his mind, quietly, as if from a huge distance. 'Another time, Sam,' it whispered, pure toneless evil. 'You can run, but you can't hide. I'll always find you.'

Then it was gone, and somehow Sam knew it would return to finish its business. He swallowed in a dry throat, his larynx protesting, then returned his gaze to the road and drew his head into the shelter of his shoulders like a turtle. Fresh despair mingled with silent fury in his mind – he sensed truth in those words. Unavoidable, inescapable, relentless truth.

But Sam Stevens had his own truth. 'I'll be ready,' he oathed. He eased off on the throttle, letting the sound of the engine mirror the subdued roar of his anger. 'And next time it'll be *my* turn to kick ass.'

CHAPTER FOUR

Timothy Johnson Has a Restless Night

December 27 1990, 5:30 p.m. London, England.

'But Mum, I don't want to go.'

'John, tell Tim he has to go and see Grandma.'

'If he doesn't want to go, let him stay.'

A worried mother's pause. 'We can't leave him alone, John. He's too young.'

A young boy seeing his opening. 'Yes you can, Mum. I'll be all right. I've done it before.'

'See? He's done it before.' An impatient man in a hurry.

'Well . . .' A reluctant mother crumbling.

'You'll be all right, won't you Tim old son?'

'Yes, Uncle John.'

A slightly shorter mother's pause. 'I don't know, John . . .'

'Sal, come on. Make a decision.'

'Are you sure Timmy?'

'Yes. Say hi to Grandma.' A young boy's dream coming true.

'Get your coat on Sal. I'll be in the car. See you later, kiddo.' An impatient man dropping hints.

'Are you sure you'll be OK Tim?'

'Oh Mum! I *am* twelve. I'm not a kid any more.'

A worried mother biting her lip. 'Well, OK then.

But lock the door when we go. And don't answer it for anybody.'

'Sure, no problem. Now *go*, before Uncle John gets mad.'

'Give your mother a hug.' A mother kissing her son. A son squirming and pulling faces. 'Right. I'll go then. 'Bye now.'

A door slamming. Just to make sure it was closed.

A young boy alone. And very pleased with himself.

'Magic! And it will be *hours* before they get back.'

A dream come true. Or so he thought . . .

Sally Johnson crossed the road and climbed into her lover's Rover. The car was moving before she had the seatbelt on.

'Do you think he'll be OK? I don't like leaving him.'

John Dane drove to the end of the road and turned right. The traffic was light, which was good news. He had a long way to go. 'Oh, stop worrying Sal. He's old enough to look after himself.' He drew to a halt at the next lights, beside the local newsagent.

'I'm not so sure,' Sally said, but her tone was already half-hearted. She examined her lipstick in the vanity mirror.

'Come on Sal. You saw the look on his face – we made his day! God only knows what sort of mischief he'll get up to.'

Sally frowned, then pushed the sun-shade back up. 'That's half the reason why I'm so worried.' She turned to look out of the window, saw the headline on the paper stand: 'PHONE BOX SUICIDE'.

Phone box suicide? That's novel. What did they do? Slash their wrists with the receiver? She frowned again, thoughts of her son already dissipating from her mind . . .

The first thing Tim did when the door slammed was fart.

It was just his way of opening up the freedom celebrations.

Tim's father had moved out over a year ago, after several months of heated arguments. Scott Johnson, thirty-seven-year-old author of horror novels, had tried and tried to live peacefully with his career-minded wife. And failed.

He was a child of the sixties and placed no stock in money. Which was just as well, since his books were as scary as washing-up liquid and were lucky to even get into print. That did not bother Scott. As long as he could sleep until noon, smoke the odd joint, play with his adorable son and write a few words every week, he was happy. He hated the values of the eighties, and despaired at the potential of the nineties. Nobody said 'vibes' any more. It was depressing.

His wife had once been a carefree, beautiful girl with long dark hair. Now she was what he called a 'paranoid, stressed, city wheeler-dealer'. She was actually Personnel Manager for a company in North London, but it was all the same to Scott. If it did not involve being your own boss and having fun – like discussing the Cosmos or sleeping – it was wheeler-dealing.

That depressed him, too.

But what depressed him most of all was the other men. He could cope with her nail-biting and violin-string nerves, but he couldn't cope with the affairs. Not that it was all her fault, of course. He would admit that he had driven her to it, with his lack of concern about financial security and his persistent and annoying habit of refusing to let go of the past.

Well, he would say to himself, I didn't actually *drive* her to it. I may have started the car, but she worked the pedals and turned the wheel. Besides, what was so wrong with holding onto values held dear? She did. Except her values were fat pay cheques and dressing for promotion. Not the joys of life, freedom of expression, and the ability to live off the Government.

But whatever the reasons, she started seeing other men (which, even in the sixties, had never been Scott's cup of tea). She had not even been very secretive or discreet. That more than anything had shown Scott the extent of her contempt for him.

Fine. Let her look down her cocaine-powdered nose at him. See how she copes with a career, a kid and no man about the house.

So he moved out, half because of her, half because of Tim. He could no longer bear to see his beloved son's tearful face whenever they argued. The divorce had been settled amicably – he could see Tim every weekend, and take him for three months a year (a trial set-up which had worked surprisingly well). Sally had worried that Tim would return from his father's house dirty, thin and spaced-out. But that had not happened. She secretly believed that Tim did the cooking and cleaning when he visited his dad, since Scott had always been incapable of even frying himself an egg.

Much to Scott's annoyance Sally had coped remarkably well on her own. Tim was a responsible boy for his age, well-balanced and capable of maintaining a sense of humour, and profoundly fond of BOTH his parents. Thus Sally's task had been eased a little. Scott had thought about asking if he could move back in again – pride had never been a word in his vocabulary – but was beaten to it by someone Tim mysteriously referred to as 'Uncle John'. Since Tim did not *have* an Uncle John, he assumed this was some lover-boy Sally had installed to fix the fuses when they blew or put up a shelf or two (and all the other things Scott had never done). From that point on he resigned himself to being an official statistic and got down to some serious work. The resulting book had sold well in the USA, and tickled his son pink. 'No washing-up liquid here, Dad,' Tim had said by page 130, looking up and smiling with genuine pleasure. 'This is real honest to God *bleach* horror.'

Scott grew fonder of his son as the months passed. At first he thought it was the sense of loss and the fact that he saw him less often. But towards Christmas 1990 he realised it was because Tim had become the sort of person Scott could love – he was happy-go-lucky but not stupid, and genuine in everything he said or did. True, living with opposing forces in his parents had made him a mild schizoid, since he felt he had to please all the people all of the time. But this only served to make him more comical, as he would play his parents off one against the other.

This was perhaps Scott's greatest triumph. Somehow he *knew* that Tim was more open and relaxed with him than he was with Sally. Scott suspected this was largely due to the presence of 'Uncle John', though he never suggested as much to Tim.

Tim, meanwhile, worshipped his father. At the same time he acknowledged the fact that Scott was a good-for-very-little ex-hippy (as his mother put it). His father was the tidal energy in his life, whereas his mother was his anchor.

Scott Johnson reciprocated that emotion. He loved his son. He would do all in his power to protect him and make him happy.

Or so he claimed.

The second thing Tim did after the door slammed was run to the window. Because you could never be sure until you actually saw them go, could you? He watched his mother climb into the car, then watched the car until it had turned the corner and vanished from sight. By that point his face was pressed hard up against the glass. It was cold outside. And dark.

As he turned away, already pulling the curtain closed, Tim caught sight of the telephone box across the street. For a moment his eyes were glued to it – every detail seemed to burn into his mind, as if a photograph was forming on the back of his skull.

The phone box was empty, the receiver idle on its cradle. The door was ajar, hung on worn hinges. The green sticker in the booth said 'Phonecard'. For a second, just for a second, Tim's eyes mistook the word. He thought it said 'Coffin'.

Behind the booth was an iron-railing fence, separating the road from a small square of lawn and flowers. This arrangement was common in the capital, where houses congregated around any patch of green like old women around gossip.

Tim did not see the flowers, or the grass. He only saw the tips of the railings. And they were dripping blood. Inside the telephone box a man was burning to death.

He closed his eyes, trying to shut out the vision, but it persisted like the after-image of a light bulb. After a while the garish colours dimmed and merged, and Tim opened his eyes again.

Across the road stood an empty telephone box. Behind the booth, the rain dripped off the railings.

It was not the first time Tim had experienced such things.

When he was eight, Tim had caught sight of a teacher from his school crossing the road a few yards away. Tim had clearly seen the blood-soaked body, the torso crushed and missing one arm. The man's head had been squashed flat, and brains oozed down his back.

Tim had been too shocked to call out. It was not every day one saw a dead man crossing the road to Woolworths. When he finally rubbed his hands over his eyes, believing himself mistaken, the image disappeared. The man who strode into the shop was just plain old Mr Rose. Not a comic-strip zombie out on a flesh eating spree.

Tim had shrugged and thought nothing of the event, putting it down to an over-active imagination and perhaps too many pickled onions. Or maybe he was just turning weird, like his dad.

That day Mr Rose had been run over and killed by a number 55 bus on Old Street.

For some months Tim had hardly said a word to anybody. He had horrible nightmares. The doctor could find nothing medically wrong, and recommended psychiatric treatment. Scott and Sally refused.

Four months after that day, on one cold and windy October night, Tim awoke from a particularly scary dream and screamed for his father. Scott was at his side in seconds. Tim screamed again when his father appeared, and cringed away from him. 'All burned, all burned,' was all Tim said before collapsing into his father's arms and crying himself to sleep. The following morning Tim had begged Scott not to leave the house. Scott had never seen such a look of anguish on his son's face. So he had told Sally to go to work, not mentioning Tim's dream or his bizarre behaviour. He then rang his agent and cancelled their lunch-time meeting in an Islington pub. He spent the rest of the day playing with his son and providing what comfort he could.

The news that day reported a gas explosion in an Islington pub. The building had been demolished by the blast, and fifteen people had been blown up or burnt to death. Scott had merely gaped at the TV pictures, while Tim wrapped his arms around his neck and gave him the fiercest hug ever. 'Thanks Dad,' Tim had said, as if that explained everything.

It had taken Scott three hours of pleading and bullying to get an answer out of his son. Then, in a flood of tears, the whole story had tumbled out. Tim's premonitions and dreams, his guilt, his sense of responsibility for all the deaths ('I did it, Dad! I saw it in my head and it happened! *I killed* those people!').

It had taken Scott another three hours to console his son and discuss the situation. Without Scott, no doubt Tim would have been guilt-ridden or mad to this day – as a hippy author of supernatural novels, Scott did not even *think* of doubting Tim's story.

His argument hinged on the fact that Tim had actually saved him from the explosion. 'You're a hero, Tim! What are you guilty about? You saved my life today and you're feeling *bad* about it?'

Tim's guilt was all cried out; he no longer carried a dark secret. In fact, as his father said, he should be PROUD of his mind, not scared or disgusted. To ram home the point, Scott did two things. First, he explained to Tim that his was a rare gift, best kept secret from the powers that be. They forged a pact to face his power together, but alone. Scott hoped this would add a touch of adventure to the proceedings, without doing any more psychological damage. It would also keep his hysterical wife out of the way.

Secondly, he sketched out the plot of a book with Tim, both suggesting ideas for the story. It was the first time Scott had ever worked with a co-author. They titled the book *The Haunting Man*, and placed a ten-year-old psychic boy as the hero. Tim's ideas all made it into the final version, and Scott was immensely proud of his son (and not in the least bothered that Tim, at eight, was a better novelist than he). Scott dedicated the book: 'To Tim, the *real* hero of this work.'

It was a truly cathartic cure for his troubled son.

Since 1988 Tim's head had been clear of visions. This was good news, given that his father had left and was no longer on call to help him through the nightmares. Scott suggested one day, when they were discussing the subject, that perhaps it had only been a temporary thing – maybe Tim would never experience them again.

After a while, Tim – reluctant at first to get his hopes up – had started to believe his father.

But now he turned away from the window, his head starting to ache. 'Thanks, Dad. Mum always said you were full of it.'

The fourth thing Tim did after the door slammed was pick up the phone. His head was agony now, despite the Aspirin raided from the bottle he was not supposed to know about or be able to open.

He had abandoned all hope of having an enjoyable evening. The menace of the vision and the certainty that something was going to happen poured a bucket of iced water over his high spirits.

Tim felt lost. The premonition was the first in over eighteen months, and had arrived totally out of the blue. He had expected anything but the renewed touch of his curse.

Why me? Won't it ever end?

He dialled the number of his father's flat in Hackney. As he stood there, listening to the tone, his eyes were drawn back to the window. The curtains were drawn but Tim could see right through them in his mind's eye. Outside a man was impaled on the railings. Another thrashed in agony as he burned alive in the telephone box.

The phone in Scott's flat began to ring.

The shrill sound filled the quiet flat. Empty beer cans littered the settee and much of the threadbare carpet.

Scott did not hear the telephone. Nor did he sense the urgency in the mental pleas of his son eight miles away. In fact, Scott did not hear anything. He lay spreadeagled on the kitchen floor. A small pool of blood had formed under his head, but it was dry now.

The sound of the telephone echoed around the house.

Mrs Abrahams, the old lady who owned the house and lived downstairs, put aside her knitting and cocked an ear.

Go on, she willed, answer it. I know you're up there.

The phone continued to ring. She pulled a face.

Drunk again, no doubt. You should go out and get a job. What kind of impression do you think you're giving your adorable little boy? A drunken lay-about for a father. Honestly. It's disgusting.

The phone fell silent, leaving only the sound of the clock on the mantelpiece. She sighed and returned to her knitting.

Tim let the phone ring forty times before he finally dropped the handset back onto its cradle. The lump of fear in his chest was larger now. For the first time in years he felt truly alone.

'It's not fair, Dad. You promised you'd *always* be there.'

For a moment his rising fear threatened to turn into hatred. By force of will alone he prevented this – it was not his father's fault circumstances had intruded on their pact. When the promise had been made the situation had been very different.

Tim allowed himself a sigh and crossed to the window.

It would happen soon. He just wished that he knew

what *it* was, so that he could perhaps prevent the tragedy. That possibility did exist – after all, Tim knew he had saved his father.

As he had so many times in the past, Tim wondered why his gift never revealed anything pleasant. Death and disaster were the only images he could conjure.

Pulling back the curtains he looked down on the street. The telephone box stood there in the cold, its lonely light mingling with that of the streetlamps. A woman stood inside, talking to someone in another part of the city, perhaps even the world.

Now? Tim wondered absently. Will it happen now?

But he knew it would not. His vision had contained two men, not one woman. So he scanned the street, searching shadows for the two men who would end up dead if he could not stop them. Seeing nothing he stepped back and dropped onto the sofa like a sack of potatoes. The TV remote control fell into his hand, so he scanned the channels. As usual there was nothing worth watching so he turned it off again. Then he began to fidget.

'Get a grip, Tim,' his father would say. 'If you need to do something then do it. If you can't be bothered, then *relax*. Chewing your nails won't get you anywhere – look at your mother. Where's all that stress got her?'

Tim would not speak the answer, but thought it nonetheless. 'Well, actually Dad, it got her a well-paid job, a pension, a load of money in the bank, and something to do with her life instead of sitting around smoking and drinking all day.' He did not say anything though. Scott was touchy about such things.

Tim examined his options: he could do nothing, which was not a pleasant choice; he could keep trying his father, but knew Scott tended to go 'out' and stay out; he could try to convince his mother of his gift and persuade her to come home – doubtless an impossible task; or he could do the same to the police – equally hopeless.

Or, finally, he could handle it himself.

He slumped in the chair, disheartened. But do what? Vandalize the phone to stop anyone using it? Or just intercept all the men who pass and say 'Excuse me sirs, but I believe that your lives will come to a gruesome and bloody end if you use this telephone box'?

He started to chew his nails. Just to make bad things worse, his headache was coming back.

Scott Johnson shuddered. A low moan escaped his mouth. His abused brain struggled to regain consciousness. With a superhuman effort he opened his eyes. The lights on the ceiling swirled, doubled, dropped into focus. He squinted against the sudden glare.

'Jesus, what happened to my mouth?' He licked his lips carefully, and swallowed. The inside of his mouth tasted as if a creature of the night had crapped and then died in there.

He sat up. Green sparklers lit in his eyeballs and the top of his head fell off. A Marching Band played the *1812 Overture* in his temples, using real cannons. Thump, thump, thump.

Scott struggled to sit up while holding his head together. Eventually the throbbing abated and he relaxed. When he took his hands away they were sticky with blood. He looked up. There was a stain on the worktop which matched exactly the pain in his head.

'Congratulations, Scott.' The image in his mind's eye was that of a drunken pig staggering around a grotty Hackney flat, Scotch in one hand, joint in the other, tripping over the door-sill and going arse over tit to smash his head on the worktop.

'Beautiful. If drinking doesn't take the pain away,

Scott, why not just bang your head against the furniture instead.'

When the world around him stopped spinning and he no longer felt he had to hold on lest he fall off, Scott pushed himself to his feet. This time he was ready for the merry-go-round, and thought he did well to reach the sink before throwing up. The spasms were bad, but he'd had worse.

'Shower time,' he said eventually, wiping the vomit from his chin. 'And maybe another drink.'

But not necessarily in that order, he added.

The hot water jets made Scott feel 1000% better. A long gargle with mouthwash and a painful tooth brushing doubled that sense of well being. By the time he'd combed his hair and tied it back in a ponytail, Scott felt well enough to start drinking again.

Instead, summoning all the will power he could muster, he went back into the kitchen. It stank, and was filthy.

He sighed and reached for the mop.

Tim sat in his dad's old armchair, reading *Slaughter at Midnight*, one of his dad's novels. In the true tradition of Scott's horror stories, it was making his eyelids feel very heavy.

Outside, a car door slammed. Tim felt his heart thud once and stop. Goosebumps rose on his flesh. NOW! he thought. THIS IS IT!

He carefully set the book on the arm of the chair, rose and crossed to the window. Without really wanting to, he pulled back the curtain and looked down on the street.

A car had stopped about ten yards from the telephone box. Two men stood beside it; one bent down to lock the door then stepped up on the pavement. Before opening the door to the booth, they kissed.

Yuck, thought Tim, then mentally slapped his wrist.

It wasn't their fault they were gay, any more than it was his fault he knew they were going to die, or his father's fault for being a hippy.

One of the men went in to make a call. The other stood outside, lounging against the railings, hands in his jacket pockets.

Without warning, all of the streetlamps dimmed and went out, plunging the street into sudden darkness.

For a few moments Tim could see nothing but his reflection in the glass. He squashed his nose up against the window and cupped his hands around his eyes to close out the light. The view slowly came into focus as his eyes adjusted.

The man inside the telephone box was gazing out at the street. He held the phone in his right hand, and Tim could see his lips moving. His boyfriend had pushed himself away from the railings, surprised at the sudden failure of the lights.

Tim could not move, his gaze locked on the road with morbid fascination. He knew he should shout, ring his dad, do *something*, but was unable to tear himself away. It was his reward for having the vision – a ring-side seat at the entertainment. Tim prayed to be wrong. He prayed the two men would make their call and disappear to wherever they had intended to go. He prayed he would not have to stand there and watch it all happen, that someone would tap him on the shoulder and he would wake up and his mum and dad would still be married and John wouldn't boss him around any more and he would never have another vision again for as long as he lived. Amen.

His prayers went unanswered.

Scott Johnson put the mop away and sat down in front of the TV. Knowing he shouldn't, but enjoying it anyway, he poured three fingers of vodka into a glass and drank it in one long swallow. The liquid fire burned his stomach and made the bile rise in his throat again, but Scott felt the shakes subside and the chills recede.

He leaned back in the chair, poured himself some more vodka, and savoured the peace of his lonely life.

Tim nearly had a heart attack when the action finally began.

A shadow flowed on the far side of the railings, moving swiftly over the grass towards the road. The man outside the phone box suddenly raised his hands to his throat and staggered back onto the fence. His eyes bulged in their sockets. He opened his mouth to scream, tongue protruding like a bloated, purple maggot.

Tim felt icy fingers of fear tickle the base of his spine.

Run away! his brain screamed, but his feet would not move.

The man on the railings had his open mouth instantly stuffed with a wad of cloth. Large hands reached over the fence and grabbed the belt in his trousers. Then he was lifted up and back, bent double as his legs kicked uselessly in mid-air. The spikes on the railings speared the man's midriff, bursting through the flesh and clothing to shower his white shirt with blood.

Tim gagged on his dinner. Tears of fear and revulsion brimmed in his eyes. His bladder loosened and urine ran down his leg.

Outside, the victim thrashed on the spikes which impaled him. His hands clutched at the metal points which violated his abdomen. His legs twitched in the air, head bouncing up and down to the motion. Blood gushed from his mouth, pushing out the gag onto the grass. With a final death spasm the man went still. His arms fell to his sides. He hung there, bent both ways over the fence, feet coming to rest just inches above the pavement.

Tim felt his knees tremble and threaten to give way. He tried to move away from the window but felt glued to the spot.

Get out of the light! If whoever is down there looks up, he'll see you silhouetted in the window. *Move*, idiot!

But his muscles refused to respond.

Even before the first man was dead, the second killing had begun. By chance the other man had turned away when his friend had been attacked. The sounds of the struggle had obviously alerted him. Tim saw the receiver drop from the man's limp hand and rebound off the cubicle wall. For a second the man just stood there and stared at the railings, unable to believe his own eyes.

By the time he moved it was too late. The shadow vaulted the four foot railing and stood by the booth. The man inside threw his body against the door, ramming the glass with his shoulder. His mouth opened and closed in terrified shouts, but Tim heard nothing.

The efforts of the trapped man were futile. The door refused to budge, even though Tim could not see what was blocking the exit.

'Kick the glass,' Tim whispered. 'Get out of there.'

Dark shoes kicked at the glass panels, shattering them. The murderous shadow flickered back into view. This time it held a jerry can, which it inverted over the pavement and emptied around the telephone box. The figure inside began to scream again, but Tim heard the screams now. He knew others would hear them, too.

And then it was over. A spark of flame appeared, briefly illuminating the killer dressed all in black, and then the booth exploded into flame. The man inside was consumed instantly. His arms beat frantically at the door, and at last it broke free. The human inferno staggered out into the street, a walking pillar of fire. After wandering in aimless circles for about fifteen seconds the man went down on both knees. Then he collapsed forward onto the tarmac, motionless. Flames still leapt from his exposed body, and pieces of burning cloth and flesh spiralled up into the night.

Tim saw nothing of this. All he saw was the killer, lit by the blaze, stood on the pavement in full view of the entire street.

And all the murderer saw was Tim.

Tim felt his eyes bore into the shadows which formed the man's face. He was struck by the notion that the other man had no eyes – only deep, dark, empty pits. Those wells of horror seemed to be laughing at him. Then a cold, empty voice spoke in his head.

'You can run. You can run. But you can't hide.'

Tim ran anyway. He ran to the door and threw all the bolts. Then he ran to the back door and all the windows and checked the security locks. Finally he ran to the telephone.

Tim was a sensible, mature boy. Despite being gripped by unreasoning terror he knew exactly what to do. He ignored his beating heart. He ignored the fact that he may have just seconds to live. And he ignored the wet patch on his trousers.

He picked up the phone and dialled his father's flat.

'Dad, you'd better be awake now,' he said clearly. 'Or I'll come back and haunt you when all this is over.'

Scott Johnson tried to ignore the telephone. The last thing he needed now was to talk to somebody.

Downstairs, Mrs Abrahams pushed her knitting aside, picked up her walking stick and banged it on the ceiling.

Scott breathed a deep sigh, and reached for the phone. 'Chongs laundry service,' he drawled.

'DAD! Thank God!'

Scott shot forward in his chair, instantly alert. 'Tim? What's up, son?'

There followed a thirty-second stream of terrified, disjointed words. Scott could have said 'Hey, hold on. Take it easy and tell me from the beginning'. But he knew his son too well. So what he actually said was: 'Tim, sit tight. I'm on my way.'

He threw the phone back on its hook, missed, grabbed his coat and car keys and ran out of the door.

Tim hung up the phone, his heart already slowing. Pops was on his way, and if he drove like he usually did then he should get there with time to spare.

Tim went around the house, checking all the locks again. It took him longer this time, because he sidled up to every door and window with the blood pounding in his temples. He had seen *The Shining*, and was expecting a fire axe to appear at any moment.

It did not.

That odious task complete he returned to the living room.

He's out there somewhere, he thought. He's coming for me, and there's nothing I can do. I can run, but I can't hide.

He started to chew his nails. 'Hurry up Dad.'

Scott hammered down Upper Street, pushing the battered old car up to eighty miles an hour. He was speeding and drunk, and that was not a wise mixture. But his son was in danger and he was in a hurry.

Scott drove through another red light.

Just a few more miles, Timmy, and I'll be there.

Hang on, son. I'm coming, and I won't let you down. I promise.

It crossed his mind that Tim might have rung him earlier, when he had been completely out of it. But he pushed the thought aside, knowing it would achieve nothing.

His attention snapped back to the road when he nearly drove into a police car pulling out of a side road. He yanked on the steering wheel, struck the kerb, glanced off a bollard, swung round and rebounded backwards onto the road. He hit the brakes. The resulting skid carried him ten yards into a brick wall, and then he was rolling. The car flipped three times before coming to rest on its roof against a bus shelter. Petrol leaked from the tank. Wheels span aimlessly in the air.

Constable David Whitlock, who had spent the last three days recovering from the Christmas Eve Bloomsbury burning, sat in his Ford Sierra and stared in amazement at the wreckage of the car lying upside down about 200 yards down the road.

'Well, bugger me,' he said quietly.

His superior, Sergeant Michael Fowles, sat beside him at the wheel. 'Bloody joy riders.' Fowles put the car into gear and nosed it down towards the wreck. 'Ring for a meat wagon.'

Scott Johnson crawled out through the shattered passenger door window, cutting his hands and knees on broken glass. Despite a few cuts and a big lump on his forehead where he had hit the steering column, Scott was unharmed. He clambered to his feet, staggered a few yards, then zigzagged over to the police car.

Scott was a man with a mission.

Fowles opened his door and stepped out. Even from some yards away he could smell the drink on the man's breath. 'Evening sir. Having a spot of bother are we?'

Scott shook his head, either in denial of that statement or merely to clear away the fog of shock. 'Look, I'm in a hurry so please listen.' He held up a hand as Fowles opened his mouth to speak. 'Later. I have to get to my son. He's in trouble.'

Of course he is, thought Fowles. And you've probably got a pregnant woman in the boot. Believe me, I've heard them all, pal.

Scott saw the expression on the Sergeant's face, and knew exactly what it meant. 'Look, I don't normally do eighty miles an hour with a pint of vodka in my stomach. But you have to believe me – my kid is in danger and I need to get over there right now.'

Fowles bit back his intended quip, restrained by the desperate and honest look in the man's eyes. 'What's the problem?'

Scott shrugged helplessly. 'I don't know. He rang me a few minutes ago blabbing something about some bloke being burnt alive in a telephone box. I know it sounds crazy but— '

His voice trailed off. They were not listening to him. They were just standing there, staring at him in amazement.

Fowles was the first to react. 'Get in,' he ordered. 'Dave, get on to Daniels – he'll want to know about this.'

The two men clambered into the car, then looked back at Scott expectantly. 'Well, hurry up!' Fowles shouted.

The car was already moving by the time Scott threw himself in.

Tim sat alone in the house, his terror growing. Perhaps five minutes had passed since the phone box had been razed to the ground.

'Dad will be here soon,' he repeated to himself.

And that was when he heard the door handle turn.

The blood froze in his veins. He heart pounded once in his head, then stopped. His trembling knees turned instantly to jelly.

'*Dad! Help!*'

Tim looked up from the floor and stared at the front door. It was made of four-centimetre-thick mahogany, held in place by a security deadlock, a chain and three bolts. The door was very secure; Scott had made sure of that himself (because although he was a hippy and claimed to believe in universal love, he was no idiot).

Tim studied the locks, and thought carefully about the man outside on the porch step. He thought about a man being impaled on a set of four-foot iron railings, and another being burned to death. He thought of the vacant eye sockets in the killer's head. He thought of the emotionless voice, and that ominous message.

Tim thought about a lot of things. But most of all he thought that all the locks in the world were just not going to be enough.

He didn't need DIY house security. He needed a machine gun.

It was over five miles from the end of Upper Street, where Scott had crashed his car by the Angel tube station, to where Tim sat locked in his house. Yet the entire journey took them just six minutes. Six minutes in which Scott aged thirty years and ate his fingernails. His imagination ran riot, picturing all manner of things happening to his son while he steamed down the back streets.

In most towns there is an idiot driver wherever you turn. In London, there are a thousand. Scott lost count of the times some moron pulled out in front of them, or refused to pull over, or even tried to race them. Fowles manoeuvred around them all, nipping in and out of the growing traffic, changing lanes like a maniac. Many a dog that evening did its business earlier than expected.

It was just past nine when the car skidded to a halt outside Scott's old house, leaving a trail of rubber on the road. Fowles did not care. As he was so fond of saying when people commented on his driving, 'It's OK, it's a company car.'

Scott was first out of the car, surprising when one considered the amount of alcohol in his bloodstream. He ignored the shouted order of 'Stay here!' directed at his back. He ignored the burnt corpse in the street and pushed through the people milling aimlessly around the carnage. He headed straight for number 56, racing up the steps, barely aware that David Whitlock was hot on his heels. He skidded to a halt at the front door, for a moment so surprised he could hardly comprehend the situation.

The door had been smashed to splinters and now hung in tatters from its bent hinges. Shards of wood littered the hall. Amongst them lay a bent and battered petrol can. A brass bolt was embedded in the wall, thrown there when the door had finally given way.

Scott pulled himself together. 'Tim!'

The only answer was the sound of breaking glass upstairs.

Scott took the stairs in threes, bounding up the old staircase like a madman and nearly breaking his neck in the process. When he reached the top he realised he had acquired a three-foot piece of splintered timber from somewhere. Instinct, he thought.

'Tim!' he bawled again. No answer.

All the house lights were on, which he found surprising. The street lights had all been dark.

But where the hell was his son?

All the upstairs doors were ajar. From the bathroom came the sound of running water, a peculiar reminder of normality.

Scott felt his hopes sink. Somehow he knew they were too late, that the culprit was no longer there.

Whitlock materialized at his shoulder. His wide eyes looked resigned to finding the worse. 'Nothing downstairs,' he whispered. 'I think our man is gone.' He frowned. 'I think it best if you go down while I check these rooms – it could be messy.' The young constable did not sound too happy about that prospect.

Scott raised his makeshift spear, grinning humourlessly. 'No chance. If that bastard is here I'm having his balls.' He did not give Whitlock a chance to refuse. Using the point of the spear he pushed the bathroom door open. Whitlock peered over his shoulder.

The bathroom was a mess. Bottles of pills, toothpaste tubes, soap and make-up littered the carpet. The mirrored doors which had once fronted the wall cabinet now lay on the floor, shattered into sparkling pieces. Toilet paper had been pulled off the roll in a long strand, and was strewn haphazardly over the room. The bath taps were on, and steam rose in clouds from the cold plastic.

Tim lay on his back in the bath, two inches of hot water sloshing around his pathetically small body. His eyes were open, staring at the ceiling. His right leg hung over the rim of the bath, bent at an impossible angle. Blood flowed from a wound in his calf, streaming around the two-inch piece of bone which protruded from torn flesh. More blood ran from his nose and mouth. The blood mingled with the flow of water and swirled gently away down the plug hole. Tim gripped a razor blade in his left hand, clenched in fingers soaked with blood which was almost certainly not his own.

On the large mirror above the bath were some hastily scrawled words. The letters dripped red and ran down the glass.

'ANOTHER TIME & PLACE U CAN RUN BUT U CANT HIDE'

Scott knew instinctively they were written in Tim's blood. He dropped his weapon and sank to his knees beside the tub, weeping silent tears that ran down his cheeks and dropped into the bloody water. A low moan of utter despair escaped his lips.

Whitlock took a deep breath and stepped back, leaving the man alone with his son. He knew he should check for vital signs, just in case, but the lad looked so pale and broken. And dead. Whitlock could not bring himself to push Scott out of the way. A quick inspection of the other rooms confirmed their suspicions. The assailant had fled through the window in the back bedroom, probably climbing down the gutter and making good his escape over the garden wall. Whitlock gazed out of the broken window towards the houses which backed onto the lawn. Nothing. No running figures, no injured murderer who had fumbled his hold and fallen from the house wall. The rear was dark and deserted . . .

Scott reached trembling hands into the water, his vision blurred by tears. He lifted Tim's body from the water and cradled it in his arms. With his left hand he pushed the hair back from his son's eyes and stroked his head, rocking slowly back and forth.

'It's OK son,' he whispered. 'Daddy's here. Everything'll be all right now. I won't let you down, I promise.' He started sobbing, great racking gulps of air which burned his throat. 'Hold on Tim, just hold on. You'll be OK. I promise.'

He stayed like that for a moment, just holding the one thing he had ever achieved that was worth something. Then, rather than leave Tim in the blood spattered room that had been his final stand, Scott crouched over the bath and lifted his son from the water. He caught sight of the razor blade in Tim's hand, and a grim burst of pride swelled through his grief.

Even at the end, he thought, you were fighting. God knows how terrified you must have been. I hope you got the bastard a good one, Tim, because what you started I swear I'll finish.

He locked one hand behind Tim's head and straightened. Tim emerged from the bath, limbs hanging slack like a rag doll, water cascading from his body. Shifting his weight, Scott clutched Tim close. He tenderly kissed the clammy forehead, then buried his head in Tim's chest and gave way to the emotion erupting within him . . .

Whitlock joined Fowles outside in the street. The Sergeant cast him a questioning look from where he crouched on the road, covering the smouldering body with a tarpaulin. The other body lay alongside, also covered. Whitlock was glad he had not been around when they had lifted that from the railings.

He shook his head. 'Nothing, sir. But I called in. Daniels is on his way. May I suggest that— '

Whitlock's suggestion was destined never to be voiced.

Scott Johnson chose that moment to come running through the door at number 56, still clutching his son's body protectively in his arms. His face was alight with barely restrained emotion.

'For God's sake call a bloody ambulance!' he yelled, almost stumbling as he raced down the steps. 'He's still alive!'

BOOK TWO

STORM TROOPER

CHAPTER ONE

Trooper Awakens

December 28, 1990. Manchester, England.

Nathan Trooper thrashed in his sleep, body wrapped in the bed-clothes, neck tendons taut, face buried screaming into the pillows.

He cried out and sat bolt upright. Cold sweat drenched his skin. His bloodshot eyes were wide and frightened, merging with deathly white cheeks.

After a few moments the demonic laughter in his head faded to nothing. His racing thoughts stilled, heart rate slowly returning to normal. The clock on the bedside table glowed an eerie 3:25 a.m. Already the dream was fragmenting into disconnected images. Nathan struggled to hold onto those images, but they swept away, slipping through fingers slick with sweat. He reached for the pad and pen he had placed beside the clock.

Four nights in a row. The same dream. Four days of trying to comprehend its meaning, defeated by forgetfulness (or unwillingness to remember). But this time he had been prepared. One line was uppermost in Trooper's mind, burned there like a neon sign now faded and blurred. He wrote that line on the paper, read the words back and frowned.

The words triggered an unwelcome memory in the dark, distant recesses of his mind, and made him shudder. Some part of him recalled the message he had dreamed, and that made him suspicious.

Was that it? he thought. Or am I just making this up?

He read them again, running the line through his brain as if that would make the message clear, as if then the dream would make some sense. As if knowledge would vanquish his sense of unease.

There was no sudden understanding or flash of insight. Disappointed and exhausted, Nathan put the pad back on the table. He repeated the words once more, shrugged, and went back to sleep.

The words were still there when he woke up. He found that vaguely surprising, since he had half-expected them to disappear as swiftly and mysteriously as the nightmare. Despite a dreamless six hours sleep Trooper felt hungover and listless.

On the way to the shower he picked up the pad, then read the words aloud. Perhaps that would help, he thought.

'You can run. You can run. But you can't hide.'

He frowned. Well, what a surprise. No bloody help at all.

And the distant childhood memory, buried deep, refused to stay silent . . .

CHAPTER TWO

John Daniels Loses His Appetite

December 28, 1990. London, England.

Post-mortems. Inspector John Daniels hated them. They always made his breakfast far too interested in the outside world.

Not so Sergeant Fowles. There he stood against the wall, a half-eaten apple in his hand. The sound of his chewing grated on Daniels' already taut nerves. He'd had about three seconds sleep the night before, and his bowels would not stop telling him that this really was going to be a long week.

'Fowles!'

The Sergeant looked up, hesitating in mid-chew. 'Sir?'

'Can't you eat that some place else?'

Fowles looked at his apple, apparently confused. 'It's my breakfast, sir.' As if that was a valid excuse.

Daniels raised one eyebrow. 'And?'

Fowles opened his mouth to speak, caught the look in Daniels' eye, and closed it again. He swallowed hard. 'Er, fancy a coffee?'

Daniels grunted. 'About time. Black, three sugars.'

Fowles nodded and walked off.

'And Fowles? Have that in your gizzard when you get back.'

Fowles smiled meekly. 'Yes, sir.'

Daniels felt his breakfast churn and start to dance. He closed his eyes for a second, waiting for the sickness to pass.

The room was long and thin, lit by neon tubes which gave everyone a headache. A row of twenty tables dominated the theatre, surrounded by trolleys of equipment and various familiar-looking power tools. Daniels assumed that what looked like a paint stripper was probably designed with another purpose in mind. There was also an array of scalpels, knives, clamps and pliers on each trolley, most gleaming, all razor sharp. Only most, that is, because some of the tables were 'occupied', and the accompanying surgical implements were spattered with a variety of nameless gore. Daniels ignored these. He also tried to ignore the smell, but that was not so easy. The cloying aroma of bleached death pervaded every orifice, and even after twenty years in the force it unsettled him.

The silent occupants of the tables were partially skinned or mutilated. Daniels amended his earlier thought – perhaps that was a paint stripper after all. His roving eyes happened on an old man who no longer had a head. Looking quickly away only presented him with the view of a naked woman with multiple stab wounds. He closed his eyes – it was the only safe place to look.

'Coffee, sir,' Fowles said at his elbow, smirking.

'Don't look at me in that tone of voice, Sergeant,' Daniels said defensively. 'And wipe that smile off your face before I cut it off.' He accepted the lukewarm coffee and downed it in one swallow. The bitter-sweet acid laced his rebellious stomach, giving it something else to worry about. Then he tossed the plastic cup into the nearest bin. 'Right then, Sergeant. Lead on.'

Fowles pointed at a table down at the far end of the room. 'Over there, sir. Gunners is just finishing up.'

Daniels walked slowly down to the elderly gent leaning over a body. 'Morning, Gunners. Are you well?'

'Quite well thank you Inspector,' the man replied without looking up. 'And yourself? How are you bearing up, old boy?'

'Oh, I've been worse. How's it going?'

Dr Bartholomew Cummings, the chief pathologist, was a mystery to Daniels. Despite being a typical English old-school-tie type, with a large bushy moustache, tiny steel-rimmed spectacles and a huge pipe, Daniels was convinced Cummings was a total nut-case and capable of anything. Anyone who spent their entire life cutting up dead bodies was not to be considered sane or rational.

At that moment the doctor was up to his elbows in burnt flesh. His shoulder-length rubber gloves were smeared with blood and God alone knew what else. The Inspector grimaced and concentrated his attention on the exposed bald spot on Cummings' pate.

'Very well actually,' Cummings replied. 'I can give you causes of death, and a few clues to help you on your merry way.'

Daniels gave a derisory snort. 'Merry? You must be kidding. It's Christmas, my wife and daughter are giving me hell for not being home, I haven't had a good night's sleep for weeks, it's 11 a.m. and I've already been working for fifteen hours. If that isn't bad enough, I've just been landed with the worst case in years, my staff have no respect for me, and the last place I want to be is standing here in the middle of a stage set for *Zombies Creeping Flesh*.'

His voice, though subdued, had an angry tone which carried to the corners of the huge room. Several people looked up from their work to stare at him in surprise. He blushed.

Cummings removed his gloves and washed his hands.

'Yes, well, we all have our little cross to bear, don't we? I mean, I could be at home smoking, watching something on the telly. Instead I'm in here on your orders, doing my best to make your jolly old life a little easier. So. Don't shout at me, eh?'

Daniels grinned, shamefaced. '*Touché*. Happy New Year.'

Cummings regarded him over the rim of his glasses. 'But will it be? I wonder sometimes, you know John.' The doctor dried his hands carefully, then delved into a pocket of his blazer and extracted his pipe. 'Shall we walk while we talk? I'd rather like a smoke.'

Daniels nodded. 'Be my guest.'

Cummings called over to one of his staff. 'Sue, clear up here will you? I'll be back in an hour or so.' He took Daniels by the elbow and gently propelled him out of the lab. Once in the corridor he paused to light the rancid tobacco in the bowl of his pipe. Huge clouds of noxious smoke appeared around his head, but the look on his face was one of pure bliss. Daniels took the opportunity to light one of his own enormous cigarettes. Fowles, a dedicated non-smoker, frowned at both of them, making none too subtle coughing sounds and waving both arms in the polluted air.

Cummings and Daniels ignored him deliberately. They set off down the corridor like a pair of antique steam locomotives.

'So Bart,' prompted Daniels. 'What's the verdict?'

Cummings puffed furiously on his pipe, chewing the stem like a horse champing a bit. By the time the tobacco was burning to the doctor's satisfaction Fowles had lost sight of them both in the fog.

'Right, I'll start with the things you know already. Both men were murdered. The barbecue victim was the same M.O. as that over-cooked sausage you had me look at on Christmas Day. Wallis, wasn't it? Otherwise, well, in layman's terms one of them died of multiple burns, shock and heart failure. The other died of massive haemorrhaging. That was interesting, incidentally. The position of the body was such that, if he had not died from his wounds, he would probably have drowned.'

'Drowned?' asked Daniels, surprised. The cigarette wobbled in his mouth as he spoke, spilling ash on the floor.

'Absolutely. In his own blood – his lungs were full of it.'

Daniels glanced sideways at the look of profound interest on the doctor's face. 'Charming,' he commented drily.

'Times of death you already know – around eight last night.' He grinned. 'Both the bodies were still warm when I got here at midnight. Of course, one was slightly warmer than the other.' Cummings seemed to find that incredibly funny.

'Anything else?' Daniels interrupted.

'You mean, anything useful?'

Daniels grunted, drew on his cigarette. 'Yeah. If you hurry up and tell me the juicy bits, maybe I'll buy you a beer. But only if it's worth anything to me.' Daniels always had to barter with Cummings to get the information which Cummings was duty-bound to give him anyway. It was just another game the old-timers played.

Cummings considered the proposal, for about a second. 'Deal.'

'Good. So, get on with it.'

They resumed their measured stroll along the corridor.

'The victims were almost certainly homosexuals, practising regular sexual intercourse. Either that or they liked bananas – and not to eat.' Cummings sniggered.

'All right, all right, I get the picture.'

'The traces of fuel on the burns victim match with the Wallis murder. Petrol. Probably unleaded,' he added.

'You can be that sure?'

Cummings chuckled. 'To be honest, I didn't bother. But if you wanted to burn someone to death, what would you do? It is only waste, after all. Why spend money on expensive gas when unleaded is cheaper? I mean, you're only going to pour it down the drain, metaphorically speaking, of course.'

'Perhaps. Unless the killings were a ritual of some sort, and the killer wanted to lavish as much upon them as possible.'

Cummings shook his head. 'I think not. Ritual they may be, but lavish they most certainly are not. I think we may be dealing with something else entirely. Take Wallis: with his record of VD, I'd lay a pound to a penny he wasn't out with his wife that night. Trash of society. Then take these two – gay. Think about it.'

'I already have. If you're implying some kind of psychopathic vigilante, who thinks his mission is to rid the world of perverts, then I think you could be right. But that's only my opinion, and we should keep an open mind. Just in case.'

Cummings shrugged. 'Fair enough. Just thought I'd mention it. But I still think those murders weren't lavish. The man who was impaled was grabbed from behind, choked by a cheese cutter, and then thrust onto some rusty iron railings.' He waved his pipe expansively, billowing smoke. 'Where's the lavish ritual in that? No sacrificial knife for starters. He was killed in a very cheap and nasty manner, as if the murderer considered him to be nothing more than dog poop on the pavement. As if he didn't think it was worth spending any more money or time than strictly necessary.'

Daniels nodded. 'Given the evidence, that is the natural conclusion. But since we seem to be dealing with a complete lunatic here, I'll hesitate before trying to make order out of chaos.'

'Very wise, old boy.'

Daniels stubbed out his cigarette. 'Anything else?'

'Absolutely. And this *will* be worth a pint. The murderer was a man – the two burn victims were restrained, and that would have required great physical strength. Nobody, not even a drunken bum like Wallis, would stand still when somebody was pouring petrol all over them and waving a lighted match in their face. Also, the other man was impaled after being lifted four feet into the air. Do you have any idea how strong you have to be to lean over a four foot fence and lift a twelve stone struggling weight to chest height? We could be dealing with Mr Universe here you know, John.'

Daniels sneered. 'You call that worth a pint? Did you think I was working on the assumption that the murderer was old granny Jones from the Zimmer squadron?'

Cummings laughed. 'No – I credited you with more intelligence than that. However, from the angles and plaster casts I can tell you that the man was at least six feet six inches tall, left handed, extremely strong, weighing around fourteen stones, maybe slightly more. He was wearing a thick gold ring on his left hand, with a raised crucifix on the surface. He also had bizarre fingernails – very strong and at least an inch long.'

Daniels was impressed. 'And would you care to reveal just how you know all that? Or is it a trade secret?'

'Not at all, my friend, no secret whatsoever. Imagine what marks you would leave in someone's neck if you were tightening a garotte around it while they kicked and struggled in your hands. All sorts of scratches and bruises, believe you me. And in this particular case, one glorious little bruise shaped exactly like a crucifix, traces of gold in the skin and a splinter of fingernail embedded in the victim's earlobe. I would say that he put up a good fight, and did quite well considering the circumstances.'

'You mean, for a queer?'

It was the doctor's turn to look horrified. 'I didn't mean that! I was simply referring to the physique of the killer – he must be built like Hercules.'

Daniels chuckled. 'Should be easy to find then.' He slotted these facts away in his mind. Once there, he knew they would be processed by the machine which had made him what he was – a good copper. But for now he was too tired, too overloaded, and too hyped up on nicotine to follow any strain of logical thought. 'Well done, Bart. That's been useful. We'll make a detective out of you yet.'

'No thanks. I have this obsession with dead bodies. Death, gore, blood and putrefaction are my only pleasures in life.'

'Bart,' Daniels said flatly, 'you're weird. But thanks.'

'Good. That means I get my pint then, right?'

Daniels laughed. 'Yeah, you get your pint.'

Cummings beamed. 'Excellent. You are a real gentleman, Inspector. I owe you my liver.' He tapped out his pipe in the nearest ashtray. 'Oh, by the way, any witnesses to the killings?'

Daniels shook his head. 'Nope, we're running blind on this one. Plenty saw the fire, but no-one saw the murder or the killer.' He did not mind lying to the pathologist, since it was none of Cummings' business anyway. Besides, it was more of a half-truth than a lie. At this moment in time he really did not have an eye witness. But if young Tim Johnson ever awoke from his coma it might be a different story.

CHAPTER THREE

Trooper Breaks Through

December 28, 1990. Manchester, England.

Nathan Trooper sat alone in his house. As usual it was cold and wet outside. He was feeling much better. Despite the repeat of the dream he felt he had revealed a vital clue – the words on the pad. Being unable to decipher them was unimportant. Understanding, he knew, would come in time. He often dealt with nebulous thoughts or emotions, and believed true progress had been made when something concrete materialized. Even a few clichéd words he had dreamt but could not understand.

Nathan had thought long and hard on the matter that afternoon, repeating the phrases in his mind while he showered and shaved off four days of stubble – greying stubble, he had noticed with wry amusement. He had said the ten words out loud in various accents and tones while he cooked his breakfast. (Nathan's usual breakfast consisted of frying everything he could lay his hands on. That day it had been fried bacon, bread and old chicken with a few green peppers and chillis thrown in for bad measure. Nathan Trooper was a man dedicated to self-abuse. He ate badly, smoked about forty cigarettes a day, and drank alcohol like water. He never exercised, kept strange, irregular hours, and was a complete insomniac.)

Nathan had copied out the words onto red paper while he ate. Then, since this did not have quite the desired effect, he threw it away and tried again. And again. Until, eventually, while the remains of his breakfast went cold under a heap of screwed-up paper, Nathan held before him a sheet of cellophane with the words written on it in red ink. It was the closest he could get – the imagery was correct, but the emotion behind the words was not yet strong enough.

In a flash of inspiration Trooper dipped his fingers in cold tea and wiped them over the lettering. Then he held the cellophane vertically, and let the fluid run and distort the words.

And then he smiled. That was it. Perfect.

'Written in blood. Why didn't I think of that earlier?'

He screwed up the cellophane, put it with the other garbage and swept the whole lot into the bin. His breakfast plates went with it, but Trooper didn't care. He ate off paper plates, because it saved on washing up.

Realising he had made a breakthrough, albeit a minor one, Nathan grabbed a bottle of vodka. It was time to celebrate.

By 5 p.m., after ninety minutes of relentless loud music and a substantial volume of alcohol, Trooper was feeling positively warm towards the world. He had uncovered the key to his dream. Now all he had to do was find time to open the door.

Having isolated the emotion behind the words, Trooper tried to intuit their meaning, or anything which might trigger his reluctant memory. This was his technique when trying to rationalize the images presented by his subconscious. His dreams had always been open to external influence, images which were often terrifying and so blocked out by the safety valve in his head.

Pursuing the visions doggedly often revealed a better understanding. Since he could not sleep on the problem, Nathan had no choice but to thrash out his ideas in the waking hours. And he had plenty of those.

Trooper did not let lack of progress frustrate him. He was used to bashing his head against a brick wall, and consoled himself with the knowledge that the penny would eventually drop. If no sudden understanding came, he simply attempted another approach. If he thought an image was incorrect, he amended it. If an avenue of thought was a dead end he backtracked and went another way.

By 5:30 p.m. Nathan had two clues. First, the words written in blood on a piece of glass. Second, a tone of voice which felt right. (He could not define it any other way. He had a vague idea of what he was trying to achieve, and simply stopped if his guess matched.) Trooper had tried to determine the character of the person who had written the letters. As yet, he had no visual images. But he did have a 'resonance' with the spoken voice. He had tried many voices – threatening, sly, evil, male, female, angry, whispered – and had rejected them all. He just got the overwhelming impression that they were *wrong*. So, in another flash of inspiration he dropped all elements of tone, accent and emotion. The result: totally flat, sexless, void of any characteristic. The combination had struck him with that familiar resonance. He knew it was right.

So, what do I have so far? he asked himself, sipping his drink. A person who leaves messages written in blood. A person whose voice is to tone what vacuum is to atmosphere.

The gruesome blood angle intrigued him most. He had the impression that the images were somehow linked with violent death; murder, perhaps. Again, in his endless probing at the subject, Nathan felt that brief thrill of being *correct*. So – a murder.

That was when he first heard the voice.

It was faint at first, so he ignored it, thinking of the vodka he had consumed and the volume of the music which left his ears ringing. But the voice remained.

It did not take him long to realize that he was not hearing a voice at all. The words he sensed did not get intercepted by his eardrums – they appeared right at the centre of his mind.

Over and over again. One faint word, repeated desperately.

This was not a new experience for Trooper. He heard voices all the time. What *was* new was that the voice seemed to come from a great distance, with no hint of the speaker's physical presence.

He listened carefully, in case there was more to the message. He managed to categorize the voice – a boy, young and scared.

Nathan reached for his note pad, now covered in scrawls and a few pertinent notes. He pondered the voice for a moment, then wrote in the centre of the page the one word repeating in his head:

HELP

CHAPTER FOUR

Scott Johnson Keeps Vigil

December 28, 1990, 9 p.m. London, England.

Just outside London's Square Mile, away from the yuppies and the architecture of the money markets, stood The Fields Memorial Hospital for Children. Despite its famous Gothic façade and proximity to many of London's attractions, Fields was ignored by tourists – it appeared only on the maps of doctors and stonemasons. Within walking distance were Parliament, the brown sludge of the Thames, the West End and the art swamped vistas of the South Bank. To the north-east was Hackney, home to a mixed ethnic community. Home, too, for Scott Johnson in his seedy flat.

Scott had not returned to his flat during the last twenty-four hours. Having discovered Tim was alive – barely, a mere flicker of pulse – Scott had hardly left his side. He had sat with him as they raced from the house in the ambulance, anxiously studying his face and miserably faint heartbeat. He had run beside the stretcher as it was wheeled into the first emergency room. He had stood next to Tim while the doctor gave his diagnosis, and while he made a full statement to the police. Then he had accompanied his unconscious son in another ambulance across London to Fields. The doctors had said Tim's condition was critical but stable. They also

73

said there was little they could do, that the specialists at Fields had better facilities for his care. When Scott asked them what specialists, they had said one dreaded word: coma. Scott had paled, but not argued; he wanted the best for his son, and he wanted it *now*.

Tim, oblivious to all the fuss, lay on the beds and stretchers like a corpse. His skin was pale and cold, his heart weak. The doctors had managed to close his eyes, frozen open in terror since Scott found him in the bath, and make him more 'comfortable'. Or so they claimed. Scott did not like their definition of 'comfortable': he knew *he* would not feel comfortable if he was stretched out on a hard bed with a million tubes coming out of every hole, especially when some of those holes had not been there when Tim had arrived.

The bed on which Tim lay was surrounded by machines. A large ECG monitor reported his fragile pulse, beeping softly. Beside it was a life-support machine and artificial respirator, standing ready in case Tim's weary heart failed. An EEG monitor recorded the boy's brain activity, spilling out sheet after sheet of plotted lines. An intravenous drip fed some nameless nutrition into Tim's inert form.

Scott sat on a chair beside the bed. He had been there for eight hours, despite the pleadings of the hospital staff to go home and get some rest; when those requests had failed, they threatened him with removal from the premises. But there was no way Scott was going to leave his son, and he made sure everyone got the message. Even Sergeant Fowles, who had taken his statement and read him his rights. Scott had a look of such stubborn determination on his face that Fowles had not even bothered asking him to leave.

Despite the charges for speeding, drunk and reckless driving, Scott only regretted not having had a faster car.

Perhaps then he would have arrived in time to save his son.

The doctors who had examined Tim said he was suffering from deep shock. Tim's injuries, though serious, were not sufficient to cause his current condition. The broken leg had been re-set and cast. His cuts had been cleaned, with a few stitches applied where necessary. But all the physical medical treatment had failed to release Tim from his coma. He stayed locked away, totally withdrawn from the world which had thrust such horror upon him.

Dr Stewart McCormack, Tim's doctor and specialist in child trauma, had briefed Scott on the situation. 'Coma is a complex condition, Mr Johnson. It occurs in a wide number of cases with as many causes. Severe injury, such as in road accidents, drug abuse, diabetes and shock can all lead to coma. We know Tim is not diabetic. A young boy witnessing such horror and then experiencing such an attack is bound to suffer immense trauma. Especially after such frantic efforts to defend himself. It seems his final defence was to retreat from the onslaught. Since he had nowhere to run he locked himself away in his own mind. It is fortunate you arrived when you did. Otherwise I am sure that he would now be dead. To put it simply, he is suffering from a denial of reality. The effect on his mind was so great he collapsed in on himself.'

Scott had accepted this. 'So what are his chances?'

McCormack had paused, then shrugged. He believed in being honest with the parents of the children he treated; they had a right to know. 'I'll be honest with you, Mr Johnson. Cases of such deep trauma shock are immensely delicate. There is little we can do but wait. He'll either recover under his own steam, or he won't.'

Scott clamped down on his disappointment. It was hardly an optimistic prognosis. 'How long?'

Again McCormack shrugged. 'We cannot predict that

either. Hours, days, or even weeks. Coma patients have been known to recover years later. In the United States there have even been cases where the relatives request termination, only to find the patient wakes up after permission has been granted to turn off life support. There seems to be no hard and fast rule about duration of the condition. The only thing we can say is that the chances of recovery reduce as the period of coma increases.'

'So if he doesn't wake up soon, the more likely it is that he never will? Is that what you're saying?' Scott did not like to voice that thought, but he felt better knowing the facts.

McCormack frowned. He did not like to give pessimistic answers, particularly in circumstances where the outcome was so unpredictable. 'Possibly. I'm sorry we cannot tell you more. But this area of medicine is still virgin territory when it comes to effective treatment. We can sustain your son's life practically indefinitely, but only he can decide when to come back.'

Scott had been mildly annoyed. He had been promised the best facilities in the UK, and what could they do? Zip. 'Is he in pain?'

McCormack had smiled apologetically. 'Again, we don't know. Not physical pain, I'm sure, but inside his head? We can't say.'

Scott had bitten back his rising frustration. More immediate problems had arisen – his frantic ex-wife had returned from an evening with her mother to find the house wrecked and swarming with police. The doctors had finally put her under sedation. Her boyfriend had hovered in the background, obviously keen to be somewhere else and not in the least concerned about Tim. Scott had taken an instant dislike to the man, as had McCormack.

'I must ask you to leave, Mr Dane.'

'Why?' That one word, said with belligerence and contempt, had made Scott's blood boil. 'The brat can't hear me, he's asleep.'

McCormack had ground his teeth. 'He is not asleep, Mr Dane, he is in a coma. And it is widely accepted that coma patients are capable of hearing and smelling the objects and people around them.'

Dane had sneered. 'I don't care if he can *sing*. He's wrecked my house and I think he's faking so he won't get punished.'

McCormack had blown a silent fuse. He had personally escorted Dane from the room, leaving Tim's shocked mother shrieking.

Since then things had been quiet. Scott had remained at Tim's side, talking incessantly (now he knew Tim might be able to hear him). Policemen, doctors and nurses came and went. Father and son were sealed in a bubble, blocking out the world.

Sergeant Fowles had returned once, leaving a police constable on guard outside the door. Scott hardly noticed.

The only excitement had occurred at 5:30 in the afternoon. Tim's EEG monitor, which had spent the day drawing bland lines, suddenly went haywire. The needles shot from side to side, plotting dark traces of ink. Scott had leapt to the door, only to collide with McCormack who had been alerted by the desk steward monitoring Tim's machines. The doctor had eagerly snatched up the printout. 'Intense mental activity,' he had explained to Scott, who stood beside him wringing his hands and looking worried.

'Is that bad?'

McCormack had smiled. 'No. In fact, it could even be taken as a good sign. It shows Tim's brain is still active.' Then he had frowned slightly. 'However, it *is* rather surprising that the readings should be so extreme, and the change so sudden.' He leafed through the pages. 'The activity has been steady all day – see? – then it leaps off the scale.' He turned to Scott, eyebrow raised. 'Any movement? Did you provide any sudden stimulus?'

Scott shook his head. 'No. I was just sitting there. I wasn't even talking. I'd run out of words.'

McCormack tore off the sheets which gave the readings either side of the anomaly. Then he left, smiling reassurance.

Since then nothing had happened. Scott grew more tired; he dozed off in his chair. So he was grateful when someone entered the room and presented him with a cup of hot black coffee.

'Thanks,' he said, guilty at nodding off.

The stranger was very tall, towering over Scott. He wore a dark suit and black overcoat which fell to his knees. His face was clean shaven, handsome in a rugged way, crowned with greying cropped hair. The face was haggard, as if its owner had not slept for some time. A slight smile twisted the thin lips. Scott was struck by the clarity and perceptiveness of the man's startlingly blue eyes.

'Mr Johnson?' The stranger extended his hand. 'Chief Inspector Daniels. I'm in charge of this investigation.'

Scott rose from the chair and shook the proffered hand. The grip was firm, though brief. He realized Daniels was indeed very tall – at least six foot six. 'Any developments?' he asked eagerly, the cobwebs of exhaustion whisked from his mind. The presence of police officers usually had that effect on people.

'No, sir. I just need to ask you a few questions, fill you in on some background. I thought you might like to be kept informed. You may even be able to cast some light on a few of the facts.'

Scott nodded, disappointed but not surprised. He had not really expected an arrest this early. 'Certainly, Inspector. But I've told your men everything I know already.'

Daniels smiled again. 'I know. But you never can tell. Two people ask you two different questions about the same thing and there's a good chance you'll give two different answers. And right now, I need all the answers I can get. Do you smoke?'

The question took Scott by surprise. It also made him realize he had not had a smoke all day, had not even felt the craving. He felt it as soon as Daniels spoke.

'Shall we go outside? Perhaps we could walk while we talk.'

Scott looked over at Tim, the worry obvious on his face. 'I don't want to leave him alone. I know it sounds silly, but I think he knows I'm here and I don't want to let him down again.'

Daniels nodded. 'I understand. But it will only be for a few minutes. You need some fresh air anyway – you were practically asleep when I came in. Doctor McCormack will tell us immediately if anything happens – anything at all. Besides, one of my men will be outside all the time from now on – we're taking this very seriously, if that's any consolation.'

Scott digested that last comment. 'This security – is that because you think the killer might try again?'

Daniels raised a hand. 'First things first. Let's go outside.' When Scott still hesitated, his eyes on Tim, Daniels tried another tack – bribery. 'Come on, the walk will wake you up. Plus I've asked McCormack if he'll let you stay here. He agreed provided you don't get in his way, and I know you won't.'

Scott allowed himself a grin. 'OK, thanks.' There was real gratitude in his voice – he had intended to stay anyway, but approval always helped. He moved to the door, pausing in case Tim reacted to his departure. The EEG remained sane. 'Tim,' he said aloud, feeling foolish, 'I won't be long. I promise.' He was aware how hollow those words sounded – why should Tim be reassured by them when his father never seemed to keep his promises?

Daniels studied Scott's face, recalling the report Fowles had given him earlier. 'He reckons he let the boy down, that none of this would have happened if he'd been there when Tim needed him.' Daniels had been unable to stifle his instinctive response: 'Well, he's right, isn't he?' But now, having seen the boy with his own eyes, Daniels was more sympathetic. He had a child of his own.

'Come on, Mr Johnson. Get some perspective on this. It wasn't you who put your son in hospital, was it? If we can catch the guy who did and put him behind bars, maybe that will be some news Tim *would* respond to.'

Scott glared at the policeman, unreasonably annoyed, but found no enmity or contempt in Daniels' eyes – just understanding backed by a ruthless determination. Scott closed his eyes, trying to regain his earlier stoicism and control. 'OK, message understood. Let's go and have that smoke. I think I need it now.'

Scott closed the door behind him. As he did so, the EEG scratched a brief flutter and then fell silent, as if Tim had called out. There was nobody there to notice.

Nathan Trooper sat cross-legged on the floor, hands on knees, eyes closed. Three hours earlier he had intercepted the first faint cries for help. Since then he had pondered his dream and the words, filtering the ether in search of any further message. So far his quest had been fruitless, but he did not mind. He was used to disappointment and frustration.

He lit one of his expensive and exclusive cigarettes. On the first puff, just as he was about to give up, the voice came again.

Just one word, again very faint. But this time he was ready, and picked up the signal much easier. Without opening his eyes, he wrote his interpretation of the message:

DAD!

It was cold outside, the night sky lit by the ever present, dull red London glow. The scene depressed Scott, but Daniels' cigarette tasted good and the ensuing dizziness in his head was welcome. Daniels stood next to him, silent, exhaling smoke through his nostrils like a patient dragon. The man unnerved Scott, and not just because he was a senior police officer. There was something predatory about Daniels, something which spoke of repressed anger and energy. Scott knew his nerves, already over-stressed by a nightmare day, were at breaking point. He tried to relax, unwilling to lose his cool with the ice-cold inspector.

'So,' he began, watching the stream of smoke from his mouth mingle with the fog of his breath, 'what do you want to know?'

Daniels tapped ash from his cigarette. 'Everything. Start with your son's telephone call. What exactly did Tim say?'

Scott tried to remember the garbled message. 'Exactly? I don't know. Tim was too scared to make much sense and I was a tad drunk, without putting too fine a point on it.' He paused to marshall his thoughts, aware that his fatigue could make him careless. 'His first words were, "Dad! Thank God!" I knew right off something was wrong. Tim was witless, absolutely terrified. Then he said something like: "It's happened again, another look. And there's someone dead on the fence, the phone box burned with a gay man in it and there's a man here trying to kill me. Please Dad, come home!"' Scott's words did little to convey the terror in Tim's voice, choked as they were by the tight lid he had imposed on his emotions.

Daniels eyed Scott cautiously. Twenty years of police work convinced him Johnson was hiding something. 'And then what?'

Scott shrugged. 'I left immediately. You know the rest.'

Daniels referenced Scott's account against the facts, filing it away for later. Scott's landlady corroborated most of what he had just said. 'Why didn't you call the police?'

Scott snorted. 'Are you kidding? And say what? "Hi, my son's about to be killed and says he's just seen a homosexual burnt alive in a telephone box"? Do me a favour.'

Daniels thought it interesting that Scott said 'homosexual' – not some slang insult. Plus, of course, Scott was right – the police would have done nothing if he had called them. It would have taken too long to explain, and a lifetime to convince. Scott had been in a hurry. 'Fair enough. Did Tim say anything else?'

'No, he didn't have to – I knew I had to get over there right away. He didn't have to say why.'

Daniels nodded. 'So you left, *drunk*, and drove like a maniac?'

'Wouldn't you have?'

Daniels had to admit he might have done the same, senior police officer or not. But he said nothing.

'To be honest with you, Inspector, being convicted of drunk driving is the least of my worries. My son is in hospital with little chance of recovery. Getting done for speeding means very little.' His hands were shaking as he lit another cigarette.

Daniels regarded him quietly. Despite his detachment and a coldness instilled through years in the job, Daniels was impressed by Scott's honesty. He was not, of course, impressed by Scott's hippy appearance, alcohol and probable drug abuse. Disregarding the idea that Scott Johnson was a drop-out was hard, but his approach struck the Inspector far more than his physical appearance.

'So tell me about Tim. What did he mean by "another look"?'

Scott shrugged. 'Dunno. I thought he was just babbling.'

Daniels let the lie pass for now. His instincts told him it was not vital to pursue that subject, at least not yet. But since Scott was obviously hiding something, the comment was clearly of some importance. He filed it away. 'Have there been any previous attacks or threats made against your son?'

'No.'

'You're sure of that? Threats of any kind – phone calls, mail, people asking about him at school?'

'Nothing, Inspector. My wife and I may be divorced, but I can assure you I secured very good access. Me and Tim spend a lot of time together, and we're very close. He tells me everything.'

Daniels let that pass, too. For all he knew it might even be the truth. 'How are relations between your ex-wife and your son?'

'No problems,' Scott said tersely, on the defensive.

'No animosity over the divorce?' Daniels was pushing – he knew that. But he wanted to test Scott's emotional reflexes.

Scott laughed at his question. 'Tim is human, Inspector. He has feelings just like you and me.' Well, maybe *you* don't. 'The divorce affected him quite badly, but he quickly got used to the arrangements, and he's OK as long as he gets to see us both. He doesn't hate or resent his mother, if that's what you're inferring.'

'I'm not inferring anything, Mr Johnson. He sounds like a stable and mature boy.'

Daniels' perceptiveness surprised Scott. Again, he felt pride swell in his chest. 'He is. We're both very proud of him.'

Daniels filed away Scott's reaction. 'I would be too – he handled the situation amazingly well, under the circumstances.'

'I'm sure he would be glad to hear that,' Scott replied drily.

Daniels kept pushing, trying to keep Scott off balance. 'So what about your wife's new partner? How does Tim get on with him?'

'OK, I guess. Tim is very territorial. I know he wasn't too happy about Dane moving in, but he got used to it. He's resilient.'

'And yourself?'

Scott looked Daniels in the eye. 'What do you mean?'

'I mean, what are your thoughts on Mr Dane?'

Scott did not look away. That impressed Daniels even more. 'I have none, Inspector. I hadn't even met him until today.'

'But it must have been hard for you to know that another man is more prominent in your son's life than you are?'

Scott bristled. 'Not at all. I am still Tim's father, he knows that. Dane is part of his mother's life, not his.'

Daniels met the steady gaze, thinking: he's not lying.

Even if he's wrong, he doesn't know it. 'So no feelings of resentment?'

Scott's anger rose another notch. 'What are you getting at?'

Daniels smiled mildly. You're innocent, he decided. Either that, or you're the best actor I've come across in a long time. 'I'm not insinuating anything. But this is a peculiar case. I'm sorry we must ask such difficult questions at such a time.'

Scott was not at all mollified. 'You're looking for a motive, right? Maybe I resented my ex-wife finding another man, is that it? Well, maybe I did. So what? What am I, a machine? For God's sake, I was married to her for nearly fifteen years! Maybe I thought Dane threatened my position as Tim's father? Huh? Maybe I did all this to wreck their relationship and bring about reconciliation?'

Interesting notion, Daniels thought. 'Is that a possibility?'

'Is it hell!' Scott thrust out his chin pugnaciously. 'Do you think I'd kill two men and attack my own son? If I had a problem I'd take it up with Sally, not take it out on Tim.'

Daniels held out one hand as a placatory gesture. 'I'm sure you would.' Besides, Daniels added silently, you're too short, your fingernails aren't long enough and you weren't even there. You have a cast-iron alibi – two of my own men, in fact. 'My apologies, Mr Johnson. I am merely trying to establish the family background.' He extracted his cigarettes. 'Another smoke?'

Scott hesitated a moment, then laughed ruefully. 'You're a cold sod, aren't you? Do you enjoy winding people up?'

'No – it's just my job. You write novels, I arrest people.' He lit both their cigarettes. 'So as far as you know, there was no warning that anything like this was going to happen?'

'No. Tim was just in the wrong place at the wrong time.'

'Is it a regular event, your son being left alone?'

'I don't know. You'd have to ask Sally. But like I said, Tim can take care of himself.' His eyes narrowed. 'Why? Do you think I think Sally is an unfit mother?'

'Not at all. And as for Tim being able to take care of himself, I've already heard that.' Daniels thought of the razor blade clenched in Tim's hand. 'One last question. Are you absolutely sure your son did not mention anything about the killer? A description? Anything at all?'

Scott took a few seconds to think carefully. 'No. All he said was that it was a man, if that's any help to you.'

Not really, Daniels commented to himself. 'Everything helps. So, I think it's time I levelled with you, if you're interested.'

Scott indicated with a nod of his head that he was.

'It's not usual to release information on an investigation. But I personally believe you have a right to know, and I think I can trust you to keep quiet.' He paused, carefully editing the facts. 'This isn't the first time we've seen this particular crime. You've probably already realized that by the reaction of my men when they found you. Another man was burned in an identical way on Christmas Eve. I'm surprised you didn't read about it in the papers.'

'I don't read papers. Was it murder?'

'Possibly. There might not even be a connection. We did try to keep it out of the press, but the reporters were swarming all over the place before we could blink. If the first case was suicide this burning may have been a copy-cat offence. Someone read the reports and it sounded like a good idea, that sort of thing.'

'But you don't think so.' It was a statement, not a question.

Daniels smiled briefly. 'No. I'm Criminal Investigation, Mr Johnson, and as such I do not deal with suicides.'

'The message on the mirror – are we up against a psycho?'

It was a pertinent question. 'I don't think you are a stupid man, Mr Johnson. I'm sure you have your own ideas about sanity, and I'm equally sure they're more liberal than my own.'

Scott took that as a 'yes'. 'Is that why you posted a guard on the door? In case he tries again?'

'Partly. I'm sure he won't, but it's a wise precaution.'

Despite the admitted danger, Scott grinned. 'And Tim's the only lead you've got, right? Otherwise you wouldn't be pumping me for information I don't have. Tim's the only chance you've got.'

It was Daniels' turn to feel defensive. 'Your son is an eye-witness. It would be very useful if he could give us a description, but that is not our only "lead", as you put it.'

Scott's response was stalled by a nurse running towards them. 'Inspector? Dr McCormack wants to see you. He says it's urgent.'

Scott was running before the nurse had finished speaking.

CHAPTER FIVE

Trooper Intervenes

December 28, 1990. Manchester, England

Nathan Trooper did not have long to wait. He was now totally locked onto the source of the mental broadcasts, excluding all other thoughts, his concentration sieving the white noise for all but the essence of the transmissions. The pad in his lap was covered with scrawls. The clock on his video recorder read 9:22 p.m.

Delving deeper into the storm of thought in his mind, Nathan tried to establish a link with the unknown boy. As usual this caused a maelstrom of sudden, swirling emotion. His consciousness mingled with that of the boy; ideas clashed, feelings collided. When the cloud passed he floated motionless in darkness. Around him, thoughts clustered in the shadows, tiny pin-pricks of light and energy. Nathan had completely lost his sense of self. Nameless, faceless, pure thought, an intruder in another's mind, he relaxed and went in search of his host and some long awaited answers.

Tim Johnson lay in his hospital bed. The ECG monitor pipped peacefully, marking out a heartbeat once every other second. The EEG traced out random thought patterns.

Tim was alone. For now.

Nathan let the overwhelming sense of ALONENESS seep

through him. He moved on, filtering for relevance, examining and rejecting information as it zapped from synapse to synapse.

He went deeper, down to the bowels of the conscious mind, and sank through a confusion of collective thoughts and memories. Random images, snapshots which were stacked in a mindless jumble, passed by him at an astonishing rate. Nameless faces appeared in his path, looming before him and dropping away in his wake.

Trooper identified a mother and father, one minute young, the next older, then young again. Sequence had no meaning here, he knew. Faces swam by, some crying, some shouting, some laughing. A vortex of images swept him up: book covers, cans of drink, beds, telephones, shoulders, baths, roads, a mother's breast, a body lying on a tatty sofa, traffic lights, police cars, an aeroplane.

Memories. Disorganized, jumbled, stacked in unknown and sometimes irretrievable piles. An enormous junkyard.

Nathan ignored them all. What he wanted was a label, a tag to identify his host. From this he could work backwards and solve the riddle of his dream. He wanted to know who was broadcasting the visions, who and where this boy was. He wanted a name.

He knew where to look. He had done this sort of thing before.

He found it.

Tim remained oblivious to everything.

Beside him, the EEG marked an immeasurably small increase in mental activity. Even if anyone had been there to see it, they would have ignored the change. And never in a million years would they have guessed its true cause.

Nathan moved at the speed of thought, darting with

care among areas of Tim's mind which even Tim knew nothing about. Subtlety was his trademark, and he never abused his guest privileges.

He debated whether to make the connection two-way. It would be informative to converse on a conscious level with the terror-stricken comatose boy. But he decided against this. In all his years of furtive interior brain surgery, Nathan had never witnessed such utter internal collapse. He had caught glimpses of an event which had shocked Tim into retreat – a crime had been committed to this boy which had left him incapable of dealing with the outside world. The fear had brought down the walls of self defence, bricking up his identity within impenetrable fortifications. Tim's brain had disconnected itself from normal life and withdrawn into an imaginary safety. If Nathan contacted him there, shattering the boy's vision of immunity, the shock could easily make Tim's collapse terminal. As it was Tim stood on a knife-edge of life and death. If Nathan pushed, Tim's only retreat would be into the welcoming darkness of death or madness.

So Nathan satisfied himself with the information gleaned from his sortie and prepared to leave. He had names, details and faces with which to arm himself. He had no wish to outstay his welcome.

The uniformed guard outside Tim's door yawned. Inside, the EEG monitor suddenly went off the scale. An alarm sounded on the front desk; McCormack came running. Another alarm sounded as the ECG reported imminent heart failure. McCormack dashed down the corridor towards the startled police constable. He pushed the door open and fell into the room, closely followed by two nurses.

Tim lay on the bed, no longer motionless. His back

was arched off the sheets, head and feet pressed into the mattress. His hands beat at his face, fingernails scratching savagely, blood streaming from his nose. His mouth was open in a silent, agonized scream.

McCormack stared at the boy's violent struggles in disbelief. Coma patients just did not *do* that sort of thing.

The sudden slump of Tim's body coincided with a flat line on the ECG. The tone of the machine changed from an erratic beep to a high-pitched constant note. Tim collapsed back onto the bed, limp as a rag. His heart had stopped beating. He was dying.

Nathan had been on the point of withdrawal when it started. In an instant the organized peace of Tim's mind had exploded into violent chaos. Trooper, caught in a whirlwind of disruption, halted his retreat. It did not take a psychic to realize something was wrong. Yet the distance between his own body and Tim was taking its toll – his energy was sapped, his concentration dwindling. He would have to move fast.

Tim screamed. The impact on his subconscious had reawoken the terror, and now his body was responding. His faint voice reached Nathan across an impossibly huge gulf. The boy was weeping, fleeing from some unseen presence, heading uncontrollably towards the abyss. In that abyss, Trooper knew, lay Death.

Another voice filled Tim's mind, an awesome toneless boom, ripping through his consciousness like a red-hot sword through butter. Demonic laughter which Nathan knew well from his dreams smashed Tim's fragile barriers.

'You can run, but you can't hide. You can never hide.'

Nathan tracked across vast psychic distances, heading swiftly for the source of that voice. He knew somebody else had joined him as an unwelcome intruder, an uninvited 'guest' with rather different objectives to his own. He instinctively knew that the new voice belonged to whoever had terrorized Tim. The presence obviously required victory, a completion of his unfinished business.

Trooper sensed for the first time the massive *power* of Tim's enemy. Never before had he experienced such awesome ability and devastating psychic force. The backlash of the intruder was like the shock wave from a nuclear explosion.

Trooper found that experience utterly terrifying.

'Please.' Tim's voice, pleading. 'Please leave me alone.'

Nathan realized a conflict was inevitable. He wondered what effect the conflict would have on Tim's mind and body, and whether anyone would witness the results. Tim's defences were now spent. If Nathan did not save him, nobody would. But the tenuous link with his own body meant that his efforts would be short-lived. He was rapidly running out of time and energy.

The intruder wasted no time in idle threats, chose instead to attack swiftly. A numbing blast of psychic strength ripped Tim's fragile fortifications apart and scattered them like flower petals in a hurricane. His consciousness, battered by the impact, was sent reeling again towards the edge of the abyss.

Nathan moved in quickly, locating his enemy, shying away from the pulsating mass of thought which tore through the boy's brain. Working fast, he found the delicate trail of thought which connected the invader's unwelcome probe to his body. Sever that link and the pain would be intense, as if half the intruder's mind had been torn out. Nathan had never attempted it before, but his experience made him well prepared. He had accumulated two decades of learning in his and others' minds – twenty years of lonely specialization.

There was, however, one problem. Sever the link with what? Here, in a realm of thought without matter, the only weapons were strength of mind and mental agility. Yet the intruder demonstrated a far greater capacity for those than Nathan possessed.

His worries were cut short as his enemy dealt a second pulse of energy. Nathan heard Tim cry out one last time, now utterly defeated and waiting helplessly for the killing blow. Trooper ignored the screams for mercy and the wash of brutal force. He ignored the pain caused by his sustained psychic action. He ignored everything but the glowing line of energy he had to cut.

Nathan reached back to his own body and summoned every reserve of energy. He collected this energy, channelled it, focused it, then held it steady as he prepared his attack.

An obscure sense of melodrama consumed him as his mind filled with power. His brain swelled and felt huge, bursting with energy. He felt invincible; knew he was in danger of being swept up like a junkie in the feelings of potency. For the first time Nathan felt real danger in his gift. This new power was corrupting. Without control, it would warp his entire identity.

Perhaps that was what had happened to the invader. Perhaps he had been perverted and corrupted by his own strength. Nathan did not know. He did not have time to care.

He released a fraction of his stored energy as a message: 'Leave now,' his thoughts boomed, silencing the victorious maniacal laughter. 'You are not welcome here.'

He sensed a sudden surprise. Resistance was obviously unexpected. The intruder's beach-head offensive turned upon itself, seeking Trooper, for the moment forgetting

Tim. It was this hesitation in pushing home its advantage which saved Tim's life.

Nathan focused his energy into a tight beam of pure thought, powerful and destructive, and released it into the invader's link. With a flash of impact the cord severed, isolating his enemy.

There was a massive burst of electrical activity in Tim's brain. Synapses crackled with energy, charging and sparking in a cacophony of mental white noise. Tim's bodily functions convulsed, his heart shocked into immobility, his limbs and muscles contracting as the intruder was banished in a sudden rush of power.

There was a high-pitched scream of terror. The howl climbed up through the octaves to a wild crescendo of pain and suffering, echoing in the vaults of Tim's bruised psyche. Then the cry was suddenly cut off, terminated at its steepest point as the deadly mental probe withdrew back to its owner.

The energy which it left behind coursed through Tim's nervous system, disrupting, damaging. The electrical surge, being the basis of all nerve signals, crackled through Tim's body, transformed into heat by muscles undergoing violent spasms. As the last trickles of current were consumed and their energy released, Tim relaxed. His body slumped back, his mind fizzing with spent power.

Nathan reeled from the shock of his attack, caught in the whiplash, for a moment completely paralysed. As his perceptions returned he wondered what damage the surge had done to Tim. His worst fears were confirmed when he sensed the heart stop, the vast consumption of power too much for it to bear.

So Nathan gathered his meagre resources and released a small amount of energy into Tim's battered mind. This he fed into the organic circuits which drove Tim's bodily functions, setting up a chain reaction which led to the heart receiving a minor electric shock. Then he withdrew, unable to hold on any longer and see if his desperate measure was successful. He was too exhausted to remain. Never before had he felt so completely devastated.

His passing left a vacuum in Tim's mind. The displaced memories dropped back into place as if Trooper had never been.

The EEG machine went haywire again, obliterating the sound of the flat line on the heart monitor. McCormack turned horrified eyes on it, his right hand hesitating in its motion to inject adrenalin into Tim's inert body. His hesitation was crucial – before he could insert the needle, the flat line bounced, jerked, then steadied.

'I have a reading, Doctor,' said one nurse.

McCormack saw it, but didn't believe it. 'What?'

'Heart rate rising.'

McCormack lowered the hypodermic, angry and confused, feeling superfluous to requirements.

'Steady at sixty, Doctor stated the other nurse, her eyes locked on the machine. 'Blood pressure levelling. EEG returning to normal.'

McCormack scowled at the machines, unconvinced. Then he glared at his patient. Tim was relaxed, his mouth open, his chest rising and falling in a smooth rhythm. 'What the hell is going on here?' McCormack breathed. Patients simply did not suffer massive heart failure, only to recover themselves ten seconds later. Now the heart monitor read a well-paced sixty-five per minute. The EEG traced a lazy line on the paper, perfectly normal. McCormack looked at the hypodermic, completely baffled. He scratched his head. 'Nurse.'

'Yes Doctor?'

'Go and get Inspector Daniels. And run some tests.'

The nurse paused. 'What sort of tests, Doctor?'

McCormack shrugged. 'I don't know, any bloody tests. Find out exactly what happened here, and find out *now*. Understood?'

The young nurse looked at her companion, who simply shrugged knowingly. 'Yes, Doctor.'

Nathan fell back into his body. His eyes did not open, nor did he take a sudden breath, nor did he scream in pain. He did nothing except simply collapse on the floor, curled up like a foetus, breathing shallowly in a state of total exhaustion.

Daniels strolled slowly back into the hospital. Scott had bolted at the nurse's words, eyes widening in horror. Daniels had not bolted anywhere since he was ten. Besides, he had a cigarette to finish. 'I take it the patient is all right,' he asked quietly.

The nurse walked beside him. 'Yes, sir. There were some complications. But Doctor McCormack only asked for you because he promised to let you know if anything happened.'

'And something did? Something unexpected?'

'Yes. Very . . . peculiar.' She shrugged. 'They're running some tests now, but I've never seen the doctor so baffled.'

Daniels puffed on his cigarette, thoughtful. 'I'm sure,' he murmured. 'To be honest with you Nurse, there are an awful lot of peculiar things about this case.'

'Oh?' she asked politely. She did not know whether to enquire further, or refrain from intruding. The tall policeman – hawk-like, slim and predatory – worried her. Like most rational people, she was uncomfortable in the company of policemen.

Daniels grinned, aware he was unintentionally upsetting the young nurse. It happened. He was a cop, the sort of person even careful, law-abiding citizens were irrationally afraid of, and hated. 'Did Tim suffer any pain?'

'Some, I think. He had convulsions, lost a little blood.'

'Really? Not what you expect from a coma patient, I suppose.'

'Not exactly, sir, no.'

Daniels stubbed out his cigarette, letting the nurse lead on. He reviewed the interview he had just had with Scott.

Daniels had not called the meeting to get answers. He simply wanted to meet the man, face to face. Fowles' detailed reports had encouraged Daniels to approach this case from the bottom up. People were always the key: they were what police work was all about. Knowing the people was the first step towards solving the crime. Even this one. And Daniels had some very bad feelings – his bowels had not let up since Christmas Eve. The gloomy sensation had not lifted and that worried him more than anything else. Daniels lived on his instincts. Logic and reason may well have been the tools of his trade, but instinct was what kept those tools sharp. This week his instincts had been screaming at him incessantly, and nothing they said was good news.

Great, he thought. What a way to end a really crap year. In a really crap way. End as you mean to go on.

Daniels pushed aside his gloom and turned back to the subject of Scott Johnson. Against his better judgement he was beginning to like the man. Scott held old values, was disconcertingly honest and forthright, and was not a two-faced vicious git like most people Daniels met these days. Scott was a man who obviously loved his son, and had risked his life to save Tim. Of course, Daniels had to admit that Scott had risked others' lives as well. But however questionable his methods, Scott's intentions were sound. That made a refreshing change. He sensed no malice or ulterior motive in Scott. He trusted those perceptions – he considered himself a good judge of character.

So what of the investigation? Would Scott be of any use in the days, weeks, or – God forbid – months to come? Possibly. But only if Tim regained consciousness, and even then only if he had something useful to say. *And* even if Tim *did* know something, and even if he *did* regain consciousness, there was no guarantee he would tell any of it to a policeman. Perhaps Scott's radical attitudes had rubbed off on the boy. That, of course, was where Scott might become a vital link in the chain. Because even if Scott had no ulterior motive, Daniels certainly did. He had the Chief Superintendent squeezing his testicles – metaphorically speaking – and needed to produce results. If Tim would not speak to the police when he recovered, he would certainly speak to his father.

Daniels hoped so. He needed some help. He needed Tim Johnson, awake, sane and – above all – talkative.

Sighing, he pushed open the door to the private room and walked into day five of the Nightmare.

The room was tense and silent. 'So Doctor,' he asked, 'what happened?'

His eyes scanned the room. Nothing seemed to have changed, except for the boy. Tim's face was red with blood. His cheeks and forehead bore the marks of many scratches. Looking down, he saw that Tim's fingers were spotted and smeared with blood, and several of his fingernails were torn and bloody. The lad himself was motionless in bed and his friendly machines beeped and scratched, as they always had. Daniels found the scene striking because of its incongruity – a paradox of peace and evident violence.

Weird.

Daniels, surprised as he was by Tim's appearance, realized he had missed every word McCormack had said in answer to his question. 'I'm sorry Doctor, what was that?'

'I said, this is not as bad as it looks. The wounds are all superficial. There will be no lasting damage.'

'Good.'

Scott could obviously contain himself no longer. 'No lasting damage? What the hell does that mean? My son gets placed here, in a coma, in a guarded room, and still he gets attacked?' He rounded on Daniels. 'What's the ruddy point of posting a guard if any old loony can barge in here and assault my child?'

Daniels smiled. 'Unless I'm much mistaken Scott, these wounds are all self-inflicted. Am I right, Doctor?'

Daniels could read McCormack like a book. The doctor's open page read: Thank God someone around here has got some sense.

'Yes, Inspector, as usual you are correct.'

Scott's face was a mask of confusion and barely suppressed rage. 'What do you mean, self-inflicted?'

Daniels sighed. 'Look at his fingernails, Scott.'

Scott stepped a little closer to the bed. 'What the hell are you two talking—' he started, then broke off and blushed. 'But—' He paused. 'I don't understand,' he added lamely.

McCormack frowned. 'Neither do we, really. Tim's heart stopped, but started again with no intervention on our part. He had some sort of massive muscular spasm and convulsion. The EEG was reporting incredible mental activity, much more violent and sustained than the earlier readings. But then, as if the power was cut off, he just slumped back in his bed and everything returned to normal.' He blew out his cheeks. 'To be honest with you, I've never seen anything like it. It was most—'

'Peculiar?' Daniels finished for him, smiling grimly.

McCormack eyed him curiously. 'You don't sound surprised.'

Daniels shrugged. 'How many times has the EEG reported a surge?' he asked, ignoring the doctor's implicit question.

'Three. Once when I was here with Scott, not long after Tim arrived at about 5:30. The other two readings occurred just now – one before Tim entered spasm, just before his heart stopped, the other about ten seconds later as it started again. In fact, at just the moment I was preparing to inject him with adrenalin.'

Daniels nodded absently. Apparently irrelevant questions surfaced in his mind. 'Doctor, what does the EEG actually measure?'

'Mental activity, as I've said. EEG stands for Electro-encephalograph, if that's any help to you.'

'Yes, I know that.' Daniels' tone was waspish. 'But what does it actually *detect*, in order to give a reading?'

'Ah, I see. Well, electrodes attached to the skull measure electrical impulses, changes in voltage and current. All functions of the brain – as we understand it so far – are initiated by electrical, chemical, and electro-chemical variations. Synapses, which are basically the switches, or connections, are triggered by such activity. So the EEG detects those changes and traces them.'

Daniels digested this slowly, a plethora of thoughts and conclusions rioting in his tired mind. 'Thank you,' he said vaguely, eventually realizing people were awaiting a response.

His train of thought was interrupted by Scott. 'So?

Any ideas? Do you understand what's going on inside Tim's head?'

Daniels ignored him. 'Doctor McCormack, have you contacted the staff at the hospital which first treated Tim?'

'Of course. I was very concerned after the first EEG surge.'

'And were they monitoring Tim with similar equipment?'

'Yes, luckily they were. They suspected brain damage.'

'And?' Daniels prompted.

'And nothing, Inspector. Nothing untoward. Certainly nothing of the magnitude we have experienced here.'

Daniels raised one eyebrow. 'So the first attack came here?' The inspector assumed an intent expression. 'Peculiar,' he mused, 'most peculiar.' He glanced at his watch. It was now a quarter past ten, and he had been working non-stop for twenty-six hours. It was definitely time to call it a day. 'Doctor, may I speak privately with you for a few moments before I leave?'

'You're leaving?' Scott asked. 'But what about this?'

Daniels smiled pleasantly. 'It's all over. At least, for now. I suggest you get some sleep. Doctor?'

Then he turned and left the room before Scott could ask any more questions. McCormack joined him outside, and they talked as Daniels walked briskly towards his car. 'Doctor, I have some very strange ideas about this which may not be medically sound. However, I would appreciate it if you would listen to some of my thoughts.'

McCormack nodded. 'Certainly. And if it's any consolation, I also have some rather strange hypotheses, though mine may in fact be more medically sound than yours.'

Daniels grinned. 'I would expect nothing less.' The grin died. 'First, I believe that what we are dealing with here is not something you or I have ever witnessed before.'

'Agreed.'

'Second, I believe Tim's life is in danger.'

'Agreed also. I was very surprised by his instability – if this continues, he could go at any time and I don't think there would be much we could do to prevent it.'

Daniels chuckled. 'This is where our theories diverge, I fear. I'm not talking about Tim, as such, but some external influence. I think there is more to this than meets the eye.'

McCormack regarded him strangely. 'A danger from outside? Really? Despite the self-inflicted wounds and the guarded room?'

'Well, I'm actually thinking more along the lines of *because* of the guarded room, rather than *despite* it. Tim was attacked and almost murdered, yet the killer cannot get to him.' He shrugged. 'I'll say no more now. I don't believe half my theories myself, and I certainly can't back them up with any rational thought. However, I do believe we must do our utmost to safeguard Tim's life.'

'Agreed. I decided to have him monitored round the clock. I want someone qualified on hand in case anything else happens.'

'Excellent. Third, I want Scott to have free access to his son. Let him come and go as he pleases.'

'Any particular reason?' McCormack did not seem surprised.

'No. Do you need one?'

The doctor grinned. 'No, I don't. It may not be good for the patient, but then again it may prove beneficial. We just don't know yet. Frankly, I'm baffled.'

'And these EEGs? Are there any further tests you can apply?'

'Ah, now there I'm ahead of you, Inspector. I have already set wheels in motion. I do not expect much of the results – we can do physical tests, but that obviously won't reveal any psychological problems. We won't know those until he recovers consciousness.'

'Well, it's worth a try. Finally, I'll leave you with some questions: why is Tim's brain so active? What caused that last attack? How could he be receptive to such violent electrical discharge? And how the hell did his heart simply start again?'

McCormack smiled wryly. 'Uncanny, Inspector. Those are the questions uppermost in *my* mind. Great minds think alike.'

Daniels unlocked his car. 'Perhaps, Doctor. But don't forget – great minds may well think alike, but fools seldom differ.'

He saw McCormack grin. 'I was just thinking the same thing myself. Good night to you.'

Daniels threw the car into gear and drove away.

Trooper groaned, coughed, struggled to open his eyes. His eyelids felt as if they were made of lead and his head seemed stuffed with concrete. His nose was sore and he ached all over.

Carefully – very carefully – he stretched out his legs and arms, uncurling from his foetal position. Muscles cracked and joints popped. As sensation slowly returned his entire body was racked with pins and needles.

'Jesus, it's cold in here,' he mumbled through cracked lips. When he licked them his tongue came away with the salty taste of blood. He realized he had suffered a massive nosebleed, but was not surprised. It happened when he pushed his brain to the limit.

Groaning, he rolled over onto his back and was surprised to see the shadows of tree branches swim into focus on the ceiling.

Daylight.

When the circulation had been restored to his extremities he tried to sit up, but was utterly unprepared for the rush of blood from his head. He nearly passed out. 'Big mistake,' he whispered, collapsing back onto the carpet. He closed his eyes and let the flashes of light disappear.

Take it easy, he cautioned himself. There's no rush. You're totally blitzed and you've been lying on the floor curled up in a ball all night long. Give yourself a chance to get going again.

The desire for a hot cup of tea overwhelmed him. He realized he was chronically dehydrated and absolutely starving.

He managed a grin. First things first, Nathan. You can't cook till you stand up, and I don't think you're ready for that yet.

But his grumbling stomach would not take 'no' for an answer. It wanted some breakfast, and it wanted it *now*.

He rolled his aching and weary body over and drew his knees up beneath him. His head swam, but with a deep breath he stumbled to his feet, clutching at the mantelpiece for support. His knees trembled, his eyes refused to focus, and his head was beginning to thump like a marching brass band. He felt as weak as a kitten.

After two minutes just standing there, regaining his sense of balance and warming himself by the fire, he risked a look at the clock on the video.

At first he could not believe his eyes. So he rubbed his eyelids with bare, sore knuckles, and looked again.

The display remained the same. *SUNDAY 30–12 10:02 AM*.

'Bloody hell,' he cursed under his breath, 'I've been out cold for a day and a half.'

An hour later Nathan sat at his breakfast table, working his way rapidly through his biggest meal in years.

Recovering from the shock of his long 'sleep' had only plunged Trooper into deeper thought. He felt the time had definitely come to stand back a little, take stock of the situation and decide what action was required. The events of the past six days had thrown him so off balance that he needed to think the matter over carefully. Very carefully.

Trooper bit into a huge bacon sandwich, desperately trying to fill the gaping hole in his stomach. He was dehydrated, cold, and tired. He had also lost twelve pounds in weight. 'The Nathan Trooper Diet!' he had giggled earlier, half crazy as he stood on the scales. 'Have an out of body experience and lose weight while you sleep!'

Never before had he experienced such complete mental and physical exhaustion. But then, he reminded himself, never before had he achieved the heights of that most peculiar evening.

'OK, let's get scientific about this,' he said aloud. It often helped to talk aloud, and having spent most of his life alone, he was used to it. 'Me receiving Tim Johnson's thoughts, here, over two hundred miles away, suggests that massive psychic force is involved.' He paused to drink the warm dregs of his fifth cup of tea. 'That worries me. He is under some kind of telepathic attack, the likes of which I have never seen before.'

He paused and stared blankly at his greasy breakfast. The conclusion which rose unbidden in his mind was unwelcome, but he believed it to be unavoidable. 'Tim is in grave danger, and there is nobody with him who even knows that. He has no defences of his own. Therefore—'

He broke off, not wishing to voice the words.

But what choice was there? Could he live with himself if he sat back with his knowledge and let Tim die? Would his conscience allow him to back away without offering assistance? Because there was no doubt in his mind; Tim would die, if nobody intervened.

'Tim will be attacked again,' he resumed, 'though I don't know when. I dealt a harmful, though far from fatal, blow. If it has taken me thirty-six hours to recover from that attack, then I dare say our enemy will take even longer, since he suffered more damage.'

He remembered the immense presence in Tim's head, bubbling with untold force and corruptive power.

'I cannot let Tim die. There, I've said it. Tim will die if I do not help him. Therefore, and as much as I hate the idea, I must help him. I must protect his fragile life as best I can.'

OK, bigshot, nice words. So what exactly are you going to *do*?

Trooper finished his breakfast then threw the plates in the bin. He was on his third cigarette before an idea came to him.

He considered the notion long and hard, viewing it from every angle. Then it only took him twenty minutes to pack.

With grave misgivings and worries about the future, a two-minded Nathan Trooper finally joined the fray. He was still doubtful about the whole thing, despite having reached an undeniable conclusion. He was also less than optimistic about his chances.

The front door to his flat beckoned as if wondering

whether it would see him again. He eyed it nervously, butterflies swarming in his stomach. It was the first time he had been out of the house in days. It was also the first time he had left his sanctuary to actively seek human company in years. Trooper did not turn his back on his home without experiencing a deep distress.

But as he started his sleek black Jaguar XJRS he knew he had no choice.

BOOK THREE

CONTINUUM

CHAPTER ONE

Anne Wallis Gets a Call

Sunday December 30, 1990, 10:30 pm. London.

Anne Wallis unlocked the door to her luxury flat and let herself in. A stack of junk mail and late Christmas cards had formed just inside the door. She ignored it. She was not in the mood for reading sensational money offers, or crass greetings from people she never spoke to all year round, half of whom she could no longer remember. In fact, she was not really in the mood for anything but a bath. A long, hot, luxurious bath, and a long, brain-numbing drink. Anything to dull the tears.

It had been a nightmare week. Plucked from executive normality in a foreign exchange dealing room, Anne had been summoned to her mother's bedside and had watched, helpless, as her life turned on its head. It was the worst Christmas she could remember. As Anne kept trying to tell herself, the only positive point was that now her life was at its lowest ever ebb the only way was up.

She hoped.

Anne dumped her suitcase on the leather settee and crossed to the drinks cabinet. She poured herself a huge gin, added a dash of tonic for appearance's sake, and then slumped down in an armchair.

Bill's armchair, she thought. The grief welled within

her. Her gaze blurred out of focus, and mascara ran as warm tears coursed down her cheeks. Anne surprised herself – she thought all the tears would have been spent by now, after six days of misery and weeping.

She wiped her eyes with the back of her hand, smearing her make-up, then gulped at the drink, grimacing as the rough gin burned her throat and ripped into her stomach. Anne had not eaten for three days, relying instead on obtaining her nourishment from alcohol and grief. She felt sick and tired all the time, worn out by emotional stress and the rigours of bereavement. Anne had thought that working in the City was stressful. She knew now that trading money was a picnic compared to the loss of loved ones.

Her life was in turmoil, she felt totally out of control, she was numb and shell-shocked and could do nothing all day except sit and stare at the shattered fragments of her existence.

One week ago she had been happily married, pregnant, deeply in love with her husband, and financially very well off.

Now she was alone and rich. Nothing more.

She thought it strange that money, previously the theme around which her entire life revolved, now meant less to her than the junk mail scattered on the carpet. Its appeal had vanished in the trauma of repeated loss. First the baby, miscarried on Christmas morning. Second, the death of her mother, killed by cancer and a forty-year, sixty-a-day cigarette suicide habit. And finally, on Boxing Day, the arrival of an uncomfortable policeman, and the news that her beloved husband had been burned to death.

All in all, she had thought, the most miserable two days a person could endure. But with the collapse of her father, who even now lay in a hospital bed waiting to die, things had turned from terrible to unbearable. Upon her overburdened shoulders had fallen the responsibility to 'make the necessary arrangements': funerals, solicitors, police statements, contacting relatives – all those horrible tasks which were devastating to even the strongest survivor. The experience had left Anne shattered and defeated. She was utterly drained and totally desolate. In the space of two days her glorious life had turned to ashes in her hands.

She had returned to London with a heavy heart, knowing the flat would haunt her with images of Bill and times now lost forever. She knew that everywhere she looked, all the textures, smells and sights would remind her of her husband. Even their arguments and bad times would mellow into faded, fond memories, precious for the reason that at least he had been there. And now his humour and embrace were gone, and his child, and all her reasons for living.

With that thought she downed the rest of the gin in a rush. That, too, brought tears to her eyes, but she welcomed the shock. Anything to break the despondent mood which oppressed and depressed her. She rose and put the glass back on the cabinet, careful to avoid the photographs which adorned every surface. She was far from ready for that. Then she took her case and carried it into the bedroom, flipped open the lid and stared blankly at the contents. At times she just did not know where to start.

Her battered mind made a decision.

'Bath. Have a bath, relax, get an early night. Get some sleep, wake up, and worry about it tomorrow.'

The decision, if a little cowardly, seemed a good one. Anne knew she was not yet ready to cope with sorting out their home, sorting through Bill's things, all the paraphernalia of six years of marriage. Not yet. Soon, maybe, but not today. Besides, it was getting late and she needed some rest. She was exhausted.

Anne took her make-up bag from the case and wandered through into the bathroom. The enormous tub was very much a sight for her sore and puffy eyes. Turning the taps on full she poured a large dose of foam bath into the swirling water and watched the bubbles dance. Thoughts of baths shared with Bill rose unbidden in her mind, happy times, wet giggles and carefree evenings. She was suddenly struck by the emptiness of the flat, as if the house itself was in mourning. Beneath the sound of the water everything was silent. Bill's laughter and strength were gone, leaving a vacuum of sorrow and an empty place she knew would never be filled.

'Stop it,' she snapped at herself. Despair and self-pity would achieve nothing, she knew. But sometimes it was hard to keep going, regardless. Sometimes it was impossible.

Anne shrugged off her depression, storing it away for safe keeping. Although she was consumed by grief, although she wanted nothing more than for Bill to walk through the door, his eyes twinkling with mirth, to crush her in his usual embrace, she knew this would not happen. Like most people, Anne had a rational part to her personality which put forth irrefutable comments whenever it seemed the blackness would swallow her. Comments like 'You'll get over it' or 'Just give it time'. These were wonderfully true. They were also totally useless and not in the least comforting.

Closing her mind, too tired to chase herself in pointless circles, Anne started to undress. She was tense after the journey, and nothing was more appealing than a long soak and a night of dreamless sleep (at least, she hoped so. Recently, her dreams had been filled with sad images of Bill as a happy father, snapshots of a life she would now never have). She undid her blouse, dropped it on the floor, stepped out of her skirt. Then she regarded herself in the full-length mirror, turning slightly to view her figure.

Again, the rational part of her mind spoke. 'Not bad. You're still an attractive woman. And there are plenty of decent men in the world who like a tall, leggy blonde with a brain and a sense of humour. It won't be long before you're married again and Bill is just a distant, hazy memory.'

She frowned. Perhaps. But there would be years between then and now when the despair would possess her and there would be no light at the end of the dark, damp tunnel.

Only rats.

The shiver at that thought was suppressed by glorious immersion in steaming-hot scented water. Her muscles relaxed as she reclined in the bath, the tension ebbing away as the delicate touch of warmth caressed her skin. She lay back and closed her eyes, stretching her toes out and floating free.

She relaxed. She unwound. Then – unexpectedly – she slept . . .

The sound of the telephone woke her up.

She came to with a start, eyes snapping open, hands gripping the sides of the bath. She realized the water was cold. Through the fog of interrupted sleep she sensed she had slept for some time.

The telephone continued to ring, even after a minute of her stumbling back into wakefulness.

Anne shrank back into the water, trying to ignore the cold seeping through her skin, wishing for the phone to stop ringing. She had no desire to talk to anyone.

It did not stop.

'Oh well, no point in staying in here I suppose,' she mumbled.

She swung a graceful leg over the edge of the bath and climbed out, wrapping herself in a warm towel. The incessant shrill of the telephone pounded at her muggy head, bringing back the tenseness.

'All right, all right, I'm coming.' She stumbled through into the lounge, reached for the phone.

It stopped.

Anne stared at it for ten seconds. How dare you! she thought. You can't drag me out of sleep and bath and then ring off!

One of Bill's fatalistic lines came to her: 'If it's important, they'll ring back; if not, then I'm glad I didn't answer.'

She pushed thoughts of Bill aside. The clock on the video in the lounge informed her that she had been asleep for almost two hours. She decided to pull the plug and go to bed. Sleep beckoned, pleasant dreamless sleep, and her resistance was low.

The telephone rang again.

'Oh, make up your mind!' she snapped, but went to answer it anyway. It could be the hospital, about her father.

She snatched up the receiver. 'Hello?'

Deep, gloomy silence was her only answer.

'Hello?' Silence. 'Is there anybody there?' Silence.

Silly question, she thought. Of course there's some-body there. They dialled the unlisted number, didn't they? 'Hello?'

There was a click, then a different silence: the completely dead silence which signified a broken connection. Anne knew she was only listening in on an electronic void.

She hung up, looked thoughtfully at the phone. It was

not the first time – in London, weird phone calls were the norm. But in her present state of mind, Anne found the dark silence unsettling.

A yawn turned her mind from the call. Once again sleep was threatening to pounce and she was reluctant to resist. Her eyes were sore and gritty, her brain was only just ticking over, and her wrinkled limbs were aching to stretch out on the mattress.

On her second attempt Anne managed to pull the plug. Although one ear was cocked at the telephone, waiting suspiciously for another interruption, it did not ring. Then she cleaned the bath – half-heartedly – rubbed herself dry, and brushed her teeth.

When she turned off the lights in the bathroom and returned to the lounge, Anne paused by the phone. She looked at it, gently chewing her lower lip. 'Go on,' she whispered, 'ring. I know you—'

It rang.

Even though she had been expecting the sound, it still made her jump out of her skin. Or perhaps she jumped because it had rung on cue. She picked up the receiver. Her heart was hammering, thumping loud and hard in her heaving chest. 'Hello?' Her voice quavered and broke on the 'o'. Somehow she knew that she was not going to enjoy this call, and that knowledge scared her.

This time silence was not the only answer.

'Hello Anne. It's nice to hear your voice.'

She did not recognize the caller. In fact, the voice was hardly human at all – dead, flat, metallic down the line. The sound conjured up images of dead trees on a barren hillside in winter.

Anne shivered. 'Hello? Who's speaking please?'

There was a small laugh. 'You don't know me Anne. We have never met. But I feel that I know you.'

Anne felt a chill strike to the core of her bones. Goosebumps rose on her skin. 'Who are you?' she asked sharply.

'It is not necessary for you to know who, Anne. Only *what*.'

She began to shake violently, suddenly more terrified than she had been in her life. HANG UP! her rational mind screamed. HANG UP THE DAMNED PHONE AND TAKE IT OFF THE HOOK! But she stood there, frozen to the spot, with the receiver clenched in her right hand.

She wished with all her heart that Bill was still there.

'That's what I wanted to talk about, actually Anne.'

'Stop calling me Anne!' she shrieked. 'I'm going to hang up.'

'Oh, I don't think that's a good idea. You would miss all the fun, all the home truths I rang to tell you about. Do you like the truth Anne? Or do you prefer your life shrouded in lies?'

She frowned, her heart missing a beat. Oh Bill, where are you when I need you? 'What do you mean?'

Again, a short laugh: cold, merciless, toneless. 'What do I mean? Lies, Anne, all lies. Everything he ever said to you.'

'I don't know what you mean. I don't know who you are, and I'm not going to listen to this!' She screamed the words down the phone, consumed by panic, shaking uncontrollably. The urge to hang up was overwhelming, despite the fascination exerted upon her. By an effort of will which startled her, she pushed the phone from her face and reached down to hang it on the cradle.

The words floated up to her from the handset, tinny and quiet, but unmistakable. 'I killed him, Anne. I killed your husband.'

She froze in shock, staring at the telephone as if it

was a poisonous spider she held instead of a pound of moulded plastic.

What did he say?

Anne found the receiver pressed once again to her ear. 'What did you say?' she whispered. The blood in her body seemed to have frozen solid in her veins, curdled by fear into a thick treacle.

'I said, Anne, that I murdered your beloved Bill.'

It's true, she thought. I know it is. This is no crank.

Somehow, she knew. Yet her rational mind refused to accept anything. 'I don't think that's very funny, whoever you are.'

'You don't believe me, Anne? Got so used to his lies that you can't recognize the truth any more? Well, perhaps you'll believe me if I give you the details.'

Anne was gripped by panic. Everything was happening too quickly, she had no time to grasp the situation or gain control.

Oh Bill, what's happening to me? What's this all about? Why did you have to go and leave me like that?

Through her confusion the voice laughed and mocked. 'Oh come on, Anne. Get a grip. I only murdered your husband. There's no need to go all flaky on me.'

As her last resistance collapsed, bringing down the walls of stoicism she had built between herself and the world, Anne screamed in despair. 'Go away! Leave me alone! Stop torturing me!'

She broke down, slipping to the floor to lean against the back of an armchair. Without knowing why, she still clasped the telephone to her ear, one final act of masochism in a sadistic week.

And through that telephone came the mocking, flat, toneless sounds of her husband's soulless killer. 'Now I see why Bill used to play around, Anne. No man likes hysterical women, even one as beautiful as you. And you are beautiful, Anne. I know – I saw you naked, as you bathed. Your firm thighs and those perfect breasts. I'd like to touch your breasts, Anne. Would you like that?'

Sobbing was her only response.

'No, I suppose not. Bill liked women too, didn't he Anne? You weren't enough for him, and you didn't even realize it. He *loved* women, lots of women, all sorts of women. Two or three at a time if he had the money. And you didn't even suspect. Of course, he was very careful. He was always clean, always checked himself and his clothes for marks and infections. And always paid in cash, so you'd never notice anything suspicious on his credit card bills.' The caller laughed. 'Of course, much of the time he HAD to pay in cash. Prostitutes don't take credit, do they Anne?'

She was disgusted, speechless. What did he say? *Prostitutes*?

'Yes, Anne, prostitutes. Bill did like his tail, you know. Had no shame about paying for it. When he wasn't getting enough from you, or when you were away, he would go out and HIRE some. Sometimes he'd bring them back to the flat, not yards from where you sit now. And he'd do them on the couch, or the floor, or the bed. Maybe even the kitchen tops. Once he had two women in the bath with him – well, I say women, one was only fifteen. Blonde and nubile, just as he liked them. Maybe he thought you were too old, Anne. Or maybe he was bored with you. Whatever the reason, he went like a rabbit on amphetamines. And you didn't even know.' He laughed again. 'You really are a blind stupid bitch, aren't you Anne?'

Anne could not tear herself away. She did not have the strength or the courage to just *stop* and hang up the phone. Racked by sobs, wet with tears, she lay crumpled on the floor. Compelled to listen to the VOICE, as much as it disgusted and abused her. Unable to disbelieve or deny, unable to hold the images of Bill in her mind without them becoming soiled and corrupted.

'Why?' she wailed out loud, her face contorted by grief and fear. 'Why did he do that to me? Why are you telling me?'

The mocking laugh tore at the tatters of her self-respect. 'Grow up, Anne. He did it because he enjoyed it and didn't give a fuck about you. He didn't love you, he loved your money. He loved the fact that you were paying for him to get laid. He loved the irony of life, and the feel of a woman's flesh against his own.'

'That's a lie!' she shrieked, capable of nothing but childish denial of those facts. And in her heart she knew them to be facts, because the voice did not lie. 'He did love me,' she added lamely.

'The fuck he did, Anne. You've got the body of a goddess and the common sense of a turd. Sure, Bill was slime. But it was you who dragged him there, you and your endless nagging. You BITCH!'

The word was screamed down the telephone at her, for the first time breaking the unmodulated monotone. Anne recoiled in horror and surprise, scared back to sensibility by the venom in THE VOICE. Something bad was happening, and suddenly Anne was terrified.

ESCAPE, her mind shouted. LOCK THE DOORS, HIDE.

But the laughter on the phone gripped her, pinned her motionless on the spot. It rent the breath from her body, froze the blood in her veins. 'Be afraid, Anne. I'm coming for you. You can run. You can run, but you can't hide. You can never hide, Anne.'

The laughter, wild and demonic, buffeted her ears.

Then the line clicked, and there was silence.

For thirty seconds she just sat there. It was inconceivable, after the ranting and the threats, that the caller was gone. At any moment she expected more filth to block her ears with disgust.

But the man was gone, on his way to her. Of that she was certain. Because the voice did not lie.

That thought galvanized her into action. She rose and ran to her suitcase, ripped back the lid, pulled out the contents, a woman possessed by fear and a sudden desire to live.

'Where is it?' she moaned. The number – the Inspector who was in charge of the murder investigation. The police sergeant had given her the card after her interview, when she had promised to keep in touch and call if anything came to mind.

And now something was on her mind and the card was gone.

'Handbag!' she screamed, fleeing back into the lounge. She could sense the man about to break down the door, outside the window, looking in, a face of pure evil. She could sense him all around, closing in, coming fast, and you can RUN BUT YOU CAN'T HIDE.

She rifled through her handbag, casting the trivia of her life aside – lipstick, handkerchiefs, mirrors, pens, brushes, nail varnish, cheque-book, a tampon.

NO CARD!

'Oh sweet Jesus where ARE you?' Panic clutched at her heart.

He was close, very close, and he was coming for her. And if she did not get help, she knew he would take her.

'Clothes!' She remembered! Standing as the policeman left, slipping the card in her slacks.

'Where are they?'

Not washing the slacks, just stuffing them in the —
'SUITCASE!'

She ran back to the bedroom, her breath coming in harsh rasps.

'Come on, come on.'

There! Slacks, pocket.

'Oh sweet Mary!'

The card, in her hand.

'Thank God!'

She rushed to the telephone, snatched at the receiver, fumbled at the card and dropped it. Sobbing with fear she knelt, reached for the sliver of cardboard, grasped it, brought it to her face.

'Calm down,' she breathed.

Was that a footstep outside?

'HURRY UP!'

She read the card, dialled the number. It was ringing.

'HURRY UP!' she screamed, but no words came. Her throat was locked shut with terror.

Answer the phone, please God, make them answer the phone!

Her voice, when it came, nothing but a moan. 'Please, hurry.'

The ringing stopped. The line clicked, there was a pause. A man said: 'Sergeant Fowles.'

Anne nearly collapsed in relief. 'Oh thank GOD! Help me, please, the man who killed my husband? He's coming to kill me!'

The man was thankfully efficient. 'Your name?'

She paused, mouth open. WHAT THE HELL IS MY NAME?

Then it came to her, drifting through the terror like a falling leaf in autumn. 'Anne Wallis. My husband Bill was kill—

'Yes, ma'am.' The voice became brisk. 'And where are you?'

'Er, in our flat, in London. West London. The address is—'

'It's all right, Mrs Wallis, I have your details. This man – how did he contact you?'

'By telephone, just now. Please hurry!'

There was a brief pause, some talking in the background. 'A car is already on its way, Mrs Wallis. Lock all the doors and windows, and do not answer the door to *anybody*. Do you understand?'

'Please HURRY! He's coming now, he said he'd kill me and I believe him.'

'Mrs Wallis, we're already on our way. Did—'

The line clicked. Went completely dead. Silence filled Anne's ear. She knew, in a sudden clarity of understanding, that the line had been cut.

She looked up, cold, terrified. 'He's here,' she whispered.

CHAPTER TWO

Sam Stevens Gets Ready

Tuesday, New Year's Day, 1991, 11.30 p.m.
Arizona.

'Yes honey, I'm *fine*. I promise.'

'Are you sure, Sam? Are you eating OK?'

'Sure, hon. I *can* cook, you know.' Sam rolled his eyes. 'And you? Denise and Terry and Jenny? How's Pa?'

'Your dad's fine. The kids are missing you. Terry keeps asking when he can go home. He says Grandad's stories are boring.'

Sam chuckled. 'You better believe it. I had to put up with 'em for years, so I *know*. How was New Year?'

His wife sighed. 'OK I guess, but I missed you.' She paused. 'When can we come home, Sam? Just what is going on?'

'Look, honey, we've been through all this before.'

'Yeah, we sure have. And you never answer my questions. Not when you came home with your face cut and bleeding a week ago, not when you bundled us in the car and drove us over here, and you *still* haven't. So what's going on? Are you in trouble? Danger?'

'Honey, I'm fine. There's some work I need to sort out, and I think it best if you and the kids aren't here. That's all.'

'That's *all*? Sam, we've never had secrets before. If

you're in danger I want to help, not feel useless and lie to the kids.'

'You're NOT lying to them, hon. 'Cos you don't know either.'

'Yeah, sure, tell me about it. I feel bad enough as it is. Don't shut me out, please. *Please* Sam.'

Sam sighed. 'I'm sorry, hon. But you have to believe me when I say I know what I'm doing. The safest thing is for you to stay there with the kids. *Trust* me, OK? I care about you all too much to risk anything over something as small as this.'

His wife was silent while she digested this. Then: 'Would it make things worse if we were there? I mean, really worse?'

'Yes, Tracey. I'd be too scared about you. And that would make things a hundred times more dangerous than they should be.'

Another pause. 'You promise?'

He grinned. Sometimes, convincing his wife was harder than getting through to his father. 'I promise. Just trust me, OK?'

'When have I not trusted you? I'm only upset because I *do* trust you. I want to be there with you and the kids. As a family.'

'I know, honey. Believe me, I understand.'

She sighed. 'I love you, Sam. And so do the kids.'

'I love you all, Trace. Kiss the kids for me, OK?'

'Sure.' She paused again, this time longer. 'I'm scared, Sam.'

He was silent for a few seconds. Then he decided to be honest with her. 'Me too, hon.'

She swallowed that calm statement without verbally flinching. In fact, Sam thought he detected a lessening of her worry. 'Take care, won't you? Call me if you need anything?'

'Sure. Look after the kids. Give them my love. And Tracey? I'll be seeing you soon. You have my word on that.'

They said their goodbyes and he hung up.

Touch wood, he thought.

Then he looked around the living room. Sure is plenty of the damned stuff to touch, he added wryly, a grin creasing his cheek and distorting the livid red scar. He rubbed the wound absently, a reminder of why he was here and his wife was somewhere else.

Somewhere safe. He hoped.

Tracey would not have recognized the lounge. The furniture was piled in the centre of the floor. The drapes were pulled back and tied open, though it was dark outside. Five stacks of wood dominated the room, filling it with the sweet odour of freshly cut timber. Sawdust stood in mounds on the floor. Tools and boxes of nails littered the carpet. On the table two shotguns lay side by side on the polished surface, surrounded by cartons of shells. A carbine rested beside them, dark metal gleaming in the soft lamp light. That, too, had its accompanying case of ammunition – 400 rounds of hollow tipped bullets which could each cut a man in half. And if all that failed, Sam's trusty old .45 was tossed negligently on the bar, loaded and ready for action.

Sam, as he had so often said to himself in the past few days, was a man with a mission. Rambo, Arizona traffic-cop style.

Why then, he asked himself as he surveyed his private armoury, can I not shake off the feeling that this just won't be enough?

Because, a little voice answered him, a bullet only kills what you can *touch*, something *normal*. And I have a feeling I'm dealing with something beyond the bounds of normal combat. *Way* beyond.

He shrugged away his worries and picked up another plank. With dogged resolve he placed it over the window frame and hammered home the nails. He had already blocked the external doors, covered the upstairs windows and nailed shut most of the rooms in the house he thought he no longer needed. He was almost ready.

The telephone rang as the hammer was in mid strike. He looked at it without surprise, knowing exactly who it was, knowing what the message would be, in no hurry to answer the call. He finished off hammering in the nail, lowered the hammer, and picked up the phone.

'You can run, Sam, but you can't hide. You can never hide.'

Same old words, same old voice, a flat and toneless repetition which still managed to curdle his blood.

He did not bother to answer. The phone went dead, just as it always did.

Beside the phone was a pad. On the pad were seventy tally marks.

Sam picked up his pen, stifled a yawn, and added another mark.

'Come and get me, asshole,' he murmured. 'I'm ready.' He turned and looked around the room, eyes coming to rest on the weapons stacked on the table. He grinned.

'Boy, am I ready.'

BOOK FOUR

RETRIBUTION

CHAPTER ONE

Storm Warning

Wednesday January 2, 1991. 1:30 p.m. London, England.

The Iraqi occupation of Kuwait was now into its fifth month. Allied troops in the Gulf numbered hundreds of thousands. A war was looming on the desert horizon with no hope for peace.

Scott Johnson knew nothing about it and cared even less. All he knew was that his beloved son still lay comatose. Tim had not moved since the violent evening of December 28th. Each day his worries grew; every morning when he woke and Tim showed no sign of recovery, Scott felt his hopes fade a little further. McCormack said no news was good news, but even he could not refute his own statement: 'The longer patients stay in coma, the less likely they are to ever recover.'

The stay in hospital had at least achieved one thing: Scott was close to reconciliation with his ex-wife, Sally. She had given her callous boyfriend the elbow, and spent much of her time at Tim's bedside. She and Scott often sat talking quietly, reminiscing, sometimes even managing a laugh. McCormack was pleased, believing this might aid Tim's recovery.

Well. You never knew your luck.

Outside the hospital worldwide events swept onwards.

Unknown to Scott or Sally, the whirlwind of power first witnessed by Bill Wallis on Christmas Eve had grown. Fed by its mutated and murderous disciples the disease was spreading, like cancer, as more and more souls, more and more depravity, joined the insanity. Not just in London, not just in Arizona, but all over the world now. Spreading . . . what had happened in London was only the tip of the iceberg.

Yet there was still time to prevent disaster. As long as somebody had the insight to realize what was happening. And as long as that someone also had the power to stop it.

Scott, blissfully ignorant of this wider scope, left Tim's room to get a drink. He nodded to the plain-clothes policemen outside the door, received the usual curt nods in reply, and sauntered over to the coffee machine. It was there, without him even realizing, that events started to come to a head.

Scott selected his drink and watched as the cup was filled with tepid, bacteria-rife water. As the machine gurgled and hummed he became aware of someone standing beside him. He looked up.

The stranger was short, about five foot six, with a pale lined face. He was wearing a dark grey suit, a white shirt and a striking paisley tie. His shoes were black and immaculately polished. He stood there, stiff as a board, sweating slightly, hands in pockets. Scott estimated the man's age at around fifty.

Scott was struck by two things. First, the man's left hand twitched noticeably in his pocket, as if he were very nervous. Second, beneath the carefully combed short hair which greyed at the temples, Scott could plainly see an old scar. The mark was about six inches long, running from the man's right ear, over his crown, to the same point above his left ear. The hair which grew over the scar was bleached white. Although the man had done his best to conceal the anomaly he was unfortunately five inches shorter than Scott, so Scott had a pretty good view. It was the most peculiar scar Scott had ever seen. He could only imagine that the man's head had been split down the middle like a coconut at some point in his youth and then sewn back together again.

'Mr Johnson?'

Scott jerked, suddenly aware of how rude he was being. The voice was deep, surprisingly so for someone that short. Yet strangled, as if the man's larynx was being squeezed. 'Pardon?' Scott said lamely, blushing.

'Scott Johnson?' The tone of voice this time suggested it was a pointless question. The man knew exactly who he was talking to.

'Yes. Can I help you?' Only then did Scott remember Daniels' warning: 'Be on your guard, speak to no-one.' He cursed himself.

The man gave a nervous little twitch of his lips which could have been a smile. Scott was overwhelmed by the man's discomfort, as if he was incredibly uneasy in his presence.

'I think not, Mr Johnson. But I am sure I can help you.'

I do not want to hear this, Scott thought, it's going to be BAD. I don't want your help, you give me the creeps.

The stranger flinched slightly, rubbed at his nose, and shrugged. Then he attempted another smile. 'I understand you may not trust me, Mr Johnson. That is wise in the circumstances. But you see, I have something very valuable to offer you.'

Scott toyed with the idea of just walking away. The man's attitude was making his skin crawl. But something held him, some other instinct. 'Oh? And what might that be?' I'm going to regret asking that, his brain wailed.

The man's smile became a little more certain, as if he knew he had won the first battle. 'What could I possibly offer you of any value besides your son's life, Mr Johnson?'

John Daniels sat at his office desk. Fowles sat opposite him. 'OK but what about Anne Wallis? What's the situation there?'

Fowles gave a derisory snort. 'We moved her to a safe house and staked out her flat, but I think it's a waste of time.'

Daniels nodded. 'I'm inclined to agree with you. Mind you, I still don't think she was faking. I've never seen anyone so terrified. I reckon the call was genuine, even if the threat was never followed through. I mean, *somebody* cut the phone line.'

'Maybe. But she's becoming a real pain in the arse. Sir.'

Daniels frowned. 'Cut her some slack, Sergeant. Her husband was burned to death, she had a miscarriage, her mother died and so might her father. She's had a bad week.' He cast Fowles a warning glance. 'Enough people have died because of this psycho, Sergeant, and I'm not going to take any risks. Anne Wallis stays under guard until I'm satisfied her life is not in any danger. Understood?'

Fowles paused. He always did when Daniels asked him a question. Usually because his answer was never the one Daniels wanted to hear. As usual, after ten minutes with Daniels he was sweating. 'Sir,' he said simply.

He was saved from a lecture by the telephone. Daniels' hand whipped out like a striking snake and snatched up the receiver.

'Yes!' he barked, thunder clouds forming on his brow.

134

Fowles stared at the window. Why did I request this transfer? I'd rather still be in Northern Ireland.

'WHAT?' Daniels' shout snapped Fowles out of his reverie.

'And?' Pause. Muffled curse. 'Right. Bring him in. Now. And hurry up.' He slammed the telephone down. 'Bugger!'

'Trouble sir?' Fowles asked mildly.

Daniels looked up. 'Looks like it.' He lit a cigarette. 'Scott Johnson just reported somebody snooping around the hospital.'

Fowles was instantly alert. 'Have they got him?'

'Yes, he was just standing there, apparently. They're bringing him in now.'

'A reporter?'

Daniels snorted. 'No, nothing so trivial. Some bloody nut-case by the sound of it.' He shook his head. 'This sodding investigation gets harder and weirder by the day.' He cursed under his breath and angrily stubbed out the half-smoked cigarette. 'Get down to the hospital and make sure security stays tight. This could be a ruse.' Fowles nodded and left.

Daniels frowned at the closed door and lit another cigarette.

A constable stood watch just inside the door to Interview Room 3. The room was bare except for a table and three chairs. Outside, through the dirty windows, London was being rained on.

The man sitting at the table was smoking a cigarette. He looked up when Daniels walked in, frowned, and looked away again.

Daniels took an instant dislike to the man. He resented being ignored. But he sat down anyway. 'Mr Trooper? Nathan Trooper?'

'Correct.'

Daniels studied the man. English; clipped accent; obviously had a few pennies to his name. Strange demeanour – hunched in his chair, uncomfortable. Daniels suspected the unease was not solely due to being shut in a police interview room. Again, he felt that tightening of his bowels, a sure sign that events were about to get out of hand. 'You live in Manchester?'

'Correct.'

'Currently staying at the SkyBase Hotel in Kensington?'

'Correct.'

'Since when?'

'Six p.m., on the 30th of December.'

So far so good. Daniels had already verified that. 'Mr Trooper, do you understand why you were brought here?'

'Yes.'

'You understand your rights and why you are being questioned?'

'Yes.'

I *hate* monosyllabic answers, Daniels groaned. Can't you at least give me some information? Like, *WHY*?

'Forgive me, Inspector Daniels. I am not the world's best conversationalist.'

Daniels raised an eyebrow. How did he know my name?

'I know many things, Inspector.'

Daniels' arched eyebrow raised even further. Hold on a minute – I didn't even ASK that question! He frowned. The interview was getting out of control. 'Perhaps you would care to explain why you were in the hospital, Mr Trooper,' Daniels asked, vainly attempting to grasp the reins. 'Were you visiting sick relatives?'

'I have no relatives, Inspector. No live ones, any-way.'

'So why were you there?'

'I have already explained that.'

'To whom?'

'Scott Johnson, and your obvious plain-clothes officers.'

They're *supposed* to be obvious, Daniels thought acidly. 'So explain it to me anyway. Why the hell were you were pestering Mr Johnson when you don't know him and it was none of your business?'

Daniels checked himself, realizing he could easily start shouting if he was not careful. The frustrations of the past ten days were threatening to explode.

'I understand your concern, Inspector. But my intentions were strictly honourable, I can assure you. I meant no-one any harm.'

'So you say. But I'd still like to know *why*.'

Trooper cast an uneasy glance at the constable by the door. 'Could I possibly have a glass of water?' he asked innocuously.

Daniels took the hint. Without taking his eyes off Trooper he asked: 'Constable, a glass of water. Take your time.'

The constable nodded and left. He knew when he wasn't wanted.

When the door closed Trooper relaxed noticeably. The furrows in his brow eased, as if a weight had been lifted from his mind.

With every passing moment, Daniels became more and more convinced that Nathan Trooper was a very peculiar man indeed. 'So?' he asked. 'Talk to me, Mr Trooper.'

Nathan smiled, his headache easing. 'Glad to, Inspector. I perceive you are a man who has Tim Johnson's safety at heart.'

'Who?'

Nathan grinned. 'Don't be coy, Inspector. Tim Johnson, the twelve-year-old boy lying comatose in that guarded room. The only witness you have to the murders of two homosexual men on the night of December 27.'

Daniels was so surprised he forgot to be cautious. 'How the hell did you know that?' he blurted.

Trooper waved one nicotine stained hand in dismissal of the question. 'Like I said, I know many things. It is unimportant how I know them. You would not believe me even if I told you.'

Daniels struggled to contain himself, mentally slapping his wrist for admitting so much by his outburst. He was losing control, had already lost the initiative, and he knew it. He needed a smoke.

'Smoke?' Trooper asked innocently, offering his cigarettes.

Daniels smothered his uneasy surprise. 'I don't, thank you.'

Trooper shook his head sadly, grinning slightly. 'Yes you do, Inspector, and right now you want a cigarette. However, if you wish to waste time playing games with me, so be it. I have all the time in the world. Tim Johnson, on the other hand, does not.'

Daniels looked at the cigarettes. Damn you, he thought. I don't know how you know, but you're right. And I hate you for it.

He reached over, took one, lit it, and inhaled deeply.

Trooper grinned. 'Excellent. Now we are getting somewhere. You see, Inspector, it is extremely important that we understand one another. I know you do not trust me, and I expected nothing less. But we have little time left. You know, and I know, and I believe Scott knows as well, that Tim's life is in grave danger.'

Daniels savoured the rich taste of the tobacco. 'Nice.' *Why do I feel like it is* me *who is being questioned?*

'I know. I would offer you some to take away with you, but you would probably think I was trying to bribe you.'

Daniels grinned. 'Probably.' *I'm beginning to feel a little out of my depth here.* 'OK. So. I've admitted Tim Johnson is in our care. But what business is that of yours, Mr Trooper?'

'On the evening of the 27th Tim was witness to two gruesome murders, and was subsequently attacked by the murderer. His life was saved by the timely arrival of his father, but the damage had already been done. Tim's mind suffered a massive collapse. You have no idea of the terror he experienced, or how monumentally brave he was to put up a fight. You or I would probably have gone insane. Tim managed to survive, but only by retreating from the outside world into a coma. He will not wake until he breaks down the walls he believes are protecting him, and voluntarily returns.

'On the evening of the 28th, he was attacked again. I am sure that neither you nor any of the doctors could explain that episode. He was very lucky to survive, because he was totally defenceless. His life is now in grave danger. Do you understand, Inspector? *Very grave* danger. One more attack and he will be lost.'

Daniels exhaled smoke through his nostrils, keeping an outward calm. Within, he was a turmoil of suspicions – Trooper said nobody would have been able to explain the episode in the hospital, and he was right. Yet Trooper's tone suggested that *he* knew and *could* explain. That bothered Daniels, not because he felt ignorant, but because he believed Trooper really did know the answers. Which could only mean one of two things: either Trooper really was there to help, as he claimed, or he was the attacker.

'You still haven't answered my question,' Daniels said calmly.

Trooper sighed. 'Inspector, we are not dealing with run of the mill assault here – this is something way beyond your present comprehension.' He paused. 'I think you know that, don't you?'

Daniels hoped his eyes did not betray a sudden flicker of agreement. He had discussed as much with McCormack after Tim's EEG bursts, and since then had been unable to shake off the feeling that he was way out of his depth. The whole investigation tasted very strange when he chewed it over. As such, Trooper's final question had touched a raw nerve. 'We?' he asked innocuously.

'Yes. We.' Trooper seemed quite convinced that he was already involved, whether or not Daniels would agree. 'I've come here because I *know* what is going on – you do not. The doctors, I imagine, have no ideas.' His lips curled slightly. 'Unless, of course, you have some very strange doctors involved. I *know* what is wrong with Tim Johnson, and I *know* how to save him. You do not. All you can do is sit back and wait for him to recover, and in doing so you will inevitably wait forever. I came here to save his life, Inspector, not to take it. Can you not see that?'

'No I can't. All I see is a stranger with no business here.'

Trooper frowned. 'I have *every* business here! That fit was no *physical* attack. The murderer was not even there at the time.'

'How do you know?'

'Because it was I who intervened to save him, Inspector. I did not have to come here. But nobody seems to realize just what is happening. Nobody understands how much danger Tim is in. Those guards at the door will achieve nothing. Don't you realize that?'

'They stopped you, didn't they Mr Trooper?'

Nathan leaned forward, the frustration clear on his face. The intensity and danger in that expression scared Daniels.

'I came here to help, Inspector. To help you, to help Tim, to help myself. I meant harm to no-one.'

Daniels nodded. 'Of course. So let's just recap, shall we? You claim to have knowledge of several murders and the victims. You have given details of attacks. You also claim that you are here to help, and mean no harm. You were found approaching a member of society who neither requested nor required your assistance. You were picked up in a hospital where you had no business. I won't insult your intelligence by denying that the room is under guard. You obviously know that. So far, you have said nothing which is relevant to our enquiries – your details could have come from eavesdropping on a private conversation. So why should I believe you? Indeed, if I *did*, why should I assume anything other than that you are the attacker? Why should I assume you are here to help? Surely the obvious conclusion is that you are the murderer?'

Trooper gave a rueful smile, and then nodded grudgingly. 'Accepted. Everything you say makes sense, Inspector. I guess it was rather silly of me to expect you to believe my story, or any circumstantial remarks I make about events and my intentions.' He reached out to pick up his packet of cigarettes. 'I did not intend to waste your time, Inspector. I sought only to offer assistance.' He paused in the motion of pocketing his cigarettes. 'And that assistance I could give, in good faith, if you allowed me access to Tim Johnson. That would prove my intentions.'

Daniels shook his head and chuckled. 'Oh, I think not, Mr Trooper. I don't think that would be at all possible.'

Trooper smiled again, this time with more humour. 'As I suspected. However, I thought it worth a try.'

At that comment Daniels regarded Trooper with a puzzled frown.

'I don't understand you, Mr Trooper. On one hand, I think you're a crackpot with delusions. On the other, I can't rid myself of the suspicion that you know a little too much for your own good. And on the other, I get the feeling you might actually believe what you say.' Daniels had no idea why he gave Trooper such bald-faced opinions. Perhaps he just decided fencing was pointless.

Nathan grinned. 'Then I feel a lot safer, Inspector, since you seem to have three hands.'

Daniels returned the grin, his frown dissolving. Something about the man was reassuring – despite his obvious unease, Trooper seemed honest. Daniels' instincts screamed that Trooper could be useful, could possess some information worth hearing. Yet twenty years of experience screamed that Trooper was the best suspect they had. As such, Daniels was indecisive. 'So what should I do with you?' he asked eventually.

'Three options, as I see it. Let me go, arrest me, or check me out. You won't arrest me because you have no evidence against me. And I must tell you, Inspector, I do not think you will ever find the evidence you require. Both you and I know this is not the sort of investigation when everything comes out cut and dried, and stands up in a court of law.' Trooper's gaze, which had become intensely piercing as he spoke, softened a little. Daniels realized he had been holding his breath. 'Besides, you are a policeman, I am a stranger, and this is a delicate situation. Do as you see fit.'

Daniels started breathing again. Something about Trooper unnerved him – that intensity, that penetrating look in his stark blue eyes. There was substance in his words. But whether that substance was relevant, whether Trooper would emerge as a player in the scenario, he did not know. He opted for caution. 'How long will you be staying in London?'

'A few days, perhaps a week. I cannot see it lasting longer than that. By then it will be resolved, one way or the other.'

Daniels raised one eyebrow. 'Meaning?'

Trooper shifted his shoulders, said nothing.

Daniels regarded him silently, considering his options. He had no grounds for an arrest, as Trooper had quite rightly pointed out. 'Mr Trooper, I will be honest with you. It's not something I do often, so consider yourself blessed. I do not trust you – you know too much. That worries me. But I do believe one thing.'

'And that is?'

'I should never close off any avenue of investigation until I am sure that avenue is a dead end.'

Trooper nodded, apparently satisfied. 'Good. I shall rely on it.' He smiled slightly, an odd twist to his lips which struck Daniels as bizarre. 'Then, with your permission, I shall take my leave. I am sure you are a busy man.' He tossed another cigarette at Daniels. 'As a measure of my good faith, I shall stay away from the hospital. You know where to contact me.'

He stood, clearly thinking the interview over. Daniels was surprised to find that this dismissal did not ruffle his feathers. He would be the first to admit that the guy was weird; but there was something straight about Trooper which spoke volumes – volumes of strange knowledge and understanding which could be useful.

'Don't leave town,' Daniels joked, lighting the cigarette.

Trooper paused by the door, then turned to face him. The expression on his face was thoughtful and cautious. 'Two things, Inspector. First, if you decide to check me out, you may find some things which do not appeal to you. They may even sound crazy. Please try hard to prevent them from affecting your judgement.' He held up a hand to stall Daniels' questions. 'I could not give you any satisfactory answers. So do not ask, please.'

There was such finality in that tone that Daniels chose not to argue. He thrust the questions to one side. 'OK. And second?'

Nathan frowned. 'If you believe nothing else, Inspector, at least believe Tim is in imminent danger. Try to be quick, eh?'

Again, Daniels found that the blunt statement did not ruffle his touchy feathers. Trooper's comments commanded respect, rather than Daniels' usual flare of anger. 'I'll do my best, Mr Trooper. But I'm only a plodder, as you can see.' He did not know why he added that comment – it was out of his mouth before he could stop.

Trooper chuckled. 'Far from it, Inspector. I am relieved to learn of your perception. If anyone has a chance to sort out this mess, I believe that man is you. Just try to keep an open mind.'

Daniels did not like the way Trooper said that last sentence. It boded ill for his future. But one question did bubble to the surface of his mind as he remembered how Trooper's unease had lessened when the constable left the room. 'Mr Trooper, you don't like people, do you? You're not comfortable around them?'

Trooper appeared pleased by the question, not at all

offended as Daniels had expected, almost as if he was glad to be insulted. Or perhaps it was all some kind of test. 'No, Inspector. They give me headaches.' He nodded goodbye. 'I expect to hear from you soon.'

Then he was gone.

John Daniels sat in the chair, smoking the cigarette, looking at the closed door and churning the interview over in his mind. Something was bugging him, something he could not put his finger on, something important he had missed.

He shrugged and looked up at Trooper's chair, as if expecting the man to reappear. 'Whoever you are, Mr Nathan Trooper, and whatever your intent, I salute you. I think that is the first time I've been out-smarted in about thirty years. Because now I have you right where you want me.' He grinned, despite his unease.

At last, things were moving. The only problem was that they were moving too fast and he had no idea where they were going.

But wherever it was, he promised himself, I'll be there to meet them when they arrive.

'FOWLES!' His roar echoed down the corridors and deserted offices. The Sergeant's head appeared from a doorway. 'Sir?'

'Get me everything you can find on Nathan Trooper. I want background, records, past history, psychology profiles, signed statements from friends, references, school reports, blood samples, fingerprints, hair, shoe size – everything.'

Fowles handed Daniels a very thick envelope folder. 'I'll have the urine samples in about an hour, sir.'

Daniels glared at him, frowned at the man's straight face, and then laughed. 'Well done, Sergeant. How did you get it so fast?'

Fowles grinned. 'Because this man is positively *famous*. We've got stuff on him going back at least thirty years. I think you'll find it, well . . . interesting. To say the least.'

Daniels did not like the sound of that. He recalled Trooper's parting comment: try to keep an open mind. 'Crooked, is he?'

Fowles shrugged. 'If you mean, is this his criminal record and is it as long as your arm, then no. Weird as hell, though.'

'Is he our man?'

Fowles shrugged again. 'Who knows? Depends on who you listen to. I'm about to ask McCormack some interesting medical questions. If he confirms my suspicions, then it's possible.'

Daniels raised an eyebrow. 'That's a bit vague, Sergeant.'

Fowles looked away. 'I suggest you read that first, sir. Maybe then my questions will make some sense.'

You're beginning to sound like Trooper, Daniels thought sourly. 'OK. Get back quick as you can.'

Fowles nodded, grabbed his jacket and bolted off down the corridor. Daniels wandered on into his office.

It was now six p.m. Trooper had left at three. Daniels had spent the last three hours interviewing an irate Scott Johnson, and grilling the officer who had brought them from the hospital. Scott had wanted to get back to his son, and to have some answers: who was the man? What had he wanted? Daniels had wanted some peace and quiet to think things over, and got neither. Now it looked as if he would have another five hours work ahead of him. Damn! Another twenty-hour day. His wife would have the Dobermans out again.

He lit another cigarette. His lungs were hurting, his mouth tasted like an ashtray, but he needed all the help he could get. With mounting trepidation, he opened the Trooper folder and started to read. The sinking feeling in his stomach grew and grew until his intestines went down like the Titanic.

SUBJECT RECORDS – PRINT REQUEST 02–01–91 15:17
SECTION 1 – SUBJECT DETAILS

Subject:	NATHAN TROOPER (no middle name) MALE CAUCASIAN
Date of Birth:	24–07–1952
Registered Address:	184, MARSH LANE BOWDEN MANCHESTER, ENGLAND.
Previous Offences:	Two
	24–07–76: exceeding mandatory speed limit. Fined £100 and 3 licence penalty points
	24–07–77: driving under the influence of alcohol. Fined £1000. Licence revoked for 3 years.
Known Relatives:	None. All family deceased (see Section 3).
Marital Status:	Single
Distinguishing Marks:	1. Abdominal scar: eight inches long, spanning lower left rib to groin.
	2. Cranial scar: six inches long, spanning left to right ear. Hair discolouration surrounding scar.

Daniels paused to stub out his cigarette. 38 years old, eh? He looks a lot older. He skipped to Section 3.

Gary Haynes

SECTION 3 – FAMILY BACKGROUND

Father: Ethan Paul Trooper, Doctor. Deceased.
D.O.B.: 01–02–1928. No criminal record.
Mother: Emma Trooper, nee Barnes, Teacher. Deceased.
D.O.B.: 03–11–1930. No criminal record.
Brother: Isaac Paul Trooper. Deceased.
D.O.B.: 06–06–1950. No criminal record.

History

Subject's mother killed by subject's father on 27–07–1964. Emma Trooper died from a massive brain haemorrhage. Ethan Trooper subsequently committed suicide by hanging. Nathan Trooper sustained multiple axe wounds (see Distinguishing Marks) but survived. Suspected brain damage. Older brother, Isaac Paul, escaped injury by being absent at time of attack.

Nathan Trooper subsequently committed to mental institution at age of 12 after hospitalization and physical recovery. Psychological and neurological tests during the internment reported – quote – significant psychic potential – unquote. After intensive studies was reported to be able to – quote – read the mind of any human being in the same room. Nathan is a prime example of the TELEPATH. He reports constant blinding headaches, and has withdrawn from society. Being in the company of others causes him pain, due, he says, to the 'volume of their thoughts'. His condition has worsened significantly as his psychic ability has increased – unquote. Independent tests corroborated this evidence. Medical tests attempted to establish a link with the head injuries sustained at age 12 and the apparent psychic ability. No link was ever proved.

At age 18 Nathan Trooper obtained degree level qualifications in Psychology and Mathematical & Logistical Science. His IQ was rated at 184.

At age 20 Nathan Trooper was confirmed fit to rejoin society, after prolonged psychiatric treatment in the – then – revolutionary therapy sessions. The examining body reported their findings thus – quote –

Nathan is an extraordinarily intelligent man . . . His deep

seated anxieties about his father's death and the murder of his family have been lessened by his therapy in the institution . . . He has managed to control and co-exist with his psychic gift. Indeed, he now reports this gift has been reduced to the level whereby he believes he will be 'normal' within a few months. We have no reason to believe otherwise . . . We perceive the mental anomaly to have been the result of massive trauma and brutal head injuries . . . We now certify Nathan Trooper to be clinically sane – unquote.

On August 3rd 1972 subject left the Samuel Hall Institute. He was delivered into the custody of his brother Isaac, who had petitioned for his release. A two-year probationary period to study whether Nathan Trooper could adjust to a satisfactory degree, was successful. Nathan Trooper was re-awarded full rights as an English citizen and a capable adult. As such, he was awarded 50% of the life insurance payment previously given to his brother after the death of his father in 1964. This then amounted to some £50,000.

Other than the two minor traffic offences (see Section 1) Nathan Trooper has no criminal record. Police psychologists have reported this as being remarkable, considering his childhood and the fact that he spent eight years in an asylum.

His brother, Isaac Paul, died on 06–06–1982 from a drug overdose. The inquest recorded a verdict of suicide.

Nathan Trooper has not worked since his release from the probationary period. He subsists on a private income. He has no surviving next of kin, or claim to his estate.

Nathan Trooper is listed on police files as a potential hazard to society. However, to date he has exhibited none of his father's homicidal tendencies, nor any tendency to commit suicide. This has been confirmed by sporadic psychiatric evaluations.

At last regular vetting, Nathan Trooper was reported to be a total recluse. He lives alone, has no known friends or associates, and rarely goes out.

Unsubstantiated reports have been received concerning his so-called psychic ability being sold to relatives of brain damaged or coma patients. No further information on this topic is available at this time.

SECTION 4 – NON-UK OFFENCES

Previously Under Investigation:

In December of 1975, Nathan Trooper was arrested on suspicion of the murder of Tenessee James, in Ohio, USA. The victim in question was a thirteen-year-old girl who suffered from extreme anti-social behaviour. Unconfirmed reports stated that Trooper had been employed to ease her psychological problems. The girl died of a brain haemorrhage. Nathan Trooper was subsequently released without charge, and returned to England. The post-mortem revealed no suspicious circumstances.

Sheriff Gordon T. McTierney, who headed the investigation, was quoted as saying: 'Just because I don't have the evidence to convict Trooper, that don't mean he didn't do it.'

Nathan Trooper's solicitor filed a lawsuit against Sheriff Gordon T. McTierney for libel. Sheriff McTierney resigned as a result of his accusations and the lawsuit.

The verdict recorded at the inquest was: Death by natural causes.

Daniels returned the official police reports to the file, then flicked through a score of psychological, neurological, medical and psychometric examination reports, and doctors' diagnoses on his injuries in 1964. The injuries had been very severe – Trooper's abdomen had been torn open by one axe blow, damaging his liver and intestines, causing severe internal bleeding and breaking four ribs. The blow to the head had cleaved the skull partially in two, penetrating the protective membrane within and damaging the brain to an unknown extent. The hospital had used twenty-two pints of blood to keep the patient alive during the ten-hour operation. Nathan Trooper's survival was, in all meanings of the word, miraculous.

The psychological reports were interesting, if a little difficult to understand. What Daniels did glean from them was that Nathan had been very lucky to end up in such a forward thinking institution. He might still have been locked in a padded cell if the doctors there had not done their utmost to cure him of his trauma. Daniels was particularly intrigued by the recurring references to Trooper's 'gift'. It triggered off a myriad of thoughts in his mind, remembered comments heard over the past few days.

Such as Anne Wallis' hysterical ranting: 'It was as if he could read my mind.' Or even, Daniels thought, the interview I've just had with the man. Those niggling thoughts, like him knowing my name and that I smoked. Or how about him answering a question I hadn't even asked? And what about him knowing all about Tim? There was always the chance he had got to Sally Johnson's ex-boyfriend, but I don't think so. Dane didn't know half of what Trooper knows.

Daniels was becoming increasingly disturbed. Things were happening which he simply could not understand. Who was Nathan Trooper? What was all the psychic mumbo-jumbo? What was Trooper doing in the hospital? Why was that Yankee sheriff so convinced Trooper had killed the girl? And why had the man come all this way just to confuse and bemuse the police force?

'You don't like people?' Daniels had asked. And Trooper had said, 'No, they give me headaches'.

Daniels flicked through the folder until he found the comment he was looking for: 'He reports blinding headaches . . . causes him pain due to the volume of their thoughts . . .'

He remembered one of Trooper's parting comments: 'You may find some things which don't appeal to you. They may even sound crazy.'

Daniels looked up. Too bloody right they did! 'Hold on a moment,' he murmured, 'stop the world. I want to get off.'

*

There was a knock on his door at about 10 p.m.
'Come in.'

Fowles opened the door and stepped into the gloom.
The office was in darkness, blinds closing out the soft
London light. The air was also thick with stale cigarette
smoke.

Daniels had been thinking.

'Turn on the light, Fowles. There's a good chap.'

There was a muted click. Harsh neon light flickered
and flooded the room. Daniels squinted against the
sudden glare.

Fowles hovered uncertainly in the doorway, both
unwilling to disturb his boss and reluctant to enter a
room filled with smoke.

'Come in, Fowles. Leave the door open, let some air
in here.'

Fowles pulled up a chair and sat down near the
doorway. He felt safer in the draught.

Daniels leaned back and stared at the yellow polystyrene ceiling tiles. 'Well? Any luck?'

'Have you read the file sir?' Fowles countered.

'I have. As you said, most interesting.'

'Isn't it just. But no luck, I'm afraid. McCormack
couldn't verify anything. I think I took him a bit by
surprise.'

Daniels grinned. 'And if I've guessed your questions
right, Sergeant, he probably went away thinking you
were a bit crazy too.'

Fowles returned the grin. 'Probably. Shall I read
them out?'

Daniels shook his head. 'No, let me guess. I need to
exercise my mind, and this telepathy lark has got me
interested.' His mind raced over the events of the day
and collated all the information he had learned. 'Fowles,
I'm going to try a little experiment. This psychic issue has

clouded things far too much for my liking, and I'd like to set the record straight. I want to give you something to think about, and show you just how much people can be fooled.'

Fowles paused, unsure what to expect from Daniels who was gazing at him askance like a lizard on a rock. 'OK. Go ahead.'

Daniels leaned back, clasped his hands behind his head and closed his eyes. He condensed what he knew about McCormack, Fowles, the Trooper files and Tim Johnson's injuries, and formed a list of probable questions – the sorts of enquiries *he* would have made if he was in Fowles' shoes. 'First, you would have asked McCormack if there was any evidence of brain haemorrhage in Tim Johnson's head.'

'Correct.'

'And he would have said absolutely not.'

'Correct.'

'And probably added in a stuffed shirt tone that he'd have told us already if there was.'

Fowles sniggered. 'Absolutely.'

'Then you would have asked if Tim's EEG scans could be interpreted as showing psychic, or otherwise paranormal, activity.'

'Close. I didn't put it quite that bluntly.' Fowles was intrigued. Daniels was spot on, so far.

'Then you would have rephrased your question, and he would have said, "Have you been drinking on duty, Sergeant?"'

Fowles laughed again. Practically word for word that time.

Daniels allowed his grin to broaden, not simply because he was right, but also because of the admiring and astonished expression on Fowles' face. 'After half an hour you may have been lucky enough to get a grudging

"Maybe" out of the miserable bastard. Although he would have denied such outlandish ideas, since he's a doctor.'

Fowles realized his mouth was open. He closed it.

Daniels preened his mental feathers.

Fowles grinned. 'Not bad, sir. Mind you, it helped to quote from the psychological and neurological reports on Trooper. I thought he might listen more if I was using the right jargon.'

'Ah. Good idea. Anyway, you would eventually have asked if a psychic attack could have caused Tim's symptoms. And he would have said, "I really could not say, Sergeant. Why don't you ask Scott? He's more experienced in these matters than I."'

Christ, Fowles thought, *exactly* word for word. How the hell did he guess that? 'I'm impressed, sir. Maybe you're psychic too.'

Daniels snorted. 'Not bloody likely, Sergeant. But I know you and McCormack, and it goes to show what you can achieve if you apply the old grey matter and some imagination, doesn't it?'

Fowles digested that, then read between the lines. 'So you don't believe Trooper's background? You think he fudged the tests, or pulled the wool over the doctor's eyes?'

Daniels did not answer for a moment. Instead he lit a cigarette and exhaled a stately stream of smoke rings, watching as they climbed to the ceiling. 'I'm a sceptic, Sergeant. I believe nothing until I see it with my own eyes. Remember that Trooper was interned in the mid-sixties, and there was all sorts of weird shit going around then. Not that you *would* remember, of course. Maybe he is, maybe not. Maybe those doctors just wanted to believe. Who knows?' He shifted in the chair. 'No, I don't believe anything at the moment. But

I wouldn't blame you if you did – this is certainly a peculiar case, and I've seen a few. My experiment was intended to demonstrate one simple fact – don't believe everything you read in the files. Doctors make mistakes and so do we. Trooper told me to keep an open mind, and that's what I'm trying to do. Trooper himself has made no claim to being psychic, so why assume it?'

Fowles shifted uncomfortably in the chair. He was beginning to feel he was being reprimanded.

It was not a new experience.

'Mind you,' Daniels mused, 'since this is such a weird case, maybe a weird explanation is what we're looking for. I mean, just examine the situation so far: two people burnt alive in call boxes. One person impaled on rusty railings. Our only witness terrorized and attacked, hospitalized with a coma he's unlikely to recover from. One relative of the first victim plagued by sick phone calls. A man who claims to know what is going on has offered his assistance, and is reported to be an expert in the paranormal. A man who does indeed appear to know a hell of a lot more about this than we do.'

Fowles shrugged. 'Well, maybe he is involved. Maybe he's finally gone wacko like the psychologists said. He is listed as a potential hazard, after all.'

'True. And that Yankee Sheriff was all fired up about him being guilty. So convinced that he lost his job over it.'

Fowles grinned suddenly. 'So why don't you ring him?'

'Who? The sheriff?'

'No. Trooper. He's in.'

Daniels looked up. 'Who's watching the hotel?'

'Barker. Kicked up a fuss – said it was his wife's birthday.'

Daniels snorted. 'Tough. Mind you, I know how he feels. My wife has got the axe out on me every time I go home.' He looked at the phone, then glanced at his watch. 'No, it's too late. He might be asleep. And besides, I don't even like the guy.'

'Nope. I just checked with Barker before I came in. Trooper is up, and awake. His profile says he's an incurable insomniac.'

Daniels grunted. 'Well, that's just his tough luck, isn't it? I've been on the job since five this morning, and I've had enough for one day. I'll talk to him in the morning.'

'If he's still there.'

'Oh, he'll be there. Our Mr Trooper isn't going anywhere.' Daniels stood up and reached for his coat. 'You know Trooper says he can bring Tim out of his coma, if we let him in.'

Fowles snorted. 'And wouldn't that be convenient?'

'Quite. However, he did say one thing I agree with. Tim Johnson is still in danger. And I don't like it. I don't feel any closer to cracking this than I did on Christmas Eve.' He walked to the door then turned, as if struck by an afterthought. 'Fowles, did anyone tell Trooper who he was coming to see? Mention me by name?'

Fowles frowned. 'No, I don't think so, sir. They just asked him in to answer some questions. Why?'

Daniels shrugged. 'Oh, nothing important.' He forced a smile. 'Good night, Sergeant. See you tomorrow.'

'Good night sir.' Fowles watched Daniels leave. He had never seen him so perturbed. He chewed his lip.

Things must be bad.

Scott stood by the pay phone in the hospital reception, waiting for the old lady inside to wrap up and bug out. Like people the world over he was beginning to realize that jingling his change, pointedly looking at his watch, tutting and coughing made absolutely no difference. The person in the call box did not suddenly hang up, come out and say, 'I'm so sorry to keep you waiting'. No. They just turned their back on you and put in some more money.

'Come on, come on,' he mumbled, aching to scream the words and barely managing to restrain himself. He had been there twenty minutes already, and she was scarcely through the 'hellos'.

He managed to catch her eye. She turned her back on him and put in some more money . . .

Scott had been bothered by the Trooper incident all day, wondering if he shouldn't have rejected the offer. Maybe Trooper could have saved Tim. Maybe, if he had helped, Tim would be sitting up in bed right now smiling at his parents. Maybe he had loused it all up by shouting 'POLICE' instead of believing the split-headed weirdo.

Daniels certainly thought not – that much had been made clear during their little chat. Scott was not so sure; Trooper's attitude was bothering him, his bald-faced cheek at just wandering over and offering to save Tim's life. And his *aura* (one of Scott's favourite words) suggested that Trooper was at least sure of his own abilities – an inner confidence in stark contrast to his outward countenance.

Time was running out, even McCormack admitted that. Scott was willing to try anything, whatever the risk. Part of him realized he may well be clutching at straws, but Scott was a desperate man.

That was when he had come up with the idea.

His wife had been sceptical. She had jokingly accused him of trying to write himself into one of his silly novels. Yet the idea had caught in Scott's brain, and was fanned by his frustrated anger and guilt. By half-past nine he was pacing the room, expounding theories on Tim's condition and Trooper's offer as if he was Albert Einstein on the verge of uncovering Relativity.

'But don't you *see* Sal? It was all caused by something in Tim's mind. All the EEG irregularities, his coma, his spasms, everything. He's locked up in there, and can't get out. If Trooper really is a psychic, then he can bring Tim back to us.'

Sally had remained unconvinced. Like Daniels, she was less inclined to let a stranger tinker with her son. However, she was glad Scott had found some release for his nervous tension. He had always been 'laid back', as he put it, during their marriage. So laid back that he was practically asleep. He had clearly changed since the divorce. Sally had never truly realized the extent of his love for Tim until the recent days spent at Tim's bedside. She had to admit that Scott still had some strange ideas, but he had been more than willing to accept the responsibility of Tim's welfare. And accepting responsibility was one thing Scott had never done during their marriage.

So when he had suggested that he call one of his old contacts, a man who had provided background for some of his books, Sally had let him go. Anything to stop him wearing a groove in the tiles with his incessant pacing. Scott had kissed her soundly on the lips, then looked frankly into her eyes. 'This is it, Sal, I can feel it. Tim's going to be OK.' Then he had left.

Tim had lain in his bed and shown no signs that he heard them.

. . . By the time the old woman said her final farewells, Scott was on the verge of a coronary. He shouldered his way into the booth and glowered fiercely at the old hag.

She ignored him. He lifted the receiver and dialled the number.

'Dave Bloom.'

Scott felt his heart quicken. 'Dave, hi, it's Scott here.' There was a bemused silence. 'Scott Johnson? You helped me out with my novel, *The Man Inside his own Mind*?'

'Oh, yes, sorry Scott. I didn't recognize your voice.'

Maybe because I didn't say 'Hi man, are you in tune with the universal vibes?' Scott thought sourly, and surprised himself with his self-loathing. 'That's OK. How's tricks?'

'Fine. Everything's OK. And you?'

'Well, I've been better to be honest with you. But I'm in a call box, and I have a favour to ask.'

'Sure, ask away. I'll invoice you later.' There was inquisitive humour in the voice.

Scott grinned. 'You do that. Listen, you remember you dug up a whole load of background for me on the book about the paranormal?'

There was a tinny laugh in the earpiece. 'How could I forget? Yes, I remember. I was pleased to see that most of it got used.'

'Of course. It was good stuff.' Better than the novel, anyway. 'I'm toying with another idea, and I've got a lead. Off the top of your head, do you recognize the name Nathan Trooper?'

Dave Bloom had a photographic memory, and was his own walking reference library. In normal circumstances Bloom would have raced through a university education and ended up a professor. Instead he had discovered the occult, and heroin. One or both of those factors had resulted in a car crash which left him paralysed and half blind. So now he read books, remembered everything he ever read, and sold it to authors who detested doing research themselves. By a peculiar twist of fate, Dave Bloom was incredibly well off and very content.

Scott knew that if anyone would know, Bloom would know. Without even looking it up.

'Trooper, eh?' There was a slight pause. 'Nathan Trooper? Psychic genius and all-round strange guy?'

Bingo! Pay dirt, Scott thought. 'Yes, that's right,' he said calmly, his voice betraying none of the emotion which hammered in his chest. 'The idea I'm kicking around is about psychic cures for coma patients. Somebody mentioned that name as a possible source.'

Bloom laughed. 'Nice idea. He's certainly got the background – *very* mysterious. Some tragedy in his youth, very secretive and dark. During the seventies there were a few reports in the obscure press about him supposedly curing people who had been comatose for years.' Bloom was paraphrasing the wealth of information stored in his head. 'Usually comas caused by psychology or mental trauma, rather than physical injury. I mean, he wasn't a doctor or anything. He couldn't cure brain damage. But his name was some sort of Talisman in the States for a while. Everybody wanted Nathan Trooper. Nothing concrete, but a lot of circumstantial evidence.'

'Sounds promising.'

'Well, no, I doubt it. There were never any photographs or interviews. Nobody ever managed to trace him, though enough tried. He turned up here and there, did his thing and vanished again. I guess his name was on some weird underground list, passed on more by reputation than fact. Then in about '76 he just disappeared off the face of the planet. There were even some explanations for that – like UFOs abducting him because of his psychic abilities. Some people reckoned he had made telepathic contact with an alien race. Of course, none of that was ever proved either,' Bloom added wryly. 'If he ever existed, God knows where he is now. You know how it is in these supernormal circles, Scott – ten-minute wonders, half of them, load of bull the other. Look at Geller. Whatever happened to him? Besides, it was in the early seventies. There was an awful lot of weird shit around then, believe you me. I was into half of it, and I used to believe all sorts of stupid things.'

Scott was too excited to have his hopes dampened. 'Thanks Dave, no problem. That's great.'

'Any use to you?'

'Could be. I mean, you know me. It doesn't have to be fact for me to use it. Quite the opposite, really.'

Bloom laughed again. 'Sure. Listen, I can send you some of the texts if you like. Then you can read it all through and see if you want to chase the idea. Give me a ring sometime, eh?'

'Great. I owe you one.'

'No, forget it. You did me a far better deal than most. If you decide to use it, then maybe we can talk numbers. OK?'

'Sure. And Dave? If I do, I don't think you'll ever know how grateful I am.'

There was a confused silence. 'Are things OK there, Scott?' It was a cautious question. Dave Bloom was not the sort of person who liked to pry – he was convinced he did not want to know most of the weirdo authors with whom he came into contact.

'Yeah. Thanks again Dave. I'll be in touch.' Scott hung up, unwilling to be asked questions. GOD KNOWS WHERE HE IS NOW.

Damn! Scott cursed himself. I know where he *was*, a few hours ago. But where the hell is he now? I

161

need to talk to him. But should I place any hope in him? Is his name really Nathan Trooper? Or did he just adopt that, knowing that if I checked it out it might just influence my decision? Where the hell is he?

Scott smiled. Daniels would know.

He rooted around in his pocket for another coin, then dialled the number Daniels had given him. It rang for so long he was about to hang up, but then: 'Inspector Daniels' office.'

'Is he there?'

'Sorry, he just left. This is Fowles. Is that Scott? Is it important? Anything I can do?'

Scott chewed his lip. 'No, I just have some information, it's not important. Can you ask him to get in touch, ASAP?'

'Sure. Is this about Nathan Trooper?'

'No,' Scott lied. He sensed that Fowles was about to push for more information, so he cut him off. 'Good night.' He hung up.

When he left the booth someone else was waiting, jangling his change, hopping from foot to foot, scowling.

Scott did not even notice.

Fowles put down the receiver in Daniels' darkened office. He was frowning. Scott had been hiding something, he was sure of that.

'Anything important?'

Fowles jumped out of his skin. Daniels was standing behind him in the doorway. He had returned as silently as a cat, sneaking up on him in the gloom. Deliberately, Fowles thought bitterly.

'Jesus, sir, didn't see you there.'

'Anything important?' Daniels repeated.

'That was Scott. Said he has some information he

wanted to discuss with you as soon as possible, so could you get in touch.'

Daniels nodded. 'Thought as much. Important?'

'He said not,' Fowles remarked, a sardonic grin on his lips, 'but after his scene this afternoon, when he was cursing you up hill and down dale for turning Trooper away, I reckon it was about Trooper. He said it wasn't. I thought he was lying.'

Daniels grinned. 'I bet he rang one of his old contacts to get some data on Trooper. Now he's all fired up about it. Idiot.'

Fowles raised an eyebrow. 'How do you know that?'

Daniels chuckled, tapping the side of his nose with a long, nicotine-stained finger. 'Instinct, Sergeant. You'll get it one day if you stick around long enough. Well, good night. Again.'

Fowles nodded. 'Good night, sir.' But Daniels was already gone. Fowles heard him whistling tunelessly as he paced along the corridor. He was impressed. In the last twenty-four hours his respect for Daniels had increased sharply. He was beginning to understand why Daniels was so highly respected, and thought the transfer might yet yield fruit for his career.

Instinct. He savoured the word. *I could use some myself.*

Daniels was still whistling when he climbed into his car. For some reason, impressing Fowles had lightened his mood considerably. Maybe it was because, in this increasingly surreal world of psychic attacks, strange people and inexplicable murders, Daniels felt that he had at least retained his grasp on the reality of human nature.

Mind you, he thought with a smile, I do feel guilty about playing the old instinct card. Maybe I should have told him Sally Johnson called me on her mobile phone and told me Scott had some hair-brained idea about checking out Trooper.

Then he laughed, and threw the car into gear.

No. A little hero worship is just what I need right now.

His black Volvo nosed out into the light London traffic.

Scott came back enthused and excited. Sally smiled. It was just typical of him really, she thought, to queue up for half an hour at a call box when I have a phone in my briefcase.

On the bed Tim lay in his secure womb, oblivious to the world.

CHAPTER TWO

Dreams

Midnight.

That night Nathan slept very little.

Sergeant Barker and his fellow watcher, who had kept tabs on Trooper all day, would report that Trooper spent most of the night standing at the window looking down at their unmarked car. As if he knew they were watching him, and wanted them to know he knew.

The room was dark for only half an hour.

However, in that short time Nathan slept. And dreamed . . .

It started, as it had since Bill Wallis had been attacked, with the horrifying images and demonic laughter. Now Nathan knew what this signified: his mental detective work had revealed Tim's fate, and he knew the dream was only the backwash of fear from the boy's mind. And other minds: he knew not how many.

Nathan had that dream every time he slept, when his mind was at rest and freely wandered the channels of human consciousness.

When that dream ended Nathan fell further into those conscious channels. He entered a deeper sleep. His mind, unfettered by the restraints he imposed on it after twenty-six years of mental noise, roamed freely, following an extra-sensory scent.

He stood upon a plain of ice which stretched to the horizon in every direction. The noon sun was high, and the glare from the ice assailed his eyes and made them stream. Tears froze on his cheeks. He raised one hand to shield his view and a man appeared before him.

The man was tall, clothed in cold weather garb and wearing snow goggles. In the mirrored surface of the glasses Nathan saw his own startled face, already rimmed with frost. The man was carrying an axe, and the axe head was dark with blood.

Beneath the glasses, Nathan knew the man would have no eyes.

'Hello Nathan.' The man's voice was flat, colourless and cold, like the landscape in which it was spoken.

Trooper squinted into the glare, shocked. 'Father?' he asked.

The man stepped forward, raising the axe. 'You have sinned,' he said without emotion. 'Once I tried to cleanse the sin from your mind, but failed. Now I must try again. Make your peace with God, my son. You have run, but you found nowhere to hide.'

The axe flashed red in the sunlight. Nathan opened his mouth to scream, turned to run, but was too late. The heavy blade fell in a glittering arc and buried itself in the top of his head. His skull split, spraying gore and brain tissue over the pure snow.

Nathan was driven to his knees, every movement staining the ice. Then he pitched forward onto what was left of his face.

And died . . .

It was also a night of dreams for John Daniels. Usually his dreams were repetitive and frustrating – running from some unknown pursuer whilst stuck in treacle.

This night, however, he had a dream so vivid he would remember it for the rest of his life.

He stood in a laboratory. The harsh glare of the neon tubes was giving him a headache. He recognized the room and the stench of bleach and death. Bart Cummings hovered over the body of a short man. The corpse was covered in blood. Daniels thought it strange that Cummings had not removed the axe from the dead man's head. The weapon cleaved the skull in two and marked the carcass like a violent exclamation mark. He knew the man was Nathan Trooper.

'It was he,' Daniels said stubbornly.

'But look,' Cummings replied, shaking his head in frustration. He lifted one of Trooper's limp hands. 'He has no fingernails. These are chewed to stumps. Where are the claws you require?'

'It was he.'

'But he is only five foot six, from the soles of his feet to the axe in his head. Where is the height you require? It was not he.'

Daniels laughed. 'That is what he wanted you to believe, Doctor. It was what he wanted us all to believe.'

Cummings shook his head. 'You are paranoid, Inspector. Who are you to disbelieve all experts? What rights have you to question our testimony? You are wrong. It was not he.'

Daniels laughed again, and held out his hands. 'Evidence, Doctor.' In his left hand he held a pair of stilts. In his right a set of rigid plastic false fingertips, like a cut-price version of the steel blades used in *Nightmare on Elm Street*.

'With these he did it. With stilts he achieved the height, and with these he had the claws. Do you doubt me now, Doctor?'

Cummings nodded. 'I do, Inspector. He still did not

have the strength. How could he lift a man bodily from the pavement of life? And *stilts*? Do you have any idea of how ridiculous you sound?'

'He was not alone,' Daniels countered. 'I do not have all the answers. But I will. He used claws and wore stilts.'

Nathan Trooper sat bolt upright on the slab, his face hideously torn and scarred, his entire body awash with blood. The axe toppled from his head in a cascade of perfect ice crystals and fell to the floor. He pointed one finger accusingly at Daniels.

'I wore no stilts.' As the corpse spoke, black blood oozed from its head. In his arms he held the limp and cold body of Tim Johnson. 'It was not I,' he whispered. 'You murdered this one. You were the one who helped. You helped me murder them.'

Daniels woke with a start at those words and the apparition.

Beside him his wife lay sleeping soundly. Outside, dawn was turning the Kent darkness into a hazy grey. The birds were singing.

With practised stealth he eased out of bed and down to the kitchen. He made himself some tea and lit a cigarette. The tobacco tasted bitter in his mouth, and caused his aching lungs to protest, but he ignored them. He needed a smoke. His hands were shaking.

He slept no more that night.

CHAPTER THREE

Timothy Johnson Receives an Offer He Cannot Refuse

Thursday, January 3, 1991. London, England.

Daniels was in his office by 6 a.m., early even for him. Unable to sleep he had risen early, eyes sore and bloodshot, mind awash with the responsibilities of the day. He was determined, if not eager, to meet the next twenty-four hours head on. His stomach informed him that today events would finally take shape, his presence making the difference between Life and Death. Tim's life. Because Daniels was aware of one thing above all others – Tim had only hours left.

He did not know how he knew; perhaps it was the dream. The vision of Trooper blaming him for the death and the implication he had delayed too long disturbed him. Perhaps it was the instinct he relied so heavily upon, or the encounter with Trooper. Perhaps, he thought wryly, it was the result of some psychic connection with Scott's universal vibes. Whatever the reason, he was convinced Tim would die if he was not brought out of his coma by the end of the day. That conviction lent urgency to his actions.

Part of him wanted to believe in Trooper, to believe there was still a chance to save Tim. Yet that chance rested on him believing in a bizarre phenomenon and a man who was their only suspect.

Yet Daniels had to admit one thing. He was a policeman; he had ways of tracking criminals, finding evidence and bringing people to justice. To date, nothing had worked; his methods had failed; the investigation was a farce. He was a desperate man out of his depth. In that respect he was more like Scott than he would care to admit. The two men were linked by a common desperation, and just about ready to clutch at any passing straw.

Nathan Trooper was that straw. And he knew it.

Daniels dialled Trooper's hotel as soon as he reached his desk, without even pausing to take off his coat. 'Room 127, please.'

The phone clicked. It only rang once.

'Yes, Inspector. You would like to see me now?'

There was such certainty in Trooper's voice as he said those words, such confidence that it was Daniels on the telephone, that the policeman almost began to believe Trooper really was psychic.

And yet, he thought, I don't accept it. After all, who else would ring him at this time of day? Who else knows he's here?

But the small voice of belief grew with every passing hour.

'If that's convenient, Mr Trooper.'

'And if it's not?'

He's playing with me again, Daniels thought. To his amazement the thought did not sour his mood. He enjoyed sparring with the man. 'Then I have two men outside your hotel who would be only too happy to convince you convenience is less than important right now.'

Trooper chuckled, without rancour. 'I know. They must be very uncomfortable out there.'

Daniels ignored this comment. He was not in the least

surprised that Trooper knew he was being watched. In fact, he would have been disappointed to hear otherwise. 'Then you'll come? Now?'

'Of course. I'll be there as soon as I can.'

The line went dead. To some, Trooper may have seemed abrupt. To Daniels he merely seemed eager to get moving, and Daniels was more than willing to encourage that attitude. They had all delayed far too long.

The small voice in his mind spoke again. How does he *know* all this? How did he know what my name was, that I smoked, that it was me on the phone? It's not guesswork, I'm sure of that.

Daniels thrust these idle queries aside; they would achieve nothing. So he dialled the police operator and got himself patched through to Sergeant Baxter, on watch outside Trooper's hotel.

'Baxter? Trooper will be coming out any minute now. Bring him in right away. Anything happen last night?'

'Not really. He knew we were here though. Spent half the night watching us out of the hotel window. He didn't sleep much, either. This morning he had the hotel bring us out breakfast.'

Daniels took a moment to interpret the remark. 'Cheeky sod.'

'Yeah.' Baxter paused. 'Nice breakfast, though.'

'Did he go out at all?'

'No. Came straight here after picking up his car from the hospital and hasn't left since.' There was a muffled exclamation. 'Here he comes now. The bastard just waved to us.'

Daniels grinned. Trooper might be a peculiar and unfortunate man, but at least he had a sense of humour. 'All right, bring him in. Don't get jumpy, Baxter. I don't think he'll try anything.'

'Is he our man?'

Daniels paused before responding, his fears and instincts at loggerheads. I'm under pressure for an arrest, I need results. Wouldn't it be rosy if he was? 'Ask me again at midnight.'

'Right you are. I'll have a report on your desk by noon. It won't exactly be interesting stuff, though.'

'No matter. Take the day off, tell your wife it was my fault.'

'Very good, sir.' Daniels knew Baxter would be smiling. No-one disputed that police wives had to put up with a lot, but Daniels thought they often forgot policemen had to put up with a lot, too.

He hung up the phone, crossed the corridor to get a coffee and lit another cigarette: his seventh of the day. It tasted like cancer so he stubbed it out. 'I hope Trooper brings some more expensive ones,' he murmured to himself. 'At least then I can console myself I'm committing suicide in style.' He returned to the desk and dialled McCormack. 'Good morning, Doctor. You're up early.'

McCormack grunted. 'No rest for the wicked, Inspector.'

Daniels was perturbed. 'I take it Tim Johnson has got worse.'

'How did you guess?'

'I didn't.' He forced a grin. 'Maybe I'm just psychic.'

McCormack mumbled inaudible expletives. 'I got a call from the duty nurse about an hour ago. Tim had another spasm. Not as severe as the last one, but it doesn't look promising. Scott is doing his best to make my life hell, and succeeding pretty well.'

It never rains, Daniels thought. 'How long has he got?'

'Impossible to tell. Two days?' He paused. 'Maybe less.'

'Bugger.' Daniels rubbed his sore eyes. 'Well, good luck.'

McCormack snorted. 'Save your luck for the boy, Inspector. He needs it more than I.' Somebody spoke in the background. 'Scott just appeared. It seems he would like a word with you.'

'I'm busy.'

'Then tell him yourself.'

The disgruntled Scot made sure the telephone changed hands.

Scott's excited voice boomed through the earpiece. 'Inspector? I have some information which may—.'

'I know,' Daniels interrupted, angry. 'You rang a Mr Bloom. He told you all sorts of things about Nathan Trooper, just what you wanted to hear. Don't insult my intelligence, Mr Johnson.'

'Hey, I didn't mean to—.'

'Mr Johnson, let me get on with my job. Don't bother me with trivia. Perhaps you should know that Trooper was once arrested on suspicion of murder. A young girl died, about Tim's age. I'd guess Mr Bloom didn't tell you *that*.' Daniels ordered himself to calm down. 'Now, I appreciate your concern but I can't let Trooper see you or Tim until I'm satisfied. I'm in charge of a murder enquiry, Mr Johnson, and Trooper is a prime suspect. Do you understand?'

Scott ignored the question. 'You know he's dying, don't you? McCormack tried to fob me off, but I've been here for six days and I *know*. Do you understand *that*, Inspector?' Scott was very upset.

Daniels quashed his irritation. 'Yes, I do. But I cannot be party to this when Trooper is still a murder suspect. However, I can assure you I am pursuing all enquiries with the utmost urgency.'

Scott gave a bitter laugh. 'That's all you can give

me? Sally's terrified of losing him now, and I'm not ashamed to admit I'm bloody scared myself. We both know, Inspector, that there is something strange about Nathan Trooper. I'm willing to accept him at face value – I'll believe and try anything right now. Modern medicine achieved nothing, despite McCormack's protestations. I'm sick and tired of being lied to.' Scott sighed. 'I failed him once, Inspector. Because of that he's almost dead. If I fail him again then – well, to be honest with you I don't know what I'll do.'

'I know. I have Tim's best interests at heart too, you know. That's *why* I can't let Trooper anywhere near him. Yet.'

Scott either missed that last word, or chose not to question him on his reason for saying it.

'Scott, don't give up hope. You never know your luck.'

Scott snorted. 'Oh, I know my luck, Inspector. That's why I'm so worried.' Then he hung up.

Daniels looked at his watch: 6:45 a.m. Somewhere down the hall a door slammed, and Daniels looked up in surprise as Baxter appeared by his office. 'Ready when you are, sir. Interview Room 1.'

'What did you do, Baxter? Sirens all the way or something?'

The Sergeant blushed. 'It was his idea, sir. He said it was urgent, he had to move fast or the boy would die. Besides, you should see him drive. Bloody maniac! He makes Fowles look safe.'

'That bad?' Well, at least that explains the two traffic offences, he thought absently. He stood, grabbing his cigarettes. 'No intrusions, understand? No one knocks. For anything. If the building catches fire, leave a bucket of water outside the door.'

'Yes, sir.'

'When Fowles arrives, tell him to get down to the hospital and double security on the boy without getting in McCormack's way. If Scott becomes a nuisance, remove him.'

'Yes sir. Anything else?'

'No.' He paused, head cocked to one side. 'Yes. Get me a firearms authorization order filled out. Leave the details to me.'

Baxter's eyes widened, but he said nothing.

'Right, that's it I think. When you're finished, go home. And don't tell *anybody* about the firearms except Fowles.' He looked up into Baxter's honest face. 'So. Do *you* think he's our man?'

Baxter shrugged. 'A half hour ago I'd have said yes, he's so bloody weird. But now? No. He just doesn't fit – he's too short.'

Daniels shuddered, remembering his dream. 'Maybe he wore stilts,' he said quietly, but left before Baxter could say any more.

Trooper helped himself to coffee. 'Good morning, Inspector.'

'Is it, Mr Trooper?'

'Perhaps. I took it as a good sign that I'm here under my own steam, and not in chains. I think that's progress, don't you?' His look spoke volumes. Daniels said nothing. 'Shall I be mother?' He handed Daniels the mug. 'Black, three sugars. Correct?'

'Correct.' I won't even *ask*, Daniels thought. 'Do you mind if I record this interview? Technically speaking, you don't have to say anything, or you can have a lawyer present. Or you can leave.'

Trooper smiled. 'Inspector, I'm aware of my rights. As you now know, I have been in this sort of situation before. My legal representative is a dour old Northerner who would prevent me from saying a word and that would hardly be beneficial to either of us. I know I can leave, but I came here to talk. So carry on.'

Daniels nodded. 'Good.' He started the cassette recorder. 'January 3rd, 1991, 6:50 a.m. Present for the interview are Chief Inspector John Daniels and Mr Nathan Trooper.'

Trooper laid four packets of his cigarettes on the table and grinned. Daniels took one without prompting. 'Shall we begin?'

'Where would you like to start?' Trooper asked calmly.

'Yesterday. Why were you at the Fields Memorial Hospital?'

'To help Timothy Johnson restore himself to life.'

'You believe you are capable of that?'

'Yes. An innocent boy is doomed to die if I do not.'

Daniels changed tack. 'You understand that you are under suspicion for the murder of two men on the evening of the 27th of December 1990? And that you are also under suspicion for the attack on Timothy Johnson, the boy you claim you wish to save?'

'I understand that you may be entertaining that idea, yes.'

'So where were you on that evening?'

'At home, alone. And no, I cannot verify that.'

'Where were you on Christmas Eve?'

'At home, alone.'

'All day? All night? Nobody can verify that either?'

'No. As I said, I was alone.'

'Are you a psychic?'

'Yes.'

'Can you read minds? Can you read my mind?'

'If I choose to do so, yes. However, the process

causes me pain and I do not attempt it unless strictly necessary.'

'In the summer of 1972 you were released from the Samuel Hall Institute for the Mentally Ill. You were there for eight years.'

'Correct.' Trooper's tone, which had previously been open and unashamed, now became wary. He adopted a guarded look.

'Tell me about your father.'

Trooper paused. 'I do not see the relevance of the question.'

Daniels smiled without humour. 'Tell me anyway.'

Trooper sighed. He was in a difficult position. On one hand, he did not wish to discuss his private life. On the other, he had to admit he was under suspicion and was determined to gain some of the policeman's trust. If he refused to answer questions – however personal and irrelevant – he would do himself no good. He sensed Daniels was trying to accept him, as if he knew he was heading an investigation which made precious little sense. A life depended on Trooper playing the game according to the rules.

He decided he had no option.

'My father was a neuro-surgeon, a pioneer. He dedicated his life to research which would make modern medicine more effective.'

'And yet?'

Trooper sighed again. His background inspired mistrust, not acceptance. He had good reasons for not dwelling upon it. 'In the summer of 1964 my father committed suicide. I do not know why.'

'What of your mother?'

'Inspector, will this line of questioning achieve anything?' Trooper was growing visibly uneasy.

'Oh, I think so, yes. Perhaps I should recount the

story.' He paused to marshal his thoughts. 'In July of 1964 your father, a doctor, murdered his wife with an axe. A motiveless killing. You yourself sustained multiple injuries, leaving you scarred for life and were committed to an asylum suffering from massive trauma. You stayed there until 1972, when you were released at age twenty into your brother's custody. After a two year probationary period you inherited fifty per cent of the life insurance payment previously awarded your brother. That amounted to £50,000, a sizeable sum for a twenty-two-year-old in 1974. Tell me, did that ever cause problems with your brother?'

'No. Isaac had invested that money for me on the assumption I would be released. He never laid claim to a penny of it. Indeed, he campaigned persistently to have me released into his custody.'

Daniels knew there was no financial motive. He was just fishing for a reaction. 'Then you and your brother were close?'

'Yes. Closer still after the attack which left us orphans.'

'Are you a homosexual?'

Trooper chuckled. 'No, Inspector, I am not.'

'What are your views on homosexuality?'

'I have none. It is everyone's right to live within the law.'

Daniels let the matter drop. 'Apart from two traffic offences, you have no criminal record. However, an investigation in the United States of America barely cleared you of murder.'

'One is not *barely* cleared of murder, Inspector. I assumed you knew that. I was innocent, and the trial declared me as such.'

'Then how do you explain the incident?'

'The inquest recorded a verdict of Death by Natural Causes.'

'That didn't answer the question.'

'The girl had a brain haemorrhage. I did not kill her. If a man beside you on a train has a heart attack, did you murder him?'

'How tall are you, Mr Trooper?'

'Five foot six, or thereabouts.'

'And you deny any responsibility for Timothy Johnson's current medical condition?'

'Yes. I am in no way responsible for these crimes.'

'And have you ever had any contact with the Johnson family prior to this visit?'

'No. None whatsoever.'

'Could you name me one person who has known you socially for over two years and who would be a willing character reference?'

'No.'

'Has anyone known you socially for more than two years?'

'No.'

Daniels frowned. 'A doctor? A solicitor? Bank manager?'

'Yes. My solicitor has known my family for thirty years.'

'But he is not what you would class as a friend?'

'No.'

'Then, by normal standards, you are something of a recluse?'

'Depending on your definition of normal, yes, I suppose I am. Does that make me a murderer?'

'No. But it rules out all possibilities of any alibi.'

Trooper shrugged. 'Probably.'

'Mr Trooper, would you say that you are a lonely man?'

'No.'

'Alone, but not lonely?'

'Yes. I prefer my life as it is.'

'Have you ever taken drugs? Illegal substances of any kind?'

'Yes and no respectively. I have often been prescribed drugs, but never taken any substance illegally.'

Daniels sat back. 'Thank you. That's been very helpful.' He reached out and turned off the machine.

Trooper lit a cigarette. Daniels noticed that his hands were steady. He showed no outward sign of being unsettled by the interview. 'That was more for my records than anything else. I knew the answers to all the questions I asked.'

Trooper eyed him suspiciously. 'Then why ask them? Just to provoke me? You seemed to be fishing for a reaction more than anything else. I hope I did not disappoint you.'

Daniels grinned. 'My job is all about people, Mr Trooper. I do not need to explain the situation to you. I'm in a rather difficult position, and getting your background has cleared up very little. You have no alibi, yet are totally open about it. You have no motive for being here to help Timothy Johnson, or for committing the attack in the first place, yet here you are. In fact, to be honest, your presence has muddied the waters rather more than I like.'

'And they were murky enough before I arrived.'

'Quite.'

'I sympathize. Would I be right in thinking that Scott is eager to allow me access to his son?'

'Why don't you ask him? Better still, go ahead and read his mind.' Daniels' response was childish but he could not help it.

Trooper frowned. 'Invading other people's privacy is not my idea of fun, Inspector. I only try when an urgent need arises.'

'Is that right?' His voice dripped sarcasm and disbelief.

'Yes, it is. Like I said, being around people makes my head ache. Can you imagine spending your entire life locked in a room with people who talked incessantly, were never quiet, just babbled without stopping for breath until you want to scream and make them shut up? Over the years I have learned the art of blocking out that mental white noise – talk of cars and mortgages and sex lives. It is a technique I acquired in 1965 when I was about to go insane. I am one of the few people in England who can honestly say they are sane, Inspector. I have certificates to prove it. To open myself up to that incessant row is not something I do lightly.'

It was the longest speech Daniels had heard Trooper give. It was said easily, but with an emotion that lent substance to the words and made him believe them. He leaned back in his chair. 'Answer me honestly, Mr Trooper. Can you help Tim?'

'Of course. If I was not sure of that I would not be here.'

Daniels leaned forward again, and pierced Trooper with a demanding stare. 'Prove it,' he said quietly.

Trooper smiled. 'How? I need free access to the boy.'

'Then prove you are psychic. If you want Tim to be safe then give me something to go on.' He grinned. 'Impress me.'

Trooper sighed. He did not look surprised. 'I thought it would come to this. I tried to avoid this outcome, but I see that it was inevitable. Your scepticism does not help, Inspector.'

'Perhaps. But I have no reason to believe you, do I?'

Trooper smiled sadly. 'No, I guess not. You just

want to *see* the elephant man before you will believe he exists.'

Daniels blushed, but held firm. 'Yes. If you want me to believe you, prove it.'

Trooper closed his eyes and fell silent. His breathing slowed. 'I did not wear stilts, Inspector.'

Daniels looked up, surprised. 'Beg your pardon?'

'I did not use plastic claws. I do not, as they say, fit the bill. Only your pride lends substance to your suspicions.'

Daniels was floored.

Trooper did not open his eyes. He continued. 'You are worried that your daughter, who is just sixteen and very pretty, has no boyfriends. You are worried that she is a lesbian.'

Daniels stared at him, totally dumbstruck. It's all true, the little voice screamed, and you never told *anybody* any of that.

'Last night you had a nightmare. The case has got a lot worse, and you feel no closer to solving it. You feel inadequate.'

Daniels felt his hackles rise.

Trooper paused. He pinched the bridge of his nose. 'When you were eleven you took a packet of cigarettes from your mother's handbag and smoked in your father's garage until you were sick. When you were thirteen you hid in the bushes to watch the girl next door undress.'

Daniels coloured red to his roots.

'When you were sixteen your father died. You do not drink because you do not want to end up an alcoholic like him.'

He broke off, both hands pressed to his temples with the knuckles white. Daniels stared at him, utterly speechless, unaware of the agony he was causing Trooper to experience.

A single drop of blood fell from Trooper's nose and landed on the table top. 'Oh Jesus,' he whispered.

Daniels thought this had gone far enough.

'When you were twenty-three you—'

Daniels knew what he had done when he was twenty-three. He roared out of his chair like a missile and sent the table flying back into Trooper's tensed midriff. 'THAT'S ENOUGH!' he bellowed.

Trooper opened his mouth to complete his sentence and never managed it. His nose suddenly spewed blood like a running tap.

Daniels stepped away from the table as the liquid gushed across its surface, horrified. Trooper's long fingers gripped the edge of the table like the jaws of a vice. Every muscle was tensed.

When Trooper threw back his head in a silent scream, casting a stream of blood over the polystyrene tiles on the ceiling, Daniels knew he should call an ambulance.

Yet he could not move. He was rooted to the spot, fascinated. Seeing Trooper's violent transformation was like witnessing a molehill turn into a volcano and start spouting molten magma.

Trooper spat saliva through clenched teeth and tipped over backwards in his chair, coming to rest in his own blood on the floor. His eyes opened. 'Don't touch him!' he screamed, spraying droplets of blood all over his face. One foot lashed out and sent his chair crashing into the wall with enough force to rip the plastic seat from its frame. 'Get away from him you fucking bastard!' he roared. 'Run, Tim, RUN LIKE HELL!' Trooper spat blood like venom and went rigid. 'Get – out – of – my – FUCKING HEAD!'

His spasms stopped, but the tendons in his neck stood out like guitar strings and his hands were clenched like claws. Bloody saliva ran in a sticky stream from the corner of his open mouth. His lips drew back in a snarl of such ferocity that Daniels flinched.

'I order you,' Trooper whispered, oblivious to everything but the presence in his head, 'to get out of my head!' He sucked in a huge breath, released it in a massive yell: 'BE GONE!'

Then he tensed once more, spat a mist of red liquid from his mouth, and relaxed. His whole body seemed to melt.

For a moment Trooper's motionless body and the glazed look in his eyes were enough to make Daniels think he was dead.

Not a mark on him, thank God, was his first thought.

But then awareness returned to the pale face. Their eyes met.

'Nathan?' Daniels asked hesitantly.

'Inspector.' Trooper was obviously disoriented. Some colour rose in his face. 'Tim,' he said, as if that explained everything. 'We don't have much time.' He tried to rise, failed to get his elbows under him and collapsed again. 'Help me up, for God's sake.'

Did Trooper stage that for my benefit? Daniels thought coldly.

'No, I did not, Inspector. Now give me a bloody hand.'

Daniels extended his hand, which Trooper took gratefully. Then he pulled sharply and was surprised at how easily Trooper rose to his feet. The man was incredibly light.

Trooper immediately sank into the nearest chair and squeezed his nose. 'Bugger. That was stupid of me. I knew he was close.'

Daniels had no idea what he was talking about. 'Are you OK?'

Nathan took a handkerchief from his pocket and wiped

his face. 'Yes, I'm fine. Covered in shit and weak as a kitten, but fine.'

'You need a doctor?' Daniels asked stupidly.

'No. I'm used to it. It happens all the time.'

Daniels eyed the blood cautiously. One wrong step and he'd be up in court facing brutality charges, he knew. He lit himself a cigarette. 'What the hell was that all about?'

'Tim. That bastard's after him again. When I opened up he was on me like a shot. He was already on Tim, and Tim was fading. I managed to get in the way just in time, fortunately.' He wiped his nose. 'He's stronger now. I must see Tim immediately.'

Daniels was about to protest when the door opened. It was Fowles. 'Sir, McCormack just rang. Tim's heart just failed again.'

'WHAT?' Daniels managed to sound surprised. In a way, he really was. But deep down he had accepted Trooper's attack and explanation without question. The timing put Trooper well away from the hospital. Which, for a change, was a cast-iron alibi for him.

Plus, he admitted, there was also the slight complication of Trooper's evident abilities at mind reading. His doubts were receding like bath-water down a plug hole.

Fowles noticed Trooper and his bloody nose. He also noticed the broken chair. 'Jesus Christ. What's been going on here?'

'Why aren't you still at the hospital, Sergeant?' Daniels was losing control. He felt his grip on reality slipping. It was all too much – the irrefutable proof that Trooper was psychic, repeating things nobody else knew; the fits; the screamed conversation with Tim and his supposed attacker. It fit together like a surreal jigsaw puzzle and Daniels did not like the picture one little bit.

Everything was coming apart at the seams.

'There's been another murder,' Fowles replied. 'Same M.O.'

Daniels heaved a huge sigh of despair. 'What? When?'

'Piccadilly Circus.'

'In broad daylight?' Daniels asked, incredulous.

'How's Tim?' Nathan interjected. 'Is he dead?'

Fowles shook his head. 'No. I've just spoken to McCormack. He said Tim had another fit, went flat-line.'

'What about the murder?' Daniels demanded.

'Happened at dawn. One woman dead.' He paused for effect. 'A prostitute. Burnt alive in a telephone box.'

Daniels hesitated, uncertain of what to do. 'Oh, *shit.*'

Trooper did not give him a chance to think. 'Now, Inspector. I must see Tim now!'

'No!'

'For God's sake, what more do you want?' Trooper yelled, desperate. 'Do you *want* him to die? Just give me one chance.'

Daniels held up his hands for silence, unable to think straight. 'Fowles, did McCormack say anything else?'

'Only that if you've got a card up your sleeve, play it now.'

Now. But he couldn't.

Trooper could still be after Tim's blood. OK, so he wasn't there when the attack happened. But nobody was there last time either. This could all be a big bluff, a huge charade. He could not give the man what he wanted. Not yet. Not until he was sure.

Trooper hammered his fist on the table. 'For God's sake man, why don't you ever bloody *listen*? If you don't let me go now, it won't be that bastard out there who kills him, it'll be you!'

Daniels finally blew his stack. He was more livid than he had ever been in his life. Those words struck a raw nerve. The guilt at dragging his heels when he had no real justification exploded in his brain like napalm. 'Fowles!' he shouted. *Arrest this man*.

But the look on Trooper's face stopped him. A look of utter desolation, of lost hopes and infinite sadness.

And *then* he knew.

Something inside him snapped. He simply knew that nothing meant more to Nathan Trooper than saving Tim Johnson's life.

And as those thoughts flooded into his consciousness he saw the relief flood Trooper's face. The guilt drifted from his mind, washed away by his decision. The guilt that he was wrong to fly in the face of the evidence, wrong to let Tim die by standing on his pride, too scared to admit that there were things in this life he simply did not understand. Not understanding them did not make them any less real. Refusing to accept them when they were proven was nothing but damned bloody foolish pride. Pride because he hated to admit, even to himself, that he had failed to solve the case.

He accepted the message of the dream, accepted all the weird evidence, and at last allowed himself to be swept along by the tide.

'Fowles,' he repeated quietly. 'Get a car out front. A fast one. And a motorcycle escort, if you can find one.'

Fowles hesitated for a split second, caught in a conflict of emotions. He sensed that he had missed something important.

And he was right. He ran off.

Daniels turned back to face Trooper. 'Don't let me down.' He tried to put sternness into his voice, but it sounded no more than a desperate plea not to be wrong.

He did not give trust lightly. He knew he would go mad if this trust turned out to be misplaced.

Trooper grinned with relief. 'Trust me,' he said.

And Daniels had no choice but to do exactly that.

The journey to the hospital was not one Daniels would forget easily. Fowles drove like a maniac through the rush-hour traffic. Even with sirens blaring and a motor-cycle outrider, he spent most of the trip mounting pavements or dodging oncoming vehicles. At one point they swerved violently to avoid a crowded pedestrian crossing, leaving behind some ashen-faced people and a smell of burnt rubber.

'How the hell did you miss that?' Daniels had screamed.

'Instinct,' Fowles replied, grinning like a madman.

Trooper was out of the car the instant it screeched to a halt outside the hospital, before Daniels could even get his bearings. The Inspector managed to heave his quaking legs out of the door, and ran after him. Scott was waiting for them in the lobby, with tears in his eyes – of relief or despair, Daniels could not tell.

Nathan paused briefly to acknowledge his presence. 'I know,' he said kindly. 'But I'm here now, so let's get started.'

Scott glanced at Daniels – a look of pleading and thanks – and Daniels nodded. Then he pulled himself together. 'This way. They took him into Crash when his heart failed, then down into Intensive Care.' He rushed off, talking over his shoulder as he went. 'McCormack's with him now. I've never seen him so worried.'

They passed wards of sick and dying children. Some of the children looked up curiously as they passed; many did not have the energy to look up at all. Nathan hunched his head down between his shoulders, felt the anguish in his mind. 'So much suffering,' he mumbled, though nobody heard him, 'so much pain.'

Daniels brought up the rear of the entourage with Fowles, his coat tails flying impressively out behind him. His eyes were on Trooper's lowered head, and already he was having second thoughts. Trooper did not seem up to saving a boy's life.

The doors to Intensive Care flew open as they approached, revealing McCormack flanked by two plain-clothes policemen. The large Scot was obviously in a foul mood, and Daniels instinctively knew it would be pointless trying to talk to him.

'I absolutely forbid it!' McCormack began without pre-amble. 'Tim is in a critical condition and totally unfit to undergo some cack-handed mumbo-jumbo experiment. I'll have none of this insanity in my ward Inspector. I want you all *out* of here right now!'

Nathan flinched from the fury in McCormack's gaze, looking very small against the Scot's bulk and indignation.

Daniels stepped between them – a confrontation was the last thing he needed. 'Doctor, leave now. I have no time to argue.'

'Leave?' McCormack roared, incensed that his author-ity was being usurped. 'You give no orders here, Daniels,' he spat. 'Tim Johnson is *my* patient, this is *my* ward, and what I say *goes*. Clear?'

Bloody megalomaniac, Daniels thought. He reached a snap decision. 'Williams. Escort the doctor out of my sight.'

'WAIT!' Trooper's voice, surprisingly commanding. 'There's no need for this. Violence will get us nowhere.' He glanced at the doctor. McCormack glared at him for a few moments, then flinched and looked away. 'A word with you, Doctor.'

'I'll have no words with you, charlatan!' McCormack's accent, usually rich and mellow, now contained unbridled fury.

Trooper closed his eyes. He felt the hospital around him, pounding on his senses, *the other* still out there, probing for a way to finish his task. He ignored them all, reached only for McCormack in the maelstrom. Pages of past and personality opened before his mind's eye even as pressure mounted in his sinuses and jetted more blood from his nose. He looked up, a sad expression on his lined face. 'If I mentioned the name Karen Hughes, would you still refuse me?' The words were spoken quietly, but with determination.

McCormack stiffened. 'What do you mean?'

'Save your pride, Doctor. One minute is all I ask.'

McCormack sneered, clearly unsettled. 'You would resort to blackmail, here, in front of him?' He pointed at Daniels.

'If it works, Doctor, I'll resort to anything.'

McCormack had developed a slight, though noticeable, tic under his right eye. Trooper somehow remained impassive, despite the trickle of blood from his nose. Eventually McCormack looked away.

Everyone else stood around feeling useless and confused. Only Daniels, himself a victim of Trooper's gift, had a clue what was going on. 'Could you leave us for a moment, Inspector?' Nathan asked courteously. 'This should be done in private.'

Daniels hesitated. His dealings with Trooper always had the same result: loss of control. Once again he could feel the reins slipping through his tightly clenched fingers.

Trooper smiled. 'I won't hurt him, Inspector. I promise.'

Daniels looked at Trooper, gave him a warning glance

which was meant to be impressive but merely came out worried, then turned and walked away. 'Sometimes,' he muttered, 'I wonder why I bother coming to work. Sometimes I feel like just another spare part.'

They left Trooper and McCormack to their battle of wills and stood in the corridor feeling like lemons. Scott chewed his nails.

Two minutes later McCormack stormed by them, looking neither right nor left, scowling like a hurricane and muttering Gaelic obscenities to himself. Daniels watched the big man vanish and cleared his throat to hide his amazement. 'Right. Shall we go?'

Trooper was already by Tim's bedside when Daniels and Scott entered the cubicle. He did not look up. Sally Johnson sat beside him on a chair, a look of wonder on her face. Her eyes met Scott's as he walked in and she smiled. She wanted to tell him that she approved of his decision, that he had been right to believe in the man, but was loathe to disturb Trooper's concentration.

Daniels saw that smile. He did not like it. First himself unsettled, then McCormack infuriated, and now Sally Johnson struck mute like a disciple of Christ. He did not know what Trooper had said to the doctor or to Sally, but he could guess. Trooper had given him a dose of the same medicine.

Judging by the look on Sally's face, however, it seemed that the medicine need not necessarily always leave a bitter taste.

Daniels pulled up a chair and sat down, his eyes on Tim. The lad was wired up to an array of machines, with tubes in his right arm and electrodes on his skull. He was extremely pale and his eyes were closed. Beside him, the EEG traced a series of almost flat lines, evidence of Tim's failing will to keep up the battle for life. Daniels was struck by the change in the boy.

He looked like an embalmed corpse. Daniels felt his hopes fade.

Nathan, who had been regarding Tim through lidded eyes, looked up. His gaze focused on nothing and his lips formed silent words. One marker on the EEG skittered slightly, registering some activity.

'He knows you are here, Sally,' Trooper said quietly. 'He loves you and Scott very much. But he is very afraid.'

Scott went to stand beside his ex-wife, and – feeling awkward – draped one arm across her shoulders. Sally squeezed his hand.

'What did you do to McCormack?' Daniels asked, less awe-struck than the parents and more conscious of Trooper's dark past.

Trooper grinned faintly. 'Nothing. He'll be back in a moment. I actually think, underneath the bluster, he is interested. He is also worried for Tim, and is suffering because he feels inadequate.'

Daniels grunted. He understood only too well McCormack's feeling of inadequacy, and had not forgotten his own ambivalent emotions about Trooper's arrival. 'Is there anything we can do?'

'No, it shouldn't take long. I'm just waiting for the doctor.' With that Trooper fell silent.

They sat and waited. The EEG readout returned to its previous level of inactivity. The heart monitor beeped slowly, ominously.

McCormack arrived, took in the scene at one glance, and closed the door. He threw Daniels a meaningful look, as if to say: I'll not forget this in a hurry. 'Right Trooper. Do your worse.'

The Scot's tone was less hostile, but still held a challenge. He made it clear he was only allowing this under duress.

Nathan smiled. 'A little faith would be nice, Doctor.'

McCormack snorted. 'Bring him out safely, and you'll have all the faith you can eat. Until then, don't tell me what to think.'

Daniels looked up at the Scot, an eyebrow raised in question.

McCormack shrugged. 'Don't ask,' he said gruffly.

Daniels returned his gaze to the bed and its pale cargo. Already the suspense was killing him. So much was invested in the young boy's memories and the strange man sitting beside him.

Ignoring everyone, Nathan modulated his breathing, relaxing, entering a state of mind which had much in common with his patient. He shut down the five senses nature had given him, slipping away from the room. Voices faded and grew silent; the anxious atmosphere fell behind him, leaving only tranquillity. He entered a realm of darkness, where only his sixth sense could function. In seconds he was completely detached from the world around him.

It was a process he had once only dreamed of, when the minds of others had threatened to engulf his sanity. Years of necessity had allowed him to execute the transformation with practised ease. He concentrated his awareness on Tim's faint presence, focusing his power. Piercing Tim's consciousness, he homed stealthily in on the signals emanating from the boy's psychic core. Carefully, not wishing to alarm his host, Nathan sent out delicate threads of communication, warning the boy of his whereabouts.

Whereas the attacks Tim had experienced in the past few days were like thermo-nuclear explosions, Nathan's subtle entry was more like the sweet caress of silk on bare flesh. And yet, such was Tim's fear that the boy was instantly panic-stricken.

'Tim, don't be afraid. I'm here to help you.' Panic, anguish, terror – the raw emotions washed over Trooper in a flood of toxic disaster. He countered them with soothing reassurance. 'I won't hurt you. I've helped you once before, do you remember?'

Fear. Uncertainty.

Nathan countered with memories of love, his only weapons.

The fear turned to mere confusion – Tim was receiving emotional signals directly at the core of his brain, and these conflicted with the outright terror in his subconscious.

Nathan was encouraged. 'Tim, I won't hurt you, I promise. Your father asked me to help. He's here now, can you sense him?'

Tim could.

'Good. Now, do you remember before? When somebody else was trying to hurt you? I said "You are not welcome here". Remember?'

Recognition. Nathan sensed the swift display of memories as Tim recalled the attack and the strange voice, that second unwanted presence which had saved him. Tim was not stupid. The boy's mental and psychic receptors opened. Cautiously, but enough for Nathan to have earned a little trust and gained a little time.

He smiled in his mind. 'Good, Tim, that's very good. You're a very clever boy. Now, here's what I want you to do . . .'

Daniels studied the EEG. From time to time it registered a slight fluctuation, but on the whole remained low and steady. Beside him, Trooper's breathing became deeper and deeper until he was only inhaling once every minute. Scott and Sally shared worried looks, but said nothing. McCormack fidgeted as the minutes passed.

'I don't like this,' Daniels ventured.

'Give it time.' Surprisingly, it was McCormack who spoke.

Daniels tried to relax, but could not. They waited.

Slowly, the markers on the EEG began to trace out lines of increasing amplitude. A drop of blood appeared on the sheet by Tim's leg. Another followed it. Then another.

Daniels glanced at Trooper, saw the nosebleed taking hold. He fervently hoped Trooper's last fit would not be repeated.

McCormack handed him a paper tissue. 'Hold that under his nose. Tilt his head back, but not too far or he'll choke on his own blood.' The words were spoken quietly, almost without interest. Yet there was a twinkle of medical curiosity in his eye.

Daniels looked up in surprise. 'He warned you of this?'

'Yes. He did not want me to become alarmed.'

The blood began to drip faster and faster. As if in sympathy, Tim's nose also began to bleed. McCormack wiped the blood from the boy's upper lip. 'Nothing to worry about,' he said to Sally, who was eyeing her son with natural concern.

'How much longer?' Daniels asked.

'I don't know.' McCormack smiled. 'He didn't tell me that.'

'Why are you helping? What did he do to you?'

The doctor raised his head. There was a haunted look in his eyes. 'What did he say to *you*, Inspector?'

Daniels looked away, knowing only too well how McCormack felt.

Another few minutes passed. Blood now gushed from

Nathan's nose and soaked every tissue Daniels held there. But still he did not move, not even seeming to breathe, his eyes closed, hands clasped in his lap. Daniels thought he looked dead.

Tim's EEG continued to show increasing activity.

The atmosphere in the room was electric. Daniels found himself holding his own breath in suspense. 'Come on, Trooper,' he whispered, 'don't let me down.' Nobody heard him. They all thought the comment was merely the echo of their own thoughts.

Nathan sneezed unexpectedly. Blood showered the bed, his face, his clothes, Daniels' arm. Tim sneezed a half-second later. Daniels glanced at McCormack, and they exchanged a worried glance. Seeing that Daniels concurred, the doctor made a decision.

'Right. That's it. I'm bringing him out.'

Scott was instantly alarmed. 'Hold on – a bit more time.'

McCormack shook his head firmly. 'No, Mr Johnson. He's already had fifteen minutes, and that's quite long enough for me.'

Scott frowned. 'Listen, you've already said that you're no expert in this – give him as long as it takes.'

'No.' McCormack was emphatic. 'I am the doctor here, Scott, not Nathan Trooper. I understand your concern, but Trooper seems to be achieving nothing. All he's done is give Tim a nosebleed.'

Sally looked up, pleading in her eyes. 'Please, Doctor.'

'No. That's it.'

'But he said pulling him out might harm Tim!' Sally insisted.

'That's a risk I'll have to take.'

Daniels hesitated, lacking the doctor's conviction. The name Tenessee James sprang to mind, though he did

196

not know whether he feared a repeat of that American tragedy through action or inaction.

McCormack felt no such qualms. He grasped Nathan's arm.

Without warning Trooper's hand shot out and clamped over McCormack's wrist like a vice. Everyone jumped, even Tim.

McCormack grabbed at Trooper's hand, dropping the tissue he held to mop up the blood. He tried to prise off Trooper's fingers, but they were clenched white-knuckle tight. 'Jesus, that hurts.' But he sounded more surprised than injured.

The EEG went mad. The needles went off the scale, scratching madly at the paper, producing reams of paper almost black with ink.

McCormack glanced at the machine in alarm. 'Daniels, get me loose! Bring him out. He's killing him!'

Daniels looked from Trooper to McCormack. Nathan was cold and motionless, his face without expression. McCormack was desperate, his face a mask of genuine concern. Oh Christ, he thought, what have I done? He dropped the tissue, releasing a gout of blood onto the bed, then rose to release McCormack from Trooper's death grip.

Scott glared at him. 'Leave him alone!'

Nathan reached out with his other hand, fingers extended like claws. Daniels ducked to avoid the strike, then raised one fist to hammer down into Trooper's head. He tensed the arm to throw the punch, all the frustration of the past ten days coiled to give a blow which would probably put Trooper unconscious on the floor.

But as he did so the EEG stopped its crazy activity. The lines dropped to normal. Tim slumped, relaxed, in the bed.

Nathan's eyes opened, wide with alarm, and he seemed

to see for the first time that he was hurting McCormack, that Daniels was ready to punch his head clean off his shoulders.

'*Stop!*' Scott roared, freezing Daniels in his tracks.

Nathan immediately released his grip on McCormack's arm, and the doctor drew his hand away. Then Trooper turned and looked Daniels in the eye. 'Do it,' he whispered, his voice hoarse and subdued with exhaustion. 'I don't care any more. It's all over.'

Daniels stared at him, half of his mind eager to throw the punch and wipe the smug expression off the psychic's face. The other half held back, uncertain, forcing his eyes to Tim's face. The lad had some colour in his cheeks at last. As he watched, Tim took a deep breath, raised one hand to rub at his nose, then opened his eyes. His innocent gaze sought and found Trooper, and he smiled. Then he closed his eyes again and settled back in the bed.

Daniels, still standing with one arm raised, looked over at McCormack. The doctor took a glance at the EEG and shrugged. 'He's resting peacefully now,' McCormack stated. 'Sleep, nothing more.'

So Daniels lowered his arm and released his breath in a long, slow exhale, forcing himself to relax. Nathan closed his eyes, more weary than he had ever been in his life. He wiped the blood from his nose with the back of his hand. 'I'm very tired,' he said quietly. And collapsed, unconscious, on the bed.

Daniels sat with Scott and Sally at Tim's bedside. The boy was still sleeping, had been since the emotive 'rescue' about eight hours earlier. McCormack had assured them that Tim was doing well, and all he needed was rest. He could give no assurances about Tim's mental state when he woke, but that had not bothered his parents.

They had spent the day talking quietly, smiling, arm in arm and mooning into each other's eyes. They were so disgustingly sweet and cute apple-pie together that Daniels was feeling sick.

He looked at Tim sleeping peacefully in the bed, lips parted, chest rising slowly with the new air of health. Daniels had hoped the boy would waken, so that he could execute the callous task of asking questions. But Tim showed no signs of returning to the land of the living until he was good and ready. Meanwhile, Daniels had other business; he had delayed his responsibilities for too long.

'Let me know the minute he wakes up,' he ordered, and stood.

Scott looked up at him, face aglow with simple joy that his child was safe. 'Thank you, Inspector.'

Daniels nodded and left the room in search of McCormack. He found the Scot drinking whisky in his office. 'Boozing on duty, Doctor?' he asked mildly, a hint of a smile on his lips.

McCormack glanced up and grunted. '*Off* duty Inspector.'

'What about Tim?'

McCormack shrugged. 'Not my problem any more. Besides, I thought I deserved it. Join me for a wee dram, Inspector? Finest stuff in the world.' He indicated the bottle.

Daniels shook his head. 'No thanks, I don't.' He remembered his conversation with Trooper that morning, how uncomfortable he had felt when Nathan probed his mind and extracted his secrets. Like his abstinence from alcohol. Though Daniels understood Trooper had been obliged to prove his ability, he did not relish the memories.

McCormack seemed surprised. 'A teetotaller? How

peculiar. But then,' he added drily, 'it's been a very peculiar day.'

'And a very peculiar man. How is he, anyway?'

'Out cold. Down for the full count, as they say. His EEG is going wild – I was tempted to turn it off in case he broke it.'

Daniels grinned. 'I can imagine. I doubt that modern technology has advanced enough to develop a machine which can monitor *his* brain patterns. Going to write a paper on him?'

McCormack chuckled. 'Interesting idea. He's fascinating enough. But to do so would require me to have contact with him, and that is something I'd prefer to avoid, Inspector.'

Daniels smiled in agreement. 'Now that I can understand. Being with him is like sitting next to an unexploded bomb. He's so unpredictable.' He paused. 'Just what *did* he say to you, Doctor?'

McCormack shrugged. 'We all have our secrets, bits of our past we try to keep hidden away, even from ourselves if we can. Trooper doesn't seem to want to let us. I'm not sure I like that.' He looked at Daniels. 'What do you make of him? Do you trust him?'

'In what way?'

McCormack spread his hands. 'In any way.'

'Well, he's not lied to me yet. But would I trust him as a person, a friend? Absolutely not. He's as reliable as a guard fox in a chicken run.'

'Do you like him?'

'Not really, no.' He frowned. 'He's too different.'

'But he did save the boy. And for that we must be grateful.'

Daniels nodded a grudging 'yes'.

'Not that gratitude is something one finds easy when

Trooper is involved. You never know when he's going to cash in the favour.'

'Quite.'

McCormack raised an eyebrow. 'But was that his intention? I mean, did he only save the boy to gain our trust? Are we pawns in his game? He does seem to be the controlling influence right now.'

Daniels frowned, uneasy. He had gone along with events, but only because he had so few options. Trooper had backed him into a corner and he had surrendered. So far nothing cataclysmic seemed to have happened, but that did not mean Trooper could be trusted. 'I know what you mean, Doctor. Everything's been too easy since he showed up. Nathan Trooper has presented himself as our panacea, and so far we have no evidence to dispute that claim. But I don't like being out of control, and I know that's something I share with you.'

McCormack nodded. 'Indeed. Does it not bother you that he knows about murders and events without the benefits of forensic evidence, or witnesses, or the other stocks of your trade?'

'A little. Presumably in the same way that you dislike him diagnosing and curing patients without any medical qualifications.'

'Exactly. Most disconcerting.'

Daniels' mind switched to another tack. 'What do you make of his head wounds?'

McCormack poured himself a drink. 'Fascinating. I find it hard to believe he wasn't killed. And I refuse to believe he suffered no brain damage – his skull was split in two! He must have had a natural flaw in the bone. He's lucky to be alive.'

'Do you think that could account for his "gift"?'

McCormack snorted. 'Far be it from me to judge, Inspector. I'll only just admit he has greater than normal abilities. When I'm not actually with him, my brain finds it hard to accept that I saw what I think I saw. So don't ask me for a medical explanation. But a blow to the head like that could do literally anything.' He shrugged. 'Incidentally, he was talking in his sleep.'

'Oh?' Daniels asked, intrigued. 'Anything interesting?'

'Who knows? I wrote it down, somewhere.' McCormack rummaged in a drawer, handed Daniels some paper. 'Mean anything to you?'

Daniels read the words and felt the blood run cold in his veins. 'He said this? Today?'

'Yes. He was repeating it over and over. It didn't seem important before.' He narrowed his eyes. 'Why? Is it?'

Daniels forced himself to shrug. 'Could be. No stone unturned, eh?' He read the words again. 'You can run, but you can't hide. You can't ever hide.' Yet how could Trooper know those words? The acid in his bowels rolled over and made him queasy.

McCormack, disturbed by the look on Daniels' face, decided to change the subject. 'So. Have you read any of Scott's work?'

'No, I haven't had the time. Any good?'

'Well, I use "work" in its broadest sense, of course. They're all about as horrific as *Sesame Street*. Except one.'

'Which one's that?'

'*The Haunting Man*. It's dedicated to Tim. Most of his books are dreadful, but in that one he seemed to be writing with conviction. It's about a ten-year-old boy who has premonitions of other people's deaths, and who convinces himself he is causing the deaths by seeing the visions. Until one day he does something to avert an accident he had foreseen, and ends up saving the victim's life.' His smile broadened. 'It may sound peculiar, but all the descriptions reminded me of someone.'

Daniels groaned silently, mentally smacking himself on the forehead. 'Let me guess – Tim?'

McCormack grinned smugly. 'Indeed, Inspector. Odd, eh?'

One line careened into Daniels' mind, a snatch of conversation he could remember having with Scott some days ago. One comment he had failed to pick up on, and might regret having missed.

They had been discussing Tim's garbled telephone distress call at the time. He'd asked Scott what Tim meant by 'another look', and Scott said: 'He was just babbling.' And he had *known* Scott had been lying. He had let the matter drop, intending to chase it up later, but in all the confusion the subject had never been raised again.

Perhaps now was the time to talk it over.

He stood. 'Thanks, Doctor. I appreciate it.'

McCormack did not seem surprised that Daniels was leaving. 'You think that Scott really was writing about Tim?'

Daniels shrugged. 'Two weeks ago, Doctor, I'd have said "bull". But now? Now I'm inclined to think anything's possible.'

McCormack grinned. 'As much as I loathe to admit it, I agree.' He leaned back in his chair. 'Good luck, Inspector. I hope you get that bastard off the streets, whoever he is.'

Daniels nodded and left, glad to be back on the prowl.

An hour later he sat with a very bemused Sergeant Fowles in his office. Fowles puffed out his cheeks, venting his confusion. 'Well. At least that explains why Scott felt so guilty.'

'It certainly does. Ties up one loose end, anyway.'

Fowles grunted. 'Shame it's only the one. I know it's only been ten days, and we *are* dealing with a psycho, but I just can't shake the feeling that we're not really getting anywhere.'

'I know,' Daniels mused. 'We've got Tim back – counting my chickens, maybe, but it's something. We've got forensic evidence and a fair description of the killer. That's a lot more than some investigations I've headed. But we're still going nowhere.'

Fowles snorted. 'And, of course, we have Nathan Trooper.'

Daniels pursed his lips. 'Yes, well. Don't put too much emphasis on that. Trooper is a different can of worms. He may have helped Tim, but when it comes to a murder investigation I hesitate to rely on his methods.' He shrugged. 'We're in the midst of something I don't understand, Fowles, and I dislike not being in control. This is so close to going completely out of control that I hardly know how to stop it.' He lapsed into a worried silence.

'Tim or Trooper awake yet?' Fowles prompted.

Daniels shook his head. 'Nope. Both out cold.'

'Isn't there some drug they can give him to wake him up?'

Daniels grinned. 'Don't I wish. But McCormack said it could be dangerous. He hasn't got a clue what's going on inside Trooper's head and reckons pulling him out could kill him. So we wait, right?'

As if in answer, the telephone rang. He picked it up. 'CID.'

The voice which spoke was not McCormack's. 'Do not think the boy is safe. Do not place your hopes in the Anti-Christ Trooper. I will kill him now. Then the boy. Then his parents, and then you. You can run, but none of you can hide.' The phone went dead.

'What's up?' Fowles demanded. Daniels looked as if he had just heard a ghost.

Daniels looked up. 'That was him,' he whispered, utterly shell-shocked. 'The killer.' He knew it with utter certainty, despite the turmoil of sudden emotion. Yet through that turmoil surged the adrenalin and the ice-cold decisiveness for which he was so renowned. 'Get a car outside. Trooper's in trouble. I'll warn the hospital.' He reached for the phone.

Fowles did not hesitate, did not even consider questioning that tone of voice. He simply ran from the room.

Daniels dialled Sergeant Williams, on guard outside Tim's room. While he waited, he called for Sergeant Gardner.

'Williams,' the telephone squawked. 'What is it, Inspector?'

'We've just heard from the killer – he says he'll kill Trooper and Tim. So watch yourself – I'll be there as soon as I can. Ask McCormack to pull Trooper out, whatever the cost. Tell him Trooper doesn't stand a chance if he's out cold when he's attacked.'

'Yes, sir. Right away. Anything else?'

Daniels paused, weighing his options and the risks. 'First priority is the boy. Everything else is secondary. Understood?'

There was a brief pause as Williams digested that. 'Yes sir.'

Daniels hung up. Gardner was standing in the doorway, a worried look on his face.

'Ah, Gardner. Get some uniforms down to the hospital. And get some out to my house as well – I think my wife and daughter are in danger.' He grabbed his coat. 'Is Curtis in?'

Yes, sir. But I think he's just leaving.'

Daniels jogged off down the corridor, mind awhirl with worries and contradictory emotions. Fear and excitement were uppermost. Things were beginning to move too fast, and he was not ready. Tim and Nathan were unconscious and helpless in hospital beds. He was under-resourced – not enough men to cover all the exits, as it were. Now the killer was moving in, preaching destruction to all who stood in his way. First Wallis, then two innocent men, then a prostitute. Now his own life was threatened, and the lives of Trooper and the Johnson family. Yet he was no closer to finding the man and stopping him, and the killing would continue until he did. Where was it all going to end? And when?

Still, at least they were on the move. The scumbag had made contact, and now it was just a matter of time.

'Superintendent!' he shouted, catching sight of Curtis just as he was closing his office door.

Curtis turned to look at Daniels in surprise. 'Ah, Inspector. What can I do for you?' But he already knew – smokers like the Chief Inspector did not run unless it was absolutely necessary.

'We've just heard from the killer.'

Curtis tensed as he felt the on-rush of events. He had been following the case closely, pressing Daniels hard for results, and now he picked up the same taut excitement. 'He called you? Here?'

'Just now. He said the others were just the start, and he was going to kill Trooper, Tim, then me. I'm stretched too thin, sir.'

Curtis accepted the responsibility without flinching. He did not question Daniels' certainty or information, or his request for more men. In fact, this was exactly what he had been waiting for. 'Leave it with me. You're sure it was him?'

Daniels recalled the voice – cold and emotionless, completely lacking any tone or inflection. He recalled the sensation of snakes slithering up his spine as the man spoke. He thought of Anne Wallis' description of the caller. 'Yes sir, I'm sure.'

Curtis nodded, satisfied. He knew he could rely on Daniels. The man was as cool as ice. 'You're going to the hospital?'

'Yes. Fowles has a car waiting now.'

'Good. What about protection for your family?'

'I've asked for some uniforms to go to the house.'

'OK, I'll follow that up too. Anything else?'

Daniels handed him the firearms authorization order. 'I'd appreciate it if you'd consider that, sir.'

Curtis scanned the details, raised one eyebrow in surprise. 'A little severe isn't it, Inspector?' But he nodded. 'I'll think about it. Now, on your way. And for God's sake keep the boy safe.'

'Yes sir, I intend to.' He turned to go.

'Daniels! How did he know to call you here?'

Daniels grinned without humour. 'I don't know, sir.'

Curtis frowned. 'In your last report you skirted around the abnormal aspects of this investigation. But I've read the files on Trooper, and I've also talked to one of the doctors who examined him when he was locked away. It's pretty overwhelming evidence.'

Daniels shrugged. 'It wouldn't stand up in court.'

'But?' Curtis pressed.

Daniels hesitated. 'But yes, I think it's true.' He paused, wondering how much he could cram down Curtis' gullet without choking the man. 'I don't like it, but it is the only way I can explain things. And he did manage to pull Tim Johnson out of his coma.'

Curtis nodded, unfazed. 'I thought as much.' He took a deep breath. 'Although the odds are stacked against us, Daniels, I don't want any more deaths. I'm relying on you, so don't let me down.'

'Sir.' Daniels turned and left. He found Fowles behind the wheel of a new Jaguar, the motor purring. 'OK,' he said, climbing in. 'Curtis is handling the logistics. So let's do our jobs, eh? I want this mad bastard behind bars or on a slab by midnight.'

8.05 p.m.

Convincing McCormack to inject Trooper to wake him up, so that he could be conscious to protect himself from the imminent attack, was one of the hardest things Daniels had ever done. In the end Daniels, running out of time and patience, told the doctor flatly that he either co-operated or be removed from the building. Other doctors, probably police doctors, would be only too willing.

McCormack blustered and ranted for a while, but he was a canny Scot and knew Daniels was not making an idle threat. So eventually he agreed, as conscious as Daniels that time was running out . . . and more than a little curious to see what Trooper's mind would do next.

Daniels never found out what drug McCormack used that evening. But he was suitably impressed by its potency.

Trooper lay motionless in the bed, his EEG turned off. The heart monitor showed a disturbingly low rate – only 25 beats per minute. Daniels raised one eyebrow in question, but the doctor simply shrugged. Then he slipped a needle smoothly into the vein in Trooper's forearm. 'A few moments,' he cautioned. 'Then we'll see.'

The repetitive tone of the ECG remained stable at 25. Then, slowly, it began to rise – 26, 27, 28, 30, 32, 35, 39, 45.

McCormack seemed pleased with the steady progress. 'Hopefully it will steady at about 75.' There was silence in the room, apart from the tone of the ECG – 50, 55, 60, 65, 67, 70, 72, 73.

Another two minutes. Nathan stirred slightly, a frown creasing his brow – 75, 77, 80. Thirty seconds passed – 85, 90.

McCormack's smug smile faded – 105, 120.

The ECG tone increased rapidly in frequency, filling the room with its disturbing volume. Daniels found his own heart rate increasing as if to keep up with the stimulus.

One hundred and fifty. Nathan shook his head violently, obviously distressed.

McCormack leaned forward, frowning. 'Not good,' he murmured.

One hundred and seventy: Trooper opened his mouth and screamed, and Daniels nearly wet himself. Trooper went rigid in the bed, muscles tensed, mouth stretched wide as the howl tailed off to a strangled gargle.

'Bloody hell!' McCormack remarked. Daniels thought the doctor sounded more intrigued than worried.

'What's wrong?' Daniels asked, beginning to panic.

'Too much, too fast, too soon,' McCormack commented drily.

Nathan suddenly sat bolt upright in bed, his eyes flying open in a violent stare. His right arm shot out to point at the door and his eyes narrowed, as if someone was there.

There was not. Daniels knew because he looked, just in case.

And then Nathan's vicious glare faltered, the violence

ebbing away. His face crumpled and took on the appearance of a small boy.

Daniels and McCormack regarded the transformation
with total surprise. Nathan's ravaged features softened
and mellowed, wiping the age away so he seemed to
regress into his past.

Daniels half-expected what was to come next.
McCormack, however, had not read the police files –
he was totally taken aback.

'Daddy?' Nathan said, even his voice small now,
frightened, young. 'What are you doing Daddy?' His
eyes opened in fear. 'No Daddy!' He thrashed in the
bed. Then he began to whimper tears of absolute terror.
'Don't wanna surprise,' he mumbled, 'don't let him in
Mummy.' His movements became more agitated. He
tried to squash himself into the corner of the bed,
up against the pillow. 'No Daddy! Please don't hurt
me!' His mouth was wide now, the look on his face
so terrified that Daniels felt a sharp pang of empathy
and pity for the young boy Trooper had once been. The
young boy who had been terrorized and mutilated by his
own father, his innocence lost in the murderous blow of
an axe. 'Daddy!' he screamed.

Nathan's hands pulled back around his head, enfolding
his cranium. He flinched away in the bed, seeming to
duck, pulling his torso sideways to avoid the strike which
had hit him twenty-six years ago.

He gave one last scream, a cry of such fear and
desperation that Daniels closed his eyes so as not to
see the axe fall. Daniels' mind filled in the scene of
that horrific night, showing him a small, frightened
boy, helpless in the face of his father's madness. To
experience such things must have completely unhinged
Nathan's mind; Daniels was amazed the man was still
aiive, let alone sane.

When Daniels opened his eyes again, Trooper was lying calmly in the bed. The ECG was slowing noticeably, its frantic notes easing back to stabilize at 78. Then Nathan opened his eyes.

For a moment his gaze was out of focus, drifting across the ceiling of the room as if seeking a familiar landmark. Then he seemed to fall back into himself, and became aware of the two men at his bedside. 'Inspector,' he said, his voice croaky and quiet, but once again the voice of a man. His glance flicked sideways to McCormack, who was studying him with fascination. 'Doctor.'

Daniels was surprised, and not a little pleased, that the doctor appeared moved by the scene. His opinions of Trooper may have changed for the better because of that. 'Are you all right?'

Trooper blinked, swallowed, then nodded his head. 'Yes, I'm fine. A bad dream, I think. How's Tim? Is he awake yet?'

'He's fine, and no,' McCormack answered smoothly. He leaned forward to shine a pen torch into Trooper's left eye. 'Look up,' he murmured, 'good. Down. Other eye.' He repeated the examination on Nathan's right eye. 'OK – follow my finger.' He moved his hand in various directions, watching Trooper's eyes as they tracked the digit in mid-air. 'Good. How many fingers?' He held up four.

'Twenty-seven,' Nathan replied, struggling to rise. But as he sat up, the blood drained from his face and he fell back onto the pillow. 'Jesus! What did you give me?'

McCormack grinned. 'Enough. Now just take it easy.'

Nathan wiped a hand over his face. 'How long have I been out?'

McCormack glanced at his watch. 'About ten hours. It's 8:15 p.m.'

Nathan grunted in surprise, wiped his eyes. 'Well,

that's better than last time, at least. It was thirty-six hours then.'

Daniels decided it was time to slice through the pleasantries. He still had a suspect to apprehend. 'Nathan, we've heard from the killer. He says he's going to kill us all, you and Tim included.'

Nathan was instantly alert. 'And Tim's still asleep?' He was incredulous, angry. 'Why didn't you wake me? Where are my clothes?'

McCormack shook his head emphatically. 'Absolutely not, Mr Trooper. You're in no shape for anything – you need rest.'

Nathan shouldered aside the doctor's admonition, sat up and swung his legs out of bed. He sat there for a moment, head in his hands, the world spinning so fast he was not sure he could hold on.

Daniels' eyes were drawn to the scar on Trooper's flank. From his lower left rib down to a point beneath the sheet, a wide swathe of pale tissue marked where the axe had fallen for the second time. It was a particularly ugly scar. Once again, Daniels felt that sharp pang of pity. Poor bastard.

'You see?' McCormack pointed out. 'You can't even stand up.'

Trooper shook his head. 'Doctor,' he explained slowly, finally finding his voice. 'You have no comprehension of how vicious this man is. It is imperative Tim and I are awake.'

'But how can he attack? Tim is under guard.'

Trooper gave a short, bitter laugh. 'If only it was that easy, Doctor. The man could be miles away and still crush the brain in my head. He does not even need to touch me. Only *think* me. So,' he reached out, 'hand me my clothes. I have work to do.'

McCormack made to protest, but Trooper raised a

hand to silence him. 'Don't worry, Doctor. It will not take much to wake him now. He only needs a little nudge – I let him sleep so he could rest. He's been through more than you can imagine, and I did not wish to bring him out too fast. These things must be done gently. Don't forget that he is only a young boy.'

In the face of Trooper's determined tone McCormack acquiesced. He and Daniels left the room to give Nathan time to get dressed.

Trooper appeared some moments later, yawning, deep in thought.

'So,' Daniels prompted. 'Anything we can do to help?'

Trooper smiled apologetically. 'Already done, Inspector.' And, much to their surprise, from Intensive Care came the unmistakable sound of Scott shouting in undisguised joy.

When the trio entered Tim's room they found the boy in a crushing embrace with his parents, looking over their shoulders with an embarrassed glow in his once pale cheeks. 'I'm all right, Mum, honest. I'm fine.' He rolled his eyes. 'How are you both?'

Scott and Sally laughed. 'We're fine Tim, now you're fine.'

Then Tim caught sight of Trooper, and his young face lit up. His smile broadened. Nathan winked at him, his tired features softened by a half grin. McCormack crossed the room, at once buoyant and concerned. He examined Tim's eyes as he had Nathan's, then held up two fingers. 'How many fingers?' he asked.

Tim glanced at Trooper, and he smiled again. 'Twenty-seven,' he said, with a giggle.

CHAPTER FOUR

Vindication

Thursday, January 3, 1991. London, England

Anne Wallis sat alone, listening to the wind in the trees and the sound of her 'captors' playing cards in the kitchen.

She wondered why they were called safe houses. She certainly did not feel very safe, not now – her fourth day in isolation, hemmed in by guards there for her own 'safety', four days away from the home where she needed to be to patch her wounds, the fourth day of living hell after the sickening revelations of THE VOICE.

Anne knew she could not take much more of this punishment, the sleepless nights, the endless tears. She was not even allowed to visit her father in the hospital. She tried to console herself that her father had at least recovered from his wife's death, and should be home within a week. Some good news in a very bleak fortnight.

But her attempt failed. Her thoughts always led to THE VOICE. She spent every waking hour fearing its return, every sleeping hour reliving the nightmare. She was exhausted.

Bill, she thought in sudden anger, you two-timing bastard.

The house telephone rang.

Anne had not heard THE VOICE for four days. But every time the phone rang she was terrified it would be him.

She glanced at her watch – 10 p.m. Her father or the hospital usually rang at ten, her only contact with the outside world.

She picked up the receiver, even as one of Daniels' men appeared in the doorway and shook his head at her. 'Hello?'

'Hello, Anne.'

All the blood drained from her face. She tried to drop the handset, but it was glued to her ear. She tried to close her ears, but THE VOICE tore them open with a sickening, toneless laugh. 'I'm outside, Anne. I'm coming for you. You can't hide. Not from me.'

The phone was snatched from her hand. People were shouting in the background. 'He's here!' she screamed. 'He's outside!'

The front door slammed open, feet hitting the ground running; someone bundled her into a back room and stood guard at the door. She was crying. She wished she could stop, but it was all too much, why now? Why here? The house was supposed to be SAFE.

She just wanted to be safe. She just wanted some peace.

There was a public telephone about fifty yards from the house, the receiver swinging when Sergeant Baxter found it, seconds later.

'Jesus!' he spat, dropping the handset in disgust. Pus and mucus smeared the moulded plastic. The booth stank of death. He stepped back, and his shoe squelched in something. He looked down. 'Oh, for FUCK'S SAKE!' There were maggots and flies all over the floor of the booth. In the midst of them, green and rotten, lay a slice of skin covered with strands of long, white rancid hair.

*

'It's all a matter of perspective,' Nathan said calmly, eyeing his reflection in the window. 'Tim's mind was filled with images left there by the killer. I did a little psychic first-aid, that's all. Pulled out a few nice memories to balance the fear – early childhood, Christmas, that sort of thing. The others will trickle back and he'll have bad dreams, but I think he'll be OK. He is a mature lad.' He smiled slightly. 'When the killer cornered him, filling his mind with terror so he could hardly stand up, he grabbed a razor-blade and attacked the man.' Nathan's face expressed wonder. 'Such courage. Truly remarkable.' His voice trailed off.

'What of his gift?' Daniels asked. 'What he calls "looking"?'

Nathan sighed. 'Gift is not the word I would use, Inspector.' His eyes grew distant. 'Like my "gift", it has given him little joy. No doubt he would prefer to be free of its curse.'

Probably, Daniels thought. I know I would. 'One more question,' he asked. 'Why did you attack us when we tried to pull you out, when you were linked with Tim?'

Trooper turned to look at him, a puzzled look on his face. 'I did not *attack* you, Inspector. I just tried to *stop* you.'

'Why?'

'Because of Tenessee James, that's why.' He frowned. 'Her father never trusted me. So he knocked me out towards the end of a session, laid me out cold on the floor, because she had a nose-bleed. The girl and I were very closely linked – there was complete mental empathy. So when he hit me, and severed that link, the backwash on her was immense. She never recovered. Three days later she died.' His voice was filled with sadness. 'I had warned him, of course. I knew the risks, and I made sure he knew them before we started. But he did not listen.' He shrugged. 'I spent three days trying to pull her out of her fugue. He pleaded with me, blamed and cursed himself to hell and high heaven. But I just could not find her.'

Daniels took a moment to digest that, remembering how Trooper had lashed out at him and McCormack. Not, as Daniels had thought then, to stop himself being harmed, but to stop Tim from being harmed. Trooper had known that if the link was broken Tim may have died. 'And you never mentioned that to Sheriff McTierney, I presume?'

Nathan smiled. 'You jest, Inspector. Some outback American sheriff believing a load of mid-seventies acid psycho-drama? I think not. I would have been on trial for drug abuse as well as murder.' He shook his head. 'No, Inspector. I did not murder her. I just happened to create the circumstances in which her father caused her death. It's a fine line, I know.'

Daniels said nothing. He wasn't paid to judge, especially when the circumstances were so bizarre.

Nathan turned to face him. 'So has all the effort been worth it? Has Tim been able to give you any useful information?'

Trooper was obviously closing the subject of his psychic background, and Daniels was sensitive enough not to push the subject.

'Well,' he said, scratching his face, 'I suppose so. We got a description of the killer, which at least confirms we haven't been barking up the wrong tree for the past two weeks. We now know we're looking for someone with severe facial wounds and apparently no eyes. Tim explained that his razor-blade got the man right across the forehead and cheek, and I doubt that a wound that deep would heal without leaving a scar. Especially since the killer could hardly visit a casualty ward to have it stitched up. He may be insane, but we know he's not stupid. As for the eyes, well, I don't know. Tim said the guy seemed to be *rotting*, decomposing on his feet. It could just be Tim's imagination, but I'm not so sure.'

Trooper nodded, recalling from Tim's memories the image of the killer. 'Believe it. I saw it too and Tim's right. So what next?'

Daniels shuddered at the matter-of-fact tone Trooper used to talk about a walking corpse. But he had to admit that he was no longer very surprised. 'We wait, just as we have been. I don't see there is anything we *can* do – we're at his mercy.'

Nathan looked troubled. 'But does it not bother you that he said immediately, and so far it has been nearly three hours?'

Daniels frowned uneasily. 'Bother me? It's making me climb the walls! But I'm assured nothing is happening. Any suggestions?'

'No.' Nathan took a deep breath, then blew out his cheeks in frustration. 'It's not that I'm expecting you to do anything, Inspector. It's just that I keep looking, and there's nothing there. I just can't sense him any more.'

Daniels shrugged. 'What do you want me to say?' He reached for the telephone. 'I'll call Curtis again, just in case.'

Nathan closed his eyes and reached out with his mind. The sounds of London filled his brain – not the sounds of traffic, but the sounds of people. Screaming heads, a huge cacophony as ten million people went about their daily lives. Nearest to him he could just pick out the minds of Daniels and others he knew. As the distance increased the individual voices blurred, a vast jumble of thoughts. But that one definitive peak of psychic power which marked the position of the killer was nowhere to be seen.

Trooper opened his eyes again, aware of the headache pounding in his temples and the taste of blood in his mouth. He knew he was over-reaching himself, and should be more cautious. Daniels was talking into the telephone. 'No, he said "Now", and that was hours ago. Yes, I know you know – yes, I'll hold.' Daniels covered the mouthpiece with one hand, looked over at Trooper and noticed the bloody nose. 'You all right?'

Trooper nodded bleakly. 'Nothing, I'm afraid. He's not hiding. He's just not there any more.'

There was a squawk in the earpiece. 'Yes, I'll speak to him.' He lit a cigarette. 'Fowles. What is it?'

'Anne Wallis, sir. She got a phone call thirty minutes ago.'

Daniels frowned. 'But I thought she was at the safe-house.'

'She was.' Fowles paused. 'That's the point, sir.'

'Oh, *shit*!' Daniels cursed. What next? What the hell was going on? The killer makes threats which are not followed through. Was that a diversion? Anne Wallis gets a call at the safe-house and even I don't know exactly which one they put her in. But there has been no attack on my house, and Trooper says the swine has vanished.

Daniels did not understand. It just did not make sense.

'What was the message, Fowles?'

'Short and sweet. He said she could run but not hide.'

Daniels' frown deepened: *that* old phrase. 'Where is she now?'

'Here in your office. We've been trying to find somewhere safe to put her, but I don't really think there's any point.'

Daniels was tempted to tell him to put her in the cells, but knew that would achieve nothing. If she was to be kept safe, there really was only one place for her. 'OK. Bring her here. ASAP.'

'Right you are, sir.' The sergeant sounded relieved. 'There was one other thing. Curtis said in light of this turn, he'll think about your firearms request now. He also says that with all our eggs under one roof, you had better watch yourself.'

'Very good, Sergeant. Tell him I will.' Daniels threw the receiver back onto the cradle in disgust. 'What does he think I'm going to do? Let the madman in and escort him to Tim's room?'

'What's up?' Trooper asked.

'Plenty.' He lit one of Trooper's cigarettes. 'I was sure this had all been a diversion. After what you told me about him and what I saw this morning, I knew after half an hour he wasn't going through with it. He's made threats before and not followed them through. So I reckoned he was trying to distract our attention, so he could move in on his real objective, but nothing's happened!' He sighed. 'I just don't get it.'

'Do not try and figure out the mind of a madman, Inspector,' Trooper said sagely. 'And this man is quite mad.'

'Oh, I know that. But he's got an edge on us, hasn't he? He just phoned the wife of one of the victims and threatened her too. Nothing strange about that except she was in a safe-house at the time, and there was *no way* he could possibly have known where she was.' He looked up. 'Look, Nathan, I need a little help here. I've lost the reins and that bastard out

there is holding all the aces. Can't you give me anything?'

Nathan shrugged sheepishly. 'Sorry, Inspector. All I
know is that he is some miles away. Possibly not in
London at all.'

'So, what do you think? You probably know more
about him than anyone else. Anyone else alive, anyway.
No ideas?'

Nathan lit himself a cigarette. 'Well, let us see. He
wants me and Tim dead for the damage we did him. He
wants Scott dead because Scott foiled his first attempt
on Tim's life. And he wants you dead because you are in
his way. He is angered by our alliance – I would assume
he had not bargained for that. No doubt he thought you
would never believe my story and that you would not
stand a chance on your own. Without me you never
would have reached these conclusions, because no sane
man would.' Trooper paused. 'But most of all I think
he wants me. I am his greatest threat.'

'So how would he plan to do that?'

Nathan shrugged. 'Who knows? As I said, he is
quite insane. Before, I would have expected an outright
attack. But now he is wary. Perhaps he will opt for
something more subtle – a leverage.'

Daniels nodded. 'My thoughts exactly. It certainly
sounds reasonable enough. But then, that probably
means we're wrong, eh?'

Trooper returned the grin. 'Quite. The ball is in his
court. As you said, what else can we do but wait?'

Anne Wallis arrived about forty minutes after that.
Fowles escorted her to where Daniels sat alone, chain
smoking. To Daniels, she seemed frightened and subdued. Her eyes were haunted, puffy through tears and
lack of sleep. She was wearing a smart cream suit which

flattered her figure. Daniels was suitably impressed, which was not surprising. The last time he had seen her she had been wearing nothing but a bathrobe and on the verge of hysteria.

'Mrs Wallis, hello again.' He stood. 'I'm sorry, but we're doing everything we can to keep you safe. I hope you understand.'

She nodded, frowning. 'There really is no need to apologize, Inspector.' She remembered THE VOICE, the slime, the creeping flesh, the horror. 'I am almost getting used to the idea of living out of a suitcase. It has been a most enlightening experience.'

Daniels frowned. 'Well, consider the alternative. Rest assured we are doing our utmost to end this as soon as possible.'

She gave a humourless smile, remembering THE VOICE.

He turned to Fowles. 'Sergeant. Any updates?'

'No, but Curtis is checking on your house every fifteen minutes.'

Daniels nodded. 'Good. Mrs Wallis, would you like a cup of coffee, or anything? I'll be with you in a moment.'

She sighed gratefully. 'Please, Inspector.'

Daniels nodded at one of the uniformed men standing by the door. 'Three coffees, please.' The policeman left. 'Has Curtis authorized what I requested yet?'

'No sir. He still thinks we lack sufficient grounds.'

Daniels cursed. 'Until one of us gets killed, I suppose?'

Fowles shrugged. 'That *might* be sufficient grounds, yes.'

Daniels grinned at the deadpan humour. 'All right, Sergeant. That'll do for now. But keep yourself available.'

'Yes sir.' He looked around. 'Where's Trooper?'

'He went to sit with Tim. The boy had a nightmare.'

The uniformed policeman returned with the coffees, so Fowles took his and left. Daniels went and sat opposite Anne Wallis. 'I thought it might help if we filled you in on some of the details. Perhaps you could get a better grasp of the situation.'

'I would be grateful, Inspector,' she replied smoothly, crossing her legs. 'Being totally in the dark hardly helps.'

'I'm sure.' He paused to prepare his account, leaving out most of the detail but keeping enough to bring home the gravity of the investigation. He told her about them finding her husband on Christmas Eve, which upset her although she tried not to show it. He told her about Tim's attack. He did not tell her anything about Nathan Trooper, or discuss the psychic angle on the investigation.

He was pleased to see that her anger melted away during the conversation. The talk cost him nothing, and since her co-operation would be advantageous he thought the discussion worthwhile.

As did she. 'Thank you, Inspector. I appreciate you taking the time, and I apologize if I seemed ungrateful. But it has been the most horrible Christmas of my entire life, and it does not make it any easier to cope if you don't know *why* it's happening.'

'I understand. Now, I suggest you try and relax. Get some sleep if you can. We have rather taken over this part of the hospital, so there are some spare rooms. Take your pick.'

Behind him, the door opened.

'Ah, my apologies,' Nathan said politely. 'I did not know you were busy.' He made to leave.

'It's OK, Nathan, come in. I'd like you to meet Anne Wallis.'

Nathan's expression turned to intense concern. He crossed the room, hand extended in greeting and sympathy. 'Mrs Wallis. I was so sorry to hear of your husband's death.'

Anne, sick of crass sympathetic comments over the past week, halted her bitter retort at the last moment. Something about the stranger stalled her remark, something in his tone that expressed real understanding. For a second she was taken aback, and as a result simply stared at his hand. It stayed suspended in mid-air as if he was not sure what else to do with it.

Daniels cringed. He hated moments like that. He tried to brush over the embarrassment. 'This is Nathan Trooper. He's helping us with our enquiries.'

Anne finally grasped the hand firmly, returning the brief handshake. She fought back the emotion which always sprang to her eyes at any mention of her husband. 'Thank you.' She recovered herself. 'Forgive me, but I thought that phrase only applied to people who were under suspicion. You aren't a policeman?'

Nathan smiled warmly. 'No ma'am. And as far as being under suspicion, well, I suggest you ask the Inspector.'

Their eyes met. His were hooded and walled within, but she sensed that behind them was a pool of emotion to put her own to shame. The feeling gave her an intense sense of perspective on her life, which left her reeling with vertigo and in unexpected turmoil.

She tore herself away from Trooper's entrancing gaze, scared that if she looked too long she would lose herself in that depth. Troubled, her heart pounding, she reached for her handbag and stood up. She was surprised to find that Trooper was a good three inches shorter than she – in their moment of eye contact he had given the impression of enormous size and dimension.

But without that contact, he seemed just another small man in a world of small men.

She realized he was smiling slightly, as if at a private thought. That, too, unsettled her. 'Well, if you gentlemen will excuse me?' She left without waiting for an answer.

Nathan watched her go. When the door closed, he chuckled softly and sat down, reaching for a cigarette. 'A very perceptive woman. I'm surprised she had no suspicions about her husband. He must have been skilled at-concealing his activities.' Nathan lit a cigarette, leaned back and exhaled smoke rings through his nostrils.

'How do you do that?' Daniels asked, changing the subject entirely and glad for the diversion. 'You look like a dragon.'

Nathan looked at him blankly for a moment, and then laughed. 'I'm sorry, Inspector, I honestly have no idea. But I have been smoking for twenty-five years, so I've had plenty of practise.'

Daniels snorted. 'Well, they do say it stunts your growth.'

The words were out his mouth without thought, and he cringed at the unintended quip – realizing only as he spoke that Trooper could be sensitive about his height. But Trooper laughed at the joke, a human response which took Daniels by surprise.

For the Inspector it was an important moment. He found within Trooper in those few seconds the small reservoir of humanity which the psychic shielded from the world, vulnerable and deliberately hidden from all who came into contact with him. Nathan was not capable of opening up because exposure caused him pain. Daniels realized then that Trooper must be an incredibly lonely man. He guessed that Trooper could no longer remember what it felt like *not* to be lonely.

Once again, he experienced a sharp stab of empathy. To spend your whole life locked within the four walls of your own mind simply in order to stay alive – what a way to live.

His sense of release faded with the thought, and Nathan too seemed to lose his good humour and adopted his usual frown. He massaged his temples, feeling a headache coming on.

Daniels sat back to stare out of the window. Outside, the lights of London glowed brightly as far as the eye could see.

Nathan leaned forward suddenly, his face expressing concern. 'I am worried about Anne Wallis.'

Daniels was put off balance by the change of tack. 'Why?'

'She is close to collapse. Only stubbornness and willingness not to be seen as a weak and feeble woman are holding her together. Unlike Scott and Sally, there will be no dramatic rescue or reward for her. They got Tim back, but she has lost everything.'

This was not news to Daniels. 'Is there anything we can do?'

'Catch the bastard who – ' Trooper broke off. He looked up at Daniels suddenly, their eyes locking, Trooper's blazing.

Daniels felt that same old constriction in his bowels. Something's happening, he thought, something bad.

A single drop of blood formed in Nathan's left nostril and fell to the table. Yet he did not take his eyes off the Inspector.

'What is it?' Daniels demanded.

Nathan closed his eyes, swallowed hard. Goosepimples rose on his forearms. 'A message,' he whispered. He shuddered. 'He has hostages. He wants an exchange. Me for them. Tonight.'

'Them who?' Daniels whispered, but with a rush of ice in his blazing intestines he realized he already knew.

Trooper sighed, his eyes still closed. 'I'm so sorry.'

'Who?' Daniels bellowed, half rising in his chair and slamming both fists down on the table. The overflowing ashtray bounced, spilling ash on the veneer.

Nathan flinched, eyes rolling wildly behind closed lids. 'He is in Kent. In a large house. There is a woman and a girl. They are both terrified. Outside something is burning.' He flinched again, and a gout of blood spurted from his nose to land in the ash. 'No,' he whispered. 'Go away!' He was deathly pale. With his nose gushing blood, he calmly spread his hands palm down on the table.

Daniels went cold. The pressure in the room was immense, a massive pulsing energy making his teeth ache and his hair stand on end.

Veins throbbed in Nathan's neck, the tendons standing out like guitar strings. Outside a woman screamed.

And then it was over. Nathan slumped, exhausted, and collapsed into his chair. His nose stopped bleeding instantly.

'Nathan?' Daniels asked, shocked by the quantity of blood on the table. 'Are you OK? What's going on?'

Trooper opened his eyes slowly and looked at the Inspector. His gaze was filled with pain. His mouth worked convulsively until he found his voice again. 'He has your wife and daughter.' His voice was distant, strained, the vocal cords over-extended. 'They will die if you do not deliver me to him, tonight, at your house.'

Daniels felt his world collapse in around him.

Wife. Daughter. Hostage. Death.

Once before he had felt as desolate as this. Then he had made the mistake of surrendering to his feelings. He did not make the same mistake again. A veil as concrete as Trooper's came down and smothered his emotions before they ran riot in his mind. Ice-cold water gushed over his heart, around his inflamed intestines, filled the cavity of his skull. Red-hot anger and frustration were quenched in a violent hiss of steam. Only the smouldering fires of sworn revenge remained when he raised his eyes again.

'Fowles!' he called. His voice was a polar wind. In the paleness of his face two anger spots burned red.

Daniels' eyes met Trooper's. They regarded each other for a moment. Nathan felt his nose clot with drying blood.

'He dies for this,' Daniels whispered.

Nathan held the gaze for a few seconds, gauging Daniels' mind, measuring the extent of his hatred. Then he nodded.

Daniels took control like a man possessed. One phone call with Curtis confirmed they had lost contact with the police unit outside Daniels' house. Daniels demanded – and received – firearms. Police units scurried and screamed their way around the city.

Meanwhile, Nathan Trooper responded to a nurse's call for help. The screaming woman he had heard while casting the intruder from his mind turned out to be Anne Wallis. Nathan could hear her cries like a double echo, resounding both in his ears and his mind.

He found her huddled in the corner of a private room. A worried policewoman at the door tried to bar his entry, but one cold look from Daniels was enough to get him in. 'Do me a favour,' Daniels called down the corridor, a cigarette in one hand and a revolver in the other. 'Shut her up – I can't hear myself think.'

Nathan had been inclined to agree, but thought the Inspector was being a little harsh.

Anne was curled in a ball on the floor, arms over

her head, rocking back and forth and mumbling. The screams still echoed from her mind. Nathan knelt in front of her, reached out with his mind.

'Anne,' he called softly, 'can you hear me?' The sensitive blood vessels in his nose, already abused by the activities of the day, burst like a balloon. Blood gushed onto his clenched fists.

Through the layers of terror came a quiet response. 'Nathan?'

He surged out soothing emotion with his mind, poured oil on the tumultuous waters of her panic. 'Anne, what happened?'

Her mind filled instantly with images of her dead husband leering and laughing as he cavorted with an endless series of women. Visions of depraved sex and insanity assaulted Nathan's inner eye.

He has been here, Nathan thought. He has been here and implanted these images, to destroy her, to drive her mad.

Rage consumed him, some of it transferring down the link into her mind. She flinched in shock at the brunt of his anger.

The sequence of pictures, a triple-X sleaze movie, raped his brain. He had to stop them, and not just for her sake. The stench of madness in the intruding mind was making him feel sick.

As gently as he could Nathan tranquillized the images, erasing them from her consciousness and burying them far in the recesses of her memory. As he did so her mental screams quietened. He forced serenity into her mind like an anaesthetic, dulling her reactions, working methodically as he had with Tim Johnson until the visions were gone and only numbness remained. Like a surgeon he removed the diseased 'tissue' of unwelcome thought, cut it out and threw it away. He moved swiftly, angrily, suffering his mounting nausea and turning it into growing hatred for the man he knew he had to kill. Such illness, such depravity and criminal sickness, could not remain in his world. He vowed to remove it, or die in the attempt.

Anne's mental struggles died to a lethargic grief. She relaxed, letting free of the tension in her shoulders. Nathan took her in his arms and held her in his bloody hands while she sobbed with misery, thankful for the solid anchor he provided.

Nathan drifted, tired, aware that he had opened a door to her which had been closed for twenty-six years. For some peculiar, inexplicable reason, he did not regret letting her through his defences. To open himself up to her seemed the most natural thing in the world.

After a time of sweet calm with her in his arms, he felt a delicate tap on his shoulder. He turned. A policewoman leaned over him. 'Mr Trooper? Superintendent Curtis is here.'

Trooper nodded, reluctant to break the bond which he found strangely comforting. Yet he knew it was time – the events into which he had hurled himself were rising to a violent head. He relaxed his embrace and felt Anne move blindly from his arms. He stood. 'Take care of her, won't you?'

On impulse, he reached out one hand to touch her fine blonde hair. It seemed that only he could know how much she had suffered in the past days. 'Sleep,' he whispered, and left.

Anne felt her hold on awareness slip at that word. She felt the need to say something, to offer up thanks, but was too exhausted to move. Sleep claimed her before he had even closed the door.

'Are you sure about this?'

Nathan jumped, shocked out of his reverie by the first words Daniels had said since leaving the hospital. 'Of course I am.'

'But—' Daniels sighed. 'I'm sorry it has come to this.'

Nathan smiled. 'Look, the time for recriminations is long past. Besides, I volunteered, remember? I have lived for weeks with his sickness and terror in my head. I want him dead, whether I live to talk about it or not. Can you understand that?'

Daniels looked at him, surprised by the suppressed fury in his tone. Trooper's jaw muscles were clenched, his gaze burning with determination. 'Yes,' he said quietly. 'I can understand that.'

And he could. There was nothing he wanted more than to see the killer lying dead and his wife and daughter returned to him. After his initial shock Daniels had been driven by the same need which drove Trooper: the need to kill the man who had gone too far. For the first time in his life Daniels put his role as husband and father before his role as policeman. He did not want to bring the killer to justice; he simply wanted him dead. The risks were now too high – too many people had suffered at the hands of a man he had failed to stop. Now, if he had the chance, he would not hesitate to stop the killer from murdering again. He would simply terminate his life. Preferably with extreme prejudice.

At the hospital Daniels had taken control with iron resolve. His fury caused all around him to take one step back in fear. He had discussed the situation briefly with Curtis, answering questions with clipped monosyllables, already decided as to what action he should take. Curtis had surrendered without argument, his suggestion to storm the house with armed police vetoed when Daniels cut him off in mid-sentence. Trooper had backed him with calm acceptance.

'I will go,' Trooper had said quietly. 'There is no other way. If you refuse him he will kill them and be free, if you attack the women will be dead before your men are even in position. He can *sense* your every move and react to them. If you do anything other than what he demands, our one opportunity will be lost and they will die. He holds all the cards and makes all the rules. We can do nothing but obey those rules until an alternative presents itself.'

Curtis had not been pleased. He hated the rules, but most of all he hated the fact that Trooper was right. He acquiesced, aware that there was no point trying to argue with the psychic – without Trooper they would not have got this far. Terrorists he had dealt with before; this bizarre arena was new territory for them all.

So Daniels and Trooper had left alone, headed out of London in the midnight traffic towards Daniels' house in Kent. Daniels was armed – that much, at least, Trooper had allowed.

Trooper drove, insisting that time was of the essence.

'Left here,' Daniels instructed, then held onto the seat as Nathan threw the car wildly into the corner. The man was a complete maniac behind the wheel, and for that Daniels was grateful.

'How much further?' Trooper asked calmly.

'Another mile or so. Not long, at this rate.'

Trooper hammered his prize Jaguar down the country lane, flying over pot-holes, pushing the car to its limits.

'It's up here on the right, off the road along a grit track.'

Pitted tarmac fled under the beams of the headlights.

'Here!' Daniels barked, sure Trooper had missed the turning.

Nathan had not. Even as Daniels called out, Trooper pitched the car into the weirdest hand-brake turn Daniels had ever seen. The vehicle bucked and squealed, rear tyres slipping on loose gravel and wet road. Trooper hurled the wheel right and then left, and the car shot into the narrow driveway like a bullet from a gun.

Daniels chuckled in perverse delight, listening to the engine roar and the wing mirrors slap at overhanging branches.

Then, in the distance, they saw the house.

All lights were extinguished; it seemed to squat by the roadside like malevolence incarnate, its white walls basking in the glow of a flickering orange light. Daniels felt his heart pick up its laboured pace.

Soon, he thought, it will be over. One way, or the other.

Nathan brought the Jaguar to a halt on the forecourt. Twenty yards away, in the lee of the garage, a once pristine police car stood blackened and distorted. Flames still licked at the tyres and rose in tendrils from the shattered windows. Columns of thick, oily smoke climbed in a shower of sparks to disappear into the night sky. The air was thick with the stench of burnt rubber and flesh. Even from some distance away Daniels could feel the heat on his skin. The car had clearly been alight for some time.

'The uniformed watch?' Nathan asked quietly, his eyes squinted against the glare and heat as he probed for signs of life within. Only one blackened half-melted skull returned his gaze.

Daniels nodded. 'Curtis said they'd lost contact. Now I see why.' But far from turning his stomach, the sight only served to reinforce his resolve. He fingered the pistol in his coat pocket, found the touch of cold metal reassuring. 'Coming?'

Nathan dragged his eyes from the carnage. The killer loomed as a bloated sickness in his mind's eye. Trooper felt sick to his stomach but not because of the two dead policemen. He felt sick because the touch of evil on his mind was like the caress of living putrefaction. That touch was enough to make him cringe from the house as he would cringe from eating rotten meat.

He knew his only option was to confront this evil. Whatever his revulsion and fear, the only cure for sickness was medication. And the only medication they could offer here was death.

'It's hideous,' he said thickly. Even with his mind fully closed, the sickening nudge and probe of THE OTHER was defiling. If they did not kill it, such massive decay would soon drive him insane. And Nathan would rather be dead than locked in some forgotten room again, amongst the maddening howls of an asylum full of sick and dangerous minds. He cleared his throat, tasting bile, then squared his shoulders. 'OK, I'm ready. Let's do it.'

Daniels strode purposefully to the door, eyes darting across the blank faces of the windows. He inserted his key in the lock and opened the door. Air stale with the stench of decay poured from the hallway, assailing his nostrils like a nest of rotting snakes. He bit back his gag reaction, for a moment fearing he could smell the deaths of his family, that he had been too late.

Nathan appeared at his elbow, sensing his panic. 'The body pays the price of a sick mind, John,' he said calmly. 'What you smell is *him*, Satan himself, for no other word can describe the soul of this thing. If you see him, be warned – his body has been corrupted by power, neglect and abuse.' Then Nathan brushed past him, standing in the hall at the border between light and darkness.

Trooper changed as he stood half in, half out of the shadows. He suddenly seemed a seething mass of power, the last valiant hero in the face of an advancing, blood thirsty horde. Refracted light formed a corona around the scar on his head, like a crown of pure energy. His small body seemed to bulge at the seams, as if the power within was too much to contain. For the first time, Daniels saw beyond Trooper's physical form and noticed the giant, a colossus to stand against the onrush of hell. And he knew then that if Trooper failed there was no hope left. All would be lost.

Nathan spread and raised his arms to shoulder height, palms held upwards, and opened the floodgates in his mind. Through the jabbering horror he swam and glided, by-passing the corruption, filling his mind with raw power. The vaults of his brain suffused with energy, sparking from synapse to synapse, a vast potency that threatened to overwhelm him. Once before, when he had confronted the intruder in Tim Johnson's mind, this lust for power had almost been his downfall. Now he drank that power like a man dying of thirst, sucking at the bounty which surrounded him. The infusion of psychic energy was immense, orgasmic, horrible. He loved it, loathed it, embraced it and rejected it. And it filled him with glee and sadness.

'I have come,' he announced formally. His fragile vocal sounds were no match for the roar of his psychic voice, an outburst of white-hot radiation. Behind him Daniels screamed in pain, hands rising to his ears as if that would stop the echoes in his mind.

From the end of the hall came a revolting, hideous chuckle. It was the sound of human laughter perverted by a throat which knew nothing of humour, was thick with slime and rot. Shadows formed and drifted, a movement which brought a heightened aroma of the grave. Daniels strained his eyes to peer past Nathan but could detect nothing other than shades of darkness. His fingers closed around the revolver, itching to withdraw it and pump lead into the man who held his wife and child. He began to realize how Scott had felt, his child lost to him, terrorized by an unseen invader who gave no mercy. He began to understand the rage and the frustration.

The sickening laughter came again. 'You stand before me, Anti-Christ, and hope to confront me.' These words were liquid, as if spoken through a mouthful of custard. Daniels found the sound horrifying, not least because the same words were echoed clear and powerful in his mind. The whole conversation was occurring in the weirdest stereo he had ever heard. He felt like a pawn in a game of superpowers he could not even hope to comprehend.

'You are foolish,' the voice spoke again, 'to come here thinking of victory. Defeat shall be your only reward.'

Daniels squirmed, crushed by the awesome power of a man he had come to kill, but before whom he could now only quake in despair.

Nathan, however, clung to his resolve, shoring up his defences with power he drained from his adversary. Power which was in such supply that he doubted the killer could even detect the drain. Nathan knew he was no match for his opponent – the killer had the psychic energy of his victims coiled and chained to him in a psychic pool: Bill Wallis, the two gay men, others he could not identify – all feeding the psychopath with pure energy. But even against these odds, even knowing he could not hope to stand and win, stand he did. Better to die trying than sit back and be killed anyway.

'We have complied with your demands,' Trooper said carefully, lowering his eyes to stare along the hallway. 'I am here. Now release the woman and her child.'

The shadows flowed and the nauseating presence came closer still. Nathan forced his mind open further, pushing the capacity of his body to the limit, desperately trying to touch the other's mind. To find some intent, some reason, and use it as a weapon. All he sensed was contempt and a mild amusement.

'You seek to make demands of me?' the toneless voice boomed in their minds. There was more movement in the deep shadows. 'But no matter – they are unimportant, mere playthings. I could use them as food, but devouring you will be a greater pleasure. We awaited your coming with some anticipation. I shall enjoy consuming your soul.'

Daniels' heart leapt, his mind reluctant to accept that the bargain would be made. He dared not raise his hopes.

'Release them,' Trooper repeated.

'So be it. Later I shall claim their pathetic souls. Until then, let them delude themselves with visions of freedom.'

Nathan sensed more movement beyond the darkness. Two blurred shapes emerged from the gloom, their eyes blank.

'Catherine!' Daniels gasped, taking one step forward before Nathan motioned him back. Relief rose in his heart, just to see them alive. But then he realized they simply stood in the hallway, mindless zombies with no life. 'What have you done to them?' he cried in dismay, hand closing around the pistol.

'John!' Nathan barked. 'No!'

But it was too late. Daniels rushed past him, the gun pointed down the hall past his wife and daughter. He fired once, the report deafening in the confined space, and heard glass smash in the same instant. He coiled his finger to pull the trigger again, possessed by mad hatred and the need to end the terror once and for all.

Then he screamed in horror. In his hand he held not

a pistol but a huge tarantula, dry and hairy, wrapped around his fingers. Daniels shrieked his lungs out. He hated spiders. They gave him nightmares. This one *was* a nightmare. He glared at it, paralysed with fear. His wide eyes took in all the disgusting details – black thorax covered in hair, marked by two red stripes the colour of blood; the head, a mass of eyes; jaws and venom and death.

His mind snapped, his bladder loosened. Wildly thrashing with his hand to cast the thing off, screaming incoherently, he forgot about his family and the world around him. The spider moved up his arm, horrific and inexorable, unaffected by his frantic convulsions. Daniels opened his mouth and howled with terror.

'ENOUGH!' Trooper's voice ripped through his brain, whipping away the terror and casting it in shreds from his mind. He staggered from the blast, legs collapsing beneath him, spilling him to the floor. The spider vanished as he fell.

For some seconds he looked around himself frantically, searching for the demon in the gloom, afraid it would pounce on him from the shadows. But his battered mind slowly came to its senses, creaking into action, and his struggles ceased. He looked up at Trooper, feeling stupid and drained. 'It was never there, was it?'

Something chuckled in the darkness. Nathan shook his head sadly. 'No, John. Just an illusion. If your fear was rats, it would have been a rat. Or a thousand rats.' He smiled kindly. 'The only spiders here are in your mind, and he knows your mind.'

Daniels cursed. 'And now he has the gun.' He had dropped the gun, like an idiot, and now they were all going to die.

'It hardly matters,' Trooper assured him. 'I told you it would be useless.' He turned away. 'Release the woman and her child. Then let them all go. I will remain.'

The voice chuckled hideously. 'Of course you will.'

There was a slight pause, during which Daniels felt faint whispers in his mind. Catherine was the first to recover, coming out of the numbness as from a deep sleep. Her eyes focused slowly, scanning the hall, before finally coming to rest on her husband. 'John?' she asked huskily, obviously confused and disoriented.

Daniels felt himself consumed with relief. He stepped towards her, enfolded her in his grasp, crushed her to him. 'Yes, Cathy, it's me. Everything's all right now, you're safe.'

As she started to cry, his daughter stumbled awkwardly into his circle of comfort. He took her in his arms, holding them both, relishing the warmth of their presence and forgetting for the moment that events had yet to run their full course. When his daughter raised her head to tell him what had happened, wide-eyed and scared, he placed one finger over her lips. 'Hush now.'

His wife went suddenly stiff, startled by the ominous presence in her mind, and turned to look back down the hall. What she saw in the shadows made her gasp with fright.

The killer had stepped forwards into the gloom, so he now stood only a yard or so from Trooper. Daniels eyed him coldly, filled with rage, cursing himself again for losing the gun.

The killer was tall, at least seven feet from bare soles to bald head. He was dressed in soiled rags, bloody and rank, and he stank like stale death. His eyes were gone, leaving two black pits in his skull which gazed out at the world with unearthly darkness. From the mouth ran a stream of pus and blood, a foul mixture of decay. Daniels remembered Tim's description, and was ashamed he had not believed it. Glancing down, he saw that the man's fingernails had mutated into long yellow talons, curving to sharp, dirty points.

Nathan turned to look him in the eye. His face was aglow from within, awash with power. There was no hope in that expression, but there was fierce determination and a willingness to die trying. What Nathan said in that silent glance was a simple appeal to the man responsible for their future hopes: I cannot win, but I can weaken; use the time wisely; there will be no second chance.

Daniels said nothing. He simply nodded his understanding.

Nathan smiled sadly. 'Leave us now. It is time.'

Daniels cast one last look at the killer, expecting trickery or some foul refusal to let them leave. But the madman grinned, revealing rotten stumps of teeth which oozed decayed tissue.

'Be gone, fool, before you try my patience.'

Daniels did not hesitate. They had made the bargain, and there was nothing he could do for Trooper now – Nathan's life was in his own hands. He had blown their chance by losing the revolver, but there was no point trying to get the mushroom cloud back in the steel case. So, taking the trembling hands of his wife and daughter, he led them outside into the night. He had not realized just how sickening the stench of the corruption was until his lungs were filled with the crisp winter air. Even the lingering odour of burnt rubber was a pleasure after the interior of the house.

Behind them the door slammed firmly shut . . .

'Ah, what a sweet precious prize.' The words came thickly in the sudden darkness. 'At first I thought you weak, no threat to one such as I. But you demonstrated

your power within the boy's mind and I knew you must
be taken. There is no other like you to stand against us.
Now you must die, to link your mind with mine.'

Nathan ignored the words, concentrating only on his
power. He forced himself into a trance state, let his body
idle as he delved within his mind to seek the strength
for combat. He sensed gloating all around him, the grim
satisfaction. He readied himself for defeat, vowing he
would not be taken – his soul would not join the others
bound to the killer. If he failed and added his strength
to the pool of energy, his opponent would be invincible.
Nathan had to avoid that outcome at all costs. So he
intended to launch a brief attack, do what damage he
could to the beast and withdraw. Before he could be
overwhelmed, Nathan would destroy himself. Anything
rather than join the lost souls bound to that demon.

Trooper gathered his forces for the skirmish and
opened his mind to take the plunge. Only to find his
father standing before him, axe in hand, sightless eye
sockets laughing with glee . . .

'Who was that man?' Louise asked, still clinging to
her father's arm with one terrified eye cast back at
the house.

Daniels dragged her to the car. 'A friend,' he said
simply.

'Then why did he stay?' she asked, ducking her head
as he pushed her into the back seat. '*He* said we were
only bait. Does—'

Her words were cut off by the most agonized, soul
wrenching scream Daniels had ever heard. As he turned
to look at the house the cry died off to an inhuman
gurgle and was mercifully silenced. He hesitated, unsure
whether Nathan – whose cry it had been, he was sure of
that – would want him to interfere.

Louise huddled in the back seat, shrinking from the source of her terror. 'Let's get out of here, Dad,' she pleaded, tears running down her cheeks, 'while we still have the chance.'

Daniels turned back, locked stern eyes with his wife across the roof of the Jaguar. 'John,' she started, but gave up. He had decided, and she knew it.

'Get in the car,' he ordered. 'Now hand me that phone . . .'

The axe fell towards Nathan's head, as it did in his dreams, as it had twenty-six years ago. For over two decades he had woken in the night, bathed in sweat, screaming out a final plea as the axe-head descended again and again. He had never escaped that death blow, and knew it would haunt him to his grave.

But now he possessed a new power, drained from his opponent. He stood before his father, not turning to run or flinching from the axe, his horror balanced by determination and a need for survival. He fought the impulse to flee and watched the axe fly towards him.

It struck, splintering through bone and brain, sweeping his head into two bloody parts. He screamed – the pain unbearable, a shower of white agony in his cranium. The sight was so real his desolate cry was fuelled by a horrible remembrance.

But when the axe swung free of the shattered tissue and gouting blood, Nathan recovered himself. His head formed back around the wound as the weapon withdrew, miraculously healing until only the old scar remained and his head was whole once more.

Spiders and rats, he thought, and laughed in relief . . .

Daniels threw down the phone and uncoiled his long frame from the car. Cathy sat expectantly behind the wheel. He leaned down and looked at his wife and daughter – perhaps for the last time – not sure why he was staying. Guilt, perhaps. Guilt at not catching the killer. 'Drive. Don't stop for anything. Understand?'

Cathy frowned. 'John, why—'

He touched her lips with his fingers. 'No questions,' he murmured, then leaned in and kissed her briefly. 'Now, go.'

She knew him well enough not to argue. She backed the car up to the wall, then pulled out into the driveway. The last Daniels saw was his daughter's worried face peering out of the back window.

He stood alone in the yard, the burnt-out car warming his face. With the departure of his family and his only means of escape Daniels felt both sorrow and relief. He had no idea what he was going to do next; he just knew he was going to do *something*. Curtis was on his way and that was good news. But Daniels knew he had to act before Curtis arrived – he wanted a kill, not an arrest.

He looked over at the house, sensing the titanic struggle within. He grinned sardonically – front door security dead-locked, the keys now inside; back door security locked and bolted; windows security locked. Sometimes it was a pain being a policeman.

He sighed and went in search of a sledge hammer . . .

With the vision of his father defeated, Nathan felt his power and confidence surge. He had destroyed the demon which had shackled him since childhood. Now, with those restraints lying behind him, he stepped forward to accept his true gift. He attacked.

In THE OTHER'S mind he sensed layers; trap within trap, bluff within bluff. When Nathan attacked, the killer parried and struck back. Visions were sucked from Nathan's deepest fears, magnified a thousand times and given life on the psychic battleground. Shapeless monsters from his subconscious; his parents; doctors and patients who had abused him. Tenessee James appeared before him, screaming her hatred, her head a clot of blood. All the sights and sounds conjured from his guilt and weakness to unbalance him. The killer sought to crush him beneath the weight of his own nightmares.

But Nathan had shattered the power of the visions by seeing them for what they were: images, with no substance. So he accepted them as part of himself, felt sorrow for his failures, but put them in perspective against his successes. Once he had performed psychic surgery on Timothy Johnson; now he did it to himself.

It was a task long neglected, and Trooper found pleasure in healing himself. With every acceptance of human frailty his power grew. As each self-imposed limitation crumbled into dust, as his capacity to grow increased, the power flooded into him from the psychic net and his opponent. Until at last, after a timeless psychic battle, he and his opponent had become equals.

Then, and only then, did Trooper allow himself the first glimmer of hope. For that hope sprang from the unmistakable stench of fear in the mind of his attacker – fear of *him*, Nathan Trooper . . .

Daniels raised the garage door. The police car now only emitted occasional cracks and creaks as the metal cooled.

He stepped forward and grasped the handle of the sixteen-pound sledge-hammer firmly. Then he turned and made his way purposefully back towards the front door of the house . . .

They clashed, minds locked in irrevocable struggle. Around them, the darkness of the hall spoke nothing of the conflict taking place in their brains. They stood motionless, faces blank except for the furrows of concentration on their brows.

Within, dark and violating visions vied for supremacy on the battlefield. Nightmares unfolded, peopled by unspeakable horrors from the depths of their ids. Amongst the violence and spilled blood the two men stalked each other, pitting their wits as they battled for their lives. Nathan was outmatched, his experience in such conflict almost nil. His life had been dedicated to easing the suffering of tortured minds, not causing it. Destruction did not come easily to him. Some part of his brain still resisted using his ability as a weapon instead of a tool, and though the balance was fine his opponent exploited this reluctance to the full.

Nathan dodged a jabbering blob of protoplasm with the face of his mother, casting out a vision he plucked from the other man's twisted mind. His opponent was momentarily taken by surprise as he was confronted by a decomposing young woman.

Such was the armoury they used, and such was their defence: to accept every vision as part of yourself, however foul. In this respect Nathan had the upper hand. He sensed mind within mind in the killer's head, so many personalities, each with its own darkest fears. Nathan had by far the most ammunition.

'Andrew?' the vision said. 'Andy, did I taste nice?'

Nathan thrust aside his hesitation, sensing the opportunity, accepting the need for brutality. He seized his opponent's shocked mind, cut the supply of energy, asphyxiating him. Around him the visions faded until only the psychic link remained, that blazing thread between minds. Once he had severed that link when in Tim's mind. Now he placed a stranglehold upon it, not wanting to sever it since that would give the killer a chance of escape. Instead he grabbed it, squeezed the killer dry until his mind choked.

The man thrashed in desperation. His brain throttled, the killer howled his last breaths in mercy and rage. Nathan sobbed with pity and self-disgust, unable to maintain the killing grip, unable to let go. He loathed himself for his brutality, and yet could not stop – the lives of too many innocents had already been lost, and Nathan owed them so much. Kill. Or be killed.

The psychopath stood locked in a fierce embrace which leeched the life directly from the core of his mind. He had not anticipated this turn of events – he had not thought Trooper capable of murder. He had underestimated his foe, and it was turning out to be a fatal mistake. His mind turned and fled. If psychic power had been the killer's only weapon, then now it was surely his suicide. There were always two worlds to fight in – the psychic illusion, and the reality. He returned to reality like a meteor striking earth, shell-shocked, confused and half dead. He sensed life and oxygen return. Apart from a dark place in his head, where Trooper stood locked in a blind stranglehold, he felt alive again.

And then he felt it.

He felt the gun in his hand, recalled the spider, and laughed.

The weapon exploded between them, a bullet tearing through Nathan's midriff and erupting from his back. Tatters of flesh and cloth sprayed the wall and carpet behind him.

Trooper was taken completely by surprise. He had not even sensed his adversary's intentions. Now he was thrown back, letting go of his opponent, shocked into instant defeat. Blood gouted from the exit wound in his lower right side. He grunted as the air was squeezed from his lungs and expelled through his open mouth.

The killer staggered back, face red with agony, his mind gasping for sustenance. It would only take one more bullet, but his head was spinning and he was as weak as a new born lamb.

For a moment neither man was capable of action. They had to recover from the monumental shock of such a sudden release of power. That release had killed Tenessee James. The two men were stronger than she had been, yet both were sorely injured.

But only Nathan was dying . . .

Daniels raised the sledge-hammer, grunting with the effort.

A shot rang out. He mouthed a foul curse at himself, then rammed the hammer into the door. The lock tore free, ripping out half the door frame, and the door crashed back into the wall in a hail of plaster. He stepped forward into the darkness . . .

Nathan fought the cloud of death valiantly. He raised his head in one last effort, hand coming up to stem the flow of blood. Ahead of him the killer retreated from his demonic glare, terrified. He was still powerless, squashed senseless by Nathan's attack.

Trooper grunted in pain, took one step forward and bellowed in agony as his ruptured organs squealed in protest. Pain flamed up the nerves in his right leg, setting fire to his spine. He clamped down on his scream, biting deep into his tongue so blood gushed and filled his mouth. He lifted the foot again, planted it firmly on the floor. The pain made him weep. He resisted the urge just to lie down and die peacefully, moved another step, pursued his victim into the kitchen. His eyes blazed like stars, hungry for blood.

The killer retreated, matching step for step, until

his back was against the teak work surface. 'Stop!' he whimpered. 'You can join me. Together we shall be the greatest force on earth!'

Nathan moved ever onward, his fingers soaked with blood, his other hand scrabbling on the worktop for a weapon. He felt the blade of a carving knife slice into the pads of his fingers.

The other man raised the gun again, at last able to defend himself. But Nathan brought his angry mind to bear in a stranglehold. The weapon froze in mid-air. Nathan knocked it negligently to the floor. That act seemed to ram home to the killer how hopeless his situation had become. There was clearly no salvation here.

'Kill me then!' he spat, his fear almost as foul a stench as his decay. 'It will only make us stronger.'

Behind them, the front door crashed open in a hail of splinters. Neither of them noticed.

Nathan raised the knife, every movement a torture, only willpower keeping him going. Summoning all his strength he pulled back his arm, inverted the blade and plunged it into the killer's throat. The cold steel pierced rotting flesh, cutting through the Adam's apple, severing tendons, slicing through the jugular vein to emerge in a shower of gassy blood and decay from the back of the neck.

'Die, you bastard,' Nathan whispered. Then lunged forward and drove the point of the knife deep into the cabinet door . . .

Daniels stood in the doorway, hammer held protectively by his chest, listening to the sounds of the house. They were in there somewhere, and one of them was probably dead. He stepped forward, disturbed by the silence, his nerves at fever pitch. On impulse he reached out and fumbled for the light switch, not expecting any result. The sudden brightness as the bulbs came on startled him.

There was blood all over the floor and wall. A hole in the wall marked the resting place of the bullet.

Ignoring the stench of rotten flesh – which seemed to have grown worse – Daniels advanced stealthily into the kitchen. He made no sound as he moved. His ears strained to catch the slightest sound, eyes flicking restlessly in search of any movement. His mind sought the tell-tale whisper of the murderer, but found nothing.

As he entered the room his tension dissipated in relief. The hammer descended from his grip and stood on its head on the floor.

Hanging from a cupboard door the killer stared at him through empty eye sockets. From his throat protruded the stained and bloody handle of a kitchen knife, snatched from the worktop among some half chopped onions. Cathy had obviously been preparing dinner when the killer had struck. The corpse's mouth was open; blood and infected fluid streamed from the rotten lower lip. He stood limp and relaxed, held in place by the knife which pinned him to the cabinet, effectively nailed to the wall. The gun lay at his feet.

Nathan Trooper lay on his left side in a pool of blood, his back to the door. The whole kitchen was covered in blood, jetted out when the killer's jugular vein had been severed.

Daniels hurried over to Nathan's side and placed his index finger on Nathan's neck. No pulse. In desperate panic, he hauled himself to his feet and snatched up the telephone . . .

Daniels squatted beside Nathan, smoking a cigarette, unwilling to leave the dead man alone. While waiting for the ambulance he pieced together the scenario in his mind, but found it hard to believe Nathan had been capable of it all. The man had been a confirmed pacifist. What's more, the killer had been seven feet tall and Nathan only five foot six. Daniels felt awed.

He let his eyes drift back to Nathan's face, smiled at the peaceful expression there, lines of premature age smoothed by death.

He did not know how Nathan had done it. That was obviously one secret Trooper would take to his grave.

Daniels stood and went to the sink to stub out his cigarette. He wondered who the killer had been before mutating into a monster. He wondered if Curtis would let him tie off the loose ends. He hoped so. This had been one hell of a weird investigation, and he thought he had earned the right to put it to rest.

The faint sound of sirens reached him across the fields.

Behind him, Nathan began to cough up blood.

Daniels nearly pissed himself with fright.

CHAPTER FIVE

Unfinished Business

January 4, 1991. 12.15 pm. London, England

Post-mortems. John Daniels hated them. That was why he had decided not to attend. And if the look on Bartholomew Cummings' face was anything to go by, he had made the right decision.

They sat in their local pub, surrounded by silence. Daniels thought that probably had something to do with the smell seeping from the pathologist's every pore. Cummings had changed his clothes and showered twice since leaving the morgue, but could not get rid of the stench – it clung to him like a shroud of flies. He sipped his pint slowly, face bloodless and covered with a sheen of sweat.

'So,' Daniels prompted, 'anything to tell me?'

Cummings looked up from his beer, eyes focusing on Daniels as if from a great distance. He shook his head. 'I don't believe it, John. In thirty years I've seen nothing like it.'

Daniels had to agree.

'I mean,' Cummings continued, 'I've seen decay before. I've cut up bodies which have been dead for a long time. But *this* guy – Jesus! The state of him, and the *smell*!' He shook his head in disbelief. 'His fingers, his *eyes* . . .' He looked up, locked eyes with the Inspector. 'Tell me John – what the fuck's going on here?'

Daniels managed a tired grin. He wondered how Cummings would respond if he knew the corpse had been walking around and talking looking like that. 'What makes you think I have all the answers?'

Cummings snorted. 'Are there any?'

Daniels wondered as much himself. He was plagued by images of Nathan and their man pinned to the wall. 'So, any clues?'

Cummings shook his head dejectedly. 'Nope. Up to my armpits in filth and putrefaction, and all for nothing. Prints and dentals all gone, body completely decayed, no natural features whatsoever.' He shuddered. 'Only thing I got is that ring. You may be lucky – it's so big there may be a jeweller's stamp on it. I didn't look.'

'I'll get on it right away. Nothing else?'

'No. We cut him apart, took his rotten clothes to pieces, and nothing. No wallet, no ID, no photos, nothing. Just the ring.'

Daniels sat back in his chair, exhausted. It seemed his loose ends might remain untied after all. Having seen the killer, he knew how Cummings felt. 'Another drink?' he offered.

'So.' Anne Wallis crossed her legs, smoothed her skirt. She was nervous. Daniels could see that. 'You found him.'

He nodded. 'Yes, we found him. We got him.'

She met his gaze, eyes haunted. 'He's dead? You're sure?'

Daniels could understand how she felt. Sometimes he was not sure himself . . . not until he remembered his kitchen. 'Yes, Anne, he's dead. He won't be bothering you, or anyone else, ever again.'

Something in his voice clearly hit home. She relaxed, seemed to melt in the chair, relief flooding her face. For a while neither spoke. Then Daniels cleared his throat. 'You're free to go back to your flat, if you want to. If there's anything we can do, just ask.'

She massaged her temples. 'I can't believe it's over.'

'I know. But believe me, it is,' he said with conviction.

She looked up. 'How is he?'

'Nathan?' Daniels shrugged. 'I don't know. He lost a lot of blood. The doctors aren't saying much, but I think he'll be OK.'

Her expression was unreadable. She was thinking about that night in the hospital, when Trooper had helped her overcome the terror. She remembered feeling safe in his arms. 'Can I see him?'

He leaned back in the chair, blew out his cheeks. 'I don't see why not.' He watched her face for a reaction, detected none. Her request struck him as odd. What did she care? 'But I think there are a few things you should know about him first.'

'Oh?' She was intrigued, and not a little worried, by the Inspector's attitude. Was Trooper such an enigma? 'Such as?'

Daniels wondered how to explain it all, as if it could be explained. He smiled wearily. 'Do you mind if I smoke?'

Fowles, strangely subdued since his spell in the morgue with Cummings, was waiting for Daniels on his return. 'How's Cummings?'

Daniels grunted. 'As pale as you. Any luck with that ring?'

'I'm expecting Baxter any minute. He's chasing it up.' Fowles handed him a sheet of paper. 'Meanwhile, look at that.'

Daniels scanned the page. A stolen car with American diplomatic plates had been recovered in South London, wrecked and stripped bare. 'And?' Daniels prompted. He saw no connection, yet knew Fowles would not waste his time with trivia.

Fowles grinned. 'Never reported stolen, sir. Found this morning by some junkie who woke up in an abandoned warehouse.'

Daniels felt his bowels tighten instinctively. 'Don't tell me. The owner hasn't been seen for days?'

Fowles broadened his grin. '*Weeks*. And there's more.'

Daniels squashed a groan. 'A body in the car,' he stated.

Fowles was impressed. 'Yup. Prostitute. Mutilated.'

'Got a name?'

'For the prostitute?'

'No!' Daniels snapped. 'For the diplomat.'

Fowles grinned sheepishly. Some colour returned to his cheeks for the first time since he had seen Daniels' bloody kitchen. 'Yes sir. A junior clerk by the name of Stuart Corbett. Nobody missed him for days, then they thought he was just sick.'

'For weeks, without him calling in?' Daniels was suspicious.

Fowles shrugged. 'Like I said, very junior.'

'You got a call out for this guy?'

'Yes, sir. And photos distributed.'

Daniels re-read the report, surprised at how neatly it fit all of a sudden. 'But we won't find him, will we Fowles?'

Fowles pursed his lips. 'I think we already have, sir.'

'Got an address?'

'Yes. We were just waiting for you.'

Daniels nodded. 'Good. Let's go then.'

They ran into a very excited Sergeant Baxter on the

way out. 'Inspector! That ring – we traced it. Custom made, crucifix and all. The jeweller even remembered the man who bought it.'

Daniels was beginning to think this was all far too easy. He had a horrible feeling the ring and the car would not tie up. 'Got a name or anything?' Please, he prayed, let them match.

Baxter grinned from ear to ear. 'And an address. The man paid by credit card, had the ring delivered by courier.'

'And?' Daniels prompted, his heart hammering.

'Young American bloke by the name of Stuart Corbett.'

Daniels nearly passed out in relief. They had him at last . . .

The stench was unbelievable. Daniels could not believe the neighbours had not reported it to the police. Three of his team were forced to retire from the house, violently ill; one passed out.

The smell was not the worst of it. Maggots writhed in every corner, larvae swarmed in the cushions of the sofa, pieces of dead flesh smeared every surface. The entire place screamed neglect and decay. It was the most disgusting thing Daniels had ever seen.

Or so he thought. Until Fowles found Corbett's eyes, two weeks dead and seething with tiny flies, lying discarded in a coffee mug in the bedroom. Fowles fled in disgust – only to return some moments later, drawn by a desire to finish it once and for all.

Daniels decided his sergeant might have the makings of a true policeman after all.

Unpleasant photographs were strewn over the furniture. Tacky polaroids of poor quality, they nonetheless depicted in adequate detail the killer's foul metamorphosis. Self portraits of a man staring in horror at his reflection in the mirror, growing by the day and rotting from the inside out. These pictures, portraying inexorable and unwanted mutation, would haunt Daniels to his grave.

They found Corbett's diary. The last entry, dated November 17, 1990, read: 'Compassionate leave from tomorrow. I'm going back home to find out what all these Black dreams are about.'

Daniels had no idea what it meant.

They found many things, most of them disgusting, and carefully bagged and tagged them for examination and disposal. But Daniels left the house that night convinced it was all far from over.

January 5, 1991. 8:00 p.m.

'Is he going to be all right?' Tim asked in a small voice, sitting in a wheelchair with his leg in plaster beside Nathan's prone form.

'Oh, I think so,' Daniels replied, smiling. 'You know him better than I do – he's a tough old bird, isn't he?'

Tim managed a smile. 'Yes. He saved my life, you know.'

'I know. And mine. And my wife's, and my daughter's.'

'Are they all right?'

'Yes, they're fine, thank you. How's your father?'

'Asleep.' Tim grinned like a little devil. 'With Mum.'

Daniels laughed. He liked the boy; he liked the mischievous glint in the lad's eyes. Tim stared at Nathan, his eyes haunted and sad. 'When is he going to wake up?'

Daniels studied Trooper. His face was pale and lined, his eyes were closed, and he was still completely motionless. He looked dead, and only the EEG said otherwise. 'I don't know, Tim. When he's good and ready, I suppose. He needs the rest – it's been a long week for him.' He looked at his watch. 'I think it's bed-time for you, too. You might not be in hospital any more, but—'

'I know, I know, I'm just a kid.'

Daniels grinned. 'No, you're not. Not any more. People may think you are, but you aren't. Nathan was very proud of you.'

Tim blushed beetroot red to his roots, but smiled with pride.

Daniels stood, indicating that the visit was over. 'Come on then, Tim. I'll get my sergeant to run you home.'

Tim closed his eyes. He wished he could believe the inspector, but everytime he looked at Nathan he saw only blood and a headless corpse. He wished he could lose the vision, or change its outcome as he had with his father, but Trooper was slipping from his life and Tim knew he had no influence there. He opened his eyes, looked at Nathan. *Don't die*, he prayed silently, vainly. *I need you.*

Then he sighed and allowed Daniels to push him from the room.

Daniels stood alone on a desert plain, unarmed and naked. In the distance, a huge cloud of dust marked the advance of an enormous horde. But he could not turn, or run, or move a muscle.

From out of the dust figures appeared. Tall figures, all scrambling and clawing mindlessly. As they approached, Daniels realized with brain-numbing horror that none of them had eyes.

Behind each monster ran a score of lifeless victims, shackled to their killer, stumbling across the sand. There was no end to the line of beasts, and no end to their prey. They consumed all life in their path. Where one killer fell, he merely passed behind another beast and joined the ranks of shackled souls as they passed.

Daniels stood alone in their path, defenceless, helpless, the only surviving witness to the tide of evil which sped towards him.

Until, at long last, all but one of the creatures remained. Behind it shambled the entirety of Humanity. The eyeless mutant came to rest before him, grinning, streaks of pus leaking from every pore and orifice. 'You stopped my minions,' it said tonelessly, 'but you did not stop me. You should have learned by now never to leave any business unfinished.'

Then the creature reached out its clawed hands. As Daniels watched, unable to move, the clawed hands encircled his throat.

He opened his mouth to scream his despair and . . . the telephone rang.

He jumped in shock, temporarily disoriented, hand reaching automatically for the phone. With agonizing slowness the nightmare faded from his mind, leaving behind a sensation of impending doom.

He wiped his hand across his face, tasting stale coffee and cigarettes in his mouth. He had been smoking heavily since the night in his house, unable to ease the horror, to lose the tight feeling in his bowels. His intestines were telling him that the job was not yet finished. His lungs were telling him that one hundred and fifty cigarettes a day was pushing it.

'Daniels,' he murmured, raising the phone to his ear as he glanced at the clock. It was seven-thirty in the morning.

'Inspector, it's Fowles here. I'm at the hospital. Trooper just regained consciousness. He says he needs to talk to you. I told him you were on leave, but he was most insistent.'

Daniels groaned. 'What does he have to say for himself?'

'Not much, sir. He just told me to tell you there was some unfinished business. Does that mean anything to you?'

Daniels thought of the dream. Then he was already reaching for his clothes . . .

'So,' Daniels prompted, shifting his behind on the uncomfortable hospital chair. 'Speak.'

Trooper paused, marshalling the chaos of information in his mind. 'I learned much in my meeting with the killer, Inspector. And even more during my sleep.' Unbidden, an image surfaced in his mind – an image from Tim's mind, of himself with his head torn off and torso streaming with blood. Nathan knew Tim's gift – he knew what that image signified and why he should be afraid.

But he shrugged the thought aside and looked up.

Daniels did not notice the look flicker across Nathan's face. 'Hold it right there. Is this police business?' Trooper looked at him blankly. 'I mean, am I here in my professional capacity?'

Trooper shook his head, the movement making him wince. 'No, Inspector. This has gone way beyond your jurisdiction. While your superiors may be less than happy with your explanations they are satisfied the case is closed. I merely wish to talk to you because you understand. You may even harbour some concern for the future.'

Daniels thought of the dream. He kept thinking of the dream. 'Fine. Well, for a start you can stop calling me Inspector. We've been through enough crap together to dispense with that.' He sighed. 'Second, this is not finished at all, is it?'

Trooper opened his mouth to protest, then glumly shook his head. Daniels sighed. He had thought as much. There was, he knew, unfinished business. Trooper gave him a sombre look. 'No, it has not. And what made you say that?'

Daniels snorted. 'Dreams, bad feelings, instinct.' He shrugged. 'I just feel the first killing on Christmas Eve opened up a vast can of worms. And sticking a knife in that bastard's throat did not put the lid back on.'

Nathan flinched, unwilling to remember just what he had done to the hapless Stuart Corbett. 'Well, at least I am not alone in my fears. But I shall understand if you decide not to help – your family has suffered enough. I can ask no more of you.'

Daniels shrugged again, drew some cigarettes from his coat pocket and lit one. He had no shame – smoking in hospitals was one of his hobbies. 'All right. But I'll hear you out first. I shan't rest easy until the last nail is hammered home into this coffin either. So fire away.'

Trooper settled himself into the bed, shifting his weight to ease the pressure on his wound. He was doped up to his eyeballs with pain-killers, but his mind was still disgustingly aware.

'I do not have all the answers – the picture is clearer, but still not complete.' He drew a deep breath. 'You already know about Bill Wallis, the two gays, Corbett, and Tim. What you don't know is that on Christmas Day in Arizona, a man was attacked by another of these things. I do not know much more than that, but I *do* know he survived. And that was only the start. If you checked with Reuters you would find similar killings in Japan, Asia, Africa, Germany, Russia and Canada. All these are documented. I am amazed nobody spotted a connection. I suppose it says something for modern society that a white South African killing fifteen blacks with a chainsaw could be accepted as part of everyday life, and not even warrant a mention in the news.'

'You've seen these reports?' Daniels knew Trooper had not.

'No. I just know they happened.' He took a deep breath. 'I guess I really ought to explain what the hell is going on, otherwise you won't grasp how serious this is.' He paused. 'You know I can detect the thoughts emanating from your brain. But your brain is just part of a vast net of minds, all linked by the energy they produce. It is that energy I can sense and tap into. I know now that the killer became stronger after each killing, as if he was using the psychic power of his victims to boost his own strength. When I fought him, I could sense the dead bound to him, feeding him.' Nathan recalled the multiple minds and personalities he had used for ammunition in the battle. 'As his power increased, so did his madness. Until he was totally out of control.'

Daniels had an image of his dream – killers, thousands of them, each with countless dead behind them. It was like a modern vampire story. Yet Daniels had learned not to disregard Trooper's explanations: weird they may be, but he had not been wrong once and in these circumstances that was a pretty good track record.

'The madman I faced in your house said: "Go ahead, kill me. It will only make us stronger." Trooper looked up, his eyes bottomless pits of darkness. '*Us*, John was what he said. *Us*. That bonding, that linking of psychic power, had formed a chain within the net. These killers murdered people, grew stronger, then died. Their energy was reclaimed, and each of the others becomes more powerful as a result. Do you understand what that means? As we kill them, the others just get stronger, and then they are harder to kill. It's like catch-22, a no-win scenario.'

Daniels drank the words like poison, recalling the dream again. Killers dying, rising to join the ranks of dead . . . until only one remained. He shivered. 'How many are left?' he asked softly, not wishing to know the answer.

'The killers pull power from the net like vampires sucking blood. Personality traits, sexual hang-ups or violent tendencies become dominant characteristics. The process is mild at first, but as the power increases so does their capacity for it. With that comes a weird mutation, as if the body becomes a reflection of the corrupted mind. Tissue rots, fingernails undergo a surge of growth, the entire skeleton experiences some massive input of hormone or drug. Then you have another maniac, totally consumed by lust for souls and the desire for more power. A violent spiral towards what they see as immortality. It is as if all their social inhibitions just drop away and allow them to do exactly what they want.

'My view of the net has expanded since I confronted the killer that night – in order to beat him, I had to take some of his raw power. And yes, I know where it comes from – his victims. But you must understand that it is not people now, John, just raw energy. Besides which, the purpose I intend to use it for is rather less disgusting than the insane murder of innocents.'

Daniels waved his cigarette vaguely. 'I never said a word against you, Nathan,' he said calmly. Mainly because I don't really understand a word you're saying, he thought.

'I can see much more now, and as I slept I saw nodes vanish while others grew larger. And a lot of them were going, on cue, as if a huge experiment had come to an end. Now I can only see one.' He shook his head, horrified. 'John, you have no comprehension of the size of this thing. It is simply *huge*. An enormous bloat of psychic power the likes of which I'm sure nobody has ever seen before.' He shuddered. 'And still it kills, and grows.' He looked up. 'I must stop it. It is a violation of nature, and must be wiped from the face of this planet before it consumes everything.'

Daniels met the burning gaze, horrified, but not surprised. He thought of all he had been through to catch and kill the last psychopath. Now Trooper was telling him that had been a walk in the park. 'Is there any way you could be wrong?' he asked meekly.

'Perhaps.' He paused. 'But I do not think so. You tell me. What do *you* feel? Do *you* think I am wrong?'

Daniels did not need to think before answering that question. 'No, I think you're right.' He shrugged. 'I dunno. I just wanted a little more time. Before it all starts again.' He sighed. 'The last one was bad enough. Just what is this one going to be like?'

Trooper snorted. 'Bloody awful, I think. But the cycle can start over if we are not quick. Those killers came in a phase, appearing, killing, dying and leaving the original killer more powerful than ever. If he did it once, he can do it again. And with each person he kills, he grows stronger.' Trooper took a deep breath. 'And *that* is something I simply cannot allow.'

'You say "he". You reckon it's all down to one person?'

'I do.'

'You stopped my minions, but you did not stop me.' Daniels wondered absently if Nathan had had the same dream.

He regarded the psychic, pondering his words. The sane part of his mind thought the entire matter ridiculous. But that part of his mind had been battered in recent days, and Daniels had learned to ignore it. He could no longer accept that the world was just as he imagined – into the stagnant pond of his life had been dropped an enormous boulder, and the ripples had far from subsided. The other part of his brain, the part that acted on gut feeling and instinct, had been having a field day since Trooper had arrived. It had often been proved correct, however insane things may have seemed.

So Daniels did not reject Trooper's paranoid delusions. In fact, he accepted them without question. Because somewhere, deep down, he knew they were right. 'Where?' he asked simply.

Trooper looked up at the note of finality and decisiveness in Daniels' tone. 'America. That was where it started, and that is where it must end. In Arizona lies the only remaining loose end.'

Daniels frowned. If only it were that easy, he thought.

'Yes,' Trooper commented. 'If only.'

'Stop that!' Daniels snapped. 'My head is private property.'

Trooper blushed. 'I'm sorry. It's just that you sometimes think so clearly, so loudly, that I hear it even when I am closed.'

Daniels pulled a face. 'Well, I'll take your word for it. I'll also accept your theory, since I have a feeling you're right. And as I am currently on extended leave, staying in a hotel until the house is clean again, what's next?'

'What about your wife and daughter?' Trooper asked, surprised by Daniels' keenness. 'They need you now, surely?'

Daniels chuckled. 'Apparently not. They can hardly remember a thing. Selective amnesia, I've been told, the brain's way of protecting itself.' He sighed. 'Lucky them. My brain doesn't seem to be selective at all – I can remember everything. So the wife is staying with her folks, and Louise has gone back to college.'

Trooper picked at one of his stubby and chewed fingernails. 'She is not, you know,' he said quietly.

'Not what?' Daniels asked, confused.

'A lesbian. Your daughter.' He shrugged, embarrassed. 'Just thought you might like to know.'

Daniels looked at him blankly for a moment. Then, unable to think of anything sensible to say, he burst out laughing.

That evening, thirteen days after the killing began, Nathan discharged himself from hospital. He had to agree with the doctor who protested about his injuries. Only three days had passed since he had been shot, and he was hardly recovered. But being cooped up in a hospital full of sick people was never Nathan's idea of a good time. He was getting headaches and nosebleeds and depressed, just as he had all those years ago in the asylum, just as he always did when surrounded by people – listening to people die was no fun.

Rather than waste any more of their precious time, Nathan booked two tickets on a scheduled flight to America. By midnight, doped to the eyeballs with painkillers and vodka, Trooper sat sleeping beside Daniels as they hurtled at 600 miles an hour into the conclusion of their mutual nightmare.

Daniels did not sleep. He stared out of the window at the dark clouds, wondering just what the hell he had got himself into.

That night Anne Wallis lay in the bed in her London flat for the first time in what seemed like years, and dreamed . . .

She crouched in a stark white hospital room, sobbing

and heart broken. Her husband Bill lay naked on the floor, routinely screwing a stream of women who came and went without end.

'How could you not know?' he jibed. 'Are you blind?'

She screamed and clamped her hands over her ears to cut out his voice. She closed her eyes to cut out the sight of him inside another woman. But the words resounded in her mind, and the images were imprinted on the inside of her eyelids. 'You can run, Anne,' he laughed, 'but you can't hide. You can never hide.'

But then the door opened in a blaze of pure light to reveal the figure of a man. His hair was long and white, and flowed behind him; his eyes were the deepest pools Anne had ever seen. He pointed a long, fine finger at her startled husband. 'Leave now,' he commanded in a voice as deep as an ocean. 'You are not welcome here.'

The vision of her husband screamed, flickered and vanished.

Anne opened her eyes and ears as the man crossed to kneel beside her and embraced her. Images of happiness and laughter rose in her mind, eclipsing the horror, until her sobbing was spent. It was all she had ever wanted. It was why Bill's death had hurt her so much, not just the loss but the betrayal of her trust and dreams.

And still the images flowed. 'Remember these,' the man murmured. 'I care for you, and will not see you harmed.'

Then, without warning, he was gone.

In sudden panic she ran from the room, chasing his departing image. She ran until her lungs burned, but the source of light and hope remained beyond her grasp. Without that light her heart was desolate, lost. With it she was whole.

For years she ran, but never did the light seem any closer . . . until, when her spirits were at their lowest ebb, the light expanded to fill her eyes with warmth and comfort. And then she found him, entering a hall of such wonder that she gasped at its beauty.

On the floor of that hall the man lay dying in a pool of life-blood which pulsed with spilled power. Anne dropped in horror beside the white-haired figure, screaming her anguish as her hopes crashed around her. She took him in her arms, desperately trying to staunch the flow of blood, weeping as he died and was lost to her.

His eyes opened one last time, filled with the haunting gaze of betrayal. 'I am lost,' he whispered. 'But remember me, for I cared for you and did not let you be harmed.'

Then, smiling softly at her face, his body went limp in her arms and the last breath drifted from his lips.

Anne raised her head to wail her loss. Yet when she looked down through her tears the white-haired man was gone. In her arms she held the broken form of Nathan Trooper . . .

She woke with a gasp, the bed clothes clutched tightly to her breast, her mind filled with the dream.

'Oh, Nathan!' she whispered, her brain a turmoil of unexpected emotions. She remembered his concern for her at the hospital, when he had soothed the agony from her mind. She pieced together the broken images of that night in her grief, and she thought of her sense of loss when she had woken, and he was no longer there.

There was no guilt in her when she thought of him – *dreamed* of him. Memories of Bill were now exactly that – her grief had been tempered by the unavoidable revelations of her tormentor, of THE VOICE, the images and lies which had always been the truth.

And now Bill was gone and she was, in a way, glad. She could not have lived with him knowing what she did about him. Yet Nathan was also gone, and with him that fleeting feeling of security.

She had visited him in hospital hoping it would reconcile her feelings, but his broken form had done nothing to help. He had been at once pathetic and inspiring – she knew she owed him her life, but found it hard to believe he was capable. She had come away from her visit, and Daniels' bizarre cautionary words, more confused than ever.

All she knew was that her life, like her flat, was now empty. And that the sense of unfinished business in her thoughts and dreams was not fading with the days.

BOOK FIVE

DEATH AND VARIATIONS

CHAPTER ONE

The Lights Are Off,
But Somebody's Home

January 7, 1991, 5 a.m. Arizona, USA.

Such was the beauty of modern air travel. After spending ten hours in the air, Trooper and Daniels touched down in Arizona only three hours after leaving London. At 4 a.m. local time they took possession of a four-wheel-drive jeep and drove off into the dawn.

Daniels sat in the passenger seat, too tired to think or move, his brain a fog of jet-lagged sleeplessness. Never before had he crossed so many time zones. Never again.

On occasion Nathan cast him a troubled glance before returning his attention to the road. Groggy from pain-killers and drink, his right side in agony, he drove the jeep like a man possessed. To each side, feature-less and barren scrub passed by in the half-light. The endless tarmac sped rumbling beneath his wheels. He chain-smoked, eyes bleary in the glare of oncoming headlights.

All around him the bloated presence of the killer tugged at his sanity. Never had one node in the psychic net loomed so huge in his mind. Never had he felt so sick to his stomach.

Yet even through the stench of that decay he could

271

sense his friend's unease and pain. Trooper was unwilling to open his mind to help him – even firmly closed, the power of THE OTHER was so great he detected every trickle from the outside world, and that alone was enough to make him want to turn and run. He dared not think what would happen if he opened up to Daniels – perhaps his mind would be flooded with decay. Perhaps he would simply go insane.

So he smoked and drove, chewed his fingers to bloody stumps, and felt guilty. His one ally in the world needed his aid and he was too scared to offer any. Cursing himself for asking the man to accompany him in the first place, he battened down his hatches.

Eventually Daniels fell asleep anyway.

At 6 a.m., as the vehicle nosed into the first grey streaks of dawn, Nathan woke to the sound of a blaring horn. Hauling on the wheel, he pulled the jeep from the road and skidded to a halt in the dust. The other car rushed past him, horn fading into the night.

Daniels snored softly, unaware of the near-disaster.

Trooper eased himself out of the jeep. He forced himself to relax, monitoring his heart as the loud thud steadied. Then he spat the dry taste in his mouth out onto the yellow grass, and urinated.

What the hell am I doing here? he thought. What is this poor bastard in the car doing with me? This is *my* fight, not his. And I do not even know where I am going or what I am looking for.

He stood and looked out at the world, bemused and frustrated. A week earlier he had left his home because his nightmares told him a young boy was in trouble. Since then he had been accused of murder, shot and he had killed a man in cold blood. Now he was pushing himself to the limit to murder again.

Why? He abhorred killing, a legacy from the summer of 1964. Yet he'd had few qualms over that twelve-inch blade. What right had he to take Corbett's life? Or any other?

'All the right in the world, Nathan. We are not discussing morality, here. We are dealing with a disease which must be stamped out. You are all that stands between HIM and countless victims.'

Trooper smiled fondly, his troubled mind suddenly filled with peace. Just as it always did when he conversed with his brother. 'Hello, Isaac. It's nice to hear your voice. How are you?'

There was a whispering chuckle in his mind. 'Oh, same as usual I suppose. As well as can be expected for a dead man.'

'I have not heard from you since Christmas Eve. Why now?'

'I came because you needed some bucking up, idiot. There's no way I am going to sit back and watch you surrender to some misplaced sense of guilt. That way lies death, and all its variations.'

Nathan looked out over the scrub, basking in the dawn glow. Inside the jeep Daniels slumped against the window, his face smeared like wet putty over the glass. 'I have killed a man.'

'I know. But there is a need here which outweighs yours. That man had to die and so must the next – too much blood is upon their hands, and more will follow. The cycle will begin again when HE is ready. Will you stand by as another Tim Johnson experiences that horror, or as another Anne Wallis endures such torture?'

The words, though spoken strongly, were kind and sympathetic. And at mention of Tim and Anne, Nathan's flagging resolve hardened; his determination to do his best, whatever the cost, was restored.

'No, I will not allow that.' He sighed. 'Forgive me.'

'Do not curse yourself, Nathan. Remember that both you and I were possessed by guilt for years. In you, it led to a desire to use your gift for good and a vow against violence. In me, guilt at not being able to protect you and our mother drove me to drugs. Guilt destroyed me, brother. Do not let it destroy you as well. You must stop.'

Nathan listened to the advice, but for some reason could not tear his deepest thoughts from Anne Wallis. The mention of her name had dredged up the tangled emotions of the time he had spent with her. He wondered if she remembered the episode.

Nathan was not used to thinking about anyone except himself. He had spent so much of his life in his head that he did not even know *what* he was feeling. For him, men and women stood under one universal title: headaches. So he did not understand what was so different about Anne Wallis. Perhaps being alone was no longer enough.

His wandering mind was brought back on track by the amused and warm laughter of his dead brother, playing carelessly in his mind. 'Well, well, I'll be damned. The man of ice melts at last. You have no idea how long I've waited for this moment.'

Nathan blushed. 'Shut up, Isaac, I'm too tired for games.'

His brother's chuckles faded into the wind. 'Sorry, Nathan. Why don't you get some sleep? Follow your friend's example.'

Nathan glanced at Daniels, found the idea very attractive. 'But what about you? You always disappear when I turn my back, and are never around when I want you. You'll stay in touch?'

'When necessary,' his brother replied evasively. 'This

is the big one, Nathan. I won't let you balls it up. Get some rest, OK?'

Nathan sighed, his eyelids heavy. 'OK. Deal.'

He felt Isaac's presence slip from his mind, leaving a sad emptiness. Too exhausted to argue, he climbed back into the jeep, rolled his jacket up into a pillow, and fell asleep.

He started to dream almost immediately . . . of a red Volkswagen parked on the hard shoulder facing into the sunset, of a young policeman who had his universe turned on its head and half his face torn off, of a seven-foot beast from hell dressed in tatters of old clothing which ran with rotten food, caked blood and liquid flesh. The beast had no hair and his face was a mask of infection which ran from empty eye sockets, nose and mouth. His hands terminated in three-inch claws, curved like eagle talons, from which hung tatters of human muscle and tendon.

He dreamed of the young policeman, and just as he dreamed the name of Bill Wallis on the fate-filled night of Christmas Eve, so he dreamed the name most important to him now . . . so that he awoke, refreshed if unsettled, and at least had an objective. According to the map, a small town lay up ahead. According to his instinct, the man he sought lived in that town. And according to his dream, the man's name was Sam Stevens.

He pulled over at a garage and had the jeep filled with gas. While the attendant rang up a dent in Nathan's huge wad of bills, he crossed to the phone box. There was only one 'Stevens' in the phone book. How convenient, he thought. Then he ripped out the page and returned to the car, whistling softly.

'Are you sure this is the right place?' Daniels asked quietly.

Nathan re-checked the address on the slip of paper, and glanced over at the mailbox. 'Yes, I think so.'

'You're sure you think so? Or you think you're sure?'

Nathan grinned. 'Yes, I am sure this is the right place.'

The huge house was set back from the road and obscured by a line of trees. Long and low with a Roman roof and marble colonnade, the house looked more like a Mediterranean villa than the home of an American traffic cop. A fountain decorated the centre of a massive garden, kept lush against the elements and the dry soil by an extensive network of sprinklers. The whole area smelled sweet and cool, and stank of money. It was not exactly what Trooper had expected to find in a small Arizona town.

Daniels looked at Nathan, a wry smile on his face, one eyebrow raised in characteristic question. 'A bit flash for a traffic cop, don't you think? Maybe I'm working in the wrong country.'

Trooper returned the smile. 'You've not done badly yourself.'

'Not as well as this,' Daniels said defensively. 'It's just that my old man left me some cash when he died.'

Trooper chuckled. 'Not as much as Sam Stevens' dad. He is still alive, and he practically *owns* this town.'

Daniels pulled a face. 'So what now? It looks deserted – no car, no lights. But my guts reckon he's here, hiding. Do we sit all day and see if he comes out?'

Trooper shook his head. 'No. I suggest we go in.'

'I had a feeling you'd say that. So have you got a plan, or were you just going to walk up to the front door and ring the bell?'

Nathan grinned. 'That *was* my plan, actually.'

Daniels chuckled. 'I thought it would be.'

They left the jeep and wandered up the drive towards

the front door, Nathan slightly in the lead. He opened his mind a little to see whether his prey was in the area, but the sick crescendo was too painful. He was forced to close in on himself before he could get a bearing. However, the volume of those thoughts was such that Nathan could safely assume the killer was close.

Trooper ascended the three steps, stopped at the door and turned. He was surprised to see that Daniels had stopped some yards away, and was peering at one of the windows. 'What is it?'

'A window,' Daniels replied sourly, joining him at the door. 'Somebody's home, that's for sure. The lights are on indoors.'

'Really? I couldn't see them.'

Daniels snorted. 'No, neither did I until I looked closer. You can just see slits of light through the shutters.' He frowned. 'If I didn't know better, I'd say they were boarded up inside.'

Nathan opened his mouth to ridicule that comment, but closed it again after a moment's thought. 'Maybe they are,' he said quietly. 'If you were attacked by something huge and rotten with claws, would you not run home and board up the doors and windows?'

Daniels smiled. 'Possibly. Maybe I'd just fly to Rio.'

'Ah, no solution my friend. Because you can run, but you can't hide. Not from this thing.' He scratched his jaw. 'Mr Stevens is a remarkable man. He insulted that psycho by escaping, and two weeks later he is still alive. Quite amazing, I think.'

Daniels shrugged. 'All well and good. But are you going to stand here discussing relative psychology or ring the damned bell?'

Nathan rang the damned bell. Several times. Then he hammered on the door. Each time there was no response.

Eventually Daniels lost his patience. He shouldered Nathan aside and smashed the palm of his hand on the oak door. 'Stevens!' he shouted, 'we know you're in there.' No answer. 'Sam, open the door we want to talk to you.' Silence. 'My name is Chief Inspector John Daniels from London, England. I'm here investigating a murder.' No response. 'Mr Stevens, we know you were attacked on Christmas Day. We have good reason to believe the attacks are connected.' More silence. 'For God's sake man!' he bellowed. 'We know you're in trouble. We're here to help. It's true you can't hide. But we can at least stand together and kill the sonofabitch!'

His tirade over, Daniels stepped back from the door, face red with frustration and anger. 'If that doesn't bring the bastard out of his hole, I'll drive the bloody jeep through his front door.'

But the ploy seemed to work. From inside came the sounds of bolts being thrown back and nails being pulled from resistant wood. Slits of light appeared through the glass panels in the door.

Eventually Sam spoke. 'There's a 12-gauge aimed at your gizzard, stranger, and it's got a really light action. I ain't slept recently, so I suggest you ease back in case I decorate my garden with your intestines.'

Nathan swallowed. He disliked guns. But Daniels seemed to relax at last. 'And about time too, I must say. May we come in?'

'You got any ID? Slowly now, 'cos I'm *real* jumpy.'

Daniels carefully extracted his wallet and stepped forward, holding it up clearly. 'Can you read that?' he asked.

'Nope. But if you were who I thought you were, you'd be inside carving me up instead of fucking around on the doorstep.' A shadow moved behind the door. 'I'll have to rip these planks off. Talk amongst yourselves for a while.'

Daniels retreated from the doorway, lit two cigarettes and handed one to Trooper. 'Well, he sounds sane enough.'

Trooper grinned. 'Maybe.'

Light flooded through the door as nails were drawn and planks were torn down. It sounded like a coffin lid being removed, but Nathan supposed that was a fair comparison. Sam had, after all, shut himself away in his own tomb for the past two weeks.

Then came the sound of bolts being thrown back, of keys turning in locks. Daniels watched the door with one eye and kept the other on the road. The last thing he wanted was to have their opponent use this innocent opportunity to enter the house unawares.

Finally the door opened an inch.

'I've still got my gun. I guess I'm a tad paranoid. So come in real slow and easy, with your hands where I can see 'em.'

'We're not armed,' Nathan said lamely.

'Well, I am. Be smart, old man, 'cos old is better than dead.'

Daniels pushed the door open and walked slowly in. Nathan followed, conscious of the unseen gun. They entered a spacious hall, panelled with dark oak, decorated with photographs.

When Nathan was inside the door he felt the gun barrel prod the small of his back. The pressure made him want to turn around.

'Don't!' Stevens said sharply. The door slammed shut. Locks were thrown. Neither Daniels nor Trooper dared turn. They stood, backs to the American, hands at their sides. Daniels yawned.

'Now, don't try anything smart,' Stevens warned.

Before Sam had even finished speaking, Daniels felt the strong and professional hand of the young traffic cop travel in swift, economical arcs over his shoulders and down his sides. Then the hand sped up and down each of his legs. Trooper received the same treatment.

Quick, thought Daniels, quietly impressed. Stevens had verified that they were both 'clean' in about six seconds. He had obviously done that before – lots of times.

'OK,' Sam said cheerfully. 'I guess you are who you say you are.' He paused. 'So what are a couple of English detectives doing in my humble abode, Chief Inspector John Stewart Daniels?'

On reflex, Daniels reached into his pocket to take out his ID, in the same instant realizing that he had not told Stevens his middle name and that his wallet had gone. He laughed. 'Ever consider taking up a profession on the other side of the law, Mr Stevens?' he asked mildly. 'You're one of the slickest pick-pockets I've ever seen, and I've seen a few.'

'Nope. Around here, Inspector, I *am* the law.' The gun barrel dropped from their backs. They both felt the atmosphere in the room change noticeably. 'OK, you can turn round now.'

The first thing Daniels noticed about the traffic cop was the three-inch scar on his left cheek. The wound had healed badly, and the seam between torn flesh and face was livid and bruised. Rough stitching held the skin in place. Stevens was clean shaven, his hair was close cropped and he looked well fed. The only evidence of his ordeal was the tired purple shadow under each eye.

Stevens returned the cool stare, sizing up his visitors with a practised eye. He seemed satisfied that Daniels, a tall angular man with cold blue eyes, was a policeman. But his forehead creased in a slight frown when he switched his attention to Trooper. A question rose to his lips, but Nathan was well ahead of him.

'No, Mr Stevens, I am not.'

'What?' Stevens asked, taken aback.

Trooper smiled. 'How did I know you were thinking that?' His smile broadened. 'Yes, just what the hell is going on, Sam?' Nathan raised his eyebrows in question, pursed his lips, then turned on his heel and stalked off into the house.

Stevens looked with confusion at Daniels, who grinned. 'Don't let it worry you,' Daniels said reassuringly. 'It's just his way.'

Stevens opened his mouth to speak, but Nathan's voice from the lounge cut him off. 'Nice place, Sam. Shame about all this new woodwork, though. Rather spoils the effect, don't you think?' There was a pause. 'Ooh, guns. Ready for a siege were you?'

'What the hell *is* this?' Stevens spat. Confused, he stormed after the errant Englishman. He felt he had lost the initiative. He really did not know what to make of the short, odd, hunched-up stranger – but he was certainly no cop.

'Who the hell are you?' he demanded, confronting Nathan by the stack of planks on which his armoury had lain, unused, for nearly two weeks. 'What the hell do you think you're doing in my house?'

Nathan ignored him. 'Are your kids OK, Sam? How's Tracey? One hundred and fifty six threatening phone calls already, eh? I bet you're really tired of them now, eh?' Trooper wandered casually around the room as he spoke. The barrel of Sam's shotgun followed his every move. 'Well, I would miss her too, Sam, but at least she is safer with your dad than she is here.'

Stevens had had enough. With a casual movement he pumped the shotgun to load up a cartridge, and brought the barrel to bear on Nathan's chest. 'Five seconds to cut the crap, or I'll kill you.'

The words were said with the utmost calm sincerity. Nathan did not doubt them for a moment.

Neither did Daniels. 'Er, Nathan – perhaps you'd better—'

Nathan turned his head to look at Sam, and then opened his eyes. The pupils were very large. 'You have questions, I have questions. You want answers, as do I. I am here to help.' These words, too, were said with the utmost sincerity.

Sam sensed the truth in them. 'Two seconds,' he said.

Nathan smiled. 'Put that howitzer away, Sam. I mean you no harm. I came here to kill that thing, and I need your help.'

'Minus three seconds,' Sam said coldly, but he knew he was not going to pull the trigger. He did not understand what was going on, or how the stranger could pluck thoughts from his mind like phrases from a book, but he knew he felt no fear. The man's attitude was reassuring. He had 'straight' written all over his weird face.

Trooper paused, then smiled again. 'Good. I appreciate your restraint. I know I can be an unmitigated know-it-all bastard sometimes.' He sank wearily into a chair, rubbing at his temples. 'Sam, we have a lot to talk about.' A drop of blood formed in his left nostril and fell heavily to the carpet.

Sam opened his mouth to protest, angered that his house and life had been taken over by strangers, but stopped. Something about the huddled weirdo and his bloody nose – something sad and pathetic – threw the restraining bolts over his anger. He bit off the protest. 'You look like you need some coffee,' he said lamely.

Nathan nodded without looking up. His head was

killing him – opening his mind to read Sam's thoughts had flooded his brain with nausea and decay. The psychopath was out there polluting the ether.

From the hall came sounds of Sam securing the front door. A few moments later he returned, the shotgun laid aside. He poured three mugs of coffee and handed one to Trooper, who was clearly in pain despite a smile of thanks. 'So,' Sam prompted, 'let's talk.'

Nathan wiped his nose with the back of his hand, then sneered at the line of blood on his skin. 'Thanks for letting us in, Sam. I know what you've been through. Maybe what we tell you will make your own experiences seem rather less insane, if that is possible.' He looked up, sniffed. 'John, do you want to start?'

Daniels shrugged. 'Fair enough.' He briefly recounted the murder hunt, Tim's attack and the final confrontation with Corbett.

At mention of Corbett's physical appearance, Sam froze in mid-swallow. He scratched the scar on his cheek. 'See this? Christmas Day I got attacked by a man with claws who ran at ninety miles an hour.'

'I know,' Daniels replied calmly.

Sam nodded, a wry slant to his lips. 'Yeah, I had a feeling you were going to say that. I reckon you know all about me, huh?' He turned his head to gaze at Nathan. 'There's been somethin' weird about this since the day I stopped by that car. That – *thing* – seemed to be able to read my mind, and now so can you. Right?' He turned back to Daniels. 'You boys over there run out of ideas and enlist his help?' he asked, without venom.

Daniels shrugged, not in the least offended. 'Well, sort of.'

Nathan leaned forward in his chair, putting the coffee cup on the floor. 'Look, Sam, I know this is a bit weird . . .'

'Yeah, right, a *bit*.'

'. . . but you must watch the TV. Surely in America this kind of thing is old hat now?'

'Sure.' Sam's expression was one of guarded suspicion.

'Good. But you don't really believe it. You'd like me to prove it, yes? Well, time is an unaffordable luxury now. To save it, I want you to think of something I could not possibly know.'

Stevens frowned and Nathan smiled. 'No, Sam, calling me a bullshitter is not good enough. Try again.'

Sam glanced at Daniels, who gave an imperceptible nod.

So Sam complied with Trooper's order. He thought of an event even his wife did not know about and held the images for two seconds. 'You catch that one?' he asked, voice laden with sarcasm.

Nathan pinched the bridge of his nose before opening his eyes, 'Yes, Sam, I caught that one. You want to hear it back?'

For the first time since he had opened the door, Sam began to feel afraid. Not for his life, but because he was suddenly certain Trooper was not bluffing. He swallowed without replying.

'OK.' Nathan sniffed blood. 'When you were thirteen you stole a motorcycle parked outside your father's motel, and took it for a joyride. You were not really a thief, you were just fascinated by motorcycles and wondered what they were like to drive. When you brought it back, undamaged, you offered the owner of the bike five dollars for the gas you had used. You were so hyped up and ecstatic you did not even realize he was about three times your size. He, however, was less than happy with you. He dragged you out back and beat the crap out of you. He also took the five bucks.

Worse still, your father went crazy when you came home all beaten up, and grounded you for two months. But you loved that ride, and never regretted it. You were hooked, and you never lost the bug.'

Sam's jaw had long ago opened in amazement and disbelief. When Nathan finally drew to a close, he forced his jaws back together again. 'Well, I'll be damned!' he whispered.

Nathan returned the stare, rubbing at his nose to wipe away the blood. He managed a tentative smile. 'Convinced now, Sam?'

Stevens shook his head and grinned. 'So has all this got anything to do with what happened at Christmas?'

Nathan smiled wearily. 'Of course it does.' He pursed his lips. 'When you approached the car that day, what did you feel?'

Sam frowned as he looked away. 'Scared,' he murmured. 'I felt like I was being watched, that the car was full of something *evil*, and some part of me wanted to run like hell and not turn back.' He shuddered. 'There was a voice, but no one there to speak to me. In my head, you know? And it answered questions I didn't even *ask*.' He threw Nathan a pointed glance. 'Just like you did, eh? Except round you I don't feel threatened.'

Nathan spread his hands. 'That's the crux of it, Sam. This killer is a powerful psychic. He feeds off your mind, feeds on your fear. Of all emotions, fear gives off the most energy – electrical activity in the brain, chemical responses in the blood, adrenalin. So the killer implants terror, then your mind over-reacts and gives off more energy. The more afraid you are, the more power he has, the less likely you are to escape. You managed it because climbing on your bike and tearing off down the road eased your fear. You even enjoyed it. You basically laughed in the face of Death.'

Sam thought it was all hogwash, but he did not say so. He did not trust the little weirdo any further than he could shoot him. 'I made a few calls when I got back. Chased up the licence plate on that car. It was found in a warehouse in Bakersfield on New Year's Eve.' He paused for effect. 'There was a woman inside, torn limb from limb. The medical evidence declared no signs of weapons used in the dismemberment. Just bite marks. Was that him?'

Nathan nodded sadly. 'Yes. He was with her in the car when you passed, feeding on her. You were going to be next.' He smiled coldly. 'You have some idea now, I hope, of how lucky you were.'

Sam shrugged. 'I don't need you, pal, to tell me how lucky I was. My face has been telling me the same thing for two weeks.'

Through his pain and exhaustion, Nathan finally sensed the disbelief in Sam's voice. His hopes for an understanding ally crumbled; he began to lose what little heart he had left.

'But,' Sam continued, unaware that Nathan was losing his patience, 'you just can't *do* that. That girl was torn apart – bare handed! I can't believe all this crap. I'm just a cop.'

Nathan allowed himself a dispirited sigh. It seemed that whatever demonstrations he gave no-one ever simply believed. People were so close minded, so bloody stubborn. 'Look, Sam, you're just going to have to take my word for it. There is a whole load of other stuff, but I won't waste my breath. If you don't help, then this thing will kill us all. You've seen it – you know what it is.' He grinned cruelly, giving vent to his frustration. 'He's a heavy-weight boxer, Sam. Seven and a half feet tall with the reflexes of a world-class fencer and the IQ of Albert Einstein. His mind is wired so he can detect your every thought, predict your moves and intercept you. Everything is fine tuned and hums like the most efficient engine in the world. And his personality is that of the world's most sadistic rapist and psychopath.' He laughed, seeing the look of consternation on Sam's face. 'A tiger with the brains and cunning of a wolf, all fuelled by the desires and perversions of Jack the Ripper. That's what we're up against.'

Sam sat back in his chair.

Daniels chewed his lip, increasingly concerned. He was beginning to wonder if Nathan had finally lost his marbles.

Sam had spent his life learning people. He prided himself on being a walking polygraph, able to locate a liar at fifty paces. He had arrested people on the strength of his perceptions and had never been proved wrong. He tried to detect a lie in Trooper's words.

And failed – every word was true. Trooper's message was simple: wise up, Sam, because this *is* the way things are.

Sam turned a confused eye on Daniels. 'You buy this stuff?'

Daniels recognized the look. He nodded solemnly. 'Sam, I buy all of it. But ignore all this psychic crap and go to the roots of the problem. We had a killer in London, you have one here. There's a disease, and it's spreading. People infected by it – kill. Most of them are dead, and now there's just one left – the one who attacked you. He's the most dangerous, because he's the carrier of the disease and he must be found before it spreads again. That's what we're here to do, if we can, before it's too late.'

Nathan smiled faintly. It was a good closing speech – the disease was something tangible for Sam amongst all the gobbledegook.

Sam listened to the tale, giving more weight to Daniels' words. He was certain Daniels actually *believed* what he said, and that was something Sam could respect – a policeman doing his normal job in very abnormal circumstances.

'OK,' he said grudgingly, 'I'll accept that. You're here to stamp out a disease which makes people kill, and you want my help to track down the carrier of that disease. So what's the cure?'

Daniels grinned sourly. 'Death.'

'Yeah, I thought you were going to say that. So you came over here, way out of your jurisdiction, to kill a man. Right?'

'No. Not a man – a monster. A killer.'

Sam shook his head. 'So what now? Do we need wooden stakes, or something? Cloves of garlic? Silver bullets? Huh?'

Daniels laughed. He liked Sam – he was a man who spoke his mind and was not afraid to call you an asshole. If it wasn't for the boards on the windows, the guns and the scar on Sam's cheek, Daniels would be thinking he had gone mad. 'No, nothing quite so silly. All we need to do is find him and kill him. Any old how.'

'But from what you've said, we don't stand an ice-cube's chance in hell of even finding him, let alone killing him.'

Nathan leaned back in his chair, tired and drained, daunted by the prospect of more death. His temper was deteriorating, fuelled by a crashing headache and the frustration of having to continually defend himself. He was sick of sitting around, talking instead of *doing*. 'If we find him, I kill him. It is likely I shall fail, but I am the only one who stands a chance of getting close enough.'

Sam eyed Trooper curiously. 'Something in your tone suggests you ain't too keen on *that*.'

Nathan sighed. 'Indeed. But needs must where the Devil plays, Sam.' He looked up. 'So – will you help?'

Stevens snorted. 'Help commit murder? Me? A policeman?'

Daniels raised one eyebrow in surprise. *I am*, he thought.

'No, Sam. Help put the brakes on a killing machine.' Nathan looked around the room, waved one hand at all the fire-power. 'Or are you saying that half an hour ago you weren't happy to blow that bastard to hell and back in as many pieces as you could send him.'

Sam blushed as he looked away. 'No,' he admitted quietly. 'I was ready for him. But that would've been different.'

'How?'

'Self-defence, not premeditated murder.'

Nathan stood, furious. 'Are you trying to tell me that all this was not premeditated? That these boards just *happened* to be over the windows? That your wife and kids just *happened* to be at your father's so that they would not get in the way? That you just *happened* to be cleaning all these fucking guns at the same time?'

Sam refused to meet his eye.

'Fine! Live on your damned legal jargon. Just try and tell self-defence to the next woman who gets torn apart by that maniac!'

Stevens made to rise, but Daniels beat him to it. 'Nathan, that's enough!' he said sharply. 'Just remember that a week ago I was ready to throw you in the nick, all right? You can't expect someone to just accept your psychic super-fiction. These things take time.'

Trooper rounded on him. 'I do not *have* any more time! Don't you bloody understand that? My head is full of that creep, I can't get away from it, he makes me *sick* just by being alive!' His face was red with hurt and anger. 'Why don't you people ever *understand*? If you refuse to help me, then I'm just going to have to do it myself. Because I can't take any more of this SHIT!'

He span on his heel and stalked out, his face a mask of pain and rage. His head was aching worse than ever, he was sick to his stomach and fed up with *people*. All the company he'd had was too much to bear – he needed to be alone again, to ease the tumult in his mind. He was not used to it, had never been used to it.

Daniels read his intentions to leave, and reached out to grab his arm. 'Nathan! Give us a break, will you? Just calm—'

Trooper whirled to face him. 'Don't touch me!' he hissed. Flecks of spittle appeared on his lips.

Daniels recoiled from the rage and hatred in Trooper's eyes. This was a side he had not seen before – the look of an injured wolf in a trap. He took a step back, surprised by the sudden change.

Trooper stormed out without another word.

Daniels locked eyes with Sam. Were the warnings on Nathan's psychological reports finally coming true? he thought. Had Trooper flipped? Had the stress and the shooting been too much?

'He can't get out,' Sam said, interrupting Daniels' train of thought. 'I have the key.'

As if in denial of that statement they heard the door slam as Trooper fled. Sam rose and went to the door, only to find the mortice lock hanging from the door frame in shattered pieces.

His eyes met Daniels'. Neither man spoke.

Outside, the jeep roared off down the road.

CHAPTER TWO

Explanations

January 7, 1991, 3 p.m.

Daniels sat alone in Sam's house, reclined in one of his flash leather chairs, his feet on a stool, a cigarette in his mouth.

Sam had left three hours earlier. His wife had unexpectedly appeared on the doorstep with the children and three thousand dollars. After screaming surprise at the state of the house, she had explained what had happened. Nathan had gone to Sam's father's house and bribed her into taking Sam and fleeing before they got hurt. Anxious to act anyway, she had used that as an excuse to drag Sam away from his obsession. And Sam, unsettled by Nathan's tale and bizarre exit, had decided to go. Daniels had encouraged him to leave – as usual, Nathan was right. Sam was better off out of the way.

So now he was on his own. Sam had been all too eager to let Daniels stay in the house, no doubt guilty at deserting his refuge after such a committed seige. Daniels had nowhere else to go so he accepted the offer without qualm. Besides, he still hoped Nathan would calm down and come back, so he did not want to go far.

Before leaving, Sam had presented him with a large folder stuffed with press clippings and copies of police files. 'Like I said,' Sam murmured, keeping his back to his wife and children, 'I chased this up after my attack. Had a lot of time on my hands, right? And I found we had all kinds of shit on this going back *years*. Missing persons, mutilations, murders – any crap you can think of. This guy's been busy around here and we didn't even know enough to thread these together.' He shrugged. 'Hell, maybe they ain't connected. Maybe I'm chasing shadows.' But his eyes said otherwise. He regarded Daniels with cool anger. 'But you and I both know what's going on, right? So if I'm ducking out, you'd better be prepared. And if you and your weird friend do catch this mother,' his eyes gleamed like steel, 'give him one from me, OK?'

Daniels had taken the file without a word, and Sam had nodded sagely. 'You ain't dumb, mister, 'cos you already caught one of these sons of bitches. But you take care.' Then he had gone.

Daniels had read the file with interest. Sam had been right: the attacks were similarly violent, all unsolved, all taking place within a thirty mile radius of the nearest large town, Cordaville, about fifteen miles from Sam's house. Sam had even plotted the attacks on a local map, and the pattern was clear. They had started just over five years ago with an attack in Cordaville itself on Christmas Day. And had grown steadily more savage as the months passed.

Daniels felt close to the end of his nightmare.

As well as using Sam's house, Daniels had taken the liberty of phoning long distance to Sergeant Fowles to find out what was going on. Fowles had been more than a little surprised to discover that his boss was in Arizona, but had recovered quickly. Corbett's body had de-sensitized him to shock. He had, however, almost flipped when Daniels told him about Nathan's theories, the Reuters press clippings confirming Nathan's suspicions, and the evidence of more insanity in America. He had not been pleased. It was not easy to go through an investigation like that only to find it was the tip of the iceberg. They had all believed the nightmare over.

As soon as Fowles was over the initial shock, Daniels outlined his needs: it was time to start leading the enquiry instead of following Trooper around like a lost puppy. To do that he needed information; to get information while he was out of circulation in Arizona, he needed Fowles. Thankfully, Sam was a twentieth-century man and had his own office at home – including a fax machine. So Daniels briefed Fowles on what raw materials he wanted: 'Background. Trooper's medical history for a start. Not just what we've got, but *everything*. Hospital records, operations, right from birth. What we have only goes back to his attack, when he was twelve.'

Fowles had accepted the requests; being a dogsbody for Daniels was all part of the job. 'Will do. I can put Baxter on that one.'

'Good. Plus anything on his father. Professional record, medical papers, medical history, birth and death certs, *anything*.'

Fowles had been surprised. 'Why? Nathan's been at the heart of this from the word go – but what's his dad got to do with it?'

Daniels smiled grimly. 'Nathan let a snippet of information slip when I interviewed him, and I never picked up on it. That was a mistake. We always knew his dad was a doctor, right? But we never cared what *kind* of doctor, did we? Well, I find it a little close for comfort that he was a pioneering neuro-surgeon.'

Fowles cursed quietly. 'How the hell did we miss that?'

Daniels shrugged. 'We had a lot on our plate. Ethan

Trooper was dead and buried. We didn't even believe any of this psychic mumbo-jumbo back then. But now we know the wider scheme. I still don't know whether it's going to be important, but I'd like to find out – even if just to cross it off my list.'

Fowles blew out his breath sharply. 'All right, I'll see what I can do. But it's late here, so don't expect miracles.' Daniels had forgotten about the time difference – which surprised him, given the state of his jet lag only hours earlier. So he gave Fowles the telephone and fax numbers, then sat back to think. And wait.

Four hours later the telephone rang. Daniels picked it up.

'You can run, Sam,' a toneless voice said, 'but you can't hide. You can never hide.' The phone went dead.

Daniels looked at the receiver blankly, only then connecting the call with the log of tally marks on the table beside the phone.

Then he began to laugh, huge gales of mirth which tore at his muscles and left him gasping for breath. It was a massive release of the tension of the past few weeks. 'Only bloody human,' he announced to the world, wiping his eyes. 'When all is said and done, he's only human. And he'll make bloody human mistakes.'

He turned to the telephone. 'Sam's not here any more, you twit! But you're so damned powerful you're too stupid to even realize, aren't you? Well, I've got news for you, smart arse. I'm not running, I'm not hiding, I'm not doing anything except waiting to nail your decaying arse to the wall with Sam's .45.'

He hefted the weapon in his hand, testing its weight. The feel of cold steel brought a sadistic grin to his face. 'Come on, you fucker,' he whispered, eyes wide and challenging. 'I dare you.'

In response to that challenge, the telephone rang again.

Daniels eyed it coolly. Then he reluctantly put the gun down and picked up the receiver. 'Inspector?'

'Ah, Fowles.' His heart rate slowed. 'You sound tired.'

Fowles grunted. 'Well, it's one in the morning here, remember. I've been on this sodding job all sodding night.'

Daniels grinned. 'Good. Find anything useful?'

Fowles snorted. 'Who can tell? There's about thirty pages, with more on the way by courier from Scotland. I tell you, that guy really got around. He was a specialist, moved all over the country. It's taken ages to track him over the years.' He sighed. 'Look, the other stuff won't be here until tomorrow, and I'm knackered. So why don't I just fax it and bugger off home, eh? Then you can read it in peace, and I'll speak to you tomorrow.'

Fowles sounded exhausted. 'All right, Sergeant. Send me everything and call me back when you're ready to answer questions.'

'Right.' Fowles hung up before Daniels could change his mind.

Daniels replaced the receiver, sat back and lit himself a cigarette. After a minute, the first page crawled out of the phone line and dropped into the hopper at the back of the fax machine.

He started to read, building an image of the man who had sired Nathan. And within an hour he was convinced that it was Ethan, not Nathan, who was at the centre of the whole stinking mess . . .

Ethan Paul Trooper – born February 1, 1928. Age at death, 36. Occupation, doctor. (That much he had already known.)

Ethan Paul Trooper had been born Ethan Paul Robertson in Glasgow, Scotland. His father had been killed in an industrial accident when Ethan was four. The mother had died of heart failure six months after that. After four years of bad luck, going from home to home and living with a variety of relatives who did not want him, Ethan was adopted by a wealthy English couple when he was nine. The couple, a Mr and Mrs Edward Trooper, were childless and wealthy. The family money was old. They were by all accounts a pleasant pair, and Ethan jumped at the opportunity for stability.

Ethan Trooper was immediately sent to a private school where he was pushed hard with extra tuition to make up on his deprived childhood. He proved to be an extremely gifted and intelligent student, and – much to his parent's pride – graduated from medical school at the age of 21. It was then 1949.

Six months later he married a young woman from London, Emma Barnes. She was just 18. Two months after securing a position as a junior surgeon at a large London hospital, in November of 1949, his adoptive father was kicked by a horse and died of a brain haemorrhage. His adoptive mother had a stroke six weeks later, and spent the rest of her short life – just two more years – in a home.

Ethan, it seemed, was generally bad luck for parents.

Seven months after his adoptive father's death, in June of 1950, Ethan and Emma had a son. They named him Isaac, after Ethan's genetic father. When Ethan's adoptive mother died he inherited a modest fortune. Meanwhile, his career had progressed in leaps and bounds. Part of this meteoric rise was due to the war and staff shortages, but was mostly a direct result of his phenomenal surgical ability. Ethan was a natural; his dexterity in the operating theatre was legendary. He had also made great progress in the almost unheard of field of cranial surgery. His skill and aptitude were so renowned that he was called upon to operate throughout the country. He was outspoken in his rejection of the lobotomy, a view not widely held at that time, and frequently described it as 'barbaric'. He believed such massive tissue destruction was criminally negligent, and consistently advocated the use of finer techniques. All of which earned him a reputation, if at times a bad one.

In July of 1952 his second son, Nathan, was born.

With the gradual acceptance that the lobotomy was indeed a barbaric process, Ethan's work took on a new importance. He was a pioneer in diagnosing and treating brain tumours and anti-social disorders. He became known, not as a rebel, but as a hero.

As the years passed, Ethan dropped further out of the public eye. His work grew more and more research based, and less of any practical value. His name occasionally appeared as a specialist consultant on some complex operations, but on the whole he vanished.

There was no record in the material Fowles sent of what exactly Ethan Trooper did during his last four years, from the summer of 1960. But he did something, and Daniels knew in his guts that if he could find out *what* occurred in those four years, he would also discover *why* Ethan Trooper – child prodigy and internationally acclaimed genius – blew a mental fuse in 1964 and killed his wife and himself, and mutilated his youngest son . . .

At four in the morning, frustrated, jetlagged and stinking of cigarette smoke, Daniels had a shower. Unfortunately, his only change of clothes was in Nathan's jeep, so he washed his clothes in the bath and hung them out to dry over Sam's furniture. Then he sat back and read the fax sheets again. Halfway through, his brow furrowed and with his mind in convoluted circles of thought, he fell asleep.

At 8.30 a.m. he was dragged from a deep and dreamless sleep by the sound of the telephone. It rang three times before he remembered who he was, and another three before he realized where he was. He struggled from his cramped position to pick up the receiver.

Fowles' voice snapped him back to the real world, and his exhaustion was forgotten. 'Inspector?'

'Ah, Sergeant. What have you got for me?'

'Not much I'm afraid. One interesting anomaly, nothing more.'

'Fire away. I'll take it from here. It's time I got moving.'

'OK. Well, getting back to Ethan Trooper, it seems he had one specific colleague who he worked with exclusively. An older doctor by the name of Edward Franks. They seemed pretty much hand in glove judging by these records, both specialists in the same field.'

'Where is this Dr Franks now?'

'Six feet under, unfortunately. He died five years ago.'

Interesting, Daniels thought. 'Got a date? An exact date?'

'Hold on.' There was a slight pause. 'Christmas Eve, 1985.'

Daniels allowed himself a wry smile. The first cutting in Sam's extensive folder of unsolved crimes was dated the day after Franks died. Important? he wondered absently, then put the brakes on his runaway thoughts. 'OK. Go on.'

'Well, Franks disappeared from the public eye at the same time as Ethan Trooper. It's not hard to imagine they carried on working together, but there's no record of it. Suspicious, though.'

'Yes, too bloody suspicious. Anything else?'

'Yes. Ethan hung himself in England after killing his wife and thinking he had killed his son. But his body was flown to America after the inquest and enquiry, and was buried in Arizona. No reason is documented, but it was Franks who requested the move.'

Even more interesting, Daniels thought. Had Ethan requested that in his will? Or was Franks trying to cover something up?

'Also, Franks moved to a hospital in Manhattan twelve months after Ethan Trooper murdered his family. It's since been demolished – I checked that for you. However, I also followed up his movements with the State Medical Association, and found out he transferred.'

Daniels felt his blood freeze. He knew what was coming next.

Fowles paused. 'You know what I'm going to say, don't you?' He laughed. 'Instinct, right? Anyway, Franks transferred to a hospital in Arizona not far from you, and retired in 1975. He died out there ten years later and is buried there.'

Daniels felt his heart skip a beat, his thoughts already churning through the new information. Things were coming together.

'Great. Good work, Fowles. Is that it?'

'Yes, that's all there is. As you can see, there's a big hole where both of them vanished for four years. A dead end. Nobody knows nothing, as the man says. But I dug out Nathan's medical history last night, so I'll send that through.'

'Right. Fax me all you have, then forget about it. You've done a good job, Fowles, but the trails pick up over here and some are very cold. So if you don't mind I'd like to get on with it.'

Fowles chuckled. 'All right sir. I know when I'm not wanted. If there's anything else you need . . .'

'Will do. Thanks again.' He hung up. Then, as ever, lit a cigarette. His instincts were screaming blue murder: Ethan Trooper and Franks were buried in Arizona; they had worked in Arizona in the early sixties; Franks had transferred to Arizona after a stint in New York; the killer was in Arizona. In fact, all the answers were in Arizona . . . and some of them were bound to be in the phone book.

'FACT,' he said aloud, reclining in the armchair with his feet on the table. 'Ethan Trooper was a world-class surgeon and pioneer in the methods of modern brain science.

'FACT. His comrade in arms was Dr Edward Franks.

'FACT. After working together for some years, the young Dr Trooper and his mentor Dr Franks both vanished into obscurity.

'FACT. Four years later Ethan emerged briefly into the limelight when he murdered his family and killed himself.

'FACT. Franks had Ethan's body buried in Arizona.

'FACT. Twelve months after that, Franks left England for a medical post in New York.

'FACT. On closure and demolition of the hospital in Manhattan, Franks transferred to a hospital in Arizona, only a few miles from here. He retired from there five years later.

'FACT. Edward Franks died at the age of sixty-five from a massive heart attack on Christmas Eve, 1985 in Phoenix, Arizona. That evening a man was murdered in Phoenix, while Franks lay on a slab. Franks was buried just fifteen miles from where I'm sitting.

'FACT. A string of savage murders and rapes have taken place in Arizona over the last five years, ever since Franks died. All the attacks have common themes and M.O.s, and all are unsolved.'

He paused. 'SUGGESTION. Ethan Trooper and Ted Franks worked together after their disappearance in 1960.' He paused. 'No, make that FACT. I *know* they did, I just can't prove it. Yet.

'SUGGESTION. Their work was revolutionary, and if not illegal then at least morally suspect. They *were* pioneers, after all.'

He sighed, realized he was talking to himself. 'SUGGESTION. The man I'm looking for is responsible for all the—'

He broke off as the fax machine hummed and clicked, slowly depositing five sheets of recycled toilet paper into the hopper. He picked them up, pleased to see they told Nathan's medical history.

Three minutes later he jerked forward in the chair, one entry flying out like a boxing glove in a spring box:

> SEPTEMBER 3 1963: Admitted to Stockport General Hospital with severe head injuries arising from an automobile accident.

There followed a whole load of medical jargon which Daniels neither understood nor cared about. Then, at the bottom of the entry, one small sentence, blurred and almost obliterated by age and fax corruption, which made his heart leap:

> Supervising Surgeon: Dr Ethan Trooper.

Daniels skipped through the remaining sheets, but they only referred to things he already knew – the axe attack, medical and psychological reports, institutional profiles.

His eyes returned to that one line about the operation on Nathan's head in 1963.

Finally he sat back, mind afire with theories and hypotheses.

'FACT,' he whispered, 'ten months before his death, Ethan Trooper – neuro-surgeon and shady character – operated on his own son's brain.' He closed his eyes, deep in thought. 'Why?'

Daniels knew that in isolation none of the facts, none of the theories, not even the gobbledegook Nathan spouted about psychic webs, were enough to break the case wide open. Events were jumbled in a huge jigsaw puzzle and he had not even seen all the pieces yet. But he did know one thing: at least he'd not been barking up the wrong tree. It was simply that, when the camera panned back, he was only barking up one tree and had forgotten the rest of the forest.

So he pulled back and grabbed himself a new perspective.

Ethan Trooper operates on his son, then tries to kill him. Nathan spends half his life in a mental hospital, develops psychic ability, dedicates the rest of his life to the easing of pain. Like father, like son – Ethan Trooper's whole life was the brain. And what is Nathan's skill? The mind. Coincidence? No such thing.

Edward Franks – moves to Arizona, joins a research centre, has a heart attack and dies. On the very same day the murders begin, all bearing the hallmarks of the investigation.

Daniels felt he was on the verge of discovery . . .

Outside, the sun rose to cast shortened shadows on the earth. People went about their daily lives. The shadows lengthened into dusk. Inside, John Daniels smoked, drank coffee, and kept his mind racing through the facts. He formed hypotheses, studied them, rejected them. He ate, went to the toilet, had another shower, took a few short naps, unloaded, cleaned and re-loaded the gun.

Until at last he felt he had everything 'squared away', as Sam would say. His final theory matched the facts and the timescales. It was crazy, of course – but then the whole thing was crazy. And as Sherlock Holmes had said, when one eliminates the impossible, whatever remains – however improbable – must be the truth.

He looked up, noticing for the first time that darkness had fallen. He realized with a sick sensation in his stomach that Nathan had been missing for thirty-six hours. He wondered what the psychic was up to, out there in the wilderness, with no restraint on his rage. Yet Nathan had clearly been the catalyst for all the madness. Without him, Ethan Trooper may well have survived, scores of people would still be alive, and he would be sitting at home with his family, watching the TV and pondering entirely different matters.

He shrugged. It was all mushroom clouds and bomb cases again. People *had* died and would not be coming back, and he was *not* at home watching TV. He was sitting in a strange house in a strange country trying to piece together the fragmented history of a family which had changed his life and ended others. Now there were just a few pieces of the puzzle left to place. The empty holes stared at him like the vacant eye sockets of the man Nathan had sworn to kill.

He cast the picture aside and crossed to Sam's bookcase. From that he extracted a block of telephone directories.

It did not take him long to find what he was looking for.

January 9, 1991, 9 a.m.

The cemetery was huge, spread over the hill like commercial death. Daniels was not surprised when he saw Nathan's jeep parked outside the gates. Following the directions of the talkative caretaker, Daniels made his way down the lines of tombs and slabs. Names long forgotten passed him by, overgrown graves and rusty urns in a procession of gloom and death. Yet despite the surroundings, he was in a good mood. It was a pleasant morning, and the fresh air tasted good after two days shut up in Sam Stevens' house.

After a ten-minute walk Daniels reached his destination. It was not a large headstone, nor was it ornate, but to Daniels it was finer than the finest mausoleum. 'Hello Nathan,' he said quietly.

Nathan looked up, surprised, pulled from his reverie. He grunted. 'I should have known you would find me.'

Daniels grinned. 'It's my job.' He read the headstone.

ETHAN PAUL TROOPER

1928–1964

'Doesn't exactly pay homage to his genius, does it?'

Nathan sneered. 'It's all he deserves.'

Daniels found the vitriol in Trooper's voice disturbing. He sounded very bitter. 'How did you find it?'

Nathan shrugged. 'God knows. I drove for a day and ended up here.' There was clotted and dried blood all over his upper lip. He looked up. 'Sorry about taking off like that. I just couldn't cope with the people any more. My head couldn't take the pressure.'

'I guessed as much.'

'So why did you follow me? How did you find me?'

Daniels grinned. 'I needed my suitcase. Besides, I'm a detective, remember? It's what I get paid for. I just checked on the registers. Two minutes work, that's all.'

'That easy? It took me twenty-six years.' Nathan smiled faintly. 'Got any smokes? I used all mine.'

Daniels lit two cigarettes, handed one to Trooper.

Nathan inhaled deeply. He was unshaven, pale, and looked dreadful. 'The answers were here all along,' he said through a cloud of smoke. 'Franks left me a legacy, an explanation of why I exist.' He looked over at the Inspector. 'There are a load of files in the jeep. All the details and evidence he stole from my father's research so nobody could ever do it again.'

Daniels had expected as much. It explained why there was no record of their activities. 'Where did he leave it? The Institute?'

'Yes.' Nathan grinned sadly. 'So you found that too, eh?'

'Well, I only had to look in the phone book, Nathan. "The Ethan Trooper Memorial Institute for the Mentally Infirm". It's even printed in bold. Not exactly hard to find, was it?'

'No, I guess not.' He smiled. 'I didn't even think of that.'

Daniels pushed on. 'So. Who is this beast, do you know? Do you know where he is? Do you know how to stop him?'

Nathan shrugged. 'What difference does it make? He's out there, somewhere. He'll find me, when the time is right.'

'And then?'

'Then I shall kill him, or he me, or we'll kill each other. If you wondered whether I lost my resolve when I freaked out, well, I have not. This has gone on long enough. It is time to end it.' Nathan smiled grimly. 'That is why you're here, I suppose. If I fail then it is down to you. I am his prize. He wants me dead.'

'Because he hates you?'

'Partly. I can stop him, and he does not wish to be stopped.'

'Then you know who he is?'

'Oh, yes, I know.' There was a strange finality in his tone, as if Nathan had only existed to be standing there at that exact moment, and his allotted time was soon to end.

'Come back to the house, Nathan. We need to compare notes.'

Nathan sighed. 'I know.' He dropped the cigarette and ground it out with his heel, frowning. Then he pulled himself together. 'Come on, then. Let's get this mess sorted out.'

Daniels lit them both a cigarette, handed one to Trooper and then made himself comfortable. The heat was already rising, and he found the barren scrub depressing as it streamed past on either side. The forlorn strings of wire fencing did nothing to cheer him up, looking as abandoned as he felt. He missed seeing *green* – and would kiss the first patch of English grass he found, if he ever returned. Cordaville had dropped behind them, and they would soon be back at Sam's house. Daniels could not shake the feeling that their quest was coming to a close – probably a violent one.

'So. Let's hear your end of the story,' he prompted.

'Read those papers,' Nathan replied harshly. 'You don't need me to tell it.' He was clearly shaken by the discovery of his past.

'It might help, Nathan. You've been carrying this

baggage around with you for twenty-six years. It's time to talk it out.'

Nathan snorted at the idea. 'That bastard ruined my life with his damned bloated ego. Why should I give him any air-play?'

'Because I've been through a lot of shit with you, Nathan, and I think I deserve some sodding answers. Don't you?'

Trooper turned to look him in the eye, his expression bitter and angry. Yet he could not deny Daniels had earned an explanation.

'They met at Medical College,' he began slowly, reluctantly, as if the words were anathema to him. 'Franks had spent years in the system, unhappy with the English attitude towards "controversial" research. Pure chance brought them together – Franks could not believe his luck when Ethan arrived, rich and eager to change the world. It was the answer to his prayers.' He smiled sardonically. 'What he did not realize was that his prodigy had other ideas about who would be the boss. Ethan was a wilful arrogant shit.

'With my grandfather's money they set up a research institute at Ethan's birthplace in Scotland. Over the years they experimented on social misfits and actually achieved some success. What was never known, however, was that Ethan's surgical techniques were dangerous. Many died on the operating table. No great loss to him, of course, since they were only loonies, right?'

He shook his head sadly. 'What a bastard. I read his journal – it's one of the documents Franks had. And he talks in terms of units and experiments and objectives – not a single mention of human *life*! He used human guinea pigs who were unfortunate enough to be institutionalized.' He turned to Daniels. 'What scares me is that *I* was, too – if another Ethan Trooper had been around when I was inside, would I have died and been passed off as an unfortunate accident?' He laughed cruelly. 'It shames me to be the product of his loins. I have so very much to live down to.'

Daniels was appalled. 'What was he trying to *achieve*?'

'He was trying to enhance mental capacity by rewiring the brain. It was barbaric. Over the years they came to understand the mind, and in a way that is good. They both believed the human mind contained a massive latent potential, with perhaps fifty per cent of the brain never used or idle, hidden. Modern tests put the figure nearer eighty per cent. They were both ahead of their time. But the cost! Eighteen people died, thirty-two ended up vegetables. It was monstrous.'

'Weren't they even slightly *bothered* about all that?'

Nathan shrugged. 'Towards the end Franks thought it was going too far, and had a sudden attack of the morals. But my father was obsessed and refused to back off. He threatened Franks with all manner of horrors. So Franks towed the line.

'Anyway, in 1961 they perfected the technique. One man, an orphan called Peter Black, born here in Arizona, was the subject of the operation. He had been dumped after a life of petty crime – just another crazy mixed-up kid, as they say. They fixed his brain with scalpels until they were happy, then spent a year reviewing the results. As if by magic, his IQ rocketed up. He became able to perceive others' thoughts. Ethan and Franks were so amazed they intended to publish a paper on their findings.'

Daniels was even more disgusted by this. 'What? And reap the glory for their crimes?' He shook his head in disbelief. 'It all sounds like Frankenstein – except instead of using dead bodies they used *live* ones which nobody would miss.'

Nathan nodded. 'Quite. Anyway, they deemed the experiment a huge success. Ethan returned to England and his family, proud ego glittering. Franks stayed here to keep an eye on the patient, who seemed to have lost his criminal tendencies and developed a hunger for knowledge instead. "He's cured," they all cried.'

'So what went wrong?'

Nathan laughed. 'Hold on a minute. You haven't heard the sickest part yet. Just after Ethan got back to the UK, I was stupid enough to be hit by a car while I was out riding my bicycle.' Daniels had known that. 'My father was driving the car.'

Daniels felt his eyes widen – *that* he had not known . . .

September 3, 1963

The car turned the left corner into the street, a slight squeal of new rubber on the tarmac . . . the driver perhaps a little too eager to be home after months out of the country. The afternoon sun hit the window, dazzling him, and he failed to see the young boy come off the kerb on his bicycle, not looking where he was going . . . perhaps a little too eager to be getting along because his daddy was coming home after months out of the country.

There was no chance of stopping, no hope of steering. Neither saw each other until it was all over. The off-side wing caught the bicycle in the centre of the rear wheel, smashing it flat and taking the cycle and the rider over with it, the boy's head striking the tarmac with a sickening thwack which the driver would never forget. The screech of rending metal merged with the howl of abused tyres as the driver slammed on the brakes, just stopping the heavy car from flying over the top of the boy – but only at the expense of dragging the battered form ten yards along the road on its head.

Within seconds it was all over, and the street was filled with shocked silence. Then the driver was out of the car, shouting incoherently, his terror-stricken brain finally making sense of the sun-dazzled image and the vision of his own son disappearing under the welcome wheels of his father's car . . .

'I'll never know whether it was guilt or the desire to have a brilliant child,' Nathan continued after a moment's pause, 'but he decided to perform the operation himself. He rang Franks to tell him he was going to repeat the process on his own son. I think that was when Franks began to have second thoughts – the dregs of society was one thing, family was another. They fell out over it, but he operated anyway. I'll never know exactly *what* he did to me that day but there are chunks of my childhood I can't remember. He took something from me, and in return for childhood normality I got his damned curse.' Nathan smiled. 'But he thought it was wonderful. I believe that, given the chance, he'd have done it to himself.'

'But—' Daniels broke off. 'I don't get it. How come the first patient went psychotic and you didn't?'

Trooper's brow darkened. 'In April of 1964 their experiment suddenly went wrong. The man cast aside his studies and killed one of the guards. Franks was terrified – their patient turned from docile to psychopathic killer in the time it took the orderlies to open his door. He started to scream about voices. He battered his head against a wall to "let the people out". When they tried to restrain him he broke one orderly's neck. It took six people to get him to the floor and hold him while Franks put him to sleep. Then Franks rang my father and called him back here. He *demanded* that the subject either be operated on to reverse the surgery, or be killed. He said the man was far too dangerous. Ethan refused.'

He threw the cigarette butt out of the window. 'By then their experiment was quite mad. He screamed their own thoughts back at them and repeatedly attacked his own head. Believe me, I know how he felt. Franks had had enough and said he would go to the police if Ethan did not operate. By then Ethan had more personal worries. He had operated on me, and was flying from the States to England every week to see if I was exhibiting any of the same signs.'

'And?'

'And I was not. More withdrawn perhaps, but certainly not murdering anyone. He was torn between operating and leaving the man alone. If he admitted defeat and operated, he would have to do the same to me and that might kill me. In the end he left his decision too late. Lax security resulted in one dead nurse, a dead guard, and three dead dogs. The man escaped. They never found him.'

'Did they organize a search? Call in the police?'

'No. They would both have gone to jail if they had. So they just waited for the first killing and argued about how long it would be before I also mutated. But they never heard anything – Franks began to believe the man was dead. Ethan was not so sure. He began to crack under the strain. Guilt, I suppose. He became convinced that I would go psychotic. He returned to England a physical and emotional wreck, and then just went berserk . . .'

July 27, 1964

The man behind the counter never knew whether to

regret his decision to sell the customer the axe that hot summer morning. He had his doubts about the man as soon as he entered the shop – well dressed and clean shaven, but a crazy stoop to the shoulders and a *madness* about the eyes which was enough to trouble the steward even if the customer had only wanted a can of paint. But an *axe*?

Still. The decision had been made for him when the man walked purposefully up to the counter and held the axe protectively by his chest in both hands, as if cherishing a baby or some prized family heirloom. One hand caressed the covered sharp, grey steel blade with fine fingers – surgeon's fingers, the steward thought absently. The eyes flickered madly about the shop, dancing from object to object, bloodshot and scared . . . and guilty.

The customer dropped twenty pounds on the counter in crisp bills and walked off without waiting for his change, muttering.

The steward shuddered, rang up the cost of the axe and pocketed the change. Then he remembered those mad red eyes – and he emptied his pockets into the till, as if he knew the money would be blood money, and wanted no taint on his conscience . . .

'The rest you know. He went crazy, killed mother, tried to kill me. Whether to destroy the evidence or because he didn't want to see me go mad, I'll never know.'

Daniels blew out a deep breath in disgust. 'And Franks?'

Nathan shrugged. 'He just buried the whole thing. He assumed that if I lived there would be no comeback on him, since the axe blows would more than account for any personality disorders. He was scared and very conscious of his crimes, but he at least had the sense not to *ever* allow anyone to repeat their mistakes. He closed the Research Centre and built the Memorial Hospital with Ethan's money. I reckon he spent the rest of his life ridden with guilt, and he bloody deserved it. He was certainly guilty enough to leave me his records, in case I ever turned up looking for him. They had been sealed for years, locked away in the vaults.'

'Then he knew you would be coming back for them?'

Trooper shrugged. 'I think he half guessed. He decided their monster was dead, but deep down maybe he wasn't so sure.'

'What changed his mind?' Daniels asked, but he could guess.

Nathan grinned sourly. 'A series of telephone calls in 1985 and one repeated message: "You can run, Franks, but you can't hide. I'm coming for you, and I'll have your innards for what you did to me." Certain comments in the threats convinced Franks it was their experiment, returned and angry after twenty years of silence.

'You have to remember that Franks knew his patient had been rendered telepathic by the operation. He had also followed my life. He researched psychic phenomena, but could never explain why the experiment had been such a failure.' He shrugged. 'He didn't live to witness the murders. He died just before all that started.'

Daniels frowned. Yes, the night before to be exact. 'So when he left the records Franks simply believed the man was a homicidal maniac, and had no inkling of what he was turning into?'

'I think so. It was just his past coming back to haunt him. He wanted me to hunt the man down before he killed anyone.'

'Why didn't he do that himself?'

Trooper laughed. 'Because he was a stupid old man

who thought a life of looking over his shoulder was better than a life in jail.'

Daniels sat back in his chair and looked out of the window at the midday landscape, anxious to get back to the house. Several things made no sense: Nathan received the same operation as the killer, so why was the killer so violent and Nathan so passive? And what caused the mutation of the killer's body?

'You have some questions, no doubt,' Nathan said quietly.

Daniels smiled. 'A few. I don't understand what's different between you and Black. Why does he kill if you don't?'

For food, fool . . . and for pleasure.

The thought came unbidden to Trooper's mind, and he frowned, troubled. Was that his instinct answering? Or something more sinister, some buried remnant of that depraved egotistical disaster?

Or perhaps some subconscious symbiosis with Black?

He shifted in his seat, smothering his concern along with the rest of his emotions. 'There are two big differences between Black and I. I had a happy childhood, came from a stable background and wanted for nothing. He had a very unhappy childhood. He was unwanted, abused and at heart pretty wayward. He was only sixteen when they operated, but had already been arrested for armed robbery. He hated the world. Also, he did not have the good fortune to have his brain damaged by a large axe, wielded with surgical precision.'

Daniels stared in amazement. 'Are you saying that the attack actually *stopped* you? That it *undid* the operation?'

Nathan shrugged. 'It is the only explanation. They always suspected brain damage. True, I was left with psychic ability and a few psychological problems, but he actually did me a favour. Completely by chance, of course. You see, father believed that the potential lay in the subconscious. The weak forebrain was dominant, the backbrain only presenting itself in the animal emotions, like fear, and in dreams. So he linked the two together. The power of conscious thought with the raw energy of the id.'

'Id?'

'Yes. The instincts and memories in your subconscious, the animal behaviour that's restricted and inhibited by society. Remove the inhibitions, connect the forebrain directly to the id, and you have a massive boost to psychic and mental capacity.'

'But you also have a man driven by his deepest instincts and nature, without restrictions or any idea of what is acceptable?'

'Correct. A man who thinks killing is the law of survival, just as we did thousands of years ago when we ate raw mammoths and lived in caves. This man is so in touch with the power of his id that he has absolutely *no* compunction about killing.' Nathan shook his head sadly. 'Franks burned all the notes because he was terrified the military would get hold of it. Can you imagine? An entire army of soldiers who could quite happily *eat* the enemy? And because they are fed by raw emotion, the most successful would be those with a grudge against the world: lunatics, murderers, rapists. Think of it! Have the best army in the world *and* solve all your prison overcrowding problems!'

Daniels laughed through his horror, desperate to retain his grip on sanity. 'Do I detect a trace of cynicism there, Nathan?'

'Oh, come on. Can you honestly say that some in the police force would not give their right arm for a riot squad like that?'

Daniels felt the smile fall from his face. The saddest thing, of course, was that Nathan was right.

Nathan steered the car past the garage at the threshold to the small cluster of houses forming Sam's desert town. 'Do you remember how Corbett used your id against you? The spider?'

Daniels shuddered. Yes, he remembered.

'When I fought Corbett, we used each other's deepest fears as weapons. I nearly lost then. Peter Black has had twenty years' experience and he is a lot stronger than Corbett could ever have hoped to be.' He turned to Daniels. 'Now tell me. Am I anything but insane to even consider fighting this man?'

Daniels refused to answer. Instead he countered with his own questions. 'What causes the mutation? And why recruit allies?'

'How does a man guarantee himself life in a primitive society? By being stronger than his enemies. Black gets his strength from the psychic net by absorbing the power of his victims.

'In 1985 he must have reached a turning point. His madness became directed. Perhaps he discovered his roots, that which had made him what he was. So he went after Franks and Franks died of a heart attack. I would not be surprised if they actually came face to face, but the meeting was cut short. Franks could not cope with being faced by his own nightmares. His heart would have burst like *that*—' Nathan snapped his fingers viciously.

'Ultimate and unreasoning terror is a powerful weapon, as I'm sure you know. In the hours to come you mustn't forget that. Maybe Black stumbled across his future purely by accident – the influx of Franks' psychic energy would have given Black an immense high. So he sent out a summons, calling those who would best serve him in his lust for raw power. And when they arrived, probably following an urge they could neither understand nor resist, he changed them. He warped their minds and sent them out to kill. As each killed they grew stronger, and when they died he reaped that sick harvest. He became the embodiment of the worst aspect of himself.'

Nathan hauled on the steering to take the jeep down the side road towards Sam's isolated house. The road was deserted. They were the only people moving in the noon-time New Year apathy.

'I think that causes the mutation. His mind is so powerful, so warped, that it influences his body. Perhaps the claws are some manifestation of his concept as a hunter. But the eyes? God knows why they do that. As for the height and the muscular build – well,' he laughed, 'maybe he takes buckets of steroids.'

Daniels allowed himself a small smile in response. It was not important, anyway. But he found the entire situation scary – the reasons for all the death and terror were rooted in a dead man's ego. There was clearly no justice in any of the sorry story.

Nathan pulled up outside Sam's house and cut the engine. 'So what now? Still want to proceed?'

'Now? Now we wait. Black does not know you have no wish for his bestial supremacy. Perhaps we can turn that against him.' Daniels grinned. 'That preconception means he's put a foot forward. As you actually have a different intention we can pull the rug out from under his foot and bring him down.'

Nathan shrugged. 'If you say so, Inspector. Personally, I think that if I stand against him he will just rip out my gizzard and eat it. I find that vaguely unsettling.'

Daniels chuckled. 'I'm sure. But if he's reaching for your gizzard while you pull the rug from under his feet, maybe he'll be off balance long enough for me to blow

his brains out.' He pulled back his jacket to reveal Sam's
.45 nestling in his armpit.

Nathan opened his eyes in surprise and then laughed
with a sudden release of tension. 'You amaze me,
Inspector. And if it's any consolation, I am glad you
are here.'

'Well, to protect and to serve. Isn't that what the
Americans say?' He got out of the car and tossed Nathan
the house keys. 'You go on in. I'll bring this stuff – it's
evidence. I wouldn't want to lose it just because some
kid steals our car.'

Nathan turned and walked towards the house, his
step heavy, the stoop in his shoulders more pronounced
than usual.

Daniels watched him go, worried. Nathan's state of
mind was troubling him, as was the impending confrontation. They were far from ready for battle, and Daniels
felt useless. If Nathan believed he did not stand an
ice-cube's chance in hell, then Daniels rated their odds
at infinity to one.

Yet there was little he could do but soldier on, and
the comforting weight of the handgun restored some
determination. He would go down in a hail of bullets,
spiders or no spiders, and to hell with everything else.
Nathan may give up, but he vowed to go on, kicking
and screaming, until they tore off his legs . . .

Thus it was with some panic that they broke off their
morbid discussion that evening in answer to a loud
banging on the door. Why the mutant psychopath would
bother to knock was quite beyond them, but Daniels was
nothing if not cautious. He approached the door with the
.45 cocked at arm's length, making sure Nathan stood
to one side with a loaded shotgun. He had no idea who
the caller could be, certain that Sam would not knock
at his own front door and expecting no other. He felt

his heart hammering painfully in his chest, the adrenalin surging through his blood, that familiar tightening in his bowels.

And so they were surprised when they tore open the door and came face to face with Anne Wallis, travel-worn and tired with one small black suitcase in her hand and two purple ones under her eyes.

She took in the sight of the madmen in the doorway, huge dark gun barrels wavering in the gloom, crazy bloodshot eyes in the shadows, trigger fingers itching to pump lead, and fainted.

Anne found Nathan leaning over the sink, running a glass of cold water to alleviate the stuffy heat of the house. He looked up at her and smiled nervously, still shaking from their confrontation at the door. He wondered if she would ever know how close she had come to dying – and then assumed that she knew already. Her reaction was evidence enough for that.

Her story had surprised them both: persistent dreams, a sense that there was 'unfinished business', and panic at discovering they were gone; a chance phone call to Sergeant Fowles and a friend at the airline, a ticket booked in desperation and a wild flight across the world. She had done well to track them – her contact at Heathrow had taken her as far as Arizona, but then her native English charm had had to do the rest. She had checked the airport car-rental desks, and found Nathan immediately – everyone remembered him and the impossibly tall man at his side. She found out that he had asked about specific towns and roads, and took those routes herself. Eventually, she had come to the small town where Sam lived; and there rumours were rife – Sam had gone, face cut in two, his wife and kids scared; two Englishmen were holed up at his house with the stacks of timber Sam had bought for God knew what . . . the whole town was afire with gossip. Finding them in six million square miles of country had been surprisingly easy.

The story troubled Daniels because he thought her presence in the house would only complicate matters . . . but then he remembered the contact Nathan had with Anne before, and changed his mind. Perhaps Anne would be a welcome distraction for Trooper in his black mood.

Trooper was troubled by the news of rumour in the town; that would mean all the townsfolk were *thinking* of them, and of Sam, whom Black would know and hate. That meant a haze of thought hovering over the town – a beacon for Black as effective as setting a bonfire for him in the village square. Still; they had come for a conflict, and would not be leaving until the fight was done. Perhaps it was for the best that Black would find them sooner rather than later.

Anne closed the door and crossed to Nathan's side, fingers itching to touch him, make sure he was real. Her dreams had been persistent: it was hard to believe she had found him again.

He smiled reassuringly. 'Hi. How are you? Tired? Got over the shock?' He offered her the glass.

She shook her head. 'I'm OK. Glad to be here at last.'

He drank the water in one long swallow and then rolled the cold glass over his forehead. He was getting a headache. 'Well, I don't know how much you know but you may live to regret that decision. If you're lucky.' His tone was less than welcoming.

And it managed to offend and upset her. 'So I was wrong?' she asked tersely, inexplicably crushed. She turned away.

He looked up at her back, confused, knowing he had upset her but not knowing why, or how. Just being with her made him uneasy. 'Anne, I don't think you realize just how dangerous all this is.'

'Do you want me to go back to England?' she challenged.

He frowned. What the hell was wrong with her? Did she not understand the stakes, what was happening here?

He considered that and then mentally kicked himself. No, of course she did not understand.

Yet having her here would be total folly. Daniels he could ignore, since the man was quite capable of looking after himself. But he could spare no time to protect her. That would be suicide.

'No,' he said, and immediately cursed his stupidity. Did I really say that? I can't believe I said that.

She turned to face him, surprised. 'Pardon?'

He opened his mouth to say 'Yes, I want you to go home', but said: 'No, I don't want you to go.' He frowned. Yes I do *want* you to – now! 'It's good to see you again.' He blushed. For some reason his mouth was connected to his libido instead of his brain.

She smiled. 'Thank you.'

He looked at her steadily, noticed her long hair, her large blue eyes. He thought about that night in the hospital and of his reactions towards her. She had been in his thoughts since he had first seen her. He had to admit that he really was glad she was here, even though it was sheer lunacy. He realized, with a sinking feeling in his stomach, that he was very attracted to her.

Oh God, he thought. Not now. Not here. Not ever.

He cleared his throat nervously. 'I've been worried about you.' Why the hell did I have to go and say that?

'I had a dream the night you left England,' she said quietly, then paused. She did not know whether to say it or not. But she liked the way he blushed when he looked at her. There was an innocence about him which appealed to her, not strictly decent given that her husband was only two weeks dead. But her thoughts constantly returned to the comfort he had given that night. 'You were in it,' she added softly.

'Oh?' he repeated. Am I supposed to say something clever?

'You died,' she whispered.

He laughed nervously. 'Charmed, I'm sure.'

She rounded on him, upset again. 'I didn't *want* you to die!'

He blushed again. 'I know. I'm sorry.' He shrugged. 'Anne, look, I'm not very good with people. And I'm sorry about that too.'

Her anger subsided as suddenly as it had blossomed. 'So I've been told. The Inspector had a little "chat" with me when you were in hospital. He wanted me to know the reasons for Bill's death.'

He regarded her curiously. 'Did what he said help at all?'

'Yes. No. I don't know.' She chewed her lip. 'He said you were psychic. Is that true?' Her question was hesitant, as if she did not really want an answer at all.

He grinned slightly. 'I am afraid so, yes. But you needn't say it like that – it's not a hideous disease, you know.'

She blushed, flustered and confused by her own emotions. 'I'm sorry. I didn't mean to offend you.'

He smiled again. 'None taken.' He refilled the glass. His headache was getting worse. And his stomach was all butterflies.

'Nathan?' she asked softly. 'Are you going to die?'

He looked up, startled by the question. He noticed that her eyes were very large and full of fear. 'Why do you ask?'

She paused before answering, unsure of what to say. 'I know this isn't finished.' She shrugged. 'I just get the impression you are resigned to your fate. As if you don't care any more.'

Trooper put the glass down, his movements slow and thoughtful. He realized she was right – there was no fight left in him. He just wanted the whole thing finished; he wanted peace and quiet.

Yet her presence seemed to make those desires foolish and selfish. He realized he had once again sunk into the depths of self-pity. 'Does it matter to you?' he asked guardedly.

She opened her mouth to snap at him but the look in his eye stalled her remark. She realized that he honestly did not know. 'Yes,' she said firmly, 'of course it matters.'

Never before, in the company of any man, had she felt so uncomfortable. The intensity of her feelings was shocking.

His eyes searched hers for a moment, trying to detect a lie. He found none. 'Well,' he said, grinning, 'I'll do my best to stay alive then.' He smiled sheepishly and blushed red to his roots.

The blush was a wonder to behold. It made her laugh again.

It also made her want to give him a hug. It was her turn to comfort him. So, taking her future in her hands, she reached out and hesitantly drew herself to his side. He stiffened at her touch and she almost backed away, fearing she had overstepped the mark. But then he timidly returned her embrace.

They stood like that for about a minute. When he

finally disentangled himself she saw that his eyes were wet with tears. He smiled up at her through his sadness and joy. 'Sometimes, it is a real pain being so short.' He swallowed nervously.

She could see his heart beating through his shirt.

'Anne, I am not sure this is a good idea. Anything can happen. There's someone trying to kill me. Maybe we should let things cool off. Not that I'm suggesting anything – I mean, I may be psychic, but sometimes I can't figure out what's going on in *my* head, let alone anyone else's. I would not want to out-guess someone, because you – I mean, somebody – might get offended. If you see what I mean. Well, maybe you don't. Maybe I am wrong, hey, why not just forget all that, because—'

She placed a long forefinger over his lips. 'Nathan. Shut up.'

He swallowed again. 'Sorry. When I'm nervous I tend to just go on about things. I don't have much chance to—'

She kissed him. After a while, he stopped talking.

CHAPTER THREE

Time

Nightfall.

In his mind, a hundred tortured souls screaming their pain, captured souls, chained to his evil. In his body, decay, the sickening smell of putrefaction. Flesh decomposing into a walking monolith of maggots and rancid slime.

A lifetime of torment. Twenty-eight years of the hunt. His herd, his supply of power, gathered around him in chains of ruin, feeding him. Crying their horrors, screaming their anguish, pleading for mercy. Desperate for release, yet given none.

And always driving on, for the pleasure of rending flesh from bone. The ecstasy of sucking warm marrow from a dripping limb. The joy of gorging the brain, devouring the soul and its energy.

The price: his teeth, stained with death, gums running with infection; his hands, red with gore, clawed for the kill; his eyes, vacant sockets to view his nightmare world, crawling with maggots.

He rose from the shadows, shrouded in flies, every step a release of rotten tissue. His body was wasted, soon to be lost to him. He needed food, and a way to be free of his corpse.

But they were near. He could *smell* them on the wind

– the smell of life, of unreaped power, of fear. They would not run, could not hide.

Soon. Soon they would all be his.

He was ready.

It was TIME.

CHAPTER FOUR

From Heaven to Hell

Nightfall.

The three weary hunters sat in permanent lamplight behind the boarded windows and locked doors. Time no longer had any meaning. Tempers frayed. The house reeked of stale cigarette smoke and fear.

Nathan Trooper wandered morosely about the cellar, studying the documents bequeathed to him by Edward Franks, poring over them to extract some shred of information for a weapon in the oncoming conflict. He believed that none of the others had any concept of Peter Black's awesome size and power. Yet Black grew to dominate Nathan's thoughts as the hours slipped away.

Nathan was also scared of the feelings he had for Anne, and the speed with which they had consumed him. That closeness had been thrust upon him when he had no resources to deal with it – he was terrified of becoming involved, was sure that would destroy his ability to defend himself. His healing gunshot wound alone was enough to shatter his concentration; coupled with the memory of her kiss, he found he could give scant thought to their predicament.

And all the time the bloated mass of psychic energy which betrayed Black's presence grew and festered in his mind's eye.

*

At midnight Anne cornered Daniels in the kitchen. Beneath their feet Trooper continued his relentless pacing.

Daniels smiled kindly, but his eyes betrayed concern. Besides Nathan, only he had any inkling of what was about to happen.

'Inspector,' she said softly, 'I'm worried about Nathan.'

He shrugged. 'So am I. But he knows what's best for him.'

'I don't think he should be alone right now.'

Daniels smiled. 'Nathan has spent his life alone. He has made a career out of solitude. We'd only distract him.' He poured her a coffee. 'I know you only have his best interests at heart. But he has a tendency to ignore the social niceties you and I take for granted. Right now he's ignoring all of us, and although part of me feels offended by that, I can understand why.' He broke off, smiled apologetically. 'I'm sorry. I didn't mean to lecture.'

She sipped her coffee. 'That's all right. And don't get me wrong – I know what he's like. He's the most introverted man I know. But that's not what I meant.' She paused to reword her concerns. 'Five days ago he was shot. Since then he's been under enormous strain. He feels responsible and we let him be.' She looked up. 'Shouldn't he get some rest? Sitting in the cellar will hardly leave him in perfect condition. When did he last sleep?'

Daniels looked sheepish. 'Two or three days ago, I think.' He pulled a face. Loathe as he was to interrupt the man, Anne had a point. Insomniac psychic or not, Nathan was still human. After three days without sleep, a bad gunshot wound and all the stress of the past two weeks, tackling Black would hardly be wise.

He frowned. 'You're right, Anne. Thanks. I guess

sometimes I forget he's as mortal as the rest of us.' He glanced at his watch. 'It's midnight now. I'll ask him to take a break.'

Anne had to be content with that. 'Ask forcefully, OK?'

Daniels' grim face broke into a wry grin. With a raised eyebrow he turned and left.

The cellar was cool, smoky and dark. John did not mind the temperature or the smoke. But he was far from happy about the gloom. He could not imagine how Nathan was able to sit in the dust and watch the spiders watch him. It gave Daniels the willies. The entrance to the cellar from the outside was no more than a rickety trapdoor and a set of wooden steps, half-heartedly boarded up when Sam had been tiring of his siege mentality. Daniels could see gaps as wide as his arm in the door – and that meant spiders as wide as his arm could get in. He shuddered. 'Nathan?'

Trooper looked up from his pile of folders, his forehead marred by a deep frown. It made him look eighty years old. 'Yes?'

'Am I interrupting?'

'Yes. But as you knew you would, I assume you have a reason?'

Nathan's tone was insulting. Daniels resisted the temptation to beat some manners into him. 'I'm sorry. Anne's worried about you. We all know you've been pushing yourself pretty hard.'

Nathan shrugged. 'So?' He turned back to his papers.

'So we thought you should rest a while.'

'Really?' Nathan murmured. 'How touching.'

Daniels frowned. 'Look, Nathan, if Black is going to—'

Nathan whirled to face him. 'No, *you* look Inspector! It's all well and good to sit around, but I'd rather stand a fighting chance of coming out of this alive. Not one of you has a *clue* what is coming, but you all expect me to go up against that bloody monster for you. So why don't you just let me get on with it?' There were small anger spots in his usually pale cheeks.

'Nathan, nobody *asked* you to do this,' Daniels spat, knowing that was irrelevant. Nobody asked, but they had assumed.

'What choice did I have? Leave you to deal with it? And I thought you had some brains, Daniels.' He snorted contemptuously. 'If I left it to you we'd all be dead by tomorrow.'

Daniels flinched as if Nathan had slapped him. He realized he had not exactly achieved what he intended. But the man was intolerable. He slammed the door and stomped back into the kitchen.

'Did he listen?' Anne asked, knowing he had not by the look on the Inspector's face.

'Did he hell!' Daniels stormed, and was gone.

Nathan glared at the closed door. Great! That's all I need!

He returned to the papers scattered at his feet. But the words were blurred and his eyes so tired he could no longer read them. He pushed the folders aside in disgust and lit a cigarette.

'Bloody hell!' he hissed. 'Why don't they understand?'

He rubbed his eyes, massaged his temples to clear away the headache, and leaned back onto the steps. Smoke leaked from his nostrils. 'So little *time*.'

He sat like that for about fifteen minutes, chain-smoked four cigarettes and fell deeper into despair. His best efforts seemed worthless, his dedication meant nothing. When Black arrived, his mind would be crushed like an insect beneath a booted foot. It was all so ruddy *pointless*. Why bother? Why not just put a gun to his own head and save Black the trouble?

He sighed. Anne had complicated matters more than he liked. Why was she really here? What had she hoped to achieve? Had she been driven as much as he and Daniels? The added responsibility was unwelcome; the added emotion was confusing.

He had always been alone; he had *liked* being alone. But now he had tasted from the cup of companionship and that taste left him wanting. He began to regret accepting the responsibilities. He wished for the warmth of her concern and her touch.

Yet he knew, in his heart and Black, filth-polluted mind, that those wishes would never come true now. The memory of touching Tim's mind in the hospital, when Tim's vision showed Nathan headless and covered in blood, was evidence that his death was inevitable. He wanted her, but the risk of her pain was too much to bear.

Better to have loved and lost, they said. But Nathan believed it was better to have never loved at all. What you never had, you would not miss. Why, then, was it so hard to accept, so hard to let her go? She seemed to be his last chance at a normal life.

And then he knew he was deluding himself. A normal life? Him? With her? How long did he think she would stay with him if he screamed and shouted at her every few hours, recoiled from her touch, spouted blood from his nose when they got too close? What kind of normal life was that?

He sank his head in his hands and wept his loss: the loss of his childhood, his family, of experiences others took for granted. His entire history was of loss and nights alone. All he had ever really owned was a power he had never asked for; all he had ever wanted was to turn back the clock and be normal.

'Damn you,' he growled, 'damn you to hell, Peter Black.'

He lifted his head and bellowed his anguish into the vaults of his mind: *'Damn you father! Damn you to hell for your arrogance!'*

An hour later his mind was clear of despair, leaving him hollow and exhausted. He wanted to lie down for a while, but dared not go back up the stairs. He could not face his companions.

Yet he needed rest. And warmth. The cellar was cold.

Opening his mind, Nathan looked past the expanded blob of Black's consciousness and scanned the house. The kitchen and lounge were deserted. Daniels sat in Sam's den smoking. Anne lay in one of the many bedrooms. Her thoughts impinged on Nathan's mind. She was troubled, upset, and confused. But she did not hate him, as he had expected. Trooper stealthily ascended the steps into the house, passed through the lounge and into the first bedroom. Once inside, unnoticed, he crossed to the bed and collapsed on the mattress.

Only then did he realize how tired he was. Jetlagged, days without sleep, a hole in his side, and he was surprised at being worn out. The others had been right – he had been pushing himself too hard. Physical, psychic and emotional stresses had all taken their toll. So he lay back, kicked off his shoes and forced himself to relax. His body drifted instantly into sleep.

His mind, however, had other ideas. Such was the curse of the insomniac. Anxieties whirled in his brain. Things he had done or said, things he had yet to say or do all jumbled over themselves. Too tired to toss and turn, Nathan simply lay there and pondered life, the universe, and anything else which came to mind. Drifting, snapping aware just as he was about to sleep, he cursed his lot.

He was on the verge of giving up and having a smoke when the door opened. There was no footstep, no knock, it simply opened.

A slit of light fell on his eyes and was eclipsed by a passing shadow. His night vision was destroyed – but he did not need eyes to tell him the intruder was Anne Wallis. Her nervousness was palpable, rivalled only by his own.

'Nathan?' she whispered, 'is that you?'

'What do you want?' he asked brusquely, wishing her away. It would be easier for them all if she just left him alone.

'Are you OK?' she asked after a pause.

'Yes. Tired.'

'Do you want me to leave you alone?'

'Yes.' Somewhere in his head the lonely child who had grown into a lonely man screamed out in anguish. He felt her flinch at his denial, and her emotion pained him. 'No,' he said lamely.

Her loss and confusion turned to hope.

IDIOT! he cursed silently. What are you doing? This is pure madness. But against his better judgement he stood and crossed to the door, homing in on her thoughts. The room was pitch dark. Reaching out he found her hand and drew her gently over to the bed. She sat on the mattress, he remained standing. 'What's the matter?'

Her thoughts screamed at him, out of control, garbled. He could make no sense of them, did not even want to listen. 'I'm scared. I don't want to be alone,' she added, quietly.

'John's in the den.' Still he pushed her away. 'I could really do with some sleep.' He was hurting her, he knew it. And he just could not go on hurting her – she deserved better.

'Nathan, I don't understand. One minute you were so nice, and the next so horrible. What are you trying to do?'

'What do you want from me, Anne?' he asked harshly, squirming in agony at his own tone.

'An explanation.' Her voice was pained yet defiant.

He admired her courage and self-control. And his admiration and blossoming affection tore apart his last barricades. Sighing, he sank to his knees in front of her. 'Oh, Anne, you're not making this any easier for me,' he breathed.

He sensed her surprise. 'I'm sorry,' she said. 'I did not mean to be a burden to you. I know you're under a lot of pressure.'

He invaded her mind, not wanting to but unable to continue without knowing how she felt about him. Any other man would have known without resorting to such underhanded trickery, but not Nathan Trooper. So he scanned her thoughts, seeking there the courage to answer her questions.

What he found just made it harder. She wanted his closeness as he wanted hers, the security of his embrace. She needed an ally, someone to lean on who would want nothing in return. And most of all she wanted to ease his pain, to make him realize the world was not the hell he had always lived. Mixed with that was pity for him, but it was not pity which drove her to his side. What she wanted was to be held, to receive that gift and ease his loneliness.

Nathan did not want her heart and soul. He did not want the burden or extra responsibility. And yet he wanted it all more than anything else in the world. He wanted to *feel* life, even if it was only the once, not just to exist. He wanted *meaning*.

He leaned forward and their foreheads touched, trembling. Her scent and warmth was all he could feel, all he wanted.

'I'm sorry,' he whispered. 'I never meant to hurt you. I care for you, and never wished to see you harmed.'

She gasped. Those were his words in the dream. Hope flooded her brain. 'Nathan, don't be scared. I won't destroy you.' She thought of the dream. 'Don't push me away just because you think it will make it easier on me. Only push me away if you don't want me.'

He smiled. 'Am I that transparent?'

'You have the most striking eyes I have ever seen in a man, Nathan. Everything you think is mirrored there.'

'I still don't think you understand,' he murmured.

'You think I don't know you believe you will die?'

He looked up, surprised.

'Nathan, you have morbid doom written all over your face.' Her voice was light and alive, in total contrast to her words.

'I *know* I will, Anne. That's why you should not be here now.'

'Nathan, at least live this one evening.'

Her arms came up and wrapped around his shoulders. He returned her embrace, holding her tightly as if she would disappear if he let go. After a while they kissed, softly, hesitantly. Nathan's heart was thumping. He felt so *alive*.

When the position grew uncomfortable, Anne moved back onto the bed and lay down. Nathan, nervous as a kitten, lay down beside her.

'Stop shaking,' she whispered.

'I've never done this before,' he replied, blushing.

She took him in her arms. 'Done what?'

He cleared his throat. 'This.'

She giggled. 'Relax. Get undressed and come to bed.'

His blush extended to his feet. 'Pardon?'

'We don't have to *do* anything, Nathan. There's no pressure.' She pulled away. Trooper heard the whisper of cotton, then felt the bed move as she climbed beneath the covers. 'You can stay there if you like,' she whispered. 'But if you do I shall be offended.'

He coughed nervously. 'Er, I'm not sure about this.'

She laughed. 'I don't know, Nathan. Sometimes I do despair.'

He thought of her lying naked in the bed. He thought of all sorts of things he had never thought of before. He thought he would have a heart attack if he did not decide one way or the other fairly soon. 'Don't watch,' he said tightly, sitting up.

She laughed softly. 'Watch what? I can't *see* anything.'

Good, he thought. He undressed and climbed in beside her.

She was warm and soft and very, very close. He had never experienced anything quite like it.

'Stop shaking,' she said . . .

2 a.m.

Her hair cascaded around his face, a curtain of soft lavender.

'I've never done this before either,' he apologized.

She kissed him soundly on the lips. 'Hush.' She moved above him, legs astride his waist, every possible inch of skin touching him. Kissing, she enveloped him.

His eyes bulged in their sockets.

She felt him grow inside her. The sensation was fantastic, to be filled by him. She could feel him trembling, even then, and knew she had to relax him. 'There,' she breathed, 'was that so bad?'

'It's over?' he asked, amazed.

She collapsed on top of him, laughing uncontrollably . . .

3 a.m.

Nathan slept, curled up beside her, his face young and innocent. Even in sleep he held her tightly.

She lay in his strong embrace, content and dreamy. With one hand she gently caressed his back, continuing the motion which had soothed away his worries. If she stopped he might wake again.

Beneath the aloof exterior she had found a man whose affection and tenderness astounded her. As a lover, he lacked passion and experience. His movements were clumsy. What he lacked, however, he more than made up for with child-like wonderment and a whole-hearted offering of his feelings. He held nothing back.

She lay and looked up at the ceiling, very conscious of his closeness and his steady breathing. She had never felt that way before. She had never given and taken so much in that one, simple act. For a time, forgetting tomorrow, she was happy.

She was smiling when sleep claimed her for its own . . .

4 a.m.

Nathan disentangled himself from her arms and slipped

from the bed. His head was filled with horror, the bloat that was Peter Black so huge and close it excluded all other thought.

Around him, the house slept. He was only half aware, dazed and disoriented. Dressing hurriedly, he left the room and wandered through the house, seeking Black. The beast was close, very close, he could sense him through every pore. Stumbling, half asleep, half dead, he struggled through the house towards the cellar. Something about the cellar screamed at him, some warning, some fact he had overlooked. But the words would not come. He was exhausted. He just wanted to lie down and sleep, not fight, there was no point.

Nathan Trooper knew it was HIM. He knew HE was here, in the cellar. He knew HE had to be beaten. He could feel HIM crushing his mind with raw power.

He made it to the bottom of the steps before passing out . . .

The locomotive was huge. Steam jetted from overworked pipes as the 200 ton mass of black iron sped towards him. The roar of the pumping intestines filled his ears. The vision grew until the entire sky was blacked out by the thundering pile of death.

A nightmare face was carved into the grill: no eyes, only vacant pits darker than the metal into which they were recessed.

He stood in its path, unable to turn aside, driven to stop it before it could trample humanity beneath its red-hot wheels.

Just before the machine struck him he raised his hand in defiance. In that hand he held the weapon he had found to stop the nightmare, a talisman of good against its demonic evil.

But in the split second prior to impact, when his

ears began to bleed and his body trembled under the pounding momentum of the beast, he realized that he held only *empty air*.

The beast steamed through his inconsequential form and disappeared into the night with an eerie whistle of victory . . .

Nathan awoke with a start, his ears echoing to the sound of that unholy shrill, his brain filled with death.

He looked up, bleary eyed. The air in the cellar was chill, filled with the smell of dew and a new day. Light flooded the room.

He snapped aware in sudden panic. Daylight? In the *cellar*?

The hatch to the cellar lay open to the outside world. His heart stopped. He sniffed cautiously, detected the faint stench of death and decay. A fly buzzed wearily around his head.

Nathan felt his guts crawl like slime in his abdomen. 'He was here,' he mumbled, sensing again the foul bouquet of rotten flesh.

He rose like a zombie from his cramped sleeping place on the steps, unaware of the pain in his side where the healing gunshot wound clamoured for attention. He was only aware that Peter Black had been there during the night while he lay helpless and asleep. He had not heard the man arrive or leave, but the open door and vague smell betrayed his passing. Nathan crossed to the steps.

One wet footprint on every other step. More damp footprints in the dust. Three dead maggots on the floor, crushed into the muck of another mammoth imprint.

Nathan tasted bile in his throat and realized his hands were shaking. He climbed the steps to the house, went straight for the liquor cabinet in the lounge and pulled out a bottle of vodka. The lip of the bottle rattled against the glass when he poured himself a measure. The shakes did not lessen until he had downed the drink, and did not disappear until the glass was empty for the second time. The bottle did not rattle when he poured himself a third.

He turned in surprise when he heard footsteps behind him, his mind conjuring up images of Black prowling around the house. It was only then that he realized he had assumed Black had been and gone – what if the man was still in the house?

But the intruder was only Anne. She wandered sleepily through the living room on her way to the kitchen. She did not notice him in the corner, glass in hand, hidden in the shadows.

Nathan watched her quietly. Even first thing in the morning, when she had just risen from bed, she was beautiful. He considered calling out to her, but was not sure how she would react. Perhaps she would hate him. Perhaps she would regret the previous evening.

Pleasant thoughts of love-making vanished as he recalled the cellar. Black had been in the house while they slept, and had left without killing them. Nathan had no idea why.

He raised the glass to his mouth and downed the rest of his drink, shivering as the fire raced into his blood. He was scared. What should he do? Tell the others? Search the house?

'Bloody hell!'

Trooper raised his head in alarm. Daniels was staring at him, open mouthed. He looked tired, his eyes red, a day's growth of beard on his sallow cheeks. 'What the hell happened to you?'

'What?' Nathan asked, confused.

'Your face!' Daniels exclaimed. 'What happened to your face?'

Anne appeared in the doorway, saw Nathan and gasped in shock. The coffee cup slipped from her hand and smashed on the floor.

'What?' Nathan repeated, his confusion turning to anger and fear. 'What's the matter?' He moved into the light and saw Daniels flinch in disgust. What the hell was the matter with them?

There was a mirror on the wall. His face swam into view.

Vodka churned in his stomach. The floor dropped away from his feet. The room span. He groaned in misery.

Four finger trails of dried blood ran from his forehead, over his cheeks and down onto his jawline. Blood stained his nose and ran from the corner of his mouth. His neck and the collar of his shirt were spattered with dark clots. He raised one hand hesitantly to his head, ran his fingers through his hair and over his numb skin. *Black*. His arteries turned to ice. He watched as the little colour in his cheeks suddenly drained away.

Black's rotten stinking blood, he thought. I'm covered in it.

His eyes closed in dread. 'Oh no,' he moaned miserably. His eyes locked with Daniels. 'The cellar was open when I woke up.'

Daniels' expression of horror mirrored his own. 'Oh Christ!' he blurted. Black was here, now – in the house!

'What is it?' Anne shouted, confused. 'What's going on?'

Daniels looked at Nathan, seemed about to argue, but then backed off. His imagination was working overtime – Nathan's face was a warning to them all – it had all happened so suddenly.

Their eyes locked, Nathan's dark, Daniels' pale and wide.

Time's up, Nathan seemed to be saying. Daniels thought he could hear the words in his mind, and felt his eyes widen further.

Nathan smiled. The skin around his eyes crinkled.

Well met, Inspector. It's been . . . different.

Then those strange, dark eyes sought out Anne Wallis. A trace of regret, of sadness, flickered over them like a shadow.

Daniels felt the emotion pour through him like iced water. Then the eyes and the man had turned and gone . . .

Trooper followed his extra sense as it led him to the mass of Black's presence. His ego pulsed in Nathan's mind. Everywhere he looked he could see where the creature had been. Not just in his mind's eye, but also by the tell-tale stains of bloody footprints and nauseating odour. It sickened him. But he felt very calm.

There was a hand print on a bedroom door. He did not wait for inspiration, nor hesitate to prepare himself. He knew nothing could prepare him. Behind the door, betrayed by his power, sat Peter Black. Nathan could see him as if the wall were made of glass.

Sibilant whispers rose in his mind, distracting him, the voices of the dead. They pleaded for mercy, yearned for freedom. They warned off the young psychic, begged him to flee.

They went unheard.

Nathan grasped the door handle and turned it. Then he opened the door, pushed it inward, and stepped forward into his nightmare.

Daniels stood motionless as Nathan turned and left the room. His pent breath turned stale in his lungs. The despair in Trooper's posture, the finality in his voice, told Daniels the psychic would not be coming back.

That intuition, coupled with Nathan's statement about Black's intrusion, could mean only one thing.

Peter Black had come into their sanctuary last night to complete his unfinished business. And had never left.

So Daniels stood there, unable to act. He heard Nathan's lonely footsteps retreat down the landing. He heard a door open, then close again, softly.

It had all happened so suddenly, so unexpectedly. He had imagined that Black would arrive in a storm of violence, that Nathan would sense his arrival and they would be prepared to meet the killer on their own terms. He had imagined they would be armed and ready and at least facing the right way when Black appeared. He had pictured the monster blasting the front door open in a frenzy of wild, uncontrollable anger, a hail of gunfire, a few unpleasant images of spiders. But nothing like this. In his simplistic plan, Black would have been killed in the crossfire or pulled down by Nathan in some gargantuan psychic conflict. Then the survivors would have tidied up the mess and buried the evidence, secure in the knowledge that the horror was at last over.

But that scenario had been flawed: he had imagined a mad killer. He had not listened to Nathan's warnings or learnt the lesson of Stuart Corbett – Black was no mindless beast. He had torn down their defences and entered under cover of darkness and a deep, unnatural sleep. They were not fighting a dumb animal, but a highly intelligent psychopath: a rabid beast with the guile of a wolf.

Daniels plummeted helplessly into instant despair.

You fucked up, he accused himself. You should have listened to Nathan. He *knew* this would happen – he had no pathetic delusions about easy victory, he *knew* we we'd be lucky to even come out of this alive. You fucked up in your house when you went up against Corbett, and he was only a baby compared to Peter Black. You're *way* out of your league. This is Trooper's territory, not yours. So retire from the battleground before you screw up anything else.

Just thinking about his failure made him sick. His ideas of justice and dogged success fell. He felt useless; he *was* useless.

He knew he did not have the courage to follow Nathan into the mouth of hell. He just wanted to flee, leave the terror behind him. He wanted to return to his old charade. He wanted OUT.

He glanced over at Anne. Silent understanding passed between them. Anne wanted to cry out, to chase after Nathan and drag him back into safety. Daniels was hard pressed not to turn and flee.

But then they remembered the guns. Black *must* have seen them. Yet he had not bothered to wreck their defence – the guns were still there, undisturbed. They glared at Daniels silently, crying out to be used, arguing with his cowardice and hesitancy. They shamed him into sudden anger. He stepped towards them.

And the world exploded into madness.

Anne's eyes widened in astonishment. Her Adam's apple bobbed convulsively. 'Oh, God. Bill?' She screamed. Blood jetted from her nose. 'Look out!' she cried. 'Nathan!' Then her eyes rolled up inside her head and she collapsed unconscious on the floor.

Daniels opened his mouth to call out and found he could not breathe. His throat was clamped shut. He heaved his stomach to draw air, but his neck was in a vice. Stars burst in his eyes. His legs turned to jelly. He reached out to the guns, defiant.

His hand clenched, claw-like, around Sam's shotgun. He pulled it from the planks. It weighed more than a ton. He dropped it.

The gun fell at an impossibly slow rate. Daniels felt the world withdraw, felt his brain seize up.

And then the ground came up and hit him in the face.

He tasted blood. He lay there for a while, choking, his eyes jerking madly around the room as the world grew black. Then he saw them, thousands of them, bloated, hairy, swarming across the carpet.

The first spider reached his hand and he *felt* it touch him. He flinched away in horror. Scores more smothered him.

It's only an *illusion*, he cried.

But he could *feel* them on his skin, crawling all over him, it wasn't that he could just see them, he could feel them too.

Oh God, let me die. Let me free of this madness.

A spider appeared in front of his face. Its multi-faceted eyes shimmered, and he could see himself reflected a million times. It moved towards him. And he dropped mercifully into the darkness.

Nathan pushed the door closed quietly behind him. The room was in total darkness, the window shuttered and boarded up. He stood by the door, letting his eyes adjust to the gloom.

A lot of good those boards did, he thought calmly. Sam never knew how hopeless it was, how his survival had been no more than another twist in Black's plan – let the policeman live and draw all the enemies into the trap. Sam Stevens, human bait. Black had known all along that I would eventually track him here. And I, the great Nathan Trooper, leapt straight into the spider's web.

Trooper smiled in the darkness. At least Sam had escaped.

Or had he? The smile faded. Maybe not. Maybe Sam,

his wife and his kids lay dead in a ditch somewhere, silenced by the evil they had hoped to outrun. Black did not like to leave loose ends. He may be an animal, but he was not an idiot.

Either way, Nathan thought, I have more immediate problems.

Realizing his eyes were useless in the gloom, he reluctantly unveiled his sixth sense. His head instantly exploded into light, Black's power saturating his mind. He scanned the room, forming an image which human sight could not give. Detail sprang into focus, enhanced by the psychic glow. Everything was crystal clear.

Only then did Nathan understand why Black and his minions cut out their eyes. Nature's eyes were pathetic compared to the power of his inner eye. His view was like a night sight, mind enhanced, and he knew it would improve with psychic strength. That was why he had never been able to see before – he had been too weak, too chained to his physical senses. Now, standing there in the presence of the most powerful psychic the world had ever known, leeching some of that strength, Nathan saw his world become clearer.

He could see the furniture and all it concealed. He could see the world outside, cast in all the glorious colours of life. He could see his own body, the muscles and tissue bursting with energy. He could see thought and emotion, laid bare under his gaze. Just seeing such detail made him want to tear out his eyes for the worthless organs they were. But he controlled that hideous urge and turned his attention to that other presence.

Peter Black's mind appeared as a whirlwind, so complex and intertwined that Nathan could not decipher its meaning. Through the confusion he managed to detect pleasure, satisfaction, an all-consuming patience. But beyond that he could see nothing – Black's mind was too powerful, too shielded, too inhuman.

But where the man's mind was closed, his body was an open book Nathan read easily. The sight made him feel physically sick.

Peter Black was dead. That much was obvious at first glance. All parts of his body were riddled with decay, rot, and cancer. His veins were blocked with detritus. His main arteries could carry little blood, the thin fluid unable to pass a mass of tumours and lesions in the tissue walls. His lungs were filled with liquid, some of it normal bodily waste, most of it a thick yellow slime of infection. His heart was old and tired, unable to provide his massive body with the sustenance it required. The incredible growth of Black's skeleton had overburdened its supporting organs – his body's decline had accelerated into complete disrepair, and was close to final shutdown. The bones were brittle and riddled with fractures, over-stressed and old. Parts of his internal organs had already collapsed, and were now diseased or totally decayed. The flesh was hanging in strips. Beneath it swarmed the larvae of a hundred different insects, feeding off the nutrients contained in the dead and dying tissue. Peter Black was a walking corpse, nothing more than a nesting ground for flies.

And yet, despite the total failure of the body, Black lived. His brain was intact. There was no decay there – only raw power. His mind was vast, overflowing the bounds of his skull, reaching out into other strata. Nathan sensed other minds linked to the power, captured parts of the psychic net. They orbited Black, forever bound by chains Nathan could neither see nor understand.

The sheer *power* of the mass took his breath away.

The huge clot of energy pulsated with a life of its own. If a normal mind generated enough power for a small light bulb, then Black's mind thundered with the power of a nuclear reactor. It hummed with a sub-sonic roar which made Trooper's teeth ache.

He felt humbled and inconsequential beside it.

Black turned his head. The movement was sluggish, stirring a colony of insects nesting under Black's collar bone. The slithering motion beneath the skin turned Nathan's stomach.

Greetings.

The voice resounded in Nathan's mind, without passing through his ears. It was deep and powerful. Trooper was not surprised by this use of telepathy. Judging by the state of Black's vocal cords, the man had been unable to speak for some time. And besides, what other way should the world's greatest psychics communicate?

Standing in the shadow of Black's awesome power, Nathan began to wonder why he was still alive.

You have many questions, I see. That is good. A man who questions why he is here is less likely to act without reason.

Nathan felt threatened by the rational tone of that terrifying voice. Its humanity and normality contrasted with the decayed body and rampant evil. 'I came here to kill you.'

I know. You realize now you cannot hope to achieve that.

'Perhaps. But you disgust me – your evil is unnameable. You represent all that I detest. You murder for pleasure.'

Only those who deserved to die felt the power of my wrath.

Nathan snorted. 'What are you? God? Who are you to decide?'

I have the right of Power. They were all evil. Thieves, criminals, perverts. The dregs of society.

Nathan laughed harshly. 'Ah. Another vigilante.'

Do not mock me, Nathan Trooper. Do not tempt my anger.

The voice contained a warning and beneath that a seething rage. That rage, Nathan noted, was only thinly controlled.

'What do you want? You were the one who called me here, trapped me. Why not just kill me and have done with it?'

I do not seek your death, Trooper. We are unique, you and I.

Nathan's heart skipped a beat, his suspicions rising. 'Trying to reason with me is pointless, Black. If you thought I would listen then you made a mistake.' Nathan paused, thoughtful. 'And how many other mistakes have there been, Peter?'

None so serious as your father's, Trooper.

This time the voice was filled with malice. Nathan shuddered. 'What do you mean?'

He was an animal. He thought only of himself. He killed your mother, tried to kill you, murdered scores of innocents on the operating table. I knew your father well, Nathan. He paid me more attention than you.

For some reason that last statement hurt. 'I know. But he *created* you. That was his biggest mistake.'

Not at all. It was the only good act he ever performed.

Nathan sensed Black's anger rising, realized he was pushing too hard. For a moment, the vision of a thousand spiders filled his mind, then vanished. He could see the echo of the outburst in Black's over-active mind. 'What are you doing?' he asked quietly.

Nothing.

Nathan knew that to be a lie. His new sense could *see* the falsehood in every thought Black voiced. He knew instinctively that Black was toying with Daniels' mind. 'Leave them alone,' he ordered. 'If you wish to talk – which I can only assume you do, since otherwise I would be dead – then leave them alone.'

Black paused, his mind suddenly glowing intensely.

It is done. They are sleeping.

Nathan chewed his lip. He did not know what to do. He had come here to kill Peter Black, but now it was obvious he could not achieve that end. He was powerless in this room. He felt lost.

I mean you no harm.

'Liar!' Nathan spat. 'Stop toying with me, what do you want?'

I wanted to meet you, brother. I wanted to talk with you. I wanted you to see that I am not a monster.

Nathan looked at Black's body and laughed. What *was* he if not a monster? 'You, brother,' Nathan said the word with venom, 'are nothing more than a killer. A powerful one, yes, but a killer nonetheless. You disgust and offend me. If I had the power I would rid the world of you in an instant.' He opened his eyes. The hideous view faded into the gloom, and of that he was glad. He no longer wished to see the man. 'You make me puke.'

Black stirred again. Trooper could hear the sickening slither of his rotten flesh as it moved in the chair.

You disappoint me. I had expected more of you, of the son of Ethan Trooper. You have a huge potential, an ability you do not understand. That ability could serve you well.

'In what? Destruction?'

The quest for life, and power. And power is life.

'I have only sought to safeguard life, Black, not end it.'

I know. Therein lies your weakness. Alongside me you could have been a force for Mankind to reckon with.

The penny dropped in Nathan's overburdened mind. 'Join you?' He laughed. 'You know me not at all if you hoped for that.'

You have power I want. How I obtain it is of no importance. You can give it to me, or I can snap your mind and take your strength. I could bind you to me as I have bound others.

'I would never serve you.'

This time it was Black who laughed. A psychic mocking.

Fool. You cannot comprehend my ability to control others.

'You could never control me.' It was a pointless statement, Nathan knew that. He also knew it was untrue.

It is unwise to tempt my wrath with such brash claims.

'Look, I'm not scared of you, Black. I—'

You should be. I tire of you, Trooper. I thought you would be stimulating, but you are as boring as your companions. So look upon me, witness my power.

As Black finished, Nathan heard the bed springs squeak. Turning in surprise he was terrified to see Stuart Corbett, back from the dead, a rotten corpse with a black grin. 'You useless fuck,' Corbett accused, 'you fell asleep on the job.'

Nathan eyed the illusion warily. He knew it had to be an illusion. Didn't it? Corbett was dead. He *knew* that.

Corbett's hand snaked out and punched Trooper in the stomach. Nathan flinched in shock and unexpected pain. 'Hey! That hurt!'

Corbett climbed from the bed, his dead eyes never leaving Nathan's face. 'Fuck you, Trooper.' And then his hand was in Nathan's stomach, pushing through the skin to grasp at the entrails.

Nathan screamed in agony. Corbett laughed in his face, tore out his guts and threw them on the bed.

Anne regained consciousness and awareness slowly.

She lay on her side. Stacks of timber rose up around her like skyscrapers. Across the floor John Daniels lay spreadeagled on the carpet on his stomach. His eyes were closed, his face a mask of blood. For a moment Anne thought he had been attacked, but then she noticed the blood stain on one of the planks. He had collapsed and struck his head on the timber; he was either out cold, or dead.

She groaned in misery and closed her eyes. She remembered looking at Daniels, torn between fear and the need to help Nathan. Then things had changed – instead of Daniels she had found herself looking at her dead husband. He had appeared in the blink of an eye and simply stood there, motionless, a cold smile on his face. The image had sparked in her a sudden grief, anger and guilt. But in another instant, Bill had vanished. Nathan stood in his place, beaten and bruised with his face a mass of cuts and spilled blood. He had smiled at her fondly. 'Forgive me, Anne,' he had said, 'for I cared for you. Now I am lost. Hope is lost.' Caught in that flickering cinema-show of souls, Anne had been helpless to act, unable to move in defence when a nightmare figure had reared up behind Nathan and punched his intestines clear through his abdomen.

As those images flooded back into her waking mind, Anne cringed in terror. She struggled to her knees, head swimming and unsteady, stomach protesting at the sudden movement. She held onto the back of a chair, holding down the queasiness until her balance was restored. Then she staggered over to Daniels.

The Inspector was alive. A large flap of skin had been torn from his forehead to reveal red-stained bone below. His breathing was steady, if shallow. The wound had already turned purple, and the flow of blood was now nothing more than a slight ooze from the deepest part of the cut. His skin was very pale. Judging by the bruising and the amount of dried blood on the carpet, Anne surmised they had both been unconscious for some time.

She was alone. Daniels was of no use to her.

She studied the room, aware that time was running out, and her eyes fell on the stack of guns. She regarded them warily. A bullet would probably stop even a monster like Black; but she had never handled a gun before. She hesitated, caught between a desire to help Nathan and a deep loathing and mistrust of weapons.

In that split second of indecision there was a loud crash from the bedroom. Somebody screamed – or something. The cry was so wild and primitive that it hardly sounded human; more the howl of an animal being torn to pieces. The scream made all of her hair stand on end, and goosebumps rose on her forearms.

'Oh God,' she whispered, 'this is no time to debate morality.'

She stuffed her indecision in the back of her head, grabbed the first gun which came to hand and fled before she had a chance to change her mind. The weapon was heavy and unwieldy in her grip. She glanced at it, noticed it was the revolver Daniels had taken to polishing habitually, and thanked her luck. She had watched him clean and load it the night before, and knew how the mechanism worked. She also understood, in an instant, why he had felt better caring for the gun in the dark hours before Black's arrival.

Silence had returned to the house.

She moved out of the lounge, entered the hall which led to the bedrooms and slid carefully along the wall to the only closed door. She could *feel* the charge of their reciprocated hate and anger.

Her heart beat like a Rolling Stones concert in her rib cage.

Gripping the gun tightly, she reached out to open the door . . .

Nathan screamed in terror, clutched at his abdomen, and the pain vanished. He stared at the room, amazed. Nothing had changed – he stood just inside the door, Black sat in the far corner.

Peter Black laughed in his mind.

Nothing is as it seems. I am not what I seem.

Nathan blushed in shame. The vision had been so *real*. He had *felt* the blow, felt the agony as his vitals had been torn out. With Corbett he had experienced many visions, but none so convincing. Nathan had known them to be images plucked from his mind.

With Black it was violently different. The sensations were all so *concrete* he was not sure whether they were vision or reality. Despite knowing Corbett had been dead, he still felt the pain.

He began to doubt all that he saw and felt. If Black was powerful enough to convince him of that, then what else was real?

Black laughed again, interrupting his train of thought.

Yes, Trooper. Are you really here? Are you really alive?

*How can you be sure I am not merely toying with
your soul? How do you know you are not already
chained to me?*

He laughed again.

*This game amuses me. To see you fallen and beaten
amuses me.*

The gloating tone of that hideous voice made Nathan's
anger blossom above his shame. He brought his mind
back from the brink with raw fury. He had come here
to do a job, not to be ridiculed by some arrogant corpse.
Nathan knew he was still a threat to Black. Why else
would the man have gone to such lengths? Above
all others, Nathan represented the greatest danger to
Black's mission in life.

But what danger? Black may think Nathan had the
knowledge required to win, but Nathan could not imagine what that knowledge was. He was weaker, less
experienced, had fewer resources to call upon and lacked
his opponent's all-consuming passion for survival. Black
needed to win – it was the meaning of his life. Nathan
was not even sure he wanted to go on living.

Perhaps that was his strength. Perhaps Black would
not take the risks, would always put survival before
victory.

Perhaps; perhaps not. Only one thing was certain –
the longer they sparred, the more chance Black would
have to read his intentions and prepare against them.
Although Nathan was boosting his energy by leeching
it from his enemy, he sensed this was not going to be
a battle of strength – he would have to wait thirty years
and slaughter a hundred people before he could hope to
rival Black in the power game. So he needed something
besides raw power. He needed to find out exactly what
it was that scared Peter Black.

'So what now?' Trooper asked, aware that Black was

reading his mind and moving to intercept his every thought.

He sensed Black's ominous amusement in the darkness.

Now, brother? Now I tire of these solitary mind games. Now we fight.

And the world turned in on itself. The room vanished. The corpse vanished. They stood in a dark void of pure thought, and Nathan saw for the first time the psychic image of his enemy, a Peter Black before the mutation. With his body restored, Nathan could see Black had once been a handsome man. That thought caused him a pang of regret which he could neither explain nor welcome.

Always the violent path, he thought. Quick to judge, swift to anger, never understand. He sighed. 'As you wish.'

Then let us do battle.

Black struck immediately, giving Nathan no chance to prepare.

As ever, the war-ground was dictated by their fears. Scenes came and went: pictures of Nathan's childhood, images of his father wielding an axe with demonic red eyes and a mouth insane with froth. But Nathan had faced these fears before and avoided them smoothly. He countered with images from Black's own dark mind, and dark they were: victims in their last, terrible moments, childhood nightmares and teenage tortures. But Black, too, had lived with these moments. Witnessing those terrors did nothing to lessen his power.

They moved against each other, minds filled with images of the id. Each tested the mettle of his opponent, probing the shield of power to locate a weakness and thrust the needle-point home.

For a time the testing remained on even terms. Nathan had the advantages of determination and a new strength, though his technique was poor and he lacked the killer instinct. His experience was limited to his conflict with Corbett. Black had spent much of his life tormenting others. Even so, his pursuit of Trooper had severely depleted his reserves, and he felt strangely limited and disjointed.

So they circled, seeking the upper hand. Stalemate . . .

Anne grasped the door handle, turned it cautiously . . .

In that realm of thought it took a lifetime for the balance to tip. Black's knowledge of battle and his ability to take pleasure from terror proved the deciding factors.

It was Nathan who eventually tired.

Cracking Nathan's thin defence, Black spied the secrets locked within and exerted all his power to retrieve them. The move cost him dearly, for Trooper was now fighting for his soul. Trooper's valiant counter-attacks, however, were in vain. Black pinned him to the barriers of the psychic net and slashed Nathan's defences to ribbons. Such was his fury and hatred that Nathan fell under the onslaught to collapse, finally, at Black's feet.

Kneeling there, mentally exhausted, Trooper gasped for existence and felt Peter Black reach into his mind to pluck out his deepest anxieties. There was nothing Nathan could do to stop him – his greatest efforts had been for nothing. He experienced his old despair and sank into it gratefully. It seemed that however hard he battled the psychopath, in whatever form or manner, it was never enough. Black always retained the upper hand.

Who stands the victor now, brother? Black crooned.

Nathan reached his fingernails into the psychic net,

clawing for a handhold. All he found was the presence of his nemesis.

'Do your worst, creep,' Nathan gasped. 'If nothing else, I have at least made you pay for your arrogance.' He managed a tired smile. 'I have so depleted your strength that you barely have enough to retain the integrity of your foul body.'

Black snorted. *What need have I of that body now? I am ready to free myself of its bonds. Such irony that you, my greatest threat, should have shown me the way to true glory.* He laughed. *Think on that as you die, brother, and may it sicken you.*

Nathan looked up, cursing himself.

Yes, he had failed, and badly. Now there was nothing to do but release his hold on awareness and die.

'Be done with it,' he whispered. 'I tire of life.'

Black smiled, almost fondly. *So be it, brother. It was an honour to confront you. Such a change from the pathetic struggles of my other victims. I salute you.*

'I'm touched,' Nathan said sarcastically.

Black laughed. And then the pain began . . .

Grand Central Station, rush hour on a Friday afternoon.

One and a half million people, milling in apparently aimless circles, all rushing to get home or away. A hideous cacophony of worry and anxiety, of being late, arguing with a husband or wife, eyeing up the men or the women, sexual interest inflamed by an instant of eye contact. A vaulted chamber filled with the sound of the tannoy, passing feet and megawatts of thought power.

Into that madness fell Nathan's mind, cast into the image by a vindictive Peter Black. Without defence, the roar of those thoughts blasted his sanity to shreds. He collapsed on the floor, ears and nose bleeding, screaming his anguish to the world as swarms of people trod unfeeling on his outstretched limbs.

One of his deepest fears. People, and the volume of their thoughts. A million decibels of pure, raw, psychic volume.

Unable to defend himself, unable to block out the noise, Nathan fell in on himself like a collapsing star. Screaming blue murder, crying tears of blood, he begged for silence and release.

His only answer was the echo of Black's vicious laughter.

Until, when he could literally take no more and his mouth ran with saliva and rabid horror, his mind snapped.

The voices stopped in an instant, leaving him in an awful silence. Grieving for his lost life, his bastard father, his wasted dreams and hopes, Nathan Trooper was locked once again in a padded cell. His arms were lashed securely behind his back. His feet were bare, the toenails clipped painfully short. He sat, screaming and crying, kicking pointlessly at the walls. Doctors stood at the door, looking through the glass panel, laughing at him. He was nothing more than a circus freak, an object of malicious insult.

He rolled on his back, kicking, screaming. After a while the doctors grew bored with his antics and departed, shaking their heads and smiling in contempt.

He was alone. The mental silence was complete – no noise outside or inside him, no tell-tale whispers of other minds. Everything was peaceful and calm. In that gentleness – asylum or not – his horror receded and dissipated as a soft summer breeze.

It was only then that Nathan truly understood how

badly his life had been affected by the incessant, nerve-jarring chatter. He was at last truly alone, not plagued by the thoughts of others.

Am I free now? he wondered. Have I left the pain behind?

But through the peace the doubts and worries came gnawing back. He began to fidget and squirm on his backside. He realized he missed the telepathy, the nosebleeds, the possession of raw psychic *power*. And he was rapidly growing to hate this seclusion – Black was still out there, somewhere, and Nathan had a responsibility for that. It had been his task to stop Black, and he had failed. He disliked the idea of being remembered as a failure.

That worry alone caused him to go still for an instant. He suddenly had the most hideous thought.

What if this was merely an extension of the horrors Black had conjured up for him? What if his deepest fear was that he would one day lose his gift and find life afterwards unbearable? What if he had always been afraid that being psychic, however bad it affected his life, was infinitely preferable to *not* being psychic? What if he was not rid of Black at all, but this was merely the final agony?

Those thoughts made his flesh crawl. Such humiliation, such defeat. Total annihilation by the man he had failed to kill.

Trooper struggled against his restraints, wrenching his arms to free them from the jacket. He called out, but received no reply. The air in his lungs wheezed through tubes constricted by fear and desperation. He beat against the wall, trying to gain his feet.

'For God's sake!' he screamed. 'Let me out of here!'

With a mammoth, rib-wrenching heave he climbed to his feet. Crossing to the door he stood on tip-toe to peer through the glass. He could just see the corridor – saw nothing but an endless line of similar closed doors, behind each an image of himself peering out. The expressions on those faces were so grotesque that he cried out in surprise and despair. All the other faces cried out in response.

Trapped in a hall of mirrors.

A tug on his back made him scream in shock. He span around, lost his footing, and collapsed on the floor. He lay for a moment, squirming away from the door, gasping for breath.

And then he recognized the presence in his nightmare, and his fear vanished in a flash of astonishment. 'Tim?' he asked, amazed.

Tim Johnson stood by the door, an impish smile on his twelve-year-old face, his hands stuffed into the pockets of his oversized jeans with one of his father's oversized 'Hawkwind' T-shirts reaching down to his knees. The plaster cast was gone from his leg. 'Hi Nathan,' he said, his voice rich with emotion – fear, anxiety, happiness, youth and premature age in an impossible mix.

Nathan forced himself into a sitting position, recovering his composure. 'Tim. What the hell are you doing here?'

Tim grinned. 'Nice to see you too, boss,' he joked.

Nathan frowned, confused, then shook his head. 'No, I didn't mean that Tim. It's good to see you. But isn't this my nightmare?'

Tim shrugged. 'More than you think, it seems.'

'What do you mean?' Nathan struggled in the straitjacket.

Tim squatted on his haunches to bring himself down to Nathan's eye level. 'You're probably wondering why I'm here? Why something pleasant has intruded into your horror? Why I'm not off with Mum and Dad having a good time after all the . . . well, all of it. Eh?'

Nathan looked at the boy askance. 'Yes. And?'

Tim frowned. 'I heard you, Nathan. From all the way over in England. And – I saw you, when you were still in the hospital.' He met Nathan's puzzled eyes, recalling his vision. 'You know – *saw* you. *Looked*.' The pain was obvious in his old young eyes.

Nathan wanted to reach and hold the boy, take away that pain, comfort his mind as he had before. But his arms were pinned behind his back. 'I know, Tim. I saw you see me.' He shrugged and smiled bravely. 'It's not happened yet though, eh? You could be wrong.'

Tim nodded eagerly, his eyes bright. 'That's what I'm hoping for. Like with Dad. I've been waiting to hear you, listening for when you were in danger. And as soon as I heard – I came. I don't know how. I've never done this before. I just *had* to see you before it was too late. Do you understand?'

Nathan nodded. He didn't know how the boy had done it either, but he was grateful: this meant nothing was quite as it seemed, that Black's hold over his mind was far from total. Was there yet hope?

Tim looked at the room, at the strait-jacket. 'And there are a few things I've found out that maybe you don't know.' He blushed. 'It may sound like I've been going behind your back, Nathan, but it's not like that really. Someone came to me, one night. Talked to me.' He gave a crooked smile. 'He looked like you, but not so old. He said you were his brother.'

Nathan was surprised. Isaac? Visiting Tim? He had thought himself the only one capable of that contact. The thought made him both joyous and jealous. 'Well,' he whispered, 'you have been busy, haven't you Tim?'

He softened the words with a smile. 'And I may look older, but I'm actually younger than he is.'

Tim grinned, his cheeks dimpling. 'I know. He said that was because he's had an easy life compared to yours. Or mine,' he added quietly, looking away for a moment. Then he shivered and pulled himself together. 'Anyway. He told me to carry on listening, and told me to tell you this if we met – and I think he knew we would. Your brother's not stupid. Even if he is dead.'

Nathan chuckled. 'I like you Tim, you know that?' Tim blushed. 'So. What did Isaac have to say for himself?'

Tim drew a deep breath. 'He said this would probably happen. He said Black would trap you this way, that he was too powerful and quick for you to win. He's out there now, revelling in his victory. I can sense him.' Tim shuddered, remembering the killer who had attacked him – like a miniature version of Black, who was too foul to imagine. 'Isaac has been trying to hold him off, trying to rally his chained troops to your aid.'

Nathan frowned. 'What do you mean?'

'Well, when those people die and become bound to him, they stop being monsters. Or so Isaac says. They're like slaves, chained to him and feeding him, but they don't want to. They want to be free, to die. Being with him is torture. Isaac has been trying to weaken the chains which bind them, and that is how you've managed to leech so much of his energy.' He shrugged. 'I don't really understand. But I do know that there is more at stake here than just you or Black – I can sense all kinds of things in my head, and there is a lot of energy mounting up to defeat Black. You are the head of that energy, Nathan, the pipe for it to be used. You are the last chance they have to be free. You *have* to win.'

Nathan pondered the words. 'But I'm stuck in here,

Tim. What can I do now? Black has me where he wants me.'

Tim shook his head, a smile on his face. 'This is why I came, why Isaac sent me. You're wrong, Nathan! You fear your greatest fears – that is what this battle has done to you. After you faced Corbett you became paranoid about being defeated by yourself. And that is the greatest protection you could ever ask for.'

'What on earth are you talking about?'

Tim laughed. 'You don't understand, do you?' He shrugged. 'Well, perhaps that's best. Since you didn't know your deepest fear then neither did Black. He did not have the power to reach that part of you. You are complex, too *bright* for him. Your light, whilst a beacon for us, offends him.'

Nathan frowned. 'I appreciate the compliment, Tim, but I still don't understand.'

'Black used your fears of people and of returning to an asylum – those were experiences which marked you with deep scars. But they were not your *deepest, darkest* fears. They used to be, before this started. But as soon as you knew Black would turn those fears against you, you developed an even greater fear: of failure, the fear of *fear*.' Tim looked around the cell. 'This isn't Black's illusion, Nathan. It comes out of your head, not his.'

Nathan was dumbstruck. 'Are you trying to tell me that I have locked myself in this cell on *purpose*?' he exclaimed, incredulous.

Tim giggled. 'Yes. Silly, isn't it?'

'It's nonsense!' Nathan spat. 'I don't *want* to be here! I would rather be back there facing Peter Black. I'd rather be alive again. Hell, I'd rather be *anywhere*.'

Tim smiled. 'Well, if that is what you wish, do it.' He reached out to grab Nathan's arms. 'Do it, Nathan! Win it! Make my vision a lie, please!' His voice was sheer desperation. 'I saved my dad, please God let me save you.'

'I can't, dammit! I'm stuck here in this ruddy strait-jacket!'

Tim shrugged. 'Then undo the straps. Take it off. Open the door. Do us all a favour and go and kill Peter Black.' His voice contained a venom Nathan did not like, but could easily understand.

'I damned well can't! I've tried that and nothing happened.'

Tim shrugged. 'You put yourself here. Put yourself out.'

Nathan began to get unreasonably angry. The calm and rational too-old voice of the young boy was really beginning to wind him up. He felt his temper rising like a volcano about to blow.

Tim cocked his head to one side in a peculiarly comical manner. 'I think you are ready to save yourself, Nathan. Kill him. The knowledge of his own fear is within him. Find it and use it. Make me wrong, Nathan. Please.'

'What knowledge?' Nathan asked. 'And I can't go anywhere!'

Tim stepped back. 'Look, I've got to go now. Do your best.'

Nathan struggled to his feet. 'Hold it right there, Tim! What the hell did Isaac say I was supposed to do?'

Tim shrugged. 'He didn't say anything.'

Nathan reached out to him, confused, angry, imploring him to stay and explain. And only then did he realize – his hands. He looked down. His arms were free, the restraints gone. He looked up in surprise and the walls vanished along with the rest of his nightmare. His anger ebbed away. He blushed.

Tim grinned and giggled. 'Twenty-seven again,' he said, laughing. Then he bounded forward into Nathan's shocked embrace, and threw his arms around the psychic's neck in a fierce hug. 'Go get him, Nathan,' he whispered. 'End all this. Then come back to us, OK? Because there's something in my head I can't control and I need you to help me through it. I feel safe with you around.'

Nathan returned the hug, feeling comforted by the presence of the boy as he had when he embraced Anne.

So much more to life, he thought, which I never knew.

'Take care, Tim,' he answered softly. 'You'll be fine. And even if—' he paused, the memory of Tim's vision somehow incontrovertible. Had anything changed yet? 'Even if something does happen, I'll be around. Like Isaac. OK?'

Tim looked up, his eyes filled with tears. 'You promise?'

Nathan forced a confident smile. Was it really that easy? He had never understood Isaac's existence himself – how could he promise to duplicate it if he died? But then how could he turn his back on Tim now? He had saved the lad's life. He smiled. 'I promise. Now go back, and rest. It seems I have some work to do.'

Tim pulled away, wiping at his eyes. 'Take care, boss,' he said, managing a tired smile. 'I'll be waiting for you.'

And then, without warning, he vanished.

Nathan blinked, surprised. It was all happening too fast. What had Isaac been talking about? How had Tim become involved? How could he manage, now, to reverse the truth of Tim's deadly vision? He had already lost. Hadn't he?

Nathan closed his eyes to ponder his next move. Black must be stopped – he had to die. His id must be completely destroyed.

Nathan did not know how. He believed that the knowledge was within Black, but he did not know how to get it or what to look for.

So many deaths, he thought. Death, and all its variations. All that responsibility is now on my shoulders, and I do not have the faintest idea how to stop the bastard. I mean, how can you scare something like that? What is *his* deepest fear?

He forced himself to relax, to sit back and think. He would have only one more chance. He had to make it count.

And then, in a flash of insight, he remembered his first encounter with Stuart Corbett in Tim Johnson's mind. He recalled the psychic link, Corbett's mental probe. And he knew what he had to do – he had to get inside Black's sick and rotten mind.

Nathan smiled, feeling his fear abate as the challenge of the game took precedence. Black had tried domination by terror, and failed. Now Nathan called the game plan.

He chose strategy, brain over brawn. He decided to play chess for his soul. It was something he had always wanted to do.

So he moved into position, whispering chess moves in his mind, a distraction for his omnipresent rival. And he rose back to consciousness, increasingly aware of Black's renewed presence.

Black pushed Trooper down into the abyss of his nightmares. He pushed him down until the psychic was kicking and screaming and begging for mercy. Then he pushed some more. In the darkness of total fear, Trooper's white psychic light grew dim, losing its brilliant glow. Still Black applied the pressure, feeding off the other man's fear. He pushed down and down until the white glow was wreathed in shadow, and Nathan could no longer even beg.

Black chuckled to himself, revelling in his victory. The battle had gone well – Trooper had been a worthy opponent, but no real match for his years of skill and his true desire for terror.

He made to push Trooper one last time.

And the entity in his hands exploded into wild light.

Rising from the abyss, blazing white, a torpedo of energy blasted into Black's head. Returned from nothingness, Nathan moved swiftly and cast his mind adrift along the psychic link between himself and Black. As he sped into the swollen mass of energy, Nathan wondered if he would ever return.

Within only a few heart-stopping moments, Nathan had crossed the void into Black's mind. The link to his own mind was stretched to an impossibly thin line. When Nathan had encountered Corbett's mental probe in Tim Johnson's head he had severed that bond. Now it seemed as if Nathan was in danger of severing his own link, such was the stress imposed upon it by his rash behaviour.

Yet the connection did not snap. He fell headlong into Black's psychic batteries, his sudden and unexpected move taking his opponent entirely unawares. While Black sensed the intrusion into his mind with amazement, withdrawing into himself like a snail to deal with the threat, Trooper took the opportunity to find some answers. Specifically, he sought the reason for Black's fear of him. He needed ammunition for his attack.

He scanned the edges of Black's awareness, skirting the areas of deepest horror which screamed madness at him. Aware of Black's approaching angry defence he moved on, constantly dodging his enemy. He fell past memories, unable to distinguish which belonged to

Black and which to his victims. All the time the howling grew closer.

Changing tack, Nathan dropped deeper and descended quickly into Black's dark subconscious. Here the psychic images were at their most distressing. What he saw would, he knew, haunt him to his grave – whether that grave would be minutes or years hence. His mind blocked some of the images, but they surfaced in his own subconscious as gibbering horrors. Yet Nathan did not hesitate; he fell ever deeper into the darkness, seeking the locked container in which he knew Black held his darkest secrets and fears.

Visions swam by him. Tentacled, nameless things which bawled their lust, demonic creatures with mutated limbs, other horrors he shunned. Nathan sank into the mire, searching, picking amongst all the detritus of Black's ill id in search of one, minute item.

Micro-seconds had passed, and Nathan knew he was out of time. Soon Black's defences would fall on him with all the unrelenting wrath of that dark brain. He knew he had to withdraw before it was too late. And yet he felt so *close*. The shadows had darkened. He was near to the very heart of Black's self, the monster's core. Here, if anywhere, would be the object Nathan sought with increasing desperation. The images had faded – only darkness and silence surrounded him. There were no thoughts here, only the biochemical impulses which drove the mind he had invaded. Here was the basis of all Black did, the reason for his actions. This was the centre of the id, the generator of all psychic energy.

At last Nathan slowed. He could sense Black gathering his energy to sever the link. He had a few moments in which to act, a few more precious nano-seconds. So he opened his mind to the answers and released the floodgates. He had no time to filter Black's filthy mind; he had to drink the whole thing and pray for salvation.

Into his mind gushed Peter Black, the *real* Peter Black, the primitive animal in human form. Into Trooper oozed the slime at the centre of Black's mind, the bilge water which kept his enemy on an uneven keel. He had no control over that influx of information – it simply blasted into his forebrain, too much. Too much, too soon.

The data overflowed Nathan's mental boundaries, pushing back his sanity. He had never expected such a volume of facts, feelings and instincts. The force of that instant knowledge, like autumn rain thundering through a storm drain, blasted him back into his own mind. Nathan was buffeted uncontrollably. His mind filled with information, unfiltered psychic ability which was simply too much to bear. Black's id was too *huge* for him, and he fell before it, crushed into insignificance beside the might of his opponent.

He tried to close his mind, but could not. His brutal mistake had hammered him backwards into the shadows and he could no longer remember where he was or how to leave. Still the id assaulted him, filled him with its pervasive power, possessed him and crushed him. He could no longer distinguish between himself and Peter Black. He was lost in the cataclysmic exchange of power. He adopted his enemy's wants, his drive, his mission. Raw psychic power drove itself into the core of his mind – too much power. He felt as if his mind was about to explode. The souls of Peter Black and his victims coursed along that link and flattened Nathan's identity in their passing, leaving only tatters of what he used to be. Like a locomotive, the combined energy of a thousand dead minds blasted into his head and almost tore off the back of his skull.

His core was shattered. He had lost.

In one final heave the energy severed Nathan's link. What remained of him fled into the recesses of his brain, crawling into the polluted shadows to lick its wounds. The transfer stopped instantly, leaving only a bruised and sullen silence.

Into that silence dropped a hesitant chuckle. Peter Black, stunned by the sudden apocalypse, found himself alone. The intruder was gone, utterly destroyed in a flash of released, pent-up power. Reaching out his own mental probes, Black searched the psychic net for Trooper's presence, and found nothing.

As a psychic entity, Trooper had simply ceased to exist.

Peter Black chuckled and returned leisurely to consciousness, ascending through awareness until he surfaced once again in the world of reality. His enemy was vanquished. Nathan Trooper had vaporized his own mind in one desperate, doomed manœuvre.

Peter Black studied the bedroom with his powerful psychic vision. Trooper's body lay broken and limp. His mind, once the brightest light Black had ever seen – a glittering beacon of power untainted by ambition or disease – was now a thoughtless vacuum.

Black laughed softly, revelling in his easy victory.

Checkmate, I think.

His thought fell into the silence and contaminated it.

Nathan's mind was gone, smashed into smithereens. His body was nothing more than a dying vessel to carry his empty head.

The hero falls. The battle is lost.

Black chuckled again. Trooper's attempt to uncover the reasons for history had miscarried – instead of raiding the ammunition dump, Nathan had simply made it explode in his face. Black's last enemy had been well and truly erased from the equation. There was nothing to stand between him and his future.

He gathered his remaining strength and hauled his body to its feet by sheer force of will. The flesh and bone frame which carried his mind was near to collapse. Soon its purpose would be served, and he would be able to discard the rotting shell.

The decay had begun soon after he had called the first unhappy souls to his side to do his bidding. When he had felt the first ripples in the psychic net he had been more than satisfied. And when the first of his spawn had died and passed to him all the new power, he had been ecstatic. Never before had he experienced such pleasure, such boundless strength. Whole vistas of possibility had opened before him, avenues of destruction waiting to be explored.

But his ecstasy had been short-lived – with the power came the corruption. First, his fingernails had changed, leaving him with brutal talons for the hunt. That had not distressed him, since the claws at least served a useful purpose. Neither had his sudden growth bothered him, as that also had its benefits. At the time, he merely concluded that his psychic hunting skills were reflected in his physical form. However, as the hours had passed and his power had grown, his flesh had begun to fail him. The fragile tissue had started to decay, as if his mind was requiring too much sustenance and his body was no longer capable of providing it. He developed gangrene. That powerful body, his greatest servant in the long years of scavenging for food in the wilderness, had wasted into a lifeless hulk. His organs had caved in on themselves. His blood thinned. Colonies of insects took to nesting in his flesh.

And he had witnessed all the mutation with mounting horror, through the gift of his cursed new sight. Every detail of growing putrefaction and slithering larvae was revealed. Day by day he had watched himself rot, powerless to reverse the process.

Only power had preserved him. As the decay worsened he had been forced to expend more strength to maintain the integrity of his ailing body. Yet as he used and acquired more power, so the decay had accelerated. So began the vicious circle of power, hunger and corruption, until he had found himself losing the battle to keep hold of his physical manifestation in this world.

The process had taken years, but now it was almost over. He knew he was very close to solving the problem once and for all. His power had increased to a point where he hardly required his body at all. Soon he would relinquish that hold and float free in the psychic net. Once there, a mind without inhibition or restriction, he would be able to consume all the power he wished.

As he stood, he realized Trooper's attack had accelerated the process. The skirmish, though brief, had lost him many chained souls. His grip on the flesh had become noticeably weaker – just standing up required a massive output of energy. Only days before he had been able to run like the wind by expending less energy than that. He had to let go of his corpse before it sucked him dry.

However, he was determined to have at least some pleasure. A small physical act was required to celebrate Trooper's demise.

The tower of decomposing flesh staggered unsteadily across the room. There was a hideous slime-ridden grin on the purple and green face as one arm reached down, the hand closing around Trooper's neck to lift the limp form easily into the air.

You would never serve me. You came here to kill me.

He punctuated the sentence by hammering Nathan's slight body into the wall. Trooper's head struck the door frame, splitting his skull. Blood and cabbage brains spilled from the wound. The tight grip of Black's claws on Nathan's throat tore the skin to shreds and severed the tendons in Trooper's neck.

I disgust you.

He let go of the body, and it flew from his hand to strike the door. Wood shattered. Nathan's head shattered like an egg. Gore and slime spattered the plaster in a shower of instant death.

Black grabbed the lifeless body and tore off the head.

Behold your master!

Still laughing, he extended one taloned finger and delicately popped the eyeballs from Trooper's sockets.

The first thing Anne saw as the door swung open was the *thing* standing in the middle of the room. She felt her stomach heave. Bit by bit her eyes consumed the image and tried to convince her numb brain it was actually true. The stench was unbearable, a thick cloying smell of decomposed flesh. Black was so *big*, so *dead*; a Hollywood zombie escaped from the special effects department. Blood and pus oozed from a score of seeping crevices and wounds, flies swarmed around his body, and parts of his flesh seemed to seethe, as if colonies of parasites feasted on the soft tissue.

Bursts of white light appeared in her eyes. Her head swam and threw the gloom into disarray. She felt sick, ill and disgusted.

Her hand sank until the .45 pointed at the floor. She did not have the strength to bring the gun to bear on the monster, and why bother? How can you kill something that is already dead? Her muscles went limp. Anne could not decide whether to throw up or just faint.

Then she caught sight of the object in Black's foul hand. A head, battered like an overripe tomato, barely recognizable.

Nathan Trooper. It was his head, his blood on the floor.

In the end, unable to make a decision, she did both.

CHAPTER FIVE

The Eye of The Hurricane

The roar of power subsided to a peaceful whisper. Ripples formed concentric circles and rebounded until all was still.

Scattered across the battleground, fragments of consciousness, of purpose, drifted to the disturbed surface. And waited.

In time, and here there was nothing but all the time in the world, isolated fragments collided and joined, for they were parts of one entity which had been shattered and now sought union.

In time, fragments encountered others, and became awareness. At the centre of the pond the awareness drew the remaining fragments to it. As they coalesced, so the awareness increased.

Still, much had been lost. But not all.

Time. The reconstruction took an eternity, but everything must end. Eventually, it was ready. HE was ready.

HE had some unfinished business. HE remembered the real world, knew his business would still be waiting for him, because nobody else was capable of stopping IT. And HE remembered HIS promise to a boy, a promise strong enough to cross any barrier.

HE paused. What now? What do I do? How do I get back? How do I finish what I started?

HE smiled. *Cheat.*

HE looked inside his mind. A secret lay within. HE had destroyed himself in the quest for that secret, but it was one of the many things which survived the cataclysm. How to destroy a man who thrives on fear? HE had the answer, at last.

Why am I here? HE asked. *To play the game.*

Why play the game? *Because checkmate is not always the end.*

HIS smile broadened. It was *time*.

CHAPTER SIX

Hurricane Nathan

Peter Black let go of the bloody head, suddenly weak, pulled down by the weight of his sagging corpse. Disoriented, he could do nothing but collapse on the floor. He lay there, gathering his resources before the final manœuvre of his earth life. For so long he had kept his body artificially alive, terrified of losing his power should his decaying heart fail. Now he had no such fears. Death was merely another step on the ladder to ultimate supremacy.

Yet still he clung to his earthly incarnation. A few more moments of its familiar joy would be pleasant.

Control returned. Black became aware of his surroundings. He became aware of the fact that he was lying in a pool of Trooper's blood, and that Anne Wallis lay unconscious outside the open door. He also noted that she was holding an extremely large hand gun.

He smiled. Some people clearly never knew when to give up.

However, the sight of her did cause him a psychic chill. He had not known she had even regained consciousness, let alone drummed up the courage to take a gun and attack him. Fortunately for him, her attachment to Nathan Trooper had saved his life: she had fainted at the sight of his bloody destruction. His conflict with Trooper had left him wide open to a far more immediate danger than psychic banishment. Her loyalty and horror had almost cost him everything.

Black scanned the rest of the house, remembering that the other Englishman was also present, but soon relaxed. Daniels was dead to the world, laid out cold by his fall.

A little time left, Black thought to himself, for a little pleasure. I have rid myself of Trooper and desecrated his body. Now I shall desecrate the body of the only woman he ever found to alleviate his loneliness. Such an exquisite punishment for her misguided alliance, an eternity in my service knowing that I slaughtered and destroyed her lover.

The thought amused and pleased him. It contained an irony and injustice which appealed to his perverse imagination. If he could not have the usurper chained to him for eternity like a dog, then the usurper's woman would have to do.

Black dragged his corpse together so that he knelt on all fours. From the palms of his hands and the skin around his kneecaps putrescent fluid squirted onto the carpet. The stench was vile. Everything squelched disgustingly as he made his way to the door. Tendons popped alarmingly, so rotten they could no longer support the weight. Joints which were once supple and moved with a fluidity of grace now scraped dead bone on bone. The only lubrication which remained was the soup of tissue sewage left by the ravages of death. His battle with Trooper had cost him dearly – it took all his power to keep himself in one piece.

But he refused to give in, would not admit defeat, not now.

He came to a halt above Anne Wallis, held unsteadily on one arm as the bone buckled and threatened to push through his shoulder. Her mind filled his, images of horror which fed him, awakening desires which had lain dormant for years. Unmanned by decay, he made do with a lecherous drool. He smothered her awareness and tugged her violently back to consciousness. When her eyes opened, dazed and confused, all she saw was his face. Her resulting screams and surge of unreasoned terror merely served to fuel his desires further. She struggled beneath him, but he blocked her with a single command and fixed her eyes back upon his ravaged features. He laughed as she squirmed and howled with disgust.

How pretty you are.

The words assaulted her brain with venomous lust. She felt like vomiting, but was incapable even of expressing her repugnance.

How wonderful it will be to spend eternity with you. Trooper chose well for his first liaison. But now you are mine.

She opened her mouth and screamed so loud that even Black's dead ear drums were stunned. To no effect, however. He enjoyed his mastery over her, and from her terror drew the strength to go on. He raised one maggot-ridden hand and clumsily caressed her cheek. Traces of slime marked her face, and the stench made her stomach do cartwheels of rampant nausea. Her view of the world consisted of purple and green flesh pocked by squirming flesh-hungry larvae. His hand began its descent towards her breasts. She cringed, tried to reach for the gun, could not move.

She cried out in despair. 'Oh, God help me! Nathan!'

The darkness closed around her mind. She felt herself dying, receding into nothingness, drawing closer to HIM as he went down like a ton of lead, dragging her with him.

Helpless, hopeless, terrified, she cried out and screamed one last time. 'NO!' Her wail was distilled desolation.

And then the darkness exploded in a blaze of white light. A blast of hot wind tore through her mind, casting her adrift.

'LEAVE HER ALONE!'

The voice, powerful as a hurricane, ripped the shadows from her mind and sent her reeling. Yet she was not afraid. The voice brought with it a howl of cleanliness which overshadowed Black's polluting touch and mind. The wind was pure, fresh, lively air, not the stale and rank closeness of her enemy. She revelled in that breeze, relishing its soft and cleansing touch. She recognized the new presence, and it made her heart sing with renewed hope.

Black recoiled from her as if he had been bitten. And the roar of his anger almost eclipsed the joy she felt.

'TROOPER!'

Anne was at last free to scrabble away across the carpet. The lock fell from her brain as Black withdrew his mind. Moving crab-like, she sped sideways until she came up against the wall, as far from Black as she could get. Only then did she open her eyes to see what was happening. What she saw took her breath away.

Standing astride Black's prone form was a figure reaching at least eight feet from floor to ceiling. Long white hair flowed from a forehead which burned with an inner fire. Every pore gleamed with power, a beacon of light. The features were unmistakably Nathan's. His mouth was firm and thin, the lips pressed together in a stern frown; his nose was classically sculpted, strong bone flaring into two angry nostrils. And his *eyes* – they blazed with outrage.

Nathan's image was the embodiment of all that his father had intended: a master of the power, not its slave. He was all that Peter Black was meant to have been. In death Trooper had gained control of the gift which had always been his bane.

Black was bemused. Trooper had been utterly destroyed. Black could not comprehend – would *never* comprehend – how anyone could recover from such complete destruction. Mixed with his alarm and sudden fear was the realization that he was ignorant of the subtleties of his skill – Trooper's grasp of all that was possible in the psychic arena shamed him. Through his arrogance, Black was forced to admit that he was not the master of souls. Compared to Trooper he was a mere apprentice, a pretender to the throne.

The admission cost him dearly; his fortitude began to crumble.

Nathan took his eyes from Black's corrupted face and looked over at Anne. Beneath the power of that gaze she seemed small and inconsequential. Despite the infinite concern and affection in his look, she backed away from the piercing glance.

He sensed her discomfort, and returned his attention to Peter Black. 'Crime upon crime, evil upon evil,' the image intoned. 'You will pay the price, Peter Black. And payment is long overdue.'

Trooper reached down and grabbed Black by the throat. Fingers no more than air closed around the rotten flesh, bursting bubbles of pus and releasing a foul stench. Black was lifted bodily from the floor. Somehow his corpse managed to stay in one piece.

For the first time in years Black had to look up. Tilting back his head to gaze upon Trooper with his vacant eye sockets hammered home his inferiority. No longer was he the strongest, the most powerful. All he had strived for over the long and lonely years had been whisked from his grasp in one impossible morning. Victory had turned to defeat, supremacy to impotency. He had made a tragic mistake – he had delayed too long, and now all was lost. Yet how could he have known? How could Trooper come back? What forces worked on his side now, to make him so perfect?

Black did not understand, and that caused him to misread the evidence. He made yet another mistake. He did not *doubt*.

Nathan grinned down at him. 'Long have I waited for this, brother. My rewards are incredible – infinite power, infinite life, and none of your pathetic decay. I shall reign eternal, and you will not even be a memory in the eye of the world.'

Black struggled in the iron grip, but his energy was dispersed in confusion. His movements were lethargic, lacking the strength on which he had grown to rely. It seemed that all his tame souls had fled his side at Trooper's reappearance. For the last time he cursed his foul body – it burdened him more than he could bear.

'I have entered your mind, Peter, and I have your nightmare. As a reward for your evil I shall place you within it.'

Black tried to struggle again. Trooper merely tightened his grip and lifted the killer from the floor, pressing him up against the wall so that the top of his skull scraped on the ceiling.

Wait, Black hissed. *I do not understand.*

'And, as part of your punishment, you never will.'

But I don't want to die! The plea was pathetic.

Nathan chuckled. 'You won't, brother mine. Look upon what I have brought with me from the bowels of your own fears.'

Black had no fight left. He simply sank into abject horror as the nightmare scene unfolded around him.

The two antagonists stood in an operating theatre, the light so bright that the white walls were indistinct under the glare. There were no windows in the room; only an operating table and a trolley covered with surgical instruments. They were alone.

What is this—?

Trooper picked him up and slammed him down on the table on his back. Fetid air was forced from his liquid lungs under the impact. Before he could recover, Trooper had locked his arms and legs with rigid steel clamps. The sound of the locks clicking home made his rotten blood freeze in his diseased veins.

Black pulled at his limbs to free them. The movement only served to slough the flesh from his wrists and ankles. It also hurt, the first physical pain Black had experienced since his nerve and tissue decay had begun. He began to feel truly afraid. Not the sort of fear which used to feed him, but a fear which ebbed his power and left him weak and shivering.

Trooper stood back from the table, smiling. 'We're ready for you now, doctor,' he called.

A door opened. Black strained to lift his head to get a look at the new arrival. But when he did, when he saw who the doctor was, he screamed in sudden comprehension. He recognized the man and the room. His struggles became more frantic, he no longer cared about the pain. He had to get out. He had to escape.

The doctor crossed the room to stand beside the table, where he looked dispassionately down at his patient. He paused to pull on his gloves, all the time his eyes boring into Black's skull.

Black continued to struggle vainly, unable to stop himself. He had to get out. He had to escape. This was torture.

'A little frisky today, isn't he?' the doctor commented drily.

'Indeed.' Nathan's voice was casual and relaxed.

'Still, never mind. He's had a hard day, and an even harder life. But we'll soon sort that out, won't we Peter?'

Black shook his head and moaned helplessly. 'No, no, please, don't. Please don't. I beg you.'

'You can run, you see, Peter,' the doctor continued without malice, 'but you can't hide. You can never hide. Not from me, anyway.' He turned to Nathan. 'Everything ready?'

'Yes.'

'And you're quite sure about this?'

'Oh, yes. There's no turning back now.'

The doctor nodded once, a firm affirmation of that statement. 'True. Things have gone on quite long enough.' He pulled the second glove on securely, the rubber snapping against his forearm. 'Do you recommend any anaesthetic today, Nathan?'

Trooper smiled coldly. 'Oh, I don't think so, Father. He needs to experience a little suffering, I think.'

Ethan Trooper nodded again, pleased. 'Good. I like a man who knows what he wants. You've grown up, I see, despite everything.'

'Thank you.'

'I'm very proud of you, son. You've done a good job, bringing him back here. I was beginning to think we'd buggered it all up.'

Nathan shrugged. 'Well, all's well that ends well, Father.'

Ethan Trooper nodded, straightened his shoulders and took a deep breath. 'Right then, let's get started. Time is money.'

Black could not believe it – this was grotesque. They were going to operate on him again, after all these years, and this time, he knew, would be the last. 'Don't do this,' he begged. 'Please.'

'Oh, hush Peter,' Ethan said absently. 'We've been through all this a dozen times. You should be used to it by now.'

'Please,' Black moaned. 'Don't do this.'

Ethan ignored him. 'I'm going to make an incision *here*.' He drew a line in Black's skull with a scalpel. Black screeched in sudden and unexpected pain. The rotten flesh parted easily. 'And *here*.' He drew the blade across another part of Black's head. Peter Black howled again, louder this time. 'Then I shall remove that section of your skin, and cut through the skull plate beneath.'

Black tried to cringe away from the icy steel on his cranium. His mouth worked mechanically as it tried to remember how to cry.

'Once through, I'll pull back the membrane. It's time I undid all the work I did last time, removed those connections, put you back to normal. Take away your power and make you just like the rest of us. That OK with you?' It was said as a deliberate taunt.

Black rose to the bait, screaming his frustration. 'NO, dammit! For the sake of God, don't DO that! Anything but that!'

Ethan laughed. 'Where did God suddenly come into this, Peter? And hold your tongue, boy, before I decide to cut it out.' His look turned in an instant from good humour to icy hatred.

'Peter always was such an uncooperative subject, you know,' he said to his son. 'Quite trying on my nerves. You, on the other hand, were a model patient. Always willing to please, always calm and helpful. Even when I split your head with an axe, you were trying to be friends with me. Remarkable, really. Not like this gibbering blob of trash here.' He shook his head sadly. 'I don't know. It just goes to show that the perfect theory is a load of cobblers when you put it into practice.' He cleared his throat. The time for conversation was clearly over. 'Saw please, Nathan.'

'STOP THIS!' Black screamed. 'This isn't even *real*. You aren't *here*, for God's sake! You're DEAD!'

Ethan chuckled. 'I know. But then, so are you, old boy. And so is Nathan. Just goes to show, don't you think?'

'I'm not afraid of this! I *know* this is just illusion. You can't win this way. Illusions only work when the subject is unaware of the illusion. But I *know* this is only my imagination.'

Nathan grinned. 'Oh, really? Would you imagine this, Peter?'

He reached out and tore back the flap of skin which his father had marked on Black's head. Pus and decay spurted from the wound.

Black screamed in agony. He knew, in that instant, that this could not possibly be his vision – he could never picture such torture, because he had forgotten what pain *was*.

Nathan laughed. 'Your imagination? Not quite, Peter. This is reality. Only the idea came from your mind. This *is* really happening. We're all dead, you see Peter. Unfortunately for you, you never did quite grasp where the boundaries lay, did you? But I've been here and I *know*.' He handed his father the surgical saw. The small circular blade gleamed in the bright light.

'I'll tell you what,' Ethan said kindly. 'I'll prove to you just how real all this is by letting you stay awake throughout the entire operation. I don't normally allow you that pleasure, do I? Because it's really rather excruciatingly painful. But these *are* exceptional circumstances. Now then,' he asked, raising both eyebrows in question, 'I can't get fairer than that, can I?'

With that, and a very evil grin, he started the saw.

Black screamed. And carried on screaming until his throat was laid open by his own terror. He screamed as Ethan Trooper laid the saw on his bone and cut away the rectangle of skull to gain access to the brain. He screamed as the membrane was torn back, as the doctor probed inside his head with a blunt scalpel, tearing apart the unnatural synapses and the delicate links in his mind. He screamed as each connection was severed and he felt his power ebbing from him like water running through his fingers. He screamed as he felt his body begin to cave in on itself. He screamed as his chest cavity collapsed into a morass of rotten fluid and decayed lungs. He bawled out his agony as the flies took flight from his wasted corpse. He cried out his unimaginable horror as all that he had gained was taken from him and cast back into the psychic ether, as all that he had stolen was reclaimed and released. He screamed as his last retainers left his side, disengaging themselves from his bondage and fleeing into the darkness, souls at last at rest.

In madness, he screamed into a void of utter darkness and squealed his agony to a universe which was glad to be rid of him . . .

Anne Wallis howled in pain as Black's hideous screams filled her head. She pressed her hands to her ears, but that did nothing to stop the sound. She opened her eyes and looked across at his prone form, the mouth thrown open in abject horror, filled with maggots. The sight was too much for her, she could not bear it any longer. She reached out and picked up Sam's .45.

John Daniels chose that moment to reel drunkenly into the corridor, both hands trying to hold his skull together as the demonic cries threatened to tear him apart. He had woken to that sound, and he wanted it silenced. Through a mask of dried blood he gazed down the hall and saw Anne Wallis scrabbling for the pistol. He saw Peter Black – as rotten and hideous as he had expected – stretched out on the carpet, taut with agony and flinching under some unseen, unnameable torture. And he saw Nathan Trooper flickering like some radiant giant above it all.

The image of Trooper turned briefly at his entrance, and there was a flicker of recognition in the eyes before the massive head turned away again to regard the writhing corpse at his feet.

John Daniels did not stop to question what it was all about, no longer surprised by anything the psychic did. He just wanted a little peace and quiet. He knew this was the last chance for them to turn the tables on the beast they had come to kill.

And John Daniels was well in the mood for some table turning. 'Kill the bastard!' he shouted, the exertion exploding in his head.

Anne looked up in surprise.

'For God's sake, Anne!' he bawled. 'PULL THE BLOODY TRIGGER!'

Her attention returned to Black – his cries of agony and terror were pitiful. She looked down at the gun, torn by indecision and a reluctance to use the weapon despite Black's crimes. She wondered briefly if there was another way to end the terror.

Then she felt Nathan's powerful eyes turn on her. The dreadful screaming in her head eased under his gaze, and she heard his soft voice as clear as day in the very centre of her mind.

'Anne, hurry, I can hold him no longer. The illusion is weakening. I have no substance here – I cannot kill him. You must do it.' She felt his reassuring and comforting touch on her hair. 'I'm sorry it had to be you,' he said sadly. 'But hurry. Or we will lose. And he will claim you for himself.'

She needed no further encouragement . . .

Black screamed until the screaming was all he could remember and he could no longer recall his fear – and at that point the operating theatre vanished. The pain vanished. Ethan Trooper vanished, a wry smile hovering in the air after his body had dissolved, like a dementedly psychopathic Cheshire Cat.

The entire illusion crumbled and collapsed and revealed that it had no substance, that it had never had any substance.

Black realized he had been cheated. In a burst of recognition he sped for sanctuary and roared out his anger. He fell back into his body screaming with fury. His head turned to gaze at the enemies around him, strength pouring back into his mind.

Anne saw the head turn, the blank sockets seeking her out. The sight of him, alive again, whipped away her reluctance and filled her with revulsion. She took a deep breath, brought the gun to bear to that hideous sight, and pulled the trigger.

The silver .45 bucked in her grasp, recoiling into her palms with such violence that she was thrown against the wall, colliding painfully with the brick. Only then did the sonic concussion of the blast reach her ears, impacting like a hammer-blow. She smelled burned steel and cordite, blue smoke drifted in the stale air.

Black's head exploded.

The soft-nosed bullet caught him directly in the centre of his face and mushroomed out as it tore splinters of bone through his skull, emerging just behind his left ear and carrying with it most of his brain. Under the thousand mile an hour blast his cranium shattered and blew backward, tearing off his head and spattering it all over the wall. Pieces of rotten tissue, rotten hair, fluid bone covered the plaster. Only a blackened and bloody stump remained on his shoulders, from which a revolting soup of maggots and green fluid oozed onto the carpet.

The screaming stopped exactly as the gun blast tore the atmosphere in the house to shreds. After the incessant noise, silence fell to shroud the survivors like a blanket of universal gratitude. The hall stank of gunfire and the grave.

Anne could not take her eyes from the leaking corpse.

John Daniels could not take his eyes from the image of Nathan Trooper. It exuded power like the corpse oozed pus. The image reached out one hand towards Anne Wallis in a futile gesture of yearning. Daniels felt the depth of Trooper's emotion wash through him, felt his breath stop in his lungs.

The fingers never quite reached her hair. The image flickered once. And Nathan Trooper disappeared.

CHAPTER SEVEN

A Light in The Black

'Ow!'

'Hold still.' Anne dabbed at the deep cut above Daniels' left eye. 'Almost done.' She wiped away the last of the blood, then taped a bandage over the wound. 'It will probably need stitches.'

He grunted. 'Yeah, don't I know it.' He grinned sheepishly. 'The most painful thing is knowing how I did it.'

She smiled faintly, which surprised her. An hour ago she thought she would never smile again.

'You OK?' he asked gently, the concern obvious on his face.

Anne shrugged helplessly, a gesture of utter emptiness. 'What do you think?' Her dreams and hopes lay in tatters around her. Just thinking about it made her want to howl at the injustice. What had Nathan ever done to hurt anyone? Why did he have to die?

Daniels reached up and enfolded her hands briefly in his own. She was very cold. 'Thanks. Now sit down. I'll get you a drink.'

She sighed. 'Are you going to ring the police?'

I *am* the police, he thought stupidly, forgetting for a moment where he was. 'Soon. Once I've figured out how to explain it all.'

He wandered unsteadily into the kitchen to make some coffee.

There remained the most God-awful mess in the other room, and a whole host of unanswered questions. Not least of which was how the hell was he going to convince the Arizona State Police that neither he nor Anne was responsible for the devastation?

'No, officer, I didn't do it. The corpse did.'

Come back butlers, Daniels thought, all is forgiven.

He carried the coffee into the lounge and almost died.

'Hello, John,' said Nathan. He sat in one of the armchairs, legs crossed, immaculately dressed in a blue suit. There was not a single spot of blood on him. Anywhere.

Daniels opened his mouth to say something, realized that there was nothing one *could* say, and closed it again.

Nathan grinned. 'Sit down before you fall down, John. And put that coffee somewhere, for God's sake. There's enough mess in this house already without coffee stains on the carpet.'

Daniels obediently dropped the coffee pot heavily onto a stack of planks and collapsed on the settee. He dared not look at Anne, aware he could not cope with the emotion playing across her face.

'No, I'm not really here,' Trooper said calmly, flicking an imaginary speck of dust from his trouser leg. He nodded his head toward the bedrooms. 'I'm in there. In pieces.' Anne flinched, mesmerized. 'Forgive me, but I am playing with your minds. I thought you would prefer to see something, rather than just hear a disembodied voice.' He looked at John. 'I may have been wrong. I'm like your spider, John. A fear imposed on your reality.'

'How could you ever be a fear, Nathan?' Anne asked in a voice strained with emotion. The sight of Nathan

– welcome as it was – caused her more pain than she would dare to admit, even to herself.

He smiled at her warmly, his eyes unreadable. 'Thank you. And I am sorry if this upsets you. I merely thought it better to retire from life in a more civilized fashion.' He shrugged. 'Plus I'm new to all this. I'm finding it hard to let go. I mean, my body is dead, but I am lucky enough to retain that which is essentially ME. Not all, as I have been told, have such a privilege.'

Isaac had explained it to him, a little, in the peace after his death. There were boundaries he would have to learn now; those boundaries included Tim Johnson – to whom he had promised his help – but excluded his two friends. Isaac had said vaguely that Tim would need his guidance, as Isaac had guided Nathan himself in his lonely life, whereas the others would only be pained by his presence. So he had been permitted this one brief moment to say goodbye . . .

Daniels raised one eyebrow. 'So how long have you got?'

'A few minutes. Is that enough? How long do you want me?'

Forever would be nice, Anne thought sadly.

Nathan looked back at her and smiled.

I'm sorry. I did not wish it to end like this. I did not want to make it hard for you. I knew today would be my last. I only hope you can find it in your heart to forgive me.

She opened her mouth to reply, realized he had been *thinking* to her alone. His lips had not moved. So she framed a reply in her mind, and thought her forgiveness.

'What happens now?' Daniels asked, unaware of their private conversation. 'How do we get away with two dead bodies? And just what happened anyway? I still don't understand how you beat him.'

Nathan laughed. 'I didn't – you two did. But don't worry, everything gets cleaned up, and you go home a hero – except nobody will ever believe you. Leaving will pose no problem. Sam Stevens has made sure the authorities are looking for Black. Plus your boss Curtis has made some calls. He feared the worst, since he hadn't heard from you for some time.' He paused. 'As for an explanation, well, I'll do my best.' He tented his fingertips.

'We all have our darkest fears – even Black. But how do you scare someone who thrives on fear? Become more powerful than he, at least in his eyes. So I conjured myself up as bigger, stronger, more powerful. To disarm him, I laid him on an operating table and had my father reverse the operation. In doing so, he lost his ability to hold on to his stolen power. Even though it was all illusion, the illusion was so horrible it diverted him long enough for you to pull the plug on his life.' He shrugged. 'Anne did the rest. I could con him with illusion but I could not kill him. I don't exist any more. He never realized that – he feared me, at the end, more than anyone ever feared him.'

'Then it's over?' Anne asked. 'Really over?'

'Yes. He is dead. Completely. His body is destroyed, and his mind has been utterly consumed by madness and decay. He won't be back – there won't be another episode in this saga. It is over.'

Daniels believed him. He breathed a sigh of relief, felt the tension ease in his shoulders. After all, if you could not believe a dead man wearing a suit, who could you believe?

'Your father?' Anne asked suddenly. '*Really* your father?'

Nathan gave an enigmatic smile. 'No. I don't think so. Just another part of the illusion. Still, at times it was so real it even had me fooled.' He shrugged. 'Part of me would like to think he interceded at the end, to end the tragedy, to try and make amends, but . . .' He shivered, then seemed to pull himself together.

'I knew that only Ethan Trooper could terrify Black into submission. Only my father possessed the power to make or break Black. His darkest fear was to have Ethan Trooper reverse the process which had made him what he was. So that was what I did.'

Trooper paused, his head cocked to one side.

'I must make my excuses, I'm afraid. It is time to go.'

'You can't stay?' Anne asked, her voice breaking.

He smiled at her sadly, remembering Isaac's words. 'This is no longer my place, Anne. I don't belong here.' But I could belong, he thought with a sudden regret. I could stay by her side, I could see her safely through her life, I could watch over her . . . but then he looked into her eyes and realized he was being silly. He was *dead* now; not destroyed, certainly, but he had a different existence and was no longer part of theirs. Isaac was right. Every sight of him would hurt her, and he could not bear that. She deserved better than a lingering, painful parting. He had to say goodbye once and for all, and not be tempted by absurdities.

'Besides,' he continued, 'the police will be here soon.'

Daniels looked up, surprised. His heart quickened its pace. He knew he would have some fast talking to do, and he was not quite ready. He also knew he was the gooseberry in the room. Removing himself would allow them some privacy, give him time to get his story together, and also take away the disconcerting image of a dead man talking as if he belonged there. 'Er, if you'll excuse me,' he mumbled, standing. 'I think I'll meet them halfway.' He looked down at Nathan. 'Er, well. All the best then Nathan.'

Keep in touch, he almost added.

Nathan smiled. 'You too, John. And thanks. For everything.'

Daniels stood there a moment longer, at a complete loss for words. As was his way, however, when he had nothing to say he said nothing. So he simply gave one curt nod and left.

Nathan watched him go, smiling. 'A good man.'

Anne sighed. 'I'm sorry, Nathan, but this is very hard for me. Last night—' She broke off. 'I'm not sure I can cope with this. You're here, but you're not. I don't know what to think.'

He nodded. 'I'm sorry too. I didn't know what was best.'

The vision of him rose from the chair and crossed over to her. He felt her confusion, and knew his presence was not easing her pain. But as he had said, he was finding it hard to let go. That one night of deep companionship, of opening up and finding pleasure rather than pain, made him reluctant to leave her side. Yet even he had to admit that a dead man had no place among the living.

'I must go, and leave you all to your lives. Perhaps I had hoped that your seeing me like this, knowing I was not utterly gone, may have lessened your grief. I was wrong. Nevertheless, I would like to say two things before I go.'

She looked up. A tear welled in her left eye.

He smiled kindly. 'First, your husband is free now. He has gone to another place, a cleaner place. He asked me to tell you in his own confused way he loved you very much.'

The tears streamed down her cheeks now.

'Second, and I am sorry if this will burden you more

than you can bear, there's something you should know. What you do about it is your decision, unless you want my help. But I thought you should hear it from me rather than worry in the months to come.'

She smiled faintly at all his circumvention. 'I'm pregnant.'

He seemed surprised. 'You knew that?'

'Yes, I knew. I knew as soon as you started speaking.' She looked up into his eyes. 'I have *always* been able to read you like an open book. You have the most astonishing eyes.'

His eyes crinkled under the sadness of his smile. 'I wish – I wish things had ended differently. I wish we'd had more time together. I wish you could know just how important you are to me, how much you changed my view of the world. You were the only person in my life who caused me anything but pain. The hours I spent with you were the finest hours. I will carry those memories with me wherever I go. I just wish the hours had been longer.'

She closed her eyes against the desolation of those words. Her grief was tempered by knowing she had at least been able to give him comfort. Such an empty life, such a tragedy that he died just when he had found something which may have filled that emptiness.

She loved him so much, loved the *idea* of him so much, that her heart was close to breaking. He was so close, and yet lost forever.

'You haven't asked me if I intend to keep the baby.'

He paused before answering. 'Would my opinion help? If you want it, I shall give it. But then the decision will not be yours.'

'It is a hard decision to make alone, Nathan.'

'I know. But it is your life, Anne, not mine. I would

not want to say anything to damage your life more than I have already.'

'So you want me to keep the baby?'

He grinned. 'I didn't say that. Would it help you to know?'

She sighed. 'I don't know. I honestly don't know.'

He paused. 'If it helps, I have ensured that whatever path you choose will be as comfortable for you as I can make it.'

She wondered what that meant.

'Just know that whatever you decide, I will be thinking of you wherever I am. In the eternity of my life in death, I shall never forget you.' She felt his warm lips lightly brush her forehead, and smelt his male scent all around her. 'I love you, Anne.'

When she opened her eyes, he was gone.

John Daniels stood at the end of the driveway, leaning against the gate smoking a cigarette. His head ached and there was a lump in his throat, but he refused to acknowledge either of them.

Four cars turned the bend in the road and passed the jeep Nathan had hired. The lead car pulled up beside him, and three men got out. They were all armed. 'Hello Sam,' Daniels said, forcing a smile. 'I see you brought the cavalry.'

Sam Stevens looked past Daniels at his house, then back at the Englishman. 'He was here?' he asked, casually pointing the barrel of his gun at the bandage on Daniels' forehead.

'He was.'

'Where is he now?'

'He's dead.' Daniels took a long drag on his cigarette.

Sam blew out his cheeks. 'You sure?'

'Oh, yes.' Daniels thought of the rotten brains all over the wall. 'Quite sure. You have my word on that.'

One of the State Policemen moved away from his car. 'All right boys. Let's check this out.'

Daniels called out after them. 'Go easy on the lady – she's still in shock.' Then he turned back to Sam. He felt dead. Two weeks or more of hypertension had left him hollow and drained of all emotion. 'We messed up your house a bit I'm afraid, Sam.'

Sam shrugged. 'So? You had a party, right?'

Daniels grinned. He could not help it, despite Black, despite Nathan, despite himself. He had always liked Sam. 'Right.'

'And you killed the bastard.'

Daniels nodded.

Sam wandered over. 'Come on. These guys will want some answers.' He grinned. 'And I want to see the looks on their faces when they find out he really *was* a walking corpse with claws.' He paused. 'You mentioned a lady. What about Trooper?'

Daniels stubbed out his cigarette with a vicious stab. 'Dead. Black tore him in two.' He sighed. 'He bought us the time we needed. Brave little bastard.'

'I'm sorry.' Sam paused briefly. 'But he knew, didn't he?'

Daniels could do nothing but nod. Yes, Nathan had known he was going to die. Sam holstered his gun, aware that he no longer needed it. He could see the death and release all over Daniels' face, and already the relief was crawling down his spine. 'Come on, Inspector. Your head's started bleeding again.'

Daniels sighed. He looked up at the noon sky, squinted his eyes against the sun, and felt the warmth seep into his cold, weary bones. He had thought the death of Peter Black would make the world seem a brighter, less menacing place. But he did not feel like that at all. He just felt tired and cold. 'You know Sam,' he said wearily, 'I'm just getting too old for all this.'

Stevens clapped him roughly on the shoulder. 'Come on, Inspector. It's all over now. Time to rest, get some sleep.'

Daniels shrugged his shoulders. 'I don't want to sleep. I want to forget. I want to wind back the clock and never come here.'

Sam pursed his lips. 'Wouldn't have helped. Trooper would still be dead – he would have come here, even without you. You know that. The only difference is that Black would have killed him and you wouldn't have been around to finish the job. We'd have lost. And Trooper would have died for nothing.'

Daniels looked down into the traffic cop's wise eyes and saw the truth within them. He sighed. 'Yeah, I know. But that doesn't help much, does it? One bullet wasn't enough for that bastard.'

Sam looked away. 'I'll let you into a secret, Inspector. One bullet is never enough.'

Daniels looked up. There was a depth to that statement which surprised him.

'Now, come on. Those guys won't wait forever.'

Daniels did not move. He felt as if there was something he had to say, but he did not know what it was. 'I never really knew him, you know.' It sounded like an apology.

Sam smiled. 'I only met him once. But he was the kind nobody ever really knows – find a man who knew him, and you find a liar.'

Daniels pondered those words as they walked into the house. He could not think of a more suitable epitaph. And somehow he knew that Nathan Trooper, wherever he was, would approve of the mystery.

Epilogue

'So when is it due?' Daniels asked, grinning like an idiot at the huge bulge in Anne Wallis' abdomen.

They sat outside on his patio, basking in the glory of a fine English summer day. On days like these, when the air was warm and the sky clear and blue, John always thought about Nathan. Perhaps it was the unconscious association with that last, hot Arizona day.

'Three more weeks,' Anne said, shifting in her chair. The weight and pressure were increasingly uncomfortable.

John smiled. 'It becomes you. You look fantastic.'

And she did. The growth of life within her made her eyes glow with beauty and barely restrained joy. Over the months she had come to terms with her sadness. She had lost the father yet gained his child, and took solace from that fact.

'*It* is a boy, actually John,' she said archly.

'Oh? Have you thought of a name?'

She laughed. It was a beautiful laugh.

'Several. But I think I shall call him Ethan.' Her face clouded momentarily. 'Do you think Nathan would approve?'

402

He smiled. 'Yes, Anne. I think Nathan would definitely approve. In fact, I think Nathan would approve if you called him Archibald, if that's what you wanted.'

Her frown cleared. 'Thank you.'

'So, how are you faring?'

'I'm fine. Nathan made sure of that, didn't he?'

Daniels laughed. He had indeed.

Trooper's last will and testament had shocked and surprised them all, not least because they were all named. They all knew that Nathan had no chance to amend his will after Christmas, before he even met them. So how could he name them as beneficiaries?

Yet the executor of Nathan's estate, a grouchy old buzzard named Cartwright, had been able to produce the necessary evidence and documentation. He could prove that Nathan had visited his offices on December 28 to add an extra five clauses to his will.

Personally, John Daniels doubted that evidence. Apart from the fact that Nathan had simply not *known* any of them on the 28th, the division of worldly goods was such that Daniels found it impossible to believe Cartwright was telling the truth.

But he said nothing. Partly because nothing Nathan did, or had ever done, surprised him any longer; partly for Anne's sake and that of the baby; and partly because of the look in Cartwright's eyes at the reading of the will. Daniels recognized that wild and scared look, and sympathized with it – he saw it every day when he looked in a mirror. He suspected foul play – not from the solicitor, of course, but from Nathan Trooper. But he kept silent about his doubts. He knew nobody would ever believe him.

Trooper's estate had been worth just over four million pounds. Some intelligent investment of his original inheritance, and a very simple lifestyle, had allowed Nathan to accumulate riches of which he was totally unaware – to Nathan Trooper, money was simply an abstract concept. Of the four million, three were bequeathed to Anne Wallis, of which half was to be invested in a trust fund for the child. The remainder had been handed over to a wide variety of charities, among them a fund for the Fields Memorial Hospital for Children, where Nathan had saved Tim's life. Sergeant Fowles – to his surprise – had been named as the new owner of Nathan's prize Jaguar car. Tim Johnson had received an undisclosed sum of money and a personal letter from Nathan, which had left the boy tearful and thoughtful – Daniels had told Tim in person of Nathan's death, and suspected foul play there as well: Tim had been upset at the news, that was true – but he had not been surprised.

Daniels himself had received a lifetime supply of Nathan's exclusive cigarettes, a footnote to the will which he had found ironic and totally in line with Nathan's wry sense of humour. Even from beyond the grave, Nathan Trooper was sharing some bizarre personal joke with them all.

So Anne had been well cared for, at least financially. The money did nothing to ease her loss, but it did ease her burden. John knew it had been a hard decision for her to keep the baby, a constant reminder of the life she might have had if Peter Black had never existed. Added to that, her complex feelings about her dead husband and miscarriage made the choice even more extraordinary. But now, eight months on, Daniels believed she had made the right decision. He also believed it was what Nathan would have wanted.

He allowed himself a smile. The Lord may well work in mysterious ways, but when compared to the devious humour of Nathan Trooper the Lord was merely an amateur.

'John?'

He snapped back to the real world. 'I'm sorry. Miles away.'

Anne smiled. 'It's OK. I get like that too. Sometimes I dream about him, about us together, and the dreams are so real I wonder where he is when I wake up. Sometimes I'd swear I can smell him around the house, in the bed.' She blushed.

Daniels could think of nothing to say. So he said nothing.

'Have you ever seen him again?' she asked quietly, pointedly averting her eyes.

'No. No, I haven't.' Of which he was glad. 'Have you?'

She shook her head. 'I think, if he's still out there, that he's decided it would be a bad idea.'

Daniels eyed her curiously. 'Is he right?'

She shrugged. 'I don't know. He told me once about his brother, and their conversations. He said they always made him feel at peace, calm. I wonder if it would be like that for me. Now I've got things sorted out in my mind, and the wound is not quite so open, I wonder if I would prefer to see him.' She shrugged again. 'Who knows? There certainly aren't any text books on this subject.'

He grinned. 'Now that I will agree with.'

They lapsed into a companionable, comfortable silence. They had had many such silences since returning from America.

The smell of cooking drifted from the house. John's daughter was back from college, and had decided to cook duck for dinner.

Anne sipped her orange juice. 'I miss him,' she said suddenly. 'I miss him more than I can say, sometimes. It's all so *unjust*. I don't know how I'm going to cope. I don't know if I'll be a worthy mother to his child.'

Daniels smiled reassuringly. 'Of course you will.'

'There's such a lot to live up to.' She paused. 'What really upsets me is that he won't be present at the birth. I think he would have liked that.'

John lit another of Nathan's cigarettes. The conversation had suddenly turned morose, and he did not think Nathan would like *that*. Trooper had said himself they had their own lives to lead – they had to get on with it, let the rest go, stop worrying about the dead.

He savoured the taste of his drink.

It would be easier to let go, he thought, if the dead had not decided to hang around like a bad smell. Sometimes, Nathan, I do despair of you. Sometimes you can be a right pain in the arse.

He leaned back and blew expensive smoke into the summer air.

Tim Johnson lay asleep in his bed, next door to the room where his dad lay reunited with his mum – if not in total happiness, then at least in mutual understanding. As usual, his dreams were dark and troubled and filled with menace. He tossed and turned and murmured shadows into the silence, much as Nathan had done when the whole sorry episode first began.

And then, through the hate and the pain, welling up from the murky depths of memories, both his and inherited, came a soft light. With it flowed a sense of peace which eased away the fear. Tim calmed in his sleep, stopped his muttering and shuddering, and relaxed. Then said aloud, very clearly, with a soft smile creasing his lips: 'Hi boss.'